MW00560750

Praise for Book One,
TENDER GRACES

An intriguing family saga that grips the audience . . .
—Harriet Klausner, an Amazon.com top reviewer

Magendie shows why plot is just the wheels of a narrative vehicle.
Without voice, character, poetry and detail also, all you've got is a go-
kart. In her debut novel, "Tender Graces," Magendie builds up the
plot — a prodigal daughter story — into a sustained entertainment
through an exuberant mountain portrayal
—Asheville *Citizen Times*

This is a novel of family, both good and bad
—Baton Rouge *Advocate*

A force of lyrical storytelling
—*Smoky Mountain News*

THIS MESSAGE IS FOR GUYS: It may have a soft, pink cover but it
ain't that kind of book. Kathryn Magendie's Virginia Kate has plenty
of what my grandmother called "brass," treats us to earfuls of
authentic dialogue, and gradually reveals a story not easily forgotten.
We will soon read more, I hope, from Magendie's pen. She's real.
—Wayne Caldwell Author of *Cataloochee* and *Requiem by Fire*

With a voice true to its source, Kathryn Magendie's Tender Graces
gathers us into its story of family loss, connection, and redemption.
Magendie knows well how we live within the chains that are both our
bondage and our empowerment. This novel weaves those chains, or
webs—as mountain women call the warp they have threaded onto
their looms—with a sturdy yet graceful hand. Its texture rests in one's
imagination like a coverlet crafted to bring warmth and, yes, comfort.
—Kathryn Stripling Byer, former North Carolina Poet Laureate

Every so often, if you're fortunate enough, you'll find a book that not
only captures your attention and imagination, it captures your heart.
—Deborah LeBlanc, Author of *Family Inheritance*

Magendie's unique fresh voice and lyrical turns of phrase are gifts she gives to readers, and which last long after the last page is read. Powerful stuff for a debut novel.
—Angie Ledbetter, Author of *Seeds of Faith*

. . . a novel that reads like a poem to childhood and growing up.
—Ed Cullen, features writer for the Baton Rouge Morning Advocate, frequent contributor to All Things Considered on National Public Radio, and author of *Letter in a Woodpile*

. . . a powerful, moving and beautifully written debut.
—Danielle Younge-Ullman, author of *Falling Under*

. . .Reminiscent of early Lee Smith and Silas House, Magendie's Virginia Kate Carey is the steady beating pulse of this beautiful narrative that sweeps through a lifetime of loss, grief, and ultimately redemption and what it means to go home again.
—Kerry Madden, author of *Gentle's Holler*

secret graces

This is a work of fiction. Names, characters, places and incidents are either the products of the author's imagination or are used fictitiously. Any resemblance to actual persons (living or dead,) events or locations is entirely coincidental.

Bell Bridge Books
PO BOX 30921
Memphis, TN 38130
ISBN: 978-0-9843256-9-6

Bell Bridge Books is an Imprint of BelleBooks, Inc.

Copyright © 2010 by Kathryn Magendie

Printed and bound in the United States of America.

All rights reserved. No part of this book may be reproduced in any form or by any electronic or mechanical means, including information storage and retrieval systems, without permission in writing from the publisher, except by a reviewer, who may quote brief passages in a review.

We at BelleBooks enjoy hearing from readers. You can contact us at the address above or at BelleBooks@BelleBooks.com

Visit our websites – www.BelleBooks.com and www.BellBridgeBooks.com.

10 9 8 7 6 5 4 3 2

Cover design: Debra Dixon
Interior design: Hank Smith
Photo credits: scene -© Konradbak | Dreamstime.com &
                  texture+forest © Irinaqqq | Dreamstime.com
                  horse dingbat © Seamartini | Dreamstime.com
:Lt:01:

secret graces

Book Two, The Graces Saga

Kathryn Magendie

B

Bell Bridge Books
Memphis, Tennessee

Dedication

In pride: To my son & his new family

&

In honor: To Peggy DiBenedetto, Barry Fraser, Stephen Craig Rowe (and there are more . . .)—for keeping the light of your smile even when old bastard cancer tried to take it away.

Acknowledgements

As always, to my blogger buddies and my friends; thank you for your encouragement and support!

Mother—the name Virginia Kate comes from you, Ruth Virginia—Rebekha is a love-letter character to all those who raise other mother's children; thank you. Frank—you've been like another Dad, buying books for your friends and all you do. Daddy, it's been fifty years that you're sober and I'm so proud of you; but St. Rene you really are a saint for putting up with even the sober man who is my dad, *teeheehee*. My brothers: Mike (keep playing in that band and don't give up), Johnny (you'll do it again but better), Tommy (I'm glad you didn't leave us), thank you for bragging about me to your friends (and angel David in the clouds—I wish I could hug you just one more time and ask if you are proud of your big sister). And thank you my handsome Good Man Roger—smooch, nuff said.

BelleBooks/Bell Bridge Books and The Debs—you let me do what I love to do, thank you, thank you, thank you!

Angie Ledbetter, VK's godmother, love and thank you. Mary Ann Ledbetter for an insightful brilliant Reader's Guide. My first readers: Phyllis Laurent Duhe and Hilda Mitchell—thank you for your help and encouragement. And always, to my NAWW Sisters—*awooooooo!*, and Kim Vickers the website goddess.

Thanks to David Gooch & Christi Gaudet of Galatoire's in New Orleans for being nice and answering questions. Adnan Mahmutovic, I'm honored you taught my book in your class at the University of Sweden. Patresa Hartman—when are you going to write it, huh?, please?

What would I do without libraries and the librarians and the book clubs—y'all are so important, and don't ever forget that! Thank you Teresa Frohock, Carol Murdock, and Mikell Webb—because. Charles Mills, thanks for the awesome TG poster (I have more tomatoes for you in this book, *snicker*). Margaret Osondu—I'll always remember your cozy bookstore, thank you for all you did for me.

And to the writers/poets who took the time to write nice blurbs: Big Huge Thanks!

Finally, to my readers—my love letter to you continues with this second book.

All the world's a stage, and all the men and women merely players. They have their exits and their entrances; And one man in his time plays many parts,
—William Shakespeare

On the wind come ghost-songs. Come home, they sing. Come home to us. I turn my head away. Listen; their laments follow the wind, over bold and important mountain, from ridge to ridge, over cold running creek, over the holler, and find me where the land is flat and hot and wet. They call to me, Come Home. And the lullaby both soothes and quickens, while the spirit-voices reach out. But I turn away to another call. The ghosts hover, never uncertain: Come back to us, come back Home. The mountain waits. The mountain cries. The mountain shadows over what once was your light. The mountain holds your kin. The ghosts know my secrets, all my inner secrets. I hear their call on the wind, the ghost-songs. Calling me home, calling me home, calling me Home . . .

I say, hush, hush now.

Chapter 1

Today

At Momma's house in the West Virginia holler

I stare out of Momma's kitchen window; those dancing curtains touch and pull away, touch and pull away, just as Momma had done all her life. Momma's house is emptied of the living, except for me. Grandma Faith rests on her star, tired from her journey back with me. She knows my heart, opened the way for me to begin so I can go on from here to what comes next.

After we released Katie Ivene Holms Carey into the West Virginia wind, other than the vials of ashes my brothers and I held to release her there and yonder as Momma wanted, I was left alone with the ghosts. My family, who'd come to the holler for Momma's memorial—Daddy, my daughter Adin, and my brothers, Micah, Andy, Bobby—lingered in the air at first, like the after-shadows that appear when looking at a flash of light that is here and then gone. As breaths of wind will scatter seeds, so they scattered. They'd all asked if I would leave with them, but I am not ready. The West Virginia mountains have again slipped into my blood, down into my marrow, running through me, rising to remind me of who I am and where I come from. My kin and me.

I can't let it end, not yet. Grandma Faith lured me here, to tell our stories.

I turn and cut on the fire for a cup of Momma's Maxwell House. Micah and Andy had made faces at the brew, but I didn't mind drinking Momma's instant coffee. The taste of it is a reminder of times in this kitchen.

While waiting for the water to boil in the kettle, I touch things:

Momma's coffee cup, the rooster-handled sugar and creamer. The kitchen is old. The house is old. The floors are sagging, the steps out the front door are cracked, the walls need paint, but the old house doesn't seem worth the effort sprucing it would take. Who would live here? Not me. This was Momma's house, and it will never hold another person such as her. It can't even hold her spirit, I bet.

I think of returning to my Louisiana house, where its empty echoes as a silent symbol. But where I do not have to think so much of Momma and all we missed as mother and daughter. (*Oh Momma! I needed you. Did you need me?*)

Before he went back to New York, his Home I reckoned, Micah said, "If you're stubborn on staying here for a while until you finish what you need to finish, then go up to the house on the hill."

I'd answered, "That old lonely house. I've never been inside it."

"It's solid."

My brother and I stared at the lonely house on the hill.

"I've got some people coming soon to work on it," he said.

"It needs love."

Micah nodded his head. Then he stuck his hand into his pocket, pulled out an old key. "Not that it's locked, but for later, just in case."

"I'm not going to live in it," I said. "I'm not staying in the holler."

The ghosts set up to excited whispering.

Micah pressed the key into my hand. "It's just for just in case." He'd hugged me, and before I could say Jiminy Christmas, he was gone. That's how my big brother did things. He appeared and disappeared as if he were a spirit his own self.

Andy and Bobby told me to call if I needed them. They'd never been able to talk me out of my ornery ways before and they weren't going to try then. Andy said, "I understand, Sister."

Bobby nodded, pushed his glasses up on his nose.

I hugged my younger brothers, wished them well and good trips back to Louisiana. Their Home.

Adin had said, "Mom, call me later." She'd pulled a scamp-face, said, "That Gary is cute. He's sweet on you, you know."

"I'm too old for all that foolishness.'

She rolled her eyes, showing me she truly was my daughter. "Haven't you heard your fifties are going to be like your thirties or something like that?"

I'd hugged Adin tight, giving her no rope to pull me to places I didn't want to go. Her blood is not my blood, our kin not related, but she is my own all the same. She wants for me, even when I don't want for myself. She climbed into the car with Bobby and Andy and Andy took off in a cloud of West Virginia dirt. I wondered if Louisiana would stay Adin's Home or if she'd soon wander.

Daddy spoke low and sad, his breath speaking of his own ironies, "My Bug. My dainty Ariel. You'll figure it all out."

I let him go on back to our good Rebekha, where she keeps him safe from his demons come to haunt him.

The coffee pot squeals; I take it off the fire and into my cup spoon a heaping teaspoon of coffee crystals, pour in the boiled water, add sugar, and then the cream my brothers bought at the grocery store in town. The click of spoon against cup is the only sound, save for Mrs. Anna Mendel's cat crying for food, and then the sound of her front screen door slamming shut. Could be her nephew come out to feed that old mangy cat. Could be, but why would I care to look to see if he's out there? I don't care a speck. Mrs. Anna Mendel always had a cat, just one, and they were always hungry and prowling. Maybe they were all the same cat, with ninety-nine lives lived in the holler.

I sip my coffee; it's good, hot, bittersweet.

The morning air is cool drifting in the windows, for the sun hasn't fully spilled its light over the ridges. I walk into the living room and before I can think to stop myself, I peek out the window. Old Mrs. Anna Mendel is in her garden and I wonder if she can see a thing. Gary steps out the door, and I hurry to slip away before he sees me. I take my coffee out back to watch the day come alive and think how later I'll mosey on over to Mrs. Anna Mendel's to ask if I can pick some of her tomatoes for my supper. That's the only thing I need from over there, things from her garden. Not a thing else.

A voice on the wind titters.

When I'd called Rebekha to check on her since she'd not felt comfortable coming to Momma's memorial, she'd talked about her own garden, and then asked how Daddy was holding up, how the boys and I were holding up. She'd been a good momma to us, and even though Katie Ivene hadn't let her adopt me, Micah, and Andy, Rebekha had treated us as if we were her own. As we chatted, I told her about Mrs. Anna Mendel's tomatoes, and how they made good tomato sandwiches thick with mayonnaise and salt and pepper.

Before we hung up, Rebekha told me she'd mailed the things I'd asked for, from the house I'd lived in with Dylan and then lived in alone for so very long after he'd packed his things and left. The rest of the letters, diaries, and photo albums I needed. I have more to set down. That's why I'm here. Why Grandma Faith poked at me so hard to come. That is what I now know. I'll write it all down, then leave the holler for good.

Someone drifts by, passes cool fingers along my neck, and I don't know who it is and what it wants from me. It's not Grandma Faith. Seems too soft a touch to be Momma, but then Momma has her surprising sides. Can it be the tiny touch of my little sweet one; no, it can't. I slip thoughts out of my brain, but I know certain thoughts will be back, because they must come back. How else will I record our stories all together in one place unless I relive the stories?

I lean against the sugar maple, feel the press of it against my shirt, sip from my cup, and think of all the years I'd felt alone. Not the alone of no family or a good friend, but that certain kind of alone of once having a husband and then not having one and then never having one again and telling myself I didn't feel lonely. My footsteps were the only footsteps in my house since Adin had moved away. Jinxie was long gone and I hadn't found another dog to replace him. And Dylan, well, Dylan said I was never his, when I'd thought it was the other way.

A breeze catches my hair and pushes it back. The thoughts of Dylan want to push me on back, too. I can feel it, that falling back back and back: the sunroom in the Louisiana house; the rocker where I'd rocked away the hours, looking out at the flowers and green grass, watching cars go by in the neighborhood; the lonely moments when I was not alone; my family and my good friends. Yet, the seclusion of the holler I'd fought against as a child has turned into something I ache for now.

I stretch out my legs and study my toes. The dark pink polish is chipped. Momma would have a fit over that. She kept her fingernails and toenails polished and if one little nick or chip showed, she'd re-do them on the spot. Momma knew how to make her pretty shine out. She knew how to dress and brush her hair and put on make-up. She learned it all from the fashion magazines she read. I suppose I didn't learn that from her, though I did try, sometimes. A sudden thought slams against me that Dylan and Momma would have been perfect for each other, even if they'd have destroyed each other. With my coffee I swallow that thought down as far as it will go into my innards.

Someone quietly calls, *Virginia Kate . . . Virginia Kate . . .*

I answer, "What do you want?"

The whispers grow. I can't sort through them. There is more than one. They rise all around me, coming from the mountains, pushing up from the ground, slipping from underneath the big rock, from inside my momma's house, down from the lonely house on the hill, rising watery from the creek. All the voices surround me, whisper, *Virginia Kate . . . Virginia Kate . . .* and then, *Stay . . . stay where you belong.*

I close my eyes. Wind rushes at me and pushes me down into the ground, as if I'd grow roots and never leave the holler again. The sugar maple presses harder into my back.

There comes an image of me standing under an oak tree clutching a crowd of sunflowers. A Louisiana hot wind blows. It is the day I meet the man who changes the way I see myself, both good and bad.

I remember that girl. That girl had been afraid all her life. That girl had tried to pretend she wasn't afraid. And she gained and she lost and she knew she never had what she thought was hers, because she never fully gave of herself.

Another bitter pill to swallow with my coffee.

There under the sugar maple, I think of that hot wind, that oak tree as I pressed my back against it, the sunflowers gripped in my hand, the coming storms.

I let myself go back again. It is what I do. I go back and I tell our stories. It is what Grandma Faith taught me, that the stories become real in the telling.

I make the stories real.

There is a sigh on the wind. The spirits quiet for a time; they know to let me do what I have to do. I look off to my sweet sister mountain—to all our yesterdays—and then beyond, over the mountain, following creek and river and road, down to the sluggish and eerie swamps.

It's come time again to return to what's gone by.

Even the things that hurt.

Grandma Faith whispers, *Be strong, little mite. Tell the stories.*

Yes, Grandma, I will tell the stories.

1976 to 1977

No sooner met but they looked; no sooner looked but they loved; no sooner loved but they sighed; no sooner sighed but they asked one another the reason; no sooner knew the reason but they sought the remedy
— William Shakespeare

Chapter 2

I'm Virginia Kate Carey

As I waited under an oak tree in front of the university theater holding onto a handful of sunflowers, I was no longer my momma's little given-up girl, but instead a nineteen-year-old who had seen, heard, and lived through the mistakes of others and thought she knew what was what in this old world.

A storm of students, teachers, and disco music with most of the words being *uh huh uh huh*, roared around me. I wasn't in the mood to be bothered by a soul, so I melted into the tree, loving how the bark pressed against my back through my cotton shirt. I slipped out of my old worn-out flip flops and dug my toes into the warm dirt surrounding the reaching roots. It wasn't full dark yet, but the translucent moon leered at me though breaks in the oak's leaves. Silly old Moon and I were buddies, even if it caused a heap of trouble when it had a mind to, what with its giving everything a shine that even fooled the night into thinking it wasn't dark and forbidding.

Late September in Louisiana Land could be as ornery, wet, and mean as July and August. All the clinging moisture settling on clothes, and skin and moods. I never was used to the soggy heat that made it hard to breathe, where everyone slow-moved so as not to break out in a soaking sweat. Whether the sun or the moon slung heavy in the sky, the air dripped heat and attitude on top of the Louisiana people; they most ways seemed unmindful to it, since wasn't much else they could do.

It was my best friend Jade's fourth theater dance performance and we were going out to celebrate the review in the university's student paper. It had her doing a jig on cloud ten while looking down at cloud nine. She had shoved the paper in my face and made me read it aloud to her—twice. The second time I'd sucked up two pieces of ice from my glass of sweet tea, and the chill pressed on my inner cheeks. "Nineteen-yearsh-old Jadeshta Shanders re-form-munce ootshines the res' of de casths'. Day dim ina light of her gloo. Brawvo."

She grabbed hold my hands and made me fool-jump around with her. I didn't mind. I liked being a fool for a friend.

My daydreaming flew away with a tap on my shoulder. I turned, but all I saw was the bark of the olden oak tree.

"Nice flowers," said a deep voice.

I turned the other way and there stood a big fella grinning down at me.

He said, "Who gave them to you?"

Miss Ornery about said, none of your business, but out croaked a frog that said, "They're for Jadesta."

"That's the pretty blonde dancer, right?"

I shrugged. It wore on my nerves how he stood next to me, so I looked over his right shoulder at a dark-haired girl with messy hair, her mouth open big and wide as she snorted and laughed with her friends; I pretended the tall fella wasn't even there.

He didn't get the hint. "I've been to all her performances."

I didn't care. Why would I?

"Name's Dylan. Yours?"

I couldn't talk right then since a bird came along and pecked out my tittering voice box.

He grinned at me, as if he could wait a million years, but wouldn't. He wore his light brown hair neat, unlike most of the others who stood flipping back their long hair as if they were boy versions of that Cher. His eyes were dark blue with lighter blue flecks, and he had long eyelashes—girl eyelashes. He had a mess of muscles, too. I didn't notice them all that much. Not much. He said, "Hello? Are you in there somewhere?"

Then out it came all prissy, "I'm Virginia Kate Carey." A heat began in my toes and seared all the way to my head. My heavy hair tugged against my scalp as it fell down my back, pulled my head back to expose my throat.

He held out his hand for me to shake.

When our palms touched, his calluses scraped against my own rough patches. I hated that it gave me a little shiver and I let go his hand quicker than a flea's blink.

"Will Jadesta be out soon so you can give her the flowers, Miss Kate Carey?"

"Why don't you wait in line with her other admirers?" I had my smart-aleck look on as I pointed to the line of boys waiting by the door. Their faces moonshined with love over Jade. "And it's *Virginia* Kate."

"Where's your line, *Virginia* Kate?"

I gripped the flowers so tight the stems were bending, so I leaned the flowers against the tree, and tried not to notice the sparkled eyes he had when he looked at me. Boys were trouble. Oh, I knew that from my own momma, saw what men did for her, and to her, and I didn't want trouble. I wiped my damp palms on my britches. My ugly old britches.

He made a soft laugh that meant more than a laugh should. He said, "You two are usually together. I've been watching you." He grinned, as if he were a naughty little boy who pretended he wasn't naughty one speck.

His words tiptoed up my spine and back down again. I was aware of myself in a way I had never been before. Aware of every molecule in my body.

"If you aren't with your friend, then you're always by yourself, standing away from everyone."

Looked over his shoulder again to see if Jade was ever going to come out of that door and rescue me—no Jade yet.

"Why don't we grab something to eat after you pass on those flowers?"

Checked to see if my fingernails still had dirt from digging under the leaves earlier—they were stubby, torn, and unpainted, but they were at least clean. Checked my feet—my toes weren't polished either, and one of my flip flops was kicked away from me, and I had a smudge of dirt on my left big toe. I snaked my foot over to try to grab the strap with that toe, but before I could, Dylan bent, picked up the flip flop, and then reached over to slip it onto my dirty foot. My face heated and the teeny hairs on the back of my neck tingled. Once he was done Cinderelling my left foot, I slid my right foot into my other shoe before he could.

He straightened, cleared his throat, said, "It's a nice night to walk, and to eat, don't you think?"

"Sure." I hated the big-mouthed frog that said *sure*.

"We'll just wait here for your friend." He pushed his hand through his hair and bits of his hair swirled out. He let his hand fall and slap up against his blue jeans.

I liked the swirled pieces of his hair more than the perfect combed ones.

He burned me with a look.

I picked up the flowers from the ground and buried my face in them. Sunflowers sure were beautiful, but they didn't have much sweet flower smell once plucked and taken far from their home. I imagined them fresh-picked, still hot from the sun and smelling of earth and fresh air, and thought of the high school class trip in the hot jumpity bus. As we rode through Kansas, we passed a giant field of sunflowers, where thousands of blossoms turned their bonnet faces to the light, except for one that looked in a different direction from the others. Or maybe it was the others that turned away from that one flower. I felt a kinship to that one the most.

"Do you always carry on such titillating conversation?"

We both laughed. I sounded a regular girl when I laughed that way. A girl who would let herself act foolish over a boy. Like I didn't have a lick of sense just as the moon didn't. If only I had something smart to say. I tried to think what the other girls twittered on about to boys, but nothing came to mind. He stood too close, so that every time he took in air he stole mine so I couldn't breathe right.

He was as tall as my daddy was, and had a twinkle to his eye just as Daddy did when he was around girls. But, unlike Daddy's bourbon-hoarse voice, Dylan's rumbled out of his chest and flew right to the stars before it drippled down warm honey over me. He stepped closer and I pressed my back into the oak, so the bark tattooed through my shirt all its story. I wondered if I could come back in seventy-seven years and ask this old oak to tell me what had gone by, where I'd gone, and who I'd gone with.

Someone called Dylan's name and he turned to wave and shout back.

Aunt Ruby slithered into my ear, from that day long ago back in her dark old house in West Virginia. I could still smell her booze breath hot on my face. *Don't you be letting men get at you, you hear me? I know. Your Aunt Ruby knows all about men. That momma of your'n could tell you a thing or two about nasty men. They's been on her since she was your age.*

"Virginia Kate!" Jade's voice jerked me away from things I didn't want to think on. She stopped in front of me. "Hey, why's your face so red?" She looked from me to Dylan, and back.

"Here." I thrust the flowers at her, my arm out stiff as a tomato-stick. One of the sunflower heads fell onto the ground where it lay pitiful, but still beautiful all the same.

She put her face into them, just as I had done, lifted her head and said, "So, what's going on?" She knew. She was snarky with her left eyebrow lifted so high it was about to get lost in her short blonde bangs. She asked, "Who's this?"

"It's Dylan." I pointed to him with my stiff arm.

Jade put on her smoky-silk voice, "Hey, Dylan."

"Nice to meet you, Jadesta." They shook hands and I wondered if he liked her soft palms better than my rough ones. He said, "We're going to get something to eat. Want to join us?" Dylan leaned into me and the heat from his body mixed with my own.

Jade pulled an *oh fiddle dee dee* face. "Darn it. I can't. Got a date."

She was a lying liar. I stared a big fiery hole in her, but she didn't look my way.

Dylan said to me, "Well, I guess it's just the two of us."

Jade grabbed my arm, pulled me closer to her. "Can you excuse us a moment, Dylan?"

"Sure. I'll be right back." He strode off towards a group of people, but not before giving me a look of a lion that's about to eat up a lamb and not feel bad about it one bit.

Jade stood in front of me, the sides of her mouth twitching in an about-to-be-smart-aleck dance. "He's really good-looking, Vee. It's about time you go out with a strapping man." She talked about him all breathless and girlish, and it wore on my nerves something fierce.

"Shush up. Besides, we're not *going out.*" I stuffed my hands into the pockets of my pedal pushers, wishing I'd worn different britches, some blue jeans, or cut offs even, instead of Rebekha's clothes she used to work in the yard. "We're just going to eat some food at the same time." I gave an eye roll just as Momma used to.

"Uh huh, whatever you want to call it. I call it a date with a bee-you-tee-ful man."

"Then you can have Mr. Strapping Man for yourself."

"Yeah, you'd like that, huh?"

"So would you," I said.

She flipped her hand through her choppy hair and the ends flew up and out, light as butterfly wings.

"Come with me so I won't be by myself."

"You won't be by yourself. You'll be with Dylan."

I made my eyes go all big and round; I was surely the most pitiful sight in the known and unknown universe.

She tore off with those flowers flapping, pieces of golden yellow flying out with her, looking back at me once with a big monkey-grin before she turned the corner and disappeared.

I took in a deep breath, deep to the bottom of my lungs, then let it out slow, clearing the shroud of Aunt Ruby, clearing thoughts of Momma and men. I watched Dylan prowl back to me, not moving any of my outsides, but my insides were fraidy-frog jumping. When he stood before me and caught up my eyes with his, his pupils reflected what he saw, and it made my messy hair, my scraggled nails, my dirty foot—my everything—shine out as if I was a ten foot tall West Virginia hick girl in torn pedal pushers.

He asked, "Where'd Jadesta go?"

I shrugged.

"I guess it's just you and me, then."

I shrugged.

A girl in bell-bottoms and a tight rib-showing shirt walked by and as she did, she turned and winked at Dylan. Dylan watched her walk away, watched her rear wiggle like two squirrels stuffed in a potato sack. She had red hair and freckled peached-cream skin. She hadn't seen me at all; it was as if I blended in with the bark of the tree, the soil of the earth.

Dylan turned to me with a funny look, which then turned into a regular look. He asked, "You ready?"

I nodded, but my innards cried, *No.*

We walked through the crowd of people and they all parted for Dylan to walk by. He waved and shouted out to someone every few steps. Some stopped him to talk and the old see-through feeling seeped into my bones all the way to my marrow. Only a few said, "And who is this, Dylan?" and Dylan answered, "This is Virginia Kate Carey," and they'd say, "Oh. Okay . . ." and then went on talking about things I didn't know a hill of beans about. Well, I could have said my own name and could have met their eyes and could have been a real live person standing on the hot sidewalk, but they weren't giving me a chance.

Only his friend Patrick looked straight at me. "Nice to meet you Virginia Kate," and then said to Dylan, "You always have had good taste in women, you lucky dog."

Dylan laughed and stepped closer to me.

I stepped one step back, for I didn't want to be one of his lucky dog women he had good taste over, and wished myself back under the oak tree before I'd decided to say yes I'd go to eat. Maybe before that, maybe I wished myself somewhere else so I'd never talked to Dylan in the first place. I sniffed the air, a wild critter, and smelled danger.

The world swirled round me and I couldn't do a thing but watch it.

∞ • ∞

When I sidled on into Soot's diner with Dylan, Soot's mouth fell open. I wanted to tell her that some bats could make a nest in there and have babies if she wouldn't close it. Of all the time I'd eaten there, and been there working for Soot and Marco, I'd never had a boy by my side or talked about one, and Soot never asked. Not like my boss at the library who tried to push her son on me, and since I always said no no no, she shushed about it, directly. People should mind their own business.

Soot hugged me, and as her pregnant belly pressed against my empty stomach, her little one kicked against me and I remembered lying in my bedroom with its blue-formerly-pink walls, silly girl dreaming of how many children I'd have with my pipe-smoking, soft-speaking husband.

"Whatchoo doing?" Soot looked at Dylan, then back at me, rubbing her belly in slow circles. It wore on my nerves how she and Jade acted just because I had a fella beside me, one who might be handsome and one who might have burning eyes, but one who was most certainly not a date.

"Hey, Soot. Hey Marco," I said.

Marco waved from where he stood at his fryer. He was always at the fryer and I don't remember ever seeing him anywhere else.

Dylan took in Soot's diner. I guessed he'd never been before, the way he looked here, there, and yonder.

Soot was saying, ". . . over here, Boo." She led the way to a table in the corner, walking her ducky pregnant walk. Her dark hair swung from side to side, slapping against her shoulders. Always, I loved her. The image of me with Daddy when we ate our shrimp po-boys rose up as happy clouds. She'd made me feel special that day. Made that little girl me forget she had been forced to leave sweet sister mountain behind and come to foreign Louisiana.

Dylan pulled out a chair for me, but I was already on the other side where he planned on sitting, had pulled out my own chair, and plopped into it. I didn't mean to ruin his gallant ways, but I'd always just set myself down without anyone pulling out my chair.

Soot stood by the table to take our order. "What'll it be?"

"Since I'm in this here parish, I'll have a hamburger, fries, and an orange-pop-softdrink-coke, please, yawwwlll."

Soot fell out laughing. She turned to Marco, "Remember how she couldn't get it right when she first moved here? Called coke a pop."

Marco peeled a potato, said, "Her eyes were big as two supper plates, looking all around up in here."

Dylan lifted his eyebrows, looked from me to Soot to Marco and back again.

Soot laughed, held onto her womb as if her baby were laughing too.

I didn't bother to explain to Dylan how I learned to call a pop a coke even if it was orange, grape, Sprite, or real Coke-Cola; how y'all had to be said just right, *yawwwl*. How Louisiana was the only state that had parishes instead of counties. How South Louisiana sloshed like the inside of Soot's pregnant womb, but squirmed with weird critters instead of a sweet baby. Micah had taught me when I moved to Louisiana after Momma gave me up, then I taught Andy when Momma abandoned him, too. That's what brothers and sisters did for each other when their parents divorced and used them as prizes.

Dylan cleared his throat over our laughing and remembering, said, "I'll have a draft with my burger and fries, please."

Soot turned to Marco, "You got that, Handsome?" She never wrote down a thing.

"I'm fixin' to fry plenty of taters for our girl." Marco threw potatoes into a basket, lowered it into the grease, and sang something I couldn't make out the words to, but it sounded French, maybe the Cajun French. He hulked over the fryer, his hands as big as my head. But he was so gentle with Soot; he was the sweetest thing ever. I day-dreamed how one day I'd find someone as good as Marco, except he'd—Soot touched me on the shoulder as she walked by to take another order. Dylan was talking and I'd not heard a word.

Dylan went on all he wanted to; since I didn't have much I wanted to say. He told how he was going to be a successful architect and that he apprenticed at a firm downtown and he was close to finishing school, and blabbity blab blab he went with his mouth just a-flapping. Soot brought our food and I started in on mine. He could let his get cold while he blabbered on if he wanted to. All the frogs squirming in my belly were hungry and once I fed them, maybe they'd go to sleep and shush their blurting out stupid things.

". . . and then we took a tour of the building and they asked my opinion and I was honored to . . ."

I nodded my head, chewed my food, held myself tight in my chair.

Soot duck-waddle-sashayed over to give Dylan a second beer. I wondered what happened to the first one.

". . . and they said I have what it takes to . . ."

I thought maybe I could tell him about my photography, but then maybe I wasn't in the mood. My art professor said I had a gift with my camera; it was the first time anyone said I had a gift and when Dr. Rowe said it, it meant even more. Micah had gifts, and I figured he held a drawing pencil before he held a baby-bottle of milk; his teachers had ohhed and ahhed over what he created, but he hadn't cared what they thought; he only cared what he thought. That made me smile.

". . . my own house one day . . ."

The tables were filling, and Soot rushed to fill orders. Every so often, she turned to give me a sly look, and I ignored her silliness.

". . . in California . . ."

I watched Marco slice a piece of French bread for a po-boy.

Dylan's jabbering, the knife slicing, Soot's calling out orders, and the customers all mixed together as a machine of sounds that whirred round me until I couldn't make out what were his words and what were someone else's and what was the buzzing of my own swirly thoughts.

We finished our supper to the tune of Marco singing a little too loud about strangers meeting in the night, while Soot tee hee'd, and I did the eye roll. I could have bust Marco a good one. When Soot brought our bill, since I never let her give me free food, I wouldn't let Dylan pay for mine. Miss Priss slapped her money on the table and preened to herself when Dylan looked surprised at a girl paying for her own supper even if he did ask her to eat. I didn't want to feel beholden to him for a thing. Maybe when I walked out of the diner, I'd want to say, "So long, see you later," without feeling as if he'd done me any favors at all by paying for my burger and fried potatoes.

As we headed out the door, Soot called out, "Y'all come back soon and not later!"

I gave her a little wave and walked out with Dylan into the full dark. The air settled on my skin. My clothes rubbed against me until I thought I'd go insane, throw off my clothes, and run howling at the old moon. From the corner of my eye, I watched Dylan's mouth form all those words he said and said and said. My body itched and jittered. I didn't care for that itchy feeling one little bit. I'd need to take care.

He asked, "What dorm are you in?"

"I stay at home."

"Do you need a ride?"

I'd forgotten Jade was supposed to give me a ride home. Her rear needed a swift mule-kick for leaving me to the lion. Yet, there was another part of me that walked a little lighter over the ground, a part that wondered how the inside of his car smelled, if he drove fast or slow, if the drive home would seem long or short.

"My car isn't far . . ." He cleared his throat, added, "I really don't mind."

That stupid frog gibberished, "I do need a ride, I guess. I don't have one. A car. Or ride."

He walked with me to the theater parking lot and led me to his car, a pretty little blue Triumph. I put out my hand to open the car door, but he hurried and opened it for me. I settled onto the leather bucket seat with my hands resting on my legs. He shut the door to close me in. His car smelled of leather, and something sweet. He slid in the car, started it, and pulled out of the parking lot.

I told where I lived, and he said, "Oh yes, I know where that is." He kept both big-knuckled hands on the steering wheel that he tapped as he said, "We could go get some ice cream or something, if you want. I mean, before I take you home."

"I have to study for a test, but thank you." I was a stone cold liar.

"Just where *are* you from? I can't place your accent."

I wondered why everyone said I had the accent when everyone else did. And if my West Virginia was mixed with my Louisiana, if I sounded different from how I did before. I said, "I'm from West Virginia."

"Oh, the mountains. It must be beautiful there. I'm from California myself."

I nodded, said, "Uh huh."

"What brought you here?"

I wanted to say, *Daddy's silly little car and Momma's greedy deal with Mee Maw,* but instead I changed up the subject by pointing out the window and asking, "What kind of tree is that?" Even though I knew. As a child, I'd learned the names of many things. It was a tupelo tree.

"What tree was that?" Dylan slowed the car to a stop, backed up.

I hurried and said, "There, that one."

"The one right there?" He pointed to a tree.

I nodded, even though it wasn't the tupelo, but a persimmon.

"That's a persimmon tree." He pulled off away. "There's one in my neighbor's yard. She fell out of it." He laughed, then said, "Well, it wasn't funny at the time, but just picturing her lying on the ground yelling for help. I mean, what was she doing climbing the persimmon tree?"

I wondered that, too.

He told me how that poor little woman was sprawled on the grass, and he'd asked her, "What were you doing in the tree?" and she'd answered him, "I just felt like climbing it to see what things looked like from a persimmon tree's perspective." He said he carried her into her house and laid her on her couch where she'd told him how her couch was her best friend, next to the persimmon tree. Dylan shrugged at that.

I said, "I'd surely like to know that woman."

He didn't hear me because he was talking about the architecture of her house.

When we pulled into the driveway, I hurried and opened my door, poured myself out.

Dylan was out, too. "I'll walk you to your door."

"I can do it by myself."

He didn't listen; he walked with me up to the steps, onto the porch.

Glancing across the street, I saw Amy Campinelle and Mr. Husband staring at me from their window. I pretended I didn't see them gawking. At the door, Dylan leaned over to kiss me and I turned my head so that his lips brushed against my ear. I shivered, and in that shivery feeling was all the telling of what was inside of me and what I'd have to deny.

Aunt Ruby tried to whisper to me again about things no girl needed to hear, so I mind-flushed her back down the toilet, where she lived in the bowels of the earth with Uncle Ar-vile. She didn't want to be flushed and clung to the sides, the stubborn old mean-spirited hag. I imagined Aunt Ruby hunted up a switch and looked for kids to beat, even though no kids were around. Uncle Arville's guts spilled out from the hole in his stomach. My deader than dead aunt and uncle fussed and argued in the forever dark, just as they always had.

Dylan cleared his throat and the sound ripped aloud in the quiet night-air. He sure cleared his throat a lot. "I said, 'Good night, Kate.'"

The moon gave its light to us, but I felt that little girl in the dark with only a sliver of filtered light streaming in through the keyhole. I said to him, "It's *Virginia* Kate."

"I'll see you later?"

Maybe I nodded, or maybe I didn't. Maybe I said goodnight, or maybe I said nothing. My breath was jaggedy against my throat as if I'd swallowed a gumball from the gumball tree. The world turned and turned and made me dizzy.

He jogged down the steps and to his car, disappeared inside, roared up his engine, backed down the drive, and sped on away.

I felt like the girls I always wondered about. The ones almost kissed in a way that made them lose all their thoughts and all their breath.

Grandma Faith said, *Be mindful . . .*

I cater-cocked my head to the left to listen to the winds sent down from West Virginia, answered, "Oh, Grandma, he's just a boy."

She blew a breath against my cheek to tell me she was right there with me so I'd be safe.

I was ornery and tried to shake Grandma Faith away to the far corners of the universe, just as the flames had, as Momma had. She sighed and sighed, but wouldn't leave me, no matter how much I shook her away.

I slipped inside, closed the door, and then stood at the window. Outside where moonlight and streetlight didn't reach held all manner of unseen things. The ground squirmed with bugs, in the sky flew bats, crawfish inside hidey-holes, in the trees rested birds, and slipping along were critters that came out only in the night since the daylight held nothing for them.

My mind kept its tilt-a-whirl as I pressed my face against the pane and searched.

I'd have to keep myself wise and not be like the ones before me, young and foolish and in love—and in worse. I'd be the smart one. The one who didn't become trapped. That what I'd do. I was Virginia Kate Carey and I was nobody's fool.

Grandma Faith whispered, *There's my girl. Love wise and well or not at all.*

Chapter 3

Remember your women-kin's past

My Louisiana family was like a broken tea-set our Rebekha had since she was a little girl, where some of the teacups didn't match, one of the plates was chipped, and a spoon was bent out of shape, yet she still loved that tea-set and said nothing could replace it, especially not a brand new one.

Our family was Micah running off to New York, me already a sophomore in college before I hardly was used to the idea of college at all, Andy shaving when most boys didn't need to, Bobby the only one who had both Rebekha and Daddy's blood, Daddy and his boozy love-in-a-bottle that he fought with as if it were another wife. And then there was Rebekha, who was the teapot ready to be filled with all of us, the woman who took in Micah, Andy, and me and gave us sanctuary. I wasn't sure where Momma fit in, since she'd given Micah, Andy, and me away. Momma wasn't a tea-set sort of woman.

I awakened early and stretched out my toes. It was quiet outside, not even a dog barked. I eased out of bed, then pulled the covers tight and neat the way Rebekha taught me when I'd come to live with her and Daddy. No lumps, bumps, sagging covers, or sheets that weren't weekly washed in Rebekha's house. Those were things she said her momma was strict about and Rebekha carried it on. There were other things Rebekha's momma was mean and strict about that Rebekha didn't carry on, and for that I was glad. I'd never tell her that, though, since reminding some girls about their mommas made their eyes pinch with sad and mad and hurt and hope all at the once.

I brushed out my hair and pulled it into a high ponytail, then sneaked quiet to the bathroom to freshen up. Passing Rebekha and Daddy's room there came no noise at all. Down the hall from Andy's room came the soft sound of his radio playing a song about black waters and the Mississippi moon shining to make things better. Sometimes he left the radio on too loud and Daddy would bang on his door or holler out how Andy had better turn it down or he'd take away the radio. Daddy was on Andy all the time to grow up, said he'd soon graduate high school and still acted like a twelve-year-old. Andy just laughed at Daddy's bluster. Andy took after Momma's itchy ways, never could be still. I bet he still slept just as Momma slept, with feet moving, face twitching, all parts shimmering and skittering.

I eased shut the door to the bathroom, took my Noxzema from the cabinet, and blobbed it on my face. Jade said Noxzema was the best thing for a girl's complexion. Her skin was perfect, so I believed her. I was to clean my face for three minutes, but I rarely made it past one minute, and sometimes not that much. I rinsed and then patted my face dry. Another Jade rule—never rub my face or else one day I'd have saggy skin. There were too many rules for girls, which was another thing, she hated me calling us *girls* and instead thought I should call us *women*.

I left the bathroom, and from Bobby's room heard a rustling sound. Bobby sometimes was up as early as I was. He'd wait for Andy to wake, and if Andy slept too late, Bobby threw things at him until he jumped out of bed and chased after him, hollering how he'd bust Bobby a good one. Ever since Andy came to Louisiana when Bobby was in diapers, Bobby had latched on to him, and being ten-years-old made Bobby no less a shadow to his big brother, maybe more so. We kids had never thought of ourselves as half siblings to Bobby's whole; we all were just brothers and sister.

Once back to my room, I slipped on my old blue jean cut-offs and a soft white t-shirt. Whisper-footing it into the kitchen, I measured out the coffee and water, plugged in the pot to percolate, and then cut on the fire for scrambled eggs. Marco taught me how to make proper scrambled eggs and once let me practice cooking breakfast when the diner was slow. Even though I didn't do so hot, he never said so.

I slapped a blob of butter into the skillet to melt, whipped eight eggs with a little milk, a spit of faucet water, salt and pepper, poured it all into the hot buttered skillet, and cut down the heat. While the eggs bubbled away, I put toast in the toaster.

From Rebekha and Daddy's room I heard Daddy blowing his

nose. Their door opened, closed, and then the bathroom door closed. Soon, Andy yelled at Bobby to let him sleep, and Bobby told him he was lazy. Something slammed against a wall. The missing piece was Micah's cranky morning eyes with paint still in his fingernails, or a touch of it on his cheek. I wondered what his New York mornings were like.

Rebekha came into the kitchen, pulling her robe close to her. "Virginia Kate, you didn't have to start breakfast. But thank you." She stirred the eggs, which I saw were too browned on the bottom.

"Just in the mood, I guess." I scraped the burned edges of the toast into the sink.

Daddy came in and poured a cup of coffee, added a bit of cream, and nothing else.

"Morning Daddy."

"Morning my beauties." He looked at the eggs in the skillet.

Rebekha asked me, "How was your date last night?" She smiled with that gap in between her front teeth, the one I was always glad she never let the dentist fix, since it made her look sincere, and less as if she were trying to be perfect.

"We're just friends, so it wasn't a date."

"I see," said Rebekha, as if she didn't see.

Daddy raised an eyebrow at me.

As the weeks passed from that night of Jade's dance, and early fall turned to late fall, and then the mild old winter was near ready to sneak its way in, I knew Rebekha and Daddy were more than kit-cat curious about what I was up to and why I didn't call Dylan my date. They'd watch me with question mark eyes as I'd rush out to Dylan's car before he could come fetch me.

"What did you do last night on your date that wasn't a date, Bug?" Daddy asked.

I finished buttering the last piece of toast and put it on a plate. "We saw *Rocky.*" I didn't say Dylan had sneaked in booze and all during the movie he tipped back that Coke-Cola that held more than Coke-Cola.

Rebekha said, "Frederick, let's go see that."

"What about seeing a movie with substance?"

"You mean to tell me you never went to see Westerns as a boy or some other show that wasn't considered Shakespearean? Hummm?" Rebekha leaned over and kissed Daddy on top of his head. She loved him, even when her eyes were red from crying or her mouth was set straight from when he came home later than he should have. I'd caught her checking the cabinets and was as surprised as a hen that laid a purple egg. I never knew she looked for his hidden booze as I did.

From the hallway came the sound of shuffling and grunts and, *stop it* and *ow* and *I'm telling*. Andy-and-Bobby stampeded into the kitchen. They piled egg, grabbed toast, pushed shoved. I was relieved they'd come in, for I didn't want to talk about Dylan. Especially because of last night and *that kiss*. The one that shot my body afire. The kind of kiss I'd heard whispered about by girls with hickeys on their necks, or seen in movies where the women panted breath.

Dylan had tangled up his hands in my hair and pulled me to him. A burn began from deep inside my innards and blew outward from my pores in a hot sweat. It wasn't likened to anything I'd ever felt before. My body had seared and burned with such a raging fire, I almost turned to ashes. Danger. Something had changed with *that kiss* and made danger. Whether that change came from inside me or him or both, I couldn't figure, but *that kiss* sent my thoughts spiraling out like a pebble tossed on water, one thought leading to another and another and beyond. It was hard to think of a fella as a friend with a kiss like that.

Grandma Faith had called out strong, *Remember your women-kin's pasts*.

I listened to Grandma, had pushed him back, said, "Dylan, we're just good friends."

He'd said, "So you say."

After breakfast was over and everyone scattered, save the usual Rebekha and me, Rebekha asked what she'd been asking since I first came to live there, "You wash; I dry?"

We picked up the dishes, took them to the kitchen, and stood at the sink together. Outside the window, there were a few changes. The bushes were thicker next door, and so was Miss Darla's garden. She grew things I'd never seen before in her flowers, herbs, and small fruits. She made teas for every kind of ailment, along with balms and lotions that healed quicker than regular medicine could, least ways seemed to me.

She wasn't home; I knew because her house felt empty. Miss Darla liked to travel, see things, and gather what she wanted and needed. I wondered if she had boyfriends scattered across the good old Earth, but I never did see her with a man.

". . . around sometime to meet us."

I handed Rebekha three forks. "I'm sorry, what'd you say?"

She dried the forks. "I was saying I'd like to meet this boy, your friend, you've been seeing so we can come to know him instead of those quick waves as he picks you up." She shook out her dishrag, then took the plates I handed her.

I knew Rebekha wanted me to talk to her about Dylan, but those feelings were easier to keep stuffed down where they were safe. If I talked about him, words would be released into the air, faster and faster until I'd be sucked asunder by a tornado, mad-whirled, scattering feelings and actions willy nilly. I changed up the subject. "Mee Maw said she wants to buy me a car for my twentieth birthday. I don't know if I can wait that long."

Rebekha dried the bowl I'd just rinsed and rinsed. She couldn't stand the thought of any trace of soap left on a dish. "That's only about eight months away. Not so long to wait, from my age standpoint anyway." She put the bowl on top of the plates. "I told her she had no need to be buying cars for y'all, but I do believe she'll do whatever it is she wants to do."

I handed her the cleaned and rinsed, rinsed, rinsed skillet. "Maybe I shouldn't accept it."

"Oh, go ahead and take her offer. Andy's already planning for his, and he'll bug her for it sooner than you're getting yours, that's for certain." She began putting away the dishes, while I let out the dirty dishwater so I could clean out the sink just how Rebekha liked it cleaned.

We were quiet for a bit. The air bulged with thoughts of Mee Maw and her antics. How she'd come visit and stir up trouble and talk about how a woman needs a tater-cooking man so a woman wouldn't have to cook her own taters, and how Rebekha was a saint and everyone knew how saints died young because they were too wound tight with all the things they wished they could do instead of denying them, and on she'd go, her lips slapping together with more foolishness than should be allowed by one old woman.

When the kitchen sparkled, Rebekha excused herself to get dressed, and I headed on to my room. I opened my underwear drawer and reached inside for the card I'd bought Momma. It was her birthday coming soon and I'd spent thirty minutes trying to find the right card for a momma who may not care whether she gets a card or not, for a momma who couldn't care less about whether her daughter remembered her birthday, and one who more times than not forgot her own daughter's birthday or was too ornery to let her know she remembered. They didn't have cards for mommas like my momma.

At last I'd found a plain card with red and blue flowers, two of her favorite colors, that read of nothing at all about mommas and daughters and how they sure were glad they had each other. I'd signed it, *Love, Virginia Kate,* instead of *Love, your daughter.* It could have been a birthday card for anyone, any old stranger at all.

I'd asked Andy if he wanted to sign the card, but he gave me a look as if I were wasting my time, and in fact, he'd said that, "Virginia Kate, you're wasting your time. I bet she throws it in the garbage after she sees there's no present or money in it."

With the card in the envelope, I also slipped in a photo of me standing in front of the student union so Momma could see I was in college, one of Andy grinning out from the driver's side window of Rebekha's serious Dodge, and one of Micah in the shadow of tall New York buildings, so Momma could see how we were growing up and going on without her. I sealed the envelope, licked the stamp and pressed it, wrote out Rebekha's return address, and walked it out to the mailbox, even though the mail wouldn't come until Monday afternoon. That way, it would crouch in there and wait, and I could change up my mind about sending it if I had a mind to, which I would not.

I pictured it riding in mail trucks, pictured it delivered, pictured Mrs. Mendel taking the mail to Momma, pictured Momma as she opened it, studied our photos, and then I pretended she'd sigh over us. I daydreamed she'd dial me up to thank me, but that's when the imagining turned fuzzy and far away, as far away as the holler where my mountain rose high and shadowed Momma.

Enough of Momma. I flapped my flip flopped feet into the living room. From the side table drawer, I took the photo album Rebekha had fashioned of all us kids since we came to live with her, and of Bobby from birth until last month. I started from the beginning that wasn't really a beginning. The first page was pictures of Daddy and Rebekha's wedding day. Then, very soon after, Micah showed up in the photos. I turned another page and there was a photo of Micah and me setting on the porch together. We were inches apart, but my foot touched his foot, an anchor. In that photo, I'd only been in South Louisiana a few weeks. There were more pictures of Rebekha, Daddy, Micah, and me. Baby Bobby came. After a time, my sorrowed-photographed face began to lift into a hint of a smile. Then came Andy, and from the beginning Andy's photo-face looked as if he belonged.

I wished there was more of a beginning instead of some starting point where Micah, Andy, and I appeared as if from the air, fully formed and of differing ages. There was infant Bobby held in Rebekha's arms as she rocked him to sleep, and Bobby toddling on chubby feet, and Bobby holding his baseball and bat, each stage of his life shown. I wanted that for the three of us West Virginia kids, but those were wishes that belonged in the fire, where they'd burn and fly away as ashes in the wind. There had to be a secret for me to figure out how to let it go, but I hadn't figured that one out yet.

Even if I had photos from when we were babies and placed them in the album, it would be fake, it wouldn't be what really was. What really was hadn't changed. Our beginnings were in the holler, not there with Rebekha.

I closed the album, put it away, and headed to the back. Such silly thoughts to be thinking on a beautiful Sunday morning with Rebekha in her garden, her knees growing dirty from the Louisiana earth, her fingernails sliver-moons of Louisiana soil that she'd scrub and scrub away, her hair tucked behind her ears. Always the same. And that's what I let myself be happy for, that I was a part of her, no matter how late I came around.

From the back screened-in porch, I took a pair of Rebekha's worn gardening gloves from the shelf; the earth had stained them dark from her good work. Also from the shelf, I took a newer pair and those I stuffed into my britches' pocket. I stepped back inside, went to my room, and put the worn-out gloves in my bottom dresser drawer, where I kept things I needed to keep.

I put on the newer gloves, a light jacket, and went outside, down the steps, and to the garden where I knelt down with her, our heads close, pale-white Rebekha contrasted against that dark earth, and me with my West Virginia kin apparent in my dark hair and eyes, in the way my skin held my heritage. We worked, pulling dead plants and weeds, soothing and loosening the ground so Rebekha could plant tulip and daffodil bulbs, and to place seeds for dormant planting for a spring growing. She often planted from October to December, since the ground didn't hard freeze. Rebekha found a way to be in her garden all seasons; it was what she loved to do.

Every so often our gloved hands touched or our hair flew out in the cool wind to mingle together. I said, "December and it's 61 degrees," and took off my jacket.

"Supposed to turn colder next week, just in time for first day of winter."

We worked away, hardly talking but hardly needing to. Like comfortable family.

How else do I wish it to be? I wished it to be just as it was right then, but I wished to have been there from the beginning, instead of along the way.

Chapter 4

Why are you so afraid?

The phone rang five minutes after I'd slumped home from a bad day at class where I'd made a C on my history test and Dr. Fraser stopped me from leaving to ask if I was okay, since my good work had slipped. That'd made me late for my shift at the library, and I'd stayed late to make up for it. My stomach growled and my tongue was thirsty. I'd barely had a bite-and-swallow of my snack, when that phone yowled at me.

No one else was home, and I wondered if Dylan had dialed and listened to ringing, dialed and listened to ringing, just waiting for when someone, namely me, would answer the phone so he could hurl out what he had to say before he died from too many words backing up in him, because we hadn't talked to each other in a few days.

Before I'd barely said a hello how are you, he'd busted wide open. "Kate, I'm thinking a barbeque is the perfect opportunity to mingle friends and family so we can take us to the next level instead of floating along not as serious as I'd like. And before it gets too hot. Already it was eighty degrees yesterday. Even spring here is a killer."

"Yes, well I—"

"My family can't make a trip from California this time, but my friends are dying to meet you."

Most of them had already met me.

"We've been a couple near eight months now. Don't you think it's time?"

"We aren't really a—"

"Patrick can't quit talking about you. I think he has a crush on my girl."

"I'm not your—"

"If it gets too warm, I have plenty of shade and plenty of sodas."

"Yes, but we—"

"Should I invite your family myself? Or do you want to ask them? What do you think?" He finally paused.

"My family has plans that day."

"But I haven't said what day."

"Oh." I asked, "What day?"

"This Saturday would be perfect. I know it's short notice, but people in Louisiana do last-minute parties all the time. It's expected, even."

"They got plans on Saturday."

"You haven't even asked them."

"I just know they do is all."

He cleared his throat, then said, "I already bought beer and food and things for a big barbeque."

"I can ask Jade and her date of the week."

He laughed, and in that rumbled laugh was the reason I almost changed up my mind about asking my family to come. But I didn't. In the movies, whenever a girl's parents met the boy, it meant things were *serious*. Serious enough to cause all manner of troubles to happen. Something changed with the boy and girl because they saw each other through their family's eyes. They'd then fight and find fault with each other more and more, and soon they weren't even friends anymore. I'd seen plenty of movies about that.

"Hello? Kate? You still on the line?"

"Yes, I am."

"I know you don't eat pork, so I was thinking chicken . . ."

The barbeque was planned. It would be the first time I'd see inside his house, since I was always afraid to be alone with him there.

Jade told me, "You can't move this slowly with guys. They are easily distracted by some other shiny thing that pays better attention to them."

"I pay attention."

"You still call him a friend; well let me tell you, guys his age don't want girls for friends." She held up her fingers and ticked off the rest, "You haven't introduced him to your dad or Rebekha, you won't sleep with him, you haven't been inside his house, you won't commit to anything. For god's sake, Vee! The man has to be a saint." She thought a minute, "Either that or he finds some way, or someone, to . . . you know . . . get *that* taken care of."

I told her to mind her own business. She told me she didn't have to because she was my friend and it was a special friend rule. I said I knew what I was doing. She said oh sure you do. And on we went. But she didn't understand. Didn't understand the power of my kin's legacy.

That Saturday, I dressed in tan shorts and a yellow cotton shirt and waited on the front steps of Rebekha and Daddy's house for Jade to come fetch me. I had my barbeque party offerings setting beside me in a box.

Jade zipped into the driveway, with her latest date whose name could have been Tom, Dick, or Harry. I grabbed my box, jumped up and ran to her cute car, and climbed into the backseat. Over the music, I shouted, "What's a squeeze box?"

She shrugged, shouted, "No one knows I guess," looked back at me, turned down the music, and shook her head.

"What?"

"Is that what you're wearing?"

I shrugged.

"I should make you go back inside and change. You look thirteen years old."

Her date said, "She does not."

Jade slapped his arm. "You shut your mouth. What do you know about it?" But she laughed and he laughed. They had a secret language behind that laugh.

When I didn't leave the car to change, Jade pulled a big sigh, backed out of the driveway, and drove on, turning the music back up.

When we parked in front of Dylan's house and piled out of Jade's car, Jade smoothed down her short flowered halter dress, leaned over and fiddled with the strap on her gold sandals, while her date-of-the-week watched her with hungry eyes.

I pulled on my too-tight shorts that were from high school, tugged on my ponytail held up with an old ponytail holder Jade had given me years ago.

While her date balanced the things we'd brought in his long thin arms, Jade shook her head again at my clothes and gave me a look cats give barking dogs.

I looked at the persimmon tree next door to see if a woman was in it, but no one was there. I had the urge to go inside her house and ask if I could lie upon her couch and miss the party.

We went straight through the back gate, as Dylan had told us to, and entered a party in full swing with music, laughter, and handsome and pretty. Dylan's yard was perfect. There were blooming red and pink azaleas against the fence, and miniature white azaleas surrounding an oak tree. He had camellia bushes, crepe myrtle, Japanese magnolia, Louisiana iris. There wasn't a blade of grass that wasn't dark green, not a speck of dirt peeked out, as if he'd laid carpet instead of grass. Rebekha would have a fit, itching to get her fingers into his yard and plant more flowers, maybe some hot peppers.

Jade's fella laid down our food on a table that held chips, salsas, and a large chocolate cake. There was another table under an umbrella, and on the patio were two smaller tables. Dylan stood across the yard talking to a girl near a table under a magnolia tree. There were many girls there, and none of them wore shorts or a cotton top like mine or a ponytail holder with a big plastic ball attached. Every one of them was dressed more like Jade was. I wished then I'd have listened to my friend.

Jade knew my worries, and gave me a look that told me to stand straight and don't fret about it. She reached inside her purse, pulled out a tube of lipstick, and quick as a bird's blink, filled in my lips with rose tint, passed her finger across the lipstick tip and then dabbed some on my cheeks. She pulled a thin strand of hair from my ponytail and let it hang down, said, "There. You look beautiful."

I pulled back my shoulders.

The girl laughed and put her hand on Dylan's shoulder. He laughed back and didn't take it away. He turned from the girl, saw me, and rushed to give me a hug. He said a hello to Jade and nodded a hello to whatever-his-name-was. Maybe Jade introduced them or maybe she didn't, but right then, a dog waggled up to me and stuck his nose in the palm of my hand and I bent to pet him, his fur soft as new-combed cotton.

I straightened when Dylan called out, "Everyone, listen up!"

Some of his friends turned to us, their eyebrows raised, their mouths opened in quirked up curious lips. They slap knew who I was and why they pretended they didn't made no mind to me. I'd been see-through most my life, so why should I let it get my goat then?

"This is Kate." He put his arm around me and squeezed.

My rose lips rose in a trembled smile.

They raised hands to wave. Some of those hands were limp as over-cooked string beans.

Patrick stepped forward and hugged me tight, then tighter. He kissed me right on the mouth, hugged me again, lifted me off the ground and swung me round, while saying, "Why don't we run away together, Virginia Kate?" His lips had my lipstick on them.

Dylan told his friend, "Now, hold on there, Patrick. That's *my* girl."

Patrick let me go, said, "Some guys have all the luck." He stood near me, but didn't touch again.

Dylan introduced Jade as a dancer, and Dylan's friends crowded round, said *ohhh* and *how interesting*. Dylan finished with, "And this is her . . . her date."

Jade's date didn't seem upset that Dylan didn't know his name and that Jade hadn't bothered to tell it.

Three girls in matching gold skirts had been doing The Bump in the grass nonstop to the disco songs, ones that repeated words over and over and lots of *doo doos*, and *uh uhs*, and, *oohh ahhs*, and *oh yeahs*. They then began dancing wild, their skirts flying up.

Dylan turned to watch the girls while I stood by feeling stiff and unsure. He finally turned back and said to us, "You guys want to see the house?"

I nodded; Jade said, "Love to," the fella-with-no-name said, "All right."

We went inside Dylan's house, and he flung his hands about as he explained how the house was built in the forties, how he'd most ways kept it original except for a few modernizations. I liked his wood-frame house with the old oak floors and big kitchen full of pots and pans dangling from an iron rack hanging from the ceiling. There was a sunroom; he said it used to be a porch or a washroom, with cypress floors and a big over-stuffed rocker to look outside while rocking away. He had architectural magazines in a big basket by the side of the rocker, and I imagined him rocking, reading, and drinking a glass of whatever he had in the cabinet with carved wood doors.

Everywhere I moved, the dog stayed by my side.

Jade and no-name-necessary held hands the entire time, every so often saying, "Oh, this is nice," or "What a nice place you have here." When we came to Dylan's bedroom, Jade gave me a sly look. I gave her the narrow-eyes that said to quit it right then and there. Jade's date looked at her as if he wanted to push Dylan and me on out of the room and then push Jade onto that big fluffy bed. My face burned with thinking on all that pushing in and out.

When the tour was over, I went with Dylan into the kitchen while Jade and her guy went outside where the others were laughing and cutting up, drinking beer they'd plucked out of a big aluminum tub. I watched out the window as Jade leaned over and kissed her guy, then as they grabbed a beer and joined Dylan's friends as if they'd all been pals for years. I envied that of Jade.

Dylan stirred a pot of his homemade barbeque sauce and I turned back to him so I'd hear what he was saying. He said since he'd moved to Louisiana, he'd learned how to cook like the locals, as he put it, preparing red beans and rice with thick bean gravy; clean out the ice-box jambalaya; dirty rice; seafood gumbo with plump sweet Louisiana gulf shrimp, crab, and oysters; spicy crawfish stew; and thick slices of butter and garlic French bread.

In Dylan's barbeque pit were halved chickens that he'd soaked overnight in buttermilk. There were potatoes and corn wrapped in foil to put into the coals. In the ice-box were potato salad; and a tossed green salad with lettuce, tomatoes, red onion, and a vinaigrette dressing made with cane syrup vinegar. There were plenty of desserts, chips and dips, and other foods his friends brought. I'd made a mandarin orange, coconut, marshmallow, fruit cocktail, pecan, and sour cream fruit salad—Rebekha's ambrosia recipe. Rebekha had baked some of her lemon squares and they were on the counter under the Saran Wrap.

There was enough food to feed twice the people there and I felt a bit guilty for not inviting my family. In Louisiana, though, it was a Rule that there always be way more food than there was stomachs, so I knew it would all work out.

Dylan was saying, ". . . isn't that the weirdest thing you've ever heard?"

I nodded my head, as if I knew what he was talking about.

"Could you take those paper plates to the table, the one that already has the forks and knives on it?"

When I stepped to the plates, he grabbed my hands. "I'm glad you're here, even when your head is somewhere else."

I said, "Thank you for inviting me."

"Of course I invited you. This is all for you."

I felt trapped by his hands.

"I'm proud of you. My friends were excited about the barbeque and you *finally* coming over after so long."

Finally coming over after so long. He sure had a way with words. I turned my head to look outside at his friends, figured they didn't give a fig seed about me and what I did or didn't do.

I pulled my hands from his, grabbed the plates, turned and headed outside. In a strange sort of way, it felt as if I lived there, as if this really was *our* party instead of his. I pushed that thought out before it took hold, rooted, and grew all kinds of odd vines, the kind that took over a garden and choked all the pretty flowers out.

The dog followed me outside. He pushed his nose against me to make me pet him, but my hands were busy. He was big as a horse, with large brown eyes, his body thick-furred brown and black. His head looked too small for his body and that made me laugh.

After everyone had eaten, boozed, laughed, cut up, one of Dylan's friends fell into a group of azaleas, and Patrick slurred out how he and I should run away to the Casbah, they all scattered away. Jade left with her guy after Dylan said he'd carry me on home. I stayed to help him clean the mess, thinking how I sure had to clean up messes all the time while other people scattered.

When only a few dishes were left to soak, Dylan asked, "Want a nightcap?"

"Some iced tea," old froggy croaked out, even though I was right tired and wanted to go home. I had a big test next week. Since I took up to being friends with Dylan, I had to work extra hard on my studies.

Dylan told me to go relax, so I strolled into the living room and onto Dylan's couch. His dog flopped at my feet as I opened the photo album that called out to me from the coffee table. I couldn't get enough of photo albums. They told stories. The way a person looked at another or didn't look. The way they stood together or apart. The gleam in an eye or the glitter in them. The set of a mouth or the loose smile of one. Pictures told the true stories; all the moods and manners of people caught before they could hide it. And even if they tried to hide it, the truth was evident. Sometimes ghosts were in the photos. They showed up as orbs or misty shapes. I studied on those, too. Spirits surrounded people, curious, I supposed, as to the goings-on of the living.

Inside his album was the still-life story of Dylan. It began at his beginning, with a boy just born in his momma's arms, and the boy in diapers, and the boy toddling about. There were two other babies to join in, and there were young parents then older parents. There were barbeques, picnics, school photos, parties, and all those happenings that flowed on from a start and to the next and the next thing.

There, a little boy stood with his hands on his hips as if he were grown, but with messy hair and chocolate all over his face. There, that same boy stood with a man and a woman beside a pool that sparkled and shimmered. I studied those two people, how they looked easy and loose into the camera. The man's left hand was on the boy's shoulder and the woman's right hand on the boy's head. They wore loose fabric that billowed around them in the wind.

Dylan came to stand beside the couch. He handed me my sweet iced tea, said, "Sorry I took so long. I only had unsweetened left, so I had to make sugar syrup to sweeten it." He pointed to the album, said, "Oh, geez. You had to open that, didn't you? Look at me."

I could tell he was glad I did open it.

He eased himself on the couch beside me, sipped his little crystal glass of some thick sweet liquor, swallowed it, licked his lips, and pointed to different pictures, telling me the story of his life. It was a good story. Just as I knew, those were his parents and he was that little boy. He showed me all his family. Lots of family. There were sisters and aunts and uncles and cousins and grandmas and grandpas, and even friends who might as well be family for all they came to stay with Dylan's parents at their big house in California.

He laughed when we came to one of him in his high school graduation cap and gown. He said, "I almost chose another university but now I'm glad I ended up here."

Beside him were his parents, and a beautiful girl with long red hair to go with the long pale arm that snaked around Dylan's arm.

Dylan said, "That's the girl I followed here."

I sipped my iced tea, swallowed down the strange feeling I had by the wistful sound of Dylan's voice when he said, *that's the girl I followed here.*

He turned the page of the album and there was Dylan with the girl again, at the beach. The photo-Dylan gazed sappy-faced down at her, and she laughed up at him in the teeniest of crocheted bikinis I'd ever seen. A breath of wind could make it fall away from her body, a body that was willowy, wispy, and pale even with all that California sun.

There were other photos on the page. Of Dylan chasing the girl. Of Dylan holding the girl in the air as if she was made of clouds. Of Dylan kissing the girl. He'd stopped talking and stared at the photos, his eyes turning a darker blue, faraway and deep as his ocean. The ocean where he swam with the girl. The waves smacking them senseless, I hoped.

I sipped tea, the cold slid down into my stomach, where it mixed with whatever that strange surging feeling was.

Dylan turned the page, shrugged, said, "Foolish boys do foolish things, but it all worked out for the best." He sipped his golden liquid, looked at me hard, as if I was supposed to figure it all out.

On that page were even more photos of Dylan and the girl. An ooze settled deep inside me, heavy and full. I leaned down and patted Dylan's dog, buried my face in his thick fur, and then lifted back up when I felt as if I had control of that feeling.

Dylan turned the page, then the next, and the next, fast flipping through them. He said, "Tina wasn't right for me anyway." He rubbed my leg, turned one more page that finally did not have Tina in it and pointed to himself with a group of other fellas. "Look at us! This was taken right before I left for Louisiana. My buddies tried to talk me out of coming here."

I said all prissy, "Well, I'm not staying in Louisiana."

"Oh yeah? Where will you go then?"

I didn't know where to say and I could imagine Micah laughing at me all the way from New York, *Sure Seestor go Bleestor, suuurrre you're leaving. Then why haven't you tried to flee, see? Why you still around, bound? Why didn't you leave the land of gator, Vee Kator?*

Dylan squeezed my knee. "Maybe there's a reason for us both to stay?" He then grabbed me and pulled me to him, pushing his lips onto mine, his teeth grinding, his tongue thrusting.

I pushed away, stood, and went into the kitchen to pour more tea. On the counter was a jar of dog treats and I fished one out, listening to the big dog's nails click as he ran in to get it. The dog set nice and polite and I gave him the treat; he crunched it in pure dog happy.

Dylan had followed me in. "You're spoiling Jinxie already, Kate." He went to the counter and poured himself another glass of the golden liquid from a sparkled decanter.

Sip, swallow, stare at me, sip swallow, then, "So when do I get to see a photo album of *your* life?"

I shrugged. Fished out another treat and fed it to Jinxie.

"Where's your family from?"

Which family? The one I had or the one I lost or did he mean where did my kin come from? It was all too confusing to explain to anyone, much less myself. I didn't know the truths of some things. The dark of my eyes and hair, the skin that everyone said was a pretty color. Momma didn't know because she said her momma, my grandma Faith, said her own momma and daddy wouldn't talk about it.

Jinxie flopped onto the floor with a big sigh, his head between his paws.

"I haven't even met your mother or father yet."

"My momma doesn't live here." I rubbed the dog's ears with my foot and he fell asleep. "I have Rebekha."

"So, Rebekha is your step-mother?"

"I guess. I mean, I just call her Rebekha."

"And what about your birth mother? Where's she?"

"In West Virginia."

He emptied his glass. When he put it down to refill it again, his lips were wet and shiny. Dylan lifted the re-filled glass to his lips and sipped.

I figured that must be some good tasting stuff seeing as how he slurped it up right and left and yonder.

He pushed back his hair. "Why's your mother there and you here? Do you see her?"

"You're sure asking a lot of questions."

"That's because you never tell me anything." He put down his glass, wiped his hands on his britches.

My lips were rubbery whenever I talked to Dylan. He made me feel childish. I didn't want to talk about Momma. I didn't want to talk about any of that.

"I'm not trying to be too personal. I just want to know all about you." He came close, put his hand on my back, rubbed it in circles.

Jinxie let out a groan, his legs jerking from a doggie-dream. I stroked him again with my foot.

Dylan kept circling circling circling his hand on my back.

I could have arched it like a satisfied cat, but instead I moved away from that circling hand.

We stood in Dylan's kitchen, sipping, swallowing, with the sounds of night slipping into the cracks of the windows. Even though it wasn't cold, I had goosepimples march their way across my arms.

"Why are you so afraid?" he asked.

I wanted to ask why he thought I was afraid. Maybe I just didn't feel like talking about it. "It's about time I get on home," I said.

Dylan took my empty glass and turned to put it with his into the sink with the soaking dishes.

While his back was to me, my big fat mouth opened and the frog setting on my tongue spilled out words. "I haven't seen Momma since I was fifteen."

Without turning to me, Dylan stepped sideways to put the stopper back into the decanter. He moved slow, taking his time. He pushed the decanter away, still not turning back to me.

I took in breaths until my lungs filled, then released the air— words rushed into the air and on the floor and floated around. All over the place went words that swelled, popped, and made more words, and those grew fat and split open to birth more. "The holler is quiet and cool and our mountains there aren't familiar to anything you'd ever imagine less you've been there. Sometimes the wind whispers secrets to me. I don't think it's wind, but people who want someone to hear them." I stared out Dylan's window, imagining the oaks, the moss, the flat of everything out there in the dark. Then the flat erupted, pushed, and grew into my mountain, great, ancient, and wonderful. Spirits peeked out at me, knowing I understood they needed someone to listen and then tell their stories, even if the stories were my own and they could only pretend they were about them.

Dylan had finished washing my tea glass and a platter, rinsed with just a trickle of water, and still slow, had put them in the drain. He finished washing and rinsing up his tiny glass and picked up a small bowl. He kept his back turned, his movements slow and measured.

"There was a sugar maple in the yard that was framed in Momma's bedroom window. The tree's colors changed every fall and our maple burned as bright as fire, not like here where so much stays green."

He put the bowl in the drain, picked up a saucepot.

I pressed my lips into a line, but they wouldn't stay pressed. West Virginia Kate wanted out. She wanted to stomp her foot and be known. West Virginia Kate was tired of hiding behind the Kate fashioned for Dylan. West Virginia Kate said, "Outside my bedroom window, my mountain watched over me. I'd snuggle under Grandma Faith's quilt and dream of riding Fionadala up my mountain. I miss it. I miss my . . . I miss the holler."

Dylan rinsed the pot, put it in the drain, picked up a glass to dry with a soft clean dishrag, put the glass in the cabinet.

"Grandma Faith died in a house fire. I don't know if she was murdered or if she did it herself. No one knows. She won't say when she visits me, but I think my grandpa did it so she couldn't leave him. I used to have awful dreams."

Dylan dried the dishes, put them away.

I wanted to float back to my sweet sister mountain where handsome boys didn't ask so many questions about things they didn't understand. I then said, "I mean it. How I hear her sometimes, Grandma Faith, whispering to me. She tries to lead me to where I should go, to do the right thing, and sometimes I falter and don't listen, and that brings trouble."

Dylan wiped down the counters.

All my breath was gone. I pressed my palms to my burning eyes, wishing to stay in that dark a while. I didn't say many other things. When my parents fussed, my brothers and I would hide in the closet. Sometimes a boozed-up Momma would throw things at Daddy and he'd stomp out. The day long past when Micah had fetched my birthday present to me, and I'd opened what revealed that dark horse, began a breathless freedom for me. When I rode Fionadala, the wind rushed against my face and my hair flew out behind me, and once we were at the top, I'd be amongst the mists, the spirits, and the quiet. How sometimes the hornets stung my head and the headaches came until I couldn't think straight.

I didn't say that Momma sent off her kids one by one after making deals with Mee Maw. That my brothers and I had ruined her life. That she drank herself into stupidity, and despite all of that, I wanted to stay in the holler with my mountain rising over me because I was a foolish girl who couldn't become a woman because she still missed her momma.

With my hands still covering my eyes, I felt Dylan's arms go around me. He stroked my hair, from scalp to ends, over and over, a lullaby, as if he were comforting a wild horse.

I took away my hands, looked up at him, and thought he was sure and true.

He hugged me close, smothered me in his soft shirt. His britches scratched on my legs, but I liked it. I pulled my face away from his shirt and tipped my chin, searched his eyes for things I needed to see.

He leaned down and touched his lips onto mine light as dragonfly wings. He didn't shove his tongue into my mouth, didn't move his lips or press hard, didn't push his body onto mine; he left his lips barely touching. He then moved his head to touch his forehead to mine and I closed my eyes again, the dark feeling much different than before.

Dylan whispered, "Kate. Virginia Kate."

In the way he said it I felt his yearnings and desires. Trouble.

A hole opened wide and I wondered if I could bury down old parts of myself so I could be new, leave West Virginia Kate behind. Leave Grandma Faith's warnings behind, leave behind my mountain, Fionadala, my memories—all the things that were the little girl my momma didn't want. With my eyes closed, I inner-eye looked down into the gaping hollowed out earth, teetered on the edge. It would be so easy to do, become another person, forget that West Virginia girl. Cut my hair, fix my nails, wear lipstick every day. Be a woman. Forget my women-kin's past. And my own.

I could give up all the befores and think only of the ever-afters, and fall so easy.

From the window, the magnolia tree leaves sad waved to me in the moonlight. Trees knew so much, if only we'd listen.

Grandma Faith cried out, *Smart girls do not fall into things. Smart girls walk in with sure steps and open eyes. Heed what I say.*

Falling falling. That's how it felt even as Dylan pulled me to him and held onto me, tight, tighter, tightest. The rushing wind against my face made it hard to breathe, so I pulled back, stopped the free-fall, listened to the otherworld laments, to Grandma Faith's warnings. I pulled up and out and away from Dylan, and said, "I need to go home now," and turned away from his burning eyes.

Chapter 5

Bozo called; he said he wants his make-up back

Over our old favorite sugar popcorn and Orange Crush, while watching *Laverne and Shirley*, Rebekha asked, "How long have you been un-dating Dylan?"

"Un-dating?"

She'd chewed her popcorn and eyed me good.

"Hey, Rebekha, remember the first time you tried sugar popcorn?"

"Um hum." She quirked her mouth a bit. "So, you and Dylan."

I let the Crush burn down my throat.

"So it's not serious enough for you to have him over to dinner? Or, it's serious and that's why you are avoiding the issue?"

I chewed, swallowed, sipped, swallowed. Laverne said something to Lenny, but Squiggy answered, "Maybe so, maybe so . . ."

"Well, Miss Virginia Kate Carey?"

"All right," I said. "I'll bring him over on Saturday so everyone can gawk over him like bug-eyed fools."

"It's about time."

I sighed a big sighing sigh.

"Way past time."

I chewed more popcorn.

"Long long past time."

"Are you being ornery on me?" I tried to raise up my eyebrow.

She laughed.

Saturday morning, on a thundery June day, I borrowed Rebekha's car to go to the beauty house Dylan sent me to. I'd never been to a hairdresser before. Rebekha always cut my hair when it needed a trim. As I passed the lakes in Rebekha's serious Dodge, I watched an egret fly and then land on the branch of a cypress tree. At night, egrets flocked on the cypress as changling-eerie ornaments. Good old moon made their white feathers glow as they perched their big bodies. Those cypress branches were strong enough to hold many birds without bending.

Rising as a bird from a branch, the memory came of me under a cypress tree with Andy, Bobby, and Bobby's best friend with the half-missing finger. Stump's older brother had been there until I made him storm off mad at me for making him look foolish. One thing for true, boys didn't like girls making them look foolish. Stump's brother had been one of my first crushes, but nothing had ever come of it, since he'd acted like a strutting banty rooster.

That day, Andy's homemade kite was beside us, its red, blue, yellow tail bold on the summer-green grass. I'd felt a settling in while we kids were under that tree, a belonging had crept up on me. That evening the phone rang and in that sound was a calling back. A return to West Virginia to help Momma after her accident. The last time I'd been to the holler. The last time I'd laid eyes on Momma.

I sighed to myself with sad thoughts and regrets gone by, parked the Dodge, and went inside a house that was turned into a hairdresser place.

The woman I had an appointment with had long red fingernails and lots of rouge and said her name was Diane. Her teased brown hair was a heaving mess, far as I was concerned, and I didn't want her fooling with mine if that's how she did her own. All over the walls were women in high fashion poses, their hair pulled, cut, and snarled into every style I could imagine, and then some I never would have. The place smelled of permanent wave, and in the back, there sure enough was a woman under the dryer with her hair in tiny curlers, holding at eye level a *McCall's* magazine on how to knit, crochet, or embroider afghans. She had an afghan over her lap, one with multi-colored circles, just like on the cover.

Diane grabbed hold of my chin to get my attention, turned my head right, then left, then up, then down. I was a bug under her microscope. She let go. "There's lots to be done, so let's get started."

I wanted to say, *lots to be done my left foot*, but I held my tongue.

She wanted to cut my hair shorter, but I pulled such a hissy fit that made the afghan-woman stare at us, Diane promised she'd only trim it.

I said, "Two inches, and that's it."

She narrowed her eyes all at me, and I narrowed my eyes all at her. We were two stray cats trying to sit on the same post. I won when she let out a sigh and said she'd cut two inches but it was a shame since my hair would look good in a shag or feathered cut.

Diane washed my hair, grumping about all of it everywhere, and then cut my allowed two inches as I told her, in a V at the bottom. After she almost all the way dried it, pointing that dryer at me as though she'd liken to shoot me with it as anything else, she said, "I'm styling it, and I don't want to hear another word out of you about it."

I let her have at it.

She slopped in hair jelly, and then rolled my hair in big fat curlers. She asked me, "So, how long have you and Dylan dated?"

I shrugged.

"Two weeks? A month? Three months? That's about as long as he usually lasts with a girl, three months."

I didn't tell her I'd lasted much more than three months because I was a friend first and friends lasted longer. Though, it was hard to call us *friends* anymore. Not long after the barbeque, Dylan finally let loose his mad. He'd said, "For christ's sake, Kate, this keeping your distance *friends* thing has to stop." He'd grabbed me up, kissed fire in my blood, and then asked, "Do friends make you feel that way? *Do they?*"

I'd had nothing ornery to say.

When my hair was full of curlers, Diane stretched her arms over her head, said, "While that's setting, I'm going to give you a manicure."

"I don't need a manicure."

"You'll like it, so just relax." She pointed to a table and chair in the corner and said, "Sit there."

I did what she asked.

She poured some liquid into a bowl, grabbed my right hand, filed and buffed my nails, shoved my fingers into the bowl, and then picked up my left hand and went to town on those nails. She took out my right-handed fingers from the bowl and plunged in the left ones. With a white stick, she pushed back the cuticles on my right hand. And on it went until she said, "Sit there quiet while I pick out a color."

I started to say I had been quiet, but I let it go.

She rifled through the bottles until she found what she wanted, then painted my nails an orangey color. She then made me slip off my flip flops, took a big wet towel and cleaned my feet even though they weren't dirty, rubbed something grainy on them, wiped that off, rubbed in something cold, then something smooth and cool, and rubbed a clean towel on them again. I fidgeted and jittered in my chair, but she kept on doing her business as if my feet were slabs of meat she had to cure. After the final rub, Diane put cotton between my toes, and then stroked on the nail polish, said, "Uh hmmm this color looks good with your skin. Not many can pull off this bold of a color."

When she was done, I lifted my feet and held up my hands. "Well, that does look pretty good."

She gave me a prissed look. "You can buy this color for touch-ups, and I suggest you do."

I didn't tell her I bet I could get a color similar to it at the TG&Y for a lot less than she sold hers.

"Now, go over there, and don't ruin your polish." She pointed me to another chair, and after I'd plopped down, she swooshed gunk on my face. While my face pinched, Diane was in the back, walking to and fro, and when I turned my head, I saw her smoking a cigarette while she yappervated to a girl who was the one giving the afghan-woman her permanent.

When I was about to storm to the sink to wash off the hardened goop, she finally came back and wiped it off with warm washrags. She then rubbed in cream. The cream felt good after the mudpack. She took the cotton from between my toes.

The afghan-woman was out from under the dryer and having her curlers plucked out of her head. Her hair sprang in little pin-curls, like my second grade teacher's dog, poor old dead Mrs. Penderpast and her poor dead poodle. I still had the photograph of her dog amongst my things. Don't know why I kept it. I kept many things. For instance, the girdle Mee Maw gave me when I was too young to be wearing a girdle kept popping up out of my dresser just as a worm will on a sidewalk after a hard rain. And other things I needed to keep.

Diane was saying, ". . . glad you agree that these eyebrows have got to be cleaned up."

"What?"

She leaned close, held my head still, and began plucking out eyebrows as if I had a forest there. All the time she pulled out tiny hairs by their roots, she hummed, or clucked her tongue as a chicken pecking in the chicken yard will, *tck tck cluck tck.*

I was afraid I wouldn't have an eyebrow left.

Diane nodded, said, "Now. There. Let's get some make-up on this face."

I heaved a sigh.

She turned me from the mirror. "I'll let you see the full effect all at once." She used a pad to cream on foundation, dabbled rouge upon my cheeks with the tips of her fingers, pressed powder over my face, slithered color across my eyelids, brushed black on my eyelashes, drew a line above and below my lashes, lined my lips with an orangey pencil, slicked orange lipstick onto my lips. She then took out the curlers, and using her hands, tossed about my hair while spraying it with hairspray until I choked from the cloud. When she turned me around letting out a, "Ta Daaa!," some woman stared at me in the mirror. She was familiar, but I couldn't quite tell who she was.

The afghan-woman said, "Look at you, now. What a difference."

The other beauty girl said, "I hope Dylan's happy with those results. He was pretty specific."

Diane slow-grinned, then said, "Oh, yes indeed, he'll be happy with my work."

The heat spread from my new-painted toes all the way to my exploded-out hair. Had Dylan come in and told them what a hicked-up girl I was who needed their help? I stared into that big mirror with taped on photographs of girls with hair and make up and attitudes that made them pooch out their lips.

Diane frowned, asked me, "Don't you like it?"

I didn't want to be rude, since she had worked so hard for so long. "I look like I ought to be on a soap opera."

She preened and prissed, and then she and the other women chattered their busy squirrel way about how I really could be in a soap opera and wasn't it a shame I hadn't done all that beautifying before and blab blabbity blab.

When I asked how much I owed her, Diane said, "Dylan already took care of it. He came in yesterday and talked all about you." She handed me a purple box with a purple ribbon. "And here are some product samples. Try them and then come back here to buy them."

I took the box, but I didn't think I'd be coming back.

"Dylan will be pleased as punch," Diane crowed out of her thin slash of hot-pink lips.

I thanked her because it was good manners. The women watched me as if they knew things I did not, and I high-tailed it out of there before they did or said something else to make me feel as if I wanted to be swallowed whole by the earth.

The thunderclouds were gone and a bright sun beamed its eye on my new hairdo, baking the hairspray. I drove home with the windows up, so I wouldn't muss my hair. When I pulled into the driveway, Bobby was setting on the porch eating an apple, his baseball bat and glove beside him as it always was. He wasn't wearing his new glasses and I knew Rebekha would set out after him for it. Bobby waved to me as I put the car in park. Most eleven-year-old boys weren't so tall. Most eleven-year-old boys were out playing and not looking to bug their big sisters who weren't in the mood.

Before I had stepped halfway out of the car, he was out of his rocking chair, hollering, "Hey! Virginia Kate! Guess what?" Then he said, "Whoa! What in the great state of Louisiana happened to you?"

"Nothing happened to me." I walked pretend-casual up the steps, feeling the heavy sprayed hair pull against my scalp as if the hair would run off to be on another girl's head who appreciated it more. Every time I blinked, my top eyelashes caught on the bottom eyelashes.

"You look like a movie star, kinda." He pinched up his eyes. "I like you the other regular old way."

I shrugged, eased myself down on the rocker next to his rocker.

He jittered, then asked again, "Guess what?"

"What?"

"Chicken-butt!" He slapped his leg and laughed up a storm.

"Don't you ever get tired of that joke, Bobby?"

"Nope, never do." He chomped his apple, smacking it loud just to get on my nerves.

"Why aren't you out playing ball with Stump? Don't boys find fun stuff to do all day once school's out?"

"He went crawfishing with his dad. I hate crawfishing. That bloody meat stuff they use is gross and after the sun bakes it, it stinks bad enough to make me puke." He made vomiting sounds, then said, "After it's been in the sun a while, all the flies get on it and it stinks even more and it's just too nasty for words."

"Sounds like it." I pushed off the rocker with my foot.

"And people eat the crawfish after the crawfish been eating that maggot-infested meat." He curled his lip as if he'd just eaten maggots and stinky meat right then and there.

"Well, I don't think I want another crawfish."

"I like boiled crawfish, and crawfish pie, and crawfish bisque, and crawfish etouffee, except I try to forget about the maggot meat."

"I think I heard enough about maggot-meat."

"Well, it's just how things are. If you live in Louisiana, you got to eat something that had maggots on it at least some of the time." He nodded his head, wise to the ways of Louisiana, since that was where he was born and it was in his blood.

I leaned my head against the rocker, then remembered my hair and lifted my head. I said, "It's so hot all my thoughts are boiling out of my head."

"Hey, Seestor?"

"Yeah?"

"I saw you and that guy kissy-facing on the porch the other night." He laughed, an annoying hyena pretending to be a little brother.

I sniffed. "So?"

"It was as gross as maggot-meat." He made kiss noises, then said in a high girlish voice, "Oh my handsome prince-a-lot from Cam-e-lot, you are *sooo* handsome and *sooo* wonderful and *sooo* good a kisser, I could kiss you all the live-long day. Look at what I've done to myself, Miss princess-a-lot, all just for you because I'm a stupid *girl*."

I reached out and smacked Bobby upside his head, but all he did was laugh.

I stood. "I'm going in."

"Aw, I'm sorry. I didn't mean to make you mad."

"I'm not mad. I just need to go help Rebekha."

He threw the apple core into the flower garden, grabbed his bat and glove, said, "See ya later, alligator," jumped up and off the porch to go whooping towards the backyard.

Inside, the house was quiet, and bright with light from the opened blinds. The wood floors were extra shiny with paste wax, and the furniture dusted within an inch of its wood. I went to my room first, still blue and white as it'd been since Rebekha and I had rid the room of all that hated pink. The same room, except where I put away some of the little girl things and added in other things that were special to me. I still kept favorites on the bookshelf, though; the *Black Stallion* books, the *Black Beauty* Rebekha had given me when I came to live in Louisiana, *The Velveteen Rabbit* that I used to read to Bobby when he was little, *The Incredible Journey*, *The Adventures of Tom Sawyer*, *Call of the Wild*, along with other book friends I'd added to my collection as I grew older. Fionadala and Fiddledeedee the Tiger were on the bookshelf, too, where they were nice and comfortable. One day I'd have those things to give to my own children, except I knew Fionadala would always be mine.

Momma's hairbrush found its place on my dresser, although I didn't use the brush much any more, since a few bristles were beginning to fall out of it. I touched my hair. Parts of it were sticky and parts were not and I had the urge to grab that old silver-handled brush and pull it from roots to ends until my hair was normal again.

I reached inside my underwear drawer and took out my journal. My girl's diaries were put away, their secrets held tight. As I'd grown older, I'd bought notebooks that were made of brown and black leather, with satiny ribbons to mark the page. Those fastened diaries I had as a girl I used to fill faster than I could turn the pages. I didn't write down things as often as I did then.

Perched on the side of my bed, I wrote:

> Today, Dylan comes over to supper. Seems the longer I waited, the harder it was to do it. I don't know what to think about it. If I'll see him different when he's up against people I love, or if I'll see people I love different up against him. I wish Micah were here so he could tell me what I should do, but he probably wouldn't tell me anyway. Everything feels strange and new. I guess I should be used to that feeling, but I never get used to it. Other people seem to do fine with all the things I seem not to do fine with. Jade seems to be fine with growing older and acting as she should. Doesn't matter how much goop is on my face, or how my hair is combed, what I feel inside is still the same.
>
> I hope Daddy doesn't drink too much in front of Dylan.

I put away the journal, and reached farther into the drawer to touch a letter from Micah. I didn't need to read it again to remember how the writing in that letter was shaky and loose, as if his fingers had turned to jelly. My worry and sorrow over Micah hurt me all the way into the marrow of my bones because I wanted to believe he was feeling better, but I couldn't believe it until I saw my brother face to face to prove it. His letters were sad and lonely and I couldn't fix it from so far away.

A pot rattled against the stove, so I shook away the worry and went to the kitchen, said, "Hey, Rebekha."

She turned and her eyes flew open wide. She said, "Oh my

goodness."

I touched my hair. "Is it that bad?"

She walked over and studied me. "Let's see, hmmmm."

"Dylan said she was the best in town."

"I see. Well." Rebekha stepped back, then stepped back again, then once more until she couldn't step back any more. "From here, it's not so bad."

We both fell out laughing, and Rebekha even let out a snort. That made us laugh louder.

Rebekha said, "You look like Bobby's Beta fish."

"Stop it!"

"Bozo called; he said he wants his make-up back."

"Rebekha!"

"Wait; hold on, I think a couple of granddaddy long leg spiders crawled on your eyelashes."

"Stop!"

Rebekha laughed and laughed, slapping her hands on her thighs. She took a breath, said, "I'm sorry . . . it's just . . . god, Virginia Kate, what did they do to you?" She laughed harder.

I laughed until I cried and all that gunk on my eyelashes ran down my face in fat black muddy tracks. Sometimes laughing and crying looked the same, but that time I was for true laughing.

കെ • ക

How silly I was for going to Diane in the morning instead of right before the party. How did other women keep themselves from messing up their pretty? They'd probably not cook and clean when they knew it would ruin everything, especially when it was hot inside and hot outside. Louisiana people liked to say there were only two seasons, hot and hotter. The weather boiled, shimmered, and made everyone feel cat-stretch lazy, except Rebekha, who whirled about the house making sure everything was perfect, then whirled to the *Bet-R* to buy groceries, then whirled back home to whirl some more.

I took a bath, and since my hair was damp at the scalp and underneath at the neck, I re-washed my hair. I had to wash off all the make-up, since it was blurred on my face from washing my hair, and laughing until I cried. After I toweled off and combed out my wet hair, I then tried to fix everything back nice, using some of Diane's products, and some make-up that Jade had given me. I next dried my hair until it glowed, and pulled it back with one of Rebekha's white hairbands.

I knocked on Rebekha's door, and when she opened the door, she said, "Oh that looks better."

We were in matching robes and slippers, like momma and daughter would be.

"Your complexion doesn't need all that make-up."

"Thanks Rebekha." I turned to go.

"Wait, hold on. Come in here and let me fix your hair."

I went into her room, which smelled like sweet almonds.

She plugged in her Clairol hot curlers. "We'll just put a little bounce back into it, shall we?"

I set myself down at her dresser in her calm green and white bedroom with its dark wood furniture. Maybe Dylan wouldn't be mad at me for spoiling his gift if I had at least some fancy to my hair. Besides, my hands, feet, nails and toenails looked good, my face felt smooth from the mudpack, and my eyebrows arched over my eyes. I wondered why he had to pay for my beauty treatment anyway. Who had asked him to do all that? Not me. I most for sure had not wanted him to and I most for sure had not wanted to go in the first place.

Rebekha fluffed my hair. "Let's see here now."

"Can you fix my hair sort of like it was this morning, but not as much floof?"

"It'll look pretty, don't you worry." Rebekha held my chin with her hand, her hand cool and soft, and added a touch of brown eyeliner above my lashes and under my lower ashes. "She did a great job plucking your eyebrows, I will say that." She brushed my eyebrows with a tiny brush. "Your arch is perfect. I'm envious. My eyebrows are too straight across."

"You have beautiful green eyes."

"Thank you," she said to the mirrored me. She touched the curlers, and satisfied they were hot enough, began rolling my hair. "I'm looking forward to a proper meeting with Dylan."

"He's ready, too."

"I know it's a big step in a relationship." She clipped on another curler.

I hoped she didn't think it was because of her that I'd waited so long. I was as proud to be Rebekha's daughter as I could be, even if we had no papers to prove it. Miss Darla had taught me that papers do not mean love, actions do, sacrifice does. I said, "I'm sorry I took so long. Just can't figure myself sometimes."

"What's the rush? Better to be sure before you take this step. I think you're smart." Rebekha picked up another curler and rolled my hair round it. "I hated bringing boys to meet my mother. She was so hard to satisfy and no one was good enough."

After a pause, I added, "Not even Daddy."

"Right. Not even your father." Then she smiled, as if to say, *so what if my momma hated most everyone, look how things turned out after all?* At least that's what I figured that smile meant.

"What happened when Daddy met your parents?"

"Oh, I hate even thinking about that night." She clipped a curler. "Frederick came to dinner and my mother grilled him. Asked him about . . . about you kids, and other things." She frowned.

"She doesn't like us, does she?"

Rebekha's frown deepened, then her face brightened when she said, "It's her big fat loss."

I remembered the first time we'd met her momma, how she'd looked at Micah and me as if we were old nasty dirt under her fingernails, and how she said it looked as if we'd come from a ditch. That day went all wrong, and after that, Rebekha rarely saw her momma and daddy. I knew what it felt like never to see your momma and to feel mixed up about it. That made us alike in ways that were sad, but alike all the same.

She picked up another curler and rolled, humming a happy tune I didn't recognize.

When the last curler was in and my hair had to cool, she put on her own make-up, using just a dab here and there. Every so often, she reached over and touched a curler to check to see if it had cooled. We chatted about Andy deciding he wouldn't move into the dorm quite yet, and how Bobby was glad he'd have his big brother still around, and how Amy Campinelle lost fifty pounds and gained back sixty-three.

Unlike being in Momma's bedroom, being in Rebekha's bedroom was like belonging to a special club. There was no rum with lemon setting on the dresser, no Pond's cream, no sly looks at Daddy when he came in to talk about Shakeybaby. With Rebekha and me, it was two girls who did girl things and talked about family and life.

When the curlers were out of my hair, and my hair brushed out again with some bounce back but without that sticky hairspray, I thanked Rebekha and left her to go to my room.

From the triangle-shaped glass bowl I took the puff and dusted on a bit of the spiced powder, then pulled on the blue dress Jade had made me from a Simplicity pattern. I was supposed to have sewn it, but never moved past pinning the pattern tissue to the fabric and then cutting it out. Since the Singer was at her house, she finished it for me. It hugged at the top and waist and then flared out and I wore the same kind of shoes from the pattern photo, canvas ones that tied around my ankle. Jade had hauled me from store to store until we found those shoes. The model in the pattern wore a scarf, but I wore a hairband instead. I knew Jade would be happy with what I wore, for once, except for the hairband.

I went into the living room where Daddy was reading, and joined him, leaned my head against him. He had a drink in his left hand and one of his books of Shakespeare in his right.

He said, "'Beauty's a doubtful good, a glass, a flower, Lost, faded, broken, dead within an hour; And beauty, blemish'd once, for ever's lost, In spite of physic, painting, pain, and cost.'" He took a swallow of his drink, and then turned a page.

I supposed Daddy had some message for me, as he most times did, but I never was in the mood for figuring out his messages. I wanted him to talk to me in his own words, words I could understand and swallow down and become a part of me. I just kept my head leaned on his shoulder while he read and sipped.

He stopped reading, looked up at me as if I were a puzzle to put together, and asked, "How old is this boy you're seeing?"

"He's only a few years older than I am, Daddy."

"Few as in more than five, or few as in less than five?"

"Less than five, okay? I'm not dating my father."

He opened his mouth about to tell me not to be a smart-aleck, but then only nodded, sipped, went back to reading.

Rebekha poked her head into the room and said, "I'm all dressed. I'm going to make another dessert." She said to me, "You look so pretty."

I smoothed my skirt over my knees. "Do you need help?"

"No, Hon. I have it. You just relax until Dylan arrives."

Daddy sipped, swallowed, stayed in his Shakesworld. I stayed in my world. We were staying-in-our-own worlds fools.

When I heard a car engine, I shot up off the couch as if I had a fire lit under my rear-end. I fluffed my hair, straightened my clothes, straightened my everything but the worry frown between my eyes.

Daddy looked from his book to me. "You look pretty, just as

Rebekha said, so don't be so nervous, Bug. He's just a boy."

"Okay, Daddy." I thought that was easy for him to say, since he knew all the secrets of boys and I didn't.

Daddy glubbed a glob of drink, went back to reading.

I nervous-stepped outside where thunderclouds hovered again as if they couldn't make up their mind whether to stay and rain or go away, walked down to the car, and when Dylan stepped out with one of his papersacks, I said, "Well, here you are."

He cocked his head at me, then said, "And there you are." He came around his car and hugged on me with the arm that wasn't holding the sack. He pulled away and studied me. "I've never seen you in a dress. You are stunning in it."

I preened.

Then he said, "But something is missing . . ."

I showed him my soft hands, my soft feet, the colored nails, and then pointed to my eyebrows. "Look at this arch."

He reached out his hand and stroked my hands one at the time, said, "Very nice. Diane's the best." Then he nodded towards his papersack. "I brought some bread and wine."

"You didn't have to do that."

"My parents taught me never to arrive empty-handed." He held onto that papersack as if it would jump out of his arms and yell yeehaw I'm free.

"Come on in. Daddy's in the living room."

As we walked up the steps, he said, "Well, I'm finally going to meet *the* Frederick Hale Carey instead of marveling from afar."

I didn't ask him why he said it that way. I was dead frog tired and the evening had just begun.

Daddy came outside before we were to the door. He placed his drink and book on the little table beside one of the rockers. The two faced each other, stray dogs in the alley. I inhaled dark earth smells from Rebekha's garden and right then wished I were digging there. The air crackled and burned with electricity. The hair on my arms stood at attention.

Dylan cleared his throat.

Daddy cocked his eyebrow.

I breathed in Daddy's bourbon, all the way into my belly where it mixed with the worry. "Daddy, this is Dylan. Dylan, this is Daddy."

Daddy said in a way that showed he wondered what Dylan had been hiding, "And I'm sure it's nice to *at last* meet your beau face to face."

Dylan let go an arm from his offerings and shook Daddy's hand with a fat grin exploding across his face. He said, "'Hell is empty and all the devils are here.'"

Daddy answered, "'One may smile, and smile, and be a villain!'"

The two dogs bared their Shakespearean teeth at each other.

I said, "We made a tasty supper and I'm hungry. Aren't you two hungry?"

Dylan and Daddy spoke at the same time, and I heard, "That's nice, Bug; Sounds good, Kate; Who's Kate?; Bug?" And all their words jumbled and I pulled on Dylan's arm to get him away from Daddy and into the house to meet Rebekha.

Seven hornets buzzed my head and I for certain did not need them to start their stinging. Inside, I bumbled out the obvious, "Here's our living room."

Still clutching his papersack, Dylan walked over to Micah's painting that held swirls of mad wild color.

"My brother painted that."

Dylan swiveled his head around to me. "You're kidding me?"

"He's a prodigy," I said, all proud.

He turned back to study it and I let him. I wanted him to find his own answers in that painting, same as I had.

I had a silent wish that Daddy would stay with his New Drinking Plan all night. He and Rebekha had a big fight over booze two weeks after I graduated from high school, and she'd told him to get out. He did, but he came back two months later with all his promises. He said he had a New Plan to cut back, if we'd just give him a chance. Rebekha wanted to believe, so she took him back. I guessed she loved him that much; I guessed I did, too. They went to meetings together again as they had years back, at least for a while.

Daddy always made all kinds of promises and said all kinds of sorry's that he always meant, and that's why we always forgave him. Except Micah. He didn't want to forgive Daddy, or Momma. Maybe he blamed them for what happened that summer when we were kids. Maybe he felt he didn't save me, and himself, from Aunt Ruby's beatings; but how could he, being a little boy? Or worse, how Uncle Ar-vile had gone after Micah and when Micah pushed him away, Uncle Arville had fallen on the rusted out pole. My big brother had dark wings fluttering and I imagined New York was bright and loud enough to help him forget what scuttled in his brain. Sometimes his letters scared me so that my insides clenched up in a big fist.

"Knock knock; who's there?" Dylan tapped my head with his right index finger. "Just where do you go when you go off like that?"

"What?" I'd been staring off into the wild blue yonder, a prime fool.

"You disappear inside that head of yours at the oddest moments."

"Let's go see Rebekha." I led him into the kitchen.

He eased his sack onto the counter, said, "There's a white in there that should be refrigerated. He took it out and showed it to me. I pointed to the ice-box, and he eased in the wine as if it were a baby to put to crib.

Rebekha waited to be introduced, wiping down the counter with a la tee dah way about her. She wore a pair of spring-morning-blue pedal pushers with a yellow blouse that had little blue dots on it. She looked like a teenager when the light was just right.

"Rebekha, here is Dylan." I pointed, idiot that I was.

She wiped her hands on a clean dishrag, and stepped to Dylan. "So good to meet you."

Dylan shook Rebekha's hand, opened his mouth and flopped out words, "Rebekha, I see where Kate gets her good looks. Well I mean, that's not exactly . . . ," he cleared his throat, " . . . what I mean is, I know you aren't her mother, but . . . that is . . . it's nice to meet you, too. Kate's told me so much about you, and of course her circumstances . . ."

I wanted to say, *Hush that flapping mouth of yours.*

He turned to the stove, "So! What smells so good? What an aroma."

Rebekha stared at him with her mouth part a ways opened.

I wanted to knock him into the backyard for being a bonehead.

She said, "That would be the baked beans. And I have an apple pie cooling."

"Well, I sure can't wait to sample all of your goods." Dylan turned red, said, "I mean . . . the food and all."

"Dylan, why don't you put on some records while Virginia Kate and I finish here?"

He breathed out, said, "That sounds like a good idea."

I took Dylan to the living room and showed him the record player and records. He said, "Well, guess I made a fool of myself in there."

"No you didn't." But he kind of did.

He looked through the records. "Should I play anything in particular?"

"Whatever you want."

"Do you think I could get a glass of wine?"

"I'll get it for you."

"I opened one of the reds before I got here," he said. "Not to be tacky, but I drank a little of it already."

I turned to go.

"Pour a hefty one for me, will you? I'm more nervous than I imagined I'd be."

"Oh. Okay," I frogged.

He studied the back of an album cover.

I slipped into the kitchen, looked into the papersack, pulled out the two bottles of red wine, the opened one and the unopened one. There was a loaf of French bread and I took out that, too. From the cabinet I grabbed a wine glass and poured from the half-empty bottle. He'd said he had one glass. He must have meant two. I asked Rebekha, "Do you want some of this?"

"No thank you, Hon." Rebekha was chopping onions. I wondered if she was making an inside face about Dylan, one that said, *Well. I see. Well now.*

When I brought Dylan his wine, he still hadn't put on a record, but had three of them spread out. He said, "Is that new lipstick?"

"Jade gave it to me."

He sipped the wine, looked at me over the rim.

"And I'll pay you back every penny." I crossed my arms over my chest.

He scrubbed his face, then said, "I don't want you to. It was a gift."

"Okay. I'm sorry. Thank you."

He picked up one of Andy's albums, slid it out of the sleeve, and set it onto the turntable.

I went on back to the kitchen. Rebekha stirred the baked beans as I slipped up next to her and hugged her good strong bones, then stepped away to help her cook. It sure was funny to think back when I first came to live with her and didn't hug her, or let her hug me, for too long to be right. How I'd called her Ma'am at every turn instead of Rebekha. Then, one day it felt as natural as rain to let her love me and let me love her. I wished things felt as natural as rain with Dylan.

There came a wondering if I was being the same way with Dylan as I had been with Rebekha. Thoughts and words, messing all up and around in my head, corralled as cows in a fence with a broken gate they hadn't discovered yet.

Rebekha put oil and butter in a skillet.

I whispered to her, "I told him a little about Momma."

"And why wouldn't you tell him about yourself?"

I shrugged.

From the living room came a song about not getting any satisfaction.

I took the loaf of French bread and split it down the middle so I could add lots of butter and garlic spread.

Rebekha put the onions into the skillet. Their sizzling gave off a sound and smell of Home. She said, "Will you hand me that clean dishcloth?"

I handed her the dishrag that didn't have a stain on it, then said all happy and go lucky, "Where's the garlic spread you made?"

"In the fridge behind the salad fixings."

Daddy came into the kitchen. I listened to the old sounds. First, the opening of the freezer, the cracking of the ice-cube tray, the cold, hard sounds of ice hitting the bottom of the glass, the top, right cabinet opening then shutting (unless he was out of that bottle and needed to find his stash he didn't think I knew about), the glub of booze filling his crystal glass, the splash of water, and his sigh of "Ahhhhh," as he took the first sip. I guessed that was Home, too.

He made another one. Must be for Dylan. Maybe they'd find a common ground over a couple of booze drinks. They could lap up a river full, the two stray dogs they were, and settle down that bristled fur scruffing their necks. I snickered to myself with picturing them that way.

Daddy went on back into the living room and soon the music changed to some piano music mixed with violin.

Together, Rebekha and I finished the chicken stew, the big loaf of garlic bread, potato salad, baked beans, green salad and a fruit salad. For dessert, there was apple pie, and she'd also prepared crisp homemade coconut cookies to go with vanilla ice cream. Louisiana was food. It always looked like too much food until everyone walked away from the table and somehow it was most all eaten, and what wasn't eaten would be sent home with the guests, or eaten as leftovers. If someone didn't want to take home food, then they were for sure outsiders or had something wrong with them.

I went into the dining room to put food on the table, looking about with pride. There were cream linen napkins to match the tablecloth and tall ivory candles lit inside silver holders of differing sizes. Everything took after a picture in one of those house and home magazines.

I was ready for Dylan to eat supper with my tea-set family.

Chapter 6

Wow, your mother is drop-dead gorgeous

The table sparkled just this side of fancy and the food offered all its good smells. In the holler, we'd eaten on Christmas paper plates in the middle of June. We scooped our mashed potatoes with tablespoons and took hippopotamus bites. Momma made cookies and we'd try to sneak in and eat the dough. She'd chase us out, snapping the washrag at us, hollering, "Git! You kids are like vultures waiting to pounce on something!" We'd eat the baked cookies right off the big wooden tray where the crumbs fell all over the floor while we laughed. Sometimes Momma would let us drink our sweet milk out of the glasses with the pink and black circles—the glasses that were usually saved for her special tonics. Those times with Momma were the best ones, when she loved her children more than she loved what she'd lost. Those were the times when Momma's chaos and itchy nature were fun for little kids who didn't understand what being a parent meant.

I settled in my seat and waited for the rest to do the same.

Dylan and Daddy came to the table arguing about which cars were better cars. When Dylan set in Micah's chair it was weird, but I knew we couldn't keep Micah's chair empty as if he were going to come right on in and plop in it, or as if he were a ghost brother setting there. I had enough spirits flying around telling me things without making a live brother into one. Bobby came in and when Rebekha told him to go wash up, he Frankenstein walked to the bathroom. Andy was nowhere to be seen. Daddy was at the head of the table. Bobby came in flinging water from wet hands; he flopped across from Dylan. Last of all, Rebekha took her seat.

Dylan took a gulp and then two of his drink, and his Adam's apple bobbed. It was so similar to Daddy that I about fell out of my chair. I sent that mischievous little mouse thought scurrying away. Everyone began talking at once, except me. I dug into the food and hoped Bobby wouldn't do anything to embarrass me.

Dylan held his glass in the air. "Rebekha, everything tastes great. Thank you."

"Why, thank you for the compliment, but you should thank Virginia Kate."

I held a forkful of stew in the air, said, "I didn't do all that much."

Rebekha gave me a look that said I should hush it and let her help me look good in front of my fella.

Dylan ogled me as if I was the cutest puppy in the pound.

We set out eating again. Every so often Dylan and Daddy gave each other measure for measure.

Bobby waited until no one was looking and then opened his mouth to show me the chewed food.

I rolled my eyes.

Bobby swallowed the mess and then mouthed, "Maggot Meat!"

Dylan told a story about California beaches, and how sand was different at different coasts. Then he talked about the ocean and how he missed it sometimes, since the Louisiana coasts, he said, weren't very nice—not like California's coast, he said. How he'd gone to the beach almost every day (with that Tina, I bet).

Daddy became wound up about the sea and what it meant as symbolism, and then asked Dylan something about Caliban. Dylan went into a long story about his studies of Shakespeare, while Daddy kept interrupting him to tell him he had it all wrong. They both had finished the drinks Daddy made and had started on Dylan's wine.

I'd forgotten to count the glasses. Or was too tired to.

Rebekha said, "I forgot to mention that Virginia Kate decorated the table. Isn't it lovely?"

Dylan said, "Well, that's unexpected. She—"

"What're you saying about my sister? That she's stoopid and can't make things look nice?"

"He's not saying that, Bobby," I said. But I wondered what Dylan was about to say.

Rebekha dabbed her lips with her napkin, then said, "Andy is late for dinner again. I've bought him three watches for three Christmases straight and he still doesn't have a one of them to tell time with." She just pretended she was mad at Andy, as she still spoke of him as the crazy, silly little boy who needed her love more than frogs needed water. Except he wasn't a little boy, he had girlfriends and muscles.

"Andy's just Andy," Daddy said.

"He gave me one of his watches." Bobby talked with his mouth full. "I have it on, see?" He held up his still-dirty wrist and showed us the Timex. He then pea-eyed Dylan. "My watch says it's time for *stoopid* boyfriends to go home."

Daddy did that inhaling a breath thing he does when he wants to laugh, but knew he shouldn't.

Rebekha said, "Bobby, that's quite enough."

Bobby snickered behind his hand and I didn't know if I loved him or was mad at him.

Dylan said, "I'm sure Bobby here is just feeling territorial over his big sister."

Bobby rolled his eyes back in his head and stuck out his tongue the way a dead cow would.

Rebekha tried again, "Bobby, I taught you better manners."

"Yes Ma'am. I'm sorry." My little brother didn't look sorry one speck.

We all bent to our plates again. There was tinkling of silverware, passing of bowls and platters, and Bobby slurping his tea as if he was so thirsty he'd drink an ocean.

When everyone had put down their forks and sighed, I scraped back my chair, and stood. "I'll go make the coffee, Rebekha." I began picking up the empty plates on the table.

She stood, too, said, "Don't do that, Virginia Kate. I'll do it."

"No, I have it. Go on and set yourself back down."

She picked up a bowl.

I came around the table with my stacked plates. "You rest a while. I got this."

She held the bowl in front of her. "You have company . . ."

I took the bowl from her and stacked it on the plates. "Please, I got it."

With her eyes, she asked, *Are you sure?*

With my eyes, I answered *yes.*

She settled back into her seat, turned her attention to Dylan, and asked him if he was born in California and what brought him to Louisiana?

"I was born in Los Angeles, but my parents didn't stay there long . . ."

The rest of what he said I didn't hear as I took the dishes into the kitchen, lowered them into the large deep sink, plugged in the stopper, squirted in Joy, cut on the faucet, and watched as the bubbles foamed up and over the dishes. The steam rose and clouded the window view. I was back in the mists that settled over mountain and cove and holler. When the sink was filled, I went back to pick up more dishes.

Daddy and Dylan were at it again, this time about Shakespeare and Montaigne.

Bobby played drums with his knife and fork on the plate, until Rebekha took them away, and handed them to me.

Still no Andy. That stinker.

Back into the kitchen, I placed the other dishes in the sink. The rest of the dishes on the table could wait for later, and those in the sink could soak a while. I measured out coffee and water and plugged in the percolator, then headed off to the bathroom, shut the door, and ran the sink faucet water, just in case anyone could hear me, even though there's no way anyone could unless someone came on down the hall, and what if they did and what if it was Dylan and he heard me? My head went twirling round as I set there, water running from me, water running in the bathroom sink, water percolating in the coffee pot, water everywhere in this land of Louisiana that someway flowed out to where Dylan came from that had water he said was better.

While washing my hands, I tried not to look in the mirror in case I found faults. Maybe the world would be better off without mirrors showing back what was messy. I smoothed my dress over my body. My hand curved here and there. There were no straight lines with me and I'd never look starved as many of the other girls on campus did. I wasn't going to quit eating to get there, as Jade did. I knew what she was up to when she picked at her food and played games with it.

From the counter I took the red lipstick and drew it thick over my lips. Looked as if I'd just eaten a mess of liver blood. I rubbed off the lipstick hard as I could, and left the bathroom. Why didn't I just wear my comfortable britches, my flip flops, and the purple blouse with the bell-sleeves? Trying to look like someone who wanted to look good for her boyfriend was tiring.

I sneaked a peek in Andy's room, which used to be Micah's, but Andy wasn't there hiding from company. Most of Micah's artwork still hung on the walls, along with Andy's posters of racecars and Farrah Fawcett in a red bathing suit. A small painting Micah did from a photograph leaned on top of the chest of drawers. It was from the day Rebekha was going to adopt us and Momma pulled her stunt. Miss Darla had taken that photo, right before she gave me the green-eyed horse pendant with the note inside that read, *pieces of paper are not love, they're just pieces of paper.* She'd known before we all did how things would turn out, how Momma would only let us kids go in body and not in the law.

When I headed back down the hall to the kitchen, the coffee found my nose before I reached it, and it smelled too strong. The happy perk sound was just like that commercial, "boo de boo de boop boop de boo de boop boop boo." I tapped my finger to the sound.

There were noises coming from the living room. Someone put on a record. I bet it was Rebekha, since it was Elvis and he was singing about a jailhouse rocking. Made me think of iron bars and people behind them and how they must feel stuck there and unhappy even though they were the ones caused themselves to be fastened up. The things people found themselves into.

I looked off and beyond. Far and far away. Turned back and then tried to see all the way forward.

A foundling ghost whispered, *Virginia Kate . . . what are you looking for? It's not here . . . it's not here . . .* Hairs on the back of my neck stirred. A fat squirrel ran up the oak tree and another one followed it. A cat jumped after a lizard. A bird turned its bright black eye on me.

There came Miss Darla to her yard. Old Sophia Loren stiff-legged ran to bark at the neighborhood stray cat that everyone fed. That cat was so fat, I didn't know how it walked. Miss Darla shoved her hands in her tan britches and I heard, "Being anti-social, aren't you?"

"What do you know?"

"More than I want to sometimes."

Then the thoughts between us slammed shut as Andy came into view holding Sophia. Miss Darla ruffled Andy's hair, and said something to him while pointing to me through the window. He turned to look at me and laughed, gave Sophia back to her. Miss Darla swayed inside her house with a parting sigh that scattered on the wind then whooshed through the back door when Andy slammed in.

"Miss Darla said to tell you she found a dead dove facing to the west on her porch this morning. And, that her left big toe hurt her all night." He pulled a big shrug. "Whatever all that means."

I took out cups, saucers, and a carafe from the cabinet, checking to see if any extra bottles of booze hid there.

"So, where for art is Romeo?"

"Shush it up."

"Aw, Seestor's shy. She's buh-lushing."

When I hit him on his formerly skinny arm, I had a flash of him as he was with his suitcase after Momma drove away with Harold, snot running from his nose as he cried. He had cried so much when he was little. Until he was shed of Momma, that is.

Sticking a spoon into the leftover stew, he stirred and sniffed, then said, "You sure took long enough before you brought him to meet everyone."

I poured sugar into the sugar bowl.

He spooned a glob of stew into his mouth and chewed with his mouth open.

I poured cream into the creamer.

He said, around a mouthful, "I guesh you were embarrashed to show ush to him."

"Well, smarty-britches, he's setting in there waiting for you to anoint him with your brother seal of approval wand."

Andy grabbed a bowl and spooned in a gallon of supper. "Later. I'm hungry." Sometimes he still said hungry like hongry, but not much anymore.

I grabbed his shirttail. "Come on, go gawk and be a prime fool and get it out of your system, like everybody else has. I can't even have a friend who happens to be a boy without all this foolishness."

He set down his bowl, groaned as if he were an old man asked to pedal to Mars on a tricycle.

I marched him into the living room. "Dylan, this is my brother, Andy."

Dylan grabbed Andy's hand and shook it. "Nice to meet you, Andy. Kate talks about her brothers all the time."

"Who's Kate?" Andy wiped his hand on his britches and turned to me.

Well, Miss Kate stood there as if she thought it was the best name in the universe. As if the name Virginia Kate for certain needed changing to suit Dylan's tongue.

"Well goddamn all day long." Andy turned to go back to the kitchen.

I followed him to the kitchen, poured the dark, heavy Community Coffee into the carafe, and reached for the cream and sugar.

Andy shoved food into his mouth, hardly chewing before he

swallowed, and burped loud and long.

"When will you grow up?"

He shoveled in more supper, opened his mouth, "Gah-uh-uh-uh." Pieces of food fell from his mouth on the floor.

"I said to grow up." But as always, I laughed.

He scrubbed at the mess he made. "I don't know why he can't call you by your real name."

"It's just his way, you don't know him yet."

"I seen him around." He chewed stew, eyed the apple pie.

I poured coffee into one of the cups and stirred in cream and sugar. I had all the time in the world, drifting on the breeze, nowhere else to be. Who needed to go back to the living room? Not me.

Andy finished his stew and attached a hunk of pie. He watched me open the cabinets to the right and then the left, and down below.

"Dear old Dad put the extra behind the cereal boxes."

"Extra what?" I picked up my cup and sipped, liking how the coffee was strong and bitter. How it heated my tongue, burning off words.

Andy poured himself a cup and drank it back without cream or sugar, wincing at the hot liquid. He fanned his mouth, said "Aye, Chihuahua."

It was no lie I was getting right tired of Andy.

He slurped down faucet water and toad-burped again.

I grabbed the coffee tray, turned to go, and was three steps into the dining room when Andy called out, "You keep your head in the clouds and don't pay attention sometimes. Then when you do pay attention, you try to forget what it is you're paying attention to. I'm just watching out for you. It's a brother rule, remember?"

Over my shoulder I said, "You are sillier than a silly moon." I took the tray into the living room, put it on the coffee table, and made myself busy pouring.

Rebekha said, "I'll get the dessert."

I remembered her no eating in the living room rule. That rule sure had flown out to the four distant corners since we kids had arrived on her doorstep, one two three, and then Bobby her own as four.

Daddy settled his bones on the couch and sipped. Bobby was on the floor looking at one of Micah's old Superman comic books. Dylan was looking at photos. Peeking over his shoulder, I saw the pictures from Hamburger and Elvis Night, the summer Andy was almost bit by the moccasin and Rebekha killed it; the summer I met Jade. Our captured faces were frozen in slap-happy while we did the Twist, the Watusi, and dances we'd made up. There was a funny one of Rebekha and Micah doing the Mashed Potato. Micah's face was concentrated on his moves, and Rebekha in the photo laughed big open wide. That Hamburger and Elvis Night had been mighty fine.

I forgot my worry mind as Dylan turned to me and said, "I'm seeing who you are better by looking at who you were. I see how you like to have fun."

I hurried to my room, grabbed a box of pictures, took them back into the living room, opened the box, and pulled out a picture of Micah, Andy, and me standing barefoot in the shade of the tree. "This is a picture from the holler. That's the sugar maple I told you about."

He took the photo, studied it, said, "Look at these kids."

There was another of us kids standing by the Rambler, and then one of me in the shadow of my mountain. I spread them out for Dylan to see.

Rebekha asked, "Y'all ready for dessert?"

Even Andy came back in sniffing around for more sweets.

I helped Rebekha with dessert, brought over ice cream and cookies to Daddy first, then to Dylan, both with a sliver of pie on the side. Dylan was intent on stirring around in my box. Soon as I had a free hand, I took the box from him and placed the lid back on it.

He picked up his dessert. "I thought earlier you were trying to get away from me, you were in the kitchen so long."

I acted as if I had mysterious ways and helped myself to ice cream and two coconut cookies, forcing myself to eat slow, but it was hard because I loved coconut so much.

Andy-and-Bobby loud chewing with their mouths open, their eyes opened wide and staring; they were idiots reincarnated into bigger idiots.

Daddy left the room, and soon ice pounded into his glass. I didn't look at Rebekha when she sighed that old hurting hopeful sigh, and then said, "Well now. Let's see here. What's next?"

The cold ice cream froze my tongue. I hoped ice cream froze everyone's tongue so we'd all just be quiet for a while.

                                    ❧ • ❧

After the dishes were done and everything back to order, with even the guys helping, Dylan and I rocked on the porch with the day pulling away and the night preparing to press itself against us. The cicadas hummed, rising up and up and then growing quiet again, up and up, then quiet. The heat rose up and down in the same way, humming and shimmering even as the night slipped around us quiet as a chicken thief.

Dylan pulled a picture from his pocket and stared at it. Turning it over, he read, "'Katie Ivene Holms Carey, June 1962.' Wow, your mother was drop-dead gorgeous!" The monster in me grabbed the photo from him and shoved it into my pocket. He held up his hands. "I'm sorry. I didn't mean to upset you. But what a waste of a beautiful woman to live as she does." His voice sounded slurry, just a little.

I stood. "Goodnight, Dylan."

He reached to touch my arm. "Hey, don't be mad. That picture was loose in the box and I figured no harm. I got one of you, too. Look." He reached back into his pocket and took out a photo of Jade and me from our high school graduation party. Jade prissed, pooching out her mouth, while I laughed at her.

"You should've asked first."

He stood. "I wasn't going to keep the one of your mother, and the other I was going to ask if I could keep it." His breath fumed wine and whatever drink Daddy had fixed him. "I didn't think you'd mind if I took them out of the box."

"I mind."

He changed up the subject. "I don't think your brothers care for me all that much."

"Bobby's just a kid. And Andy, well, Andy's just Andy."

"Bobby's your half-brother, right? His coloring is more like Rebekha. You and Andy have those unreadable dark eyes, and—"

"I'm tired, Dylan. I'll see you later."

He stepped closer, placed his palm on my cheek. "Stop pushing me away. Don't you see how crazy I am about you?" He breathed harsh booze breath, said, "I wouldn't have stuck around this long if I didn't want you so bad. Can't you understand that?"

A hot wind blew across my body while my feet planted to the porch.

Dylan trailed his fingers down to my shoulder, then across and down to my chest, and placed his palm flat where my breasts swelled. He leaned in and pressed his lips to mine, parted my lips with his tongue, pressed himself close, closer, deepened the kiss, deep, deeper. He made a throated groan.

The fire raged, and my knees were weak, my innards were weak, I was weak. I pushed him away, pointed him to his car, turned my back, went inside, and shut the door before I did something Momma would do.

Next door, Miss Darla said, "Boy, that was *some kiss.*"

I answered, "Mind your own business," and closed my thoughts to her.

From the sounds inside, I placed where everyone was. The boys were in Andy's room. Rebekha and Daddy were inside theirs. There was a radio singing. There was soft, and not so soft, talking. There were good home sounds. Rebekha had made this place a home. But my sweet sister mountain, the holler, the West Virginia wind that rushed down from the ridge, the smell of the earth, all of those things were a part of me, too. How could I let all of that go? How did I ever let Momma go? *She let* you *go*, a voice reminded, and I shook that thought away to the four corners of the universe and then to the fifth, sixth, and beyond corners.

I gathered things from my room, slipped into the bathroom, started a bath, cleaned off the make-up, brushed my hair and pulled it into a ponytail. I could still taste Dylan's kiss on my tongue. I eased myself into the tub, and as I scrubbed away the evening with a soft washrag, I imagined his skin had rubbed off on mine, leaving bits of himself on me. I put my head underwater, even though I knew my hair would take forever to dry and my pillow would be wet. The universe underwater was soothing. The sounds muffled and far away; I was muffled and far away. I opened my eyes underwater and liked how everything had no hard outlines.

After I finished my bath and let the water glug out, Dylan and the day went down the drain. I toweled off, put on the robe I'd brought in, and threw my dirty clothes into the hamper, remembered Momma's picture there, and grabbed it out of my dress pocket. Last, I brushed my teeth, including my tongue, and took a small towel from Rebekha's neat-stacked towels, all the folded ends facing out, to put on my pillow.

When I opened the bathroom door, Daddy was hollering at Andy to turn down the radio.

The music screeching from Andy's room about a swinging seesaw and feet flying and diddle diddle faded to low, and Andy yelled, "It wasn't that loud!"

Patting my hair with the towel, I listened to what would come next, since something always came next with Andy.

Daddy hollered, "I can't wait for you to move into your dorm!"

Bobby screamed, "I want him to stay here!"

"Well, he needs to learn to be quiet!"

Rebekha's voice raised just a bit, "Our Andy can stay here as long as he wants to."

"Yeah, my brother can stay here as long as for-*ever!*"

Andy called out, "See? Bobby and Rebekha love me more than fried bologna!"

"'I like your silence, it the more shows off your wonder.'"

Nothing. Daddy's Shakespeare usually made everyone hush up, except Momma.

Momma would say, *You and your Shakesweird, Frederick.*

I moved on down the hall to my room.

After I put on my pajamas, I looked at the photo Dylan had taken without asking permission. Momma stood near the little white house in the holler. She had on a red halter dress and her hair blew wild around her head. The sun showed the outline of her long, strong legs through her dress. Her red lips pouted at the camera and her eyes were deep and dark; there was no beginning or end to those eyes, they went on to eternity. It was a black and white photo, but I saw the varied colors of her. The red, the black, the dark, the light. In an afterthought to Momma, there stood a little five-year-old dark-haired girl who looked up at her momma as if her momma had the moon setting right on her head.

It was easy not to notice that little girl. I don't even think Dylan had seen me; he'd only seen Momma. That's how it was and always would be. I stashed the photo in my underwear drawer, went to bed, and dreamed I was in West Virginia, wearing the red halter dress. My lips were the color of Mrs. Mendel's tomatoes. Mrs. Mendel was in her garden and I waved to her. She waved back and said, "Why'd you leave the holler? Your momma is lonely. I'm lonely, too. I miss you chil'ren running round and making racket. Come see my nephew, he's got it bad for you. He's hiding behind that tomato." The top of a head peeked out from behind a tomato as big as a Buick.

I said back, "Momma doesn't want me anymore. I'm gone away from my kin."

Mrs. Mendel said, "Foolishness foolishness. Nothing but foolishness." Then she bent down to pick a rose, pricked her finger, and then cried as the blood dribbled onto her flowers, then flowed out and down into the creek, where the creek turned red and thick and hot and raging. As Mrs. Mendel cried and cried, she turned into Momma and the garden turned into Momma's room, where I last saw my momma.

I reached out to her and, all a sudden, my dream changed and I stood high on my mountain looking down at Dylan. He called to me, but I couldn't hear what he said. He shook his head, said louder, "I'm tired of waiting for you to be a woman," turned and walked away. I set there on my mountain and cried as Mrs. Mendel had, but I felt light, lighter than the mists that rose up around me. Fionadala appeared, nuzzled my face. I mounted my dark horse and we flew away, both free as birds flying on the good old West Virginia wind. When I looked at my hands holding her mane, they were child's hands, not a woman's hands.

The mimosa scratching at the window woke me. I knew how my room looked even in the dark.

The same. That's how I wanted things to stay and that's not how life was.

The house grew quiet, as if it had to think over my decision and see if it agreed with it. The mimosa scratched more, telling me to stay stay stay in my little girl's room. The night swarmed about me. The moon rays fell onto the roof and spilled into the windows, then the clouds covered the moon and it was dark again. I snuggled into my pillow, and knew it was time to leave another home.

Chapter 7

I hear she's lassoed a big fine man!

I was at Rebekha and Daddy's to open my presents from them, which was a check for my first two months rent and more powder to replace what I'd used in the powder vessel Micah bought me for my twelfth birthday. Every few years as I emptied it, someone gave me more so the amber glass never emptied of spicy smell.

After an early supper, we were going to have cake and ice cream with Jade, Miss Darla, Soot, Marco, and little Mae Lynn, and the Campinelles.

I heard her before I saw her. The honk honk honking of the car, then the scrape of the back bumper as she pulled a big green monster into the driveway, the screeching of her voice before she even blobbed out of the car, the slam of the car door, the re-screeching as she said, "Look what I got here for my grandbaby girl! A big car!" The clomping of her feet, the yap yap yapping of Peanut the Rat Terrier, who unlike the former Imperial, had a happy fox-face that lit up with mischief.

Mee Maw Laudine had blasted in to town full head-on-for-furious to see me on my twentieth birthday. The air was close and stifling, trying to keep her out by the very unpleasant of the weather; a ninety-degree day that caused my clothes to collapse limp against my body, but Mee Maw was bigger than the weather any old time.

In the driveway was a green Plymouth Fury station wagon that looked as if it had wood down the sides of it, but I wasn't sure if it was real wood or something else made to look woodish. A black Trans Am with gold pinstripes, gold wheels, and a big gold and black bird on the hood pulled in and parked behind the green monster. The Trans Am was young while the man who stepped out was old, but that didn't seem to bother the man, he strutted out as fine as the bird on the hood, with a big cowboy hat, cowboy boots, and string tie—that car was his stallion and he'd ridden it in from the wilds of Texas to the Land of Louisiana. But, oh that Plymouth. That was another car altogether.

I turned my attention from the car back to my grandmother. Mee Maw was still screeching, and somewhere in there she introduced me to Hank. Hank took my hand in his and shook it until my body trembled. He said in a voice that sonic-boomed, "Your granny has told me so much about you!"

I turned to hug Mee Maw, who looked this side of fetching, if you liked insane bananas, in a bright yellow pantsuit with gold heels (that right matched the gold wheels on the car), and a Dolly Parton wig that tilted to the right.

Mee Maw Laudine shot happy beams at her Hank. She said, "We left at five-thirty this morning to get your car here in plenty time for your birthday!"

I said, "That's some car, Mee Maw."

"Take a gander at it before we go inside," Mee Maw yo-old-lady-oo'd.

Peanut ran around my legs. He bit into my blue jeans and pulled, tearing a hole in them. I leaned down and grabbed his squirmy bodied self and hoped he wouldn't make a piddled mess on the floor as Mee Maw's other dog had.

Mee Maw said, "That car is yours. All yours! I picked it out myself. Hardly has any mileage on it and runs like a top! I am as tickled as tickled can be. I am just so proud of my grandbaby! In college, and, I hear she's lassoed a big fine man!"

Rebekha stood on the porch, her eyes wide and her mouth in an O.

Daddy said, "Hello Mother," then tossed back his drink to fortify himself.

After we inspected the car, with Mee Maw Laudine showing me every tiny scratch and Hank saying he tried to rub and wax them out best he could and Peanut biting a hole in my shirt so I put him down and Rebekha listening to Mee Maw screech to her about her girdle pinching her be-hind and Bobby running out to us yelling oh a puppy a puppy and then snatching up Peanut to play in his room (and Rebekha saying, "Please, Bobby, make sure he goes potty first") and after Mee Maw took a dead rabbit from under the seat and said she'd hit it not far away and it was still fresh enough for supper and after Rebekha looked at the rabbit with *Oh Lord help us* eyes and Andy stomped down the porch steps crowing about how it would be his turn next to have a car and it wouldn't be a goddamn ugly green tank and after Mee Maw found out I was moved out of the house and she carried on about that until I promised it wasn't far from Rebekha and Daddy and after Hank hugged on Rebekha and lifted her into the air while Mee Maw laughed and screeched and after Daddy went back to the kitchen to throw ice in his glass and after we had Mee Maw and Hank settled in what used to be my room, I was at last able to get in my tank, start it up, and take it for a spin.

Everyone, even Peanut, even Daddy, piled inside with us. I whooshed with all the windows open even though it was a hot exploded molten rock day. The radio sang county-western music that Mee Maw had been listening to all the way from Texas. I smelled the rabbit's blood and knew I'd be scrubbing the carpet but good.

I had a car, had moved in with Jade, had a boyfriend, was twenty years old, and almost a junior in college. There was no turning back from it all. My hair flew out the window; I put my hand out with my hair. Then just as Momma had always done when we'd flown down the road in the Rambler, I yelled out, "Wheeeee!" Someone answered with another, "Wheeeee!"

When we were back to Rebekha and Daddy's house, I parked and everyone poured out. Miss Darla stepped over to look at my car, shaking her head. She grinned at me, and I grinned back. She handed me a package wrapped in bright orange paper and a white bow, said, "For later." After Miss Darla said her hellos to Mee Maw and Hank, she went on back inside, after promising to come back at six-thirty as planned. I was going to miss looking out Rebekha's kitchen window at her and Sophia Loren. I sure was.

We headed into the house, where Mee Maw went straight to what had been my room and set right out to blubbering how her girl wasn't home anymore, and how she grew up too fast. She plopped on what used to be my bed and lay across it. She said, "I'll just take me a little nap."

I think we all were glad Mee Maw blew out enough hot air to deflate herself enough so that she felt like a nap. She could breathe in and snore out until the windows fogged and the air in my old room stagnated. Outside, the weather sighed a relief things didn't go as bad as the time Category Five Grandmother rolled in with Hurricane Camille. Mee Maw could bring hurricanes, tornadoes, and gully-washers wherever she went.

While things were quiet, I walked the house. I touched the leather couch, felt the rug under my feet, went into the dining room and trailed my hand along the table where so many breakfasts and suppers had been eaten and birthday parties had been celebrated with cakes and decorations, went into the kitchen where Rebekha was preparing supper.

She said, "That's some car."

"It sure is." I picked up a knife and began chopping stalks of celery.

"Thanks for the help." Rebekha added a hunk of butter to the skillet to melt for the shrimp etouffee.

I finished the celery, and then started on the bell pepper. "I guess I can still come help you cook sometime."

"You better." She took the celery, along with the onions she'd already chopped, and tossed them into the melted butter, stirred it to cook down the vegetables.

When I'd chopped up the bell pepper, I threw the pieces in.

"We'll get all the papers straight for you, so it'll be in your name and whatever else is necessary." Rebekha minced two cloves of garlic that would go into the mix once the onions, bell pepper, and celery wilted. "And you'll need insurance."

I'd not even thought about insurance. Between my share of rent, food, and gas, insurance would be one more thing to worry over. I figured I better ask Soot for more hours, or ask for more work at the library.

"Are you okay with money and all, Hon?" She added the garlic to the skillet, stirred.

"I'm fine. At least I didn't have to buy my own car, and the birthday rent check will help a lot, thank you."

"I have you a little something personal, too. I'll give it to you later."

I smiled to myself.

"I'll add these shrimp at the very end, so they won't overcook. I'm not thinking straight." She looked at me. "Mee Maw."

"Yup, Mee Maw."

We laughed.

She put down the spoon, and then measured out a tablespoon of flour that would go into the vegetable mix to thicken it for the roux. "My first car was a Dodge and I still have a Dodge. I just love a Dodge."

Rebekha's serious Dodge. She was always the same, but I lay bet fifty shined dimes she had surprises inside of her shivering away that no one else could see. Like when she killed the moccasin, or kicked Daddy out even if it wasn't for good, and no telling what all.

"I think this rice is done," she said. "And I want to make that coconut frosting you like for your cake."

"I took out the butter and shortening so it would be soft."

"Thank you." She then hugged my neck so hard, I near broke into pieces. "I'm going to miss you being here. Washing dishes together, all that." Her voice turned as if she had syrup in her throat and couldn't swallow it down all the way.

I blinked, once, twice, three times. My eyes stung and my heart beat both full and empty. Full from her hug, empty from how I was going to miss those things, too.

We parted, and she took up to getting the rest of the meal together. I worked side-by-side her. Later, I knew she'd ask me, "You wash? I dry?" And I'd say, "Okay," and we'd stand together at her sink and do the dishes. I'd look out her kitchen window; maybe Miss Darla and Sophia Loren would come out and wave to me; maybe Miss Darla would send over a thought.

Maybe Bobby would tear into the house making a racket, and maybe Andy would fry bologna until the house smelled like a fried bologna factory. Maybe Daddy would come into the kitchen and fix himself a drink. Maybe Micah would not come, but maybe he would again one day.

I inhaled all the smells from Rebekha's kitchen, and tried not to think about how I'd left someone and somewhere again. At least I could come here any time I wanted to. Rebekha hadn't asked me to leave, and it was still my home, anytime I wanted. I was not banished as I had been from the holler.

Rebekha added the shrimp to the skillet, stirred for a bit, then cut off the fire under the etouffee and covered it to keep in the heat to cook the shrimp the rest of the way. "Well, I didn't follow my usual schedule, but I guess it'll be okay."

"Mee Maw will eat it like there's no food tomorrow."

"I think you're right."

"What happened to the rabbit?"

"I had Bobby bury it in the backyard. Deep."

We both shook our heads.

"The things that old woman does," Rebekha said.

That was a for sure truth.

I poured us two glasses of sweet tea over lots of ice, added lemon, and headed out to the porch to rock and sip before Mee Maw awoke to create thunder and lightning.

Before she joined me, Rebekha stopped by her room and then came out with a package wrapped in wild-flowered paper, which she handed to me.

I opened her present, a beautiful mahogany-colored leather photo album.

"I know how you like to look through photo albums and thought you may want to start you own."

"Thank you, Rebekha."

We rocked away. I remembered all the time before from when I'd first come in Daddy's silly little car and blinked with little wide-girl-eyes at the place I'd be living instead of the holler. I don't know what Rebekha remembered, but a smile touched her lips.

∾ • ∿

In my car, I took the long way to Jade's, drove around the lakes sparkling under the hot old August sun, then rode by Dylan's house to feed and check on Jinxie, who was fit to be tied to see someone come pet him and make over him. Dylan was on an overnight trip to see some buildings somewhere that I couldn't remember. He'd miss my twentieth birthday, but I didn't mind. Why should I?

Jade told me a man could only wait so long for what he needs and was I sure he was out of town on a business trip?

I'd asked, "What about what a *girl* needs? Anybody think about that? And yes that's where he is because he told me so."

"Just because they say it doesn't mean they do what they say. Men can be sneaky snakes, especially when they aren't getting what they want when they want it."

Even though I rolled my eyes, her words poked me hard.

I didn't want to think about Dylan and sneaky men and Jade's blabbermouth right then. Not while I was in my own car, for even if I didn't buy it myself, I was responsible for the insurance and the gas, for my rent, groceries, my own clothes. I not only worked as Soot's waitress, but also helped her with the books and other office work and still had my job at the library. All those things said I was a Woman. When I told Jade that, she laughed, told me some people were doing those things way ahead of me; like her for instance, how she had her own car well before me and she lived in her own house before me, had boyfriends before me, had sex before me. Why remind her she had parents who gave her what she wanted when she wanted it, and those boyfriends didn't always treat her right or with respect, and I didn't see where having sex made a woman a Woman but it sometimes made a woman a fool. But I didn't say one word to her about those things.

I parked in Jade's driveway, pulled the keys from the ignition, felt how heavy they were in my hands, how it made my car even more mine, grabbed the sack that held my gifts, slipped out, and headed inside to Jade. I knew she'd laugh and think my car ugly beside her cute VW bug, but I didn't care.

Inside, Jade yapped on the phone, wrapping the long curly cord round and round her arm, then unwinding it, then twisting it, then pulling it, over and again until the cord was a big snarled mess. Sometimes she pulled the cord to its full length, climbed out the kitchen window, and set outside to talk.

She pointed to a wrapped present setting on the counter, then pointed to me, then grinned, then ignored me to talk on the phone again.

There were no messages for me on the blackboard. For someone who liked to talk, Dylan sure didn't like to dial me up when he was out of town.

While waiting for Jade, I took my so-far gifts to my room, including the unopened Miss Darla's. Then headed back to the kitchen to dance around from foot to foot as my hint for Jade to hurry it up.

She said to someone on the phone, "But how do you know you *don't* want something until you jump right on in life and *taste* it?"

I wanted to ask her, "What if it tastes bitter? What if I can't swallow it?"

I waved the keys in Jade's face; she finally told the person she was talking to she had to go. We ran outside and just as I thought, when she saw my ugly green car, she laughed, and also just as I knew, I didn't care one teeninsy bit. We both jumped inside, and I took her flying about town with the heated air whipping our hair across our faces. We stopped at Soot's and Marco's and let them gawk over the car. We then rode on over to Rebekha and Daddy's for my birthday cake and more presents, including Jade's present to me—silver dangley earrings, a photography book, and bright red fingernail polish. I ate cake, laughed, hugged, heard the happy birthday song. Without Dylan. Without a call. And I still didn't care. I sure didn't. Nope.

That night after the party, after I'd bathed and climbed into bed at Jade's, I opened the gift from Miss Darla. It was a statue of a young woman with full high breasts, a proud look about her, her hair long and dark, her eyes darker. She rode a dark and muscled buffalo horse—the Ponokamita—and there was motion all about the horse and young woman as they galloped to a place they hungered. The woman's hair flew behind her, as did the horse's thick curly mane and tail. I sucked in my breath all the way to my toes.

There was no note. Miss Darla knew I'd see what I wanted to see and feel what I needed to feel when I held her gift. The statue ripped a yearning in me that sent me falling backward. Back to where the wild things roamed, searching for the scratch that would cure our itch.

Chapter 8

Today

I read old letters while snuggled in Grandma Faith's quilt in the West Virginia holler.

Dear Katie Ivenes Girl,

I aint got nothing to give you. If it wernt for kids and a ungreatfull wife Id not been in a jail all them year. I aint never kilt nobody lessen they ask for it. If you think I kilt your granny then she ask for it. If she didnt ask for it then I aint kilt her. I got the cansur and you think I care a speck about you and them other basturds my girl and that long lanked shitter made out of their rutting? Dont no why that panty ass boy of mine give me a letter. Nothing in it but sillyness that aint never to come true. Just like your granny you dont got no sinse. When I die and that will be days and not weeks I rekon I aint calling fourth a thing for the lot of you. You all burn in hell for all I give a care. If you cant fashun what I tell you then I have told all I got to say. Now leave me to my own. And I aint calling me your granpa. Luke and thats it. Luke

Dear Veestor,

I sold a painting! For only a 100 buckeroos but I needed the money for more paint. One day that painting will be worth thousands, you wait and see you better believe it. Keep sending your letters to that post office box I sent you. That's the best thing for now. I know you want a picture of me but not right now. Maybe later. But thanks for sending the pictures of all of you. You look like a woman kind of sort of, except you don't, cause you also look the same. I can't believe how tall Bobby is. And Andy's just Andy. He almost looks blurry in the photo, like he can't be still for even a second to take a picture. Hey, last time you wrote, you mentioned you moved in with Sunbeam white bread girl. About time. Stop being afraid of change, Vee-Kator. I can see your face right now, your eyes rolling like Momma. Don't deny it, I can spy it! haha! Well, gee, I got to flee, see? Love, Micah

Dear Virginia Kate,

How are you? I am fine. I figure you want to hear about the holler. It is mostly the same. I believe some one is building up yonder to the other side since I hear things. Guess they will do that, build houses and all and blow things up. Onliest reason we got our tv working regular all this time is on account of that old rich woman what lived acrost the way, you re-collect? She had all those little birds? She passed away and I do not know who took up in her house, if any body. She was rich as Judas after the deal. Her son was some biggity big in banking. This here holler is not for every body, but I would not live no where else. I sure miss you younguns running round.

Remember my nephew I said was coming and you missed him while you was here back long time ago? Well, he called last night and asked about you again! That boy got it bad and he never laid eyes on you other than the pictures I got and the stories I tell. He was such a hurted boy and grew up to be kind. His poor daddy was killed from a drunked driver. I will tell you about that one day.

Well, any way, back to the holler. That old empty house stands lone some and no body ever goes up there no more. Except one time I spied your momma up there. Bout scared me to Jesus, since I thought her a ghost. Her white night gown was floating all round her. I watched her out from my window. She stood there a spell, then the strangest thing, she just lay her self down near the corner of the house. After a while pass, I figure I best go see about her. I stepped out my door and that is when she got offen the ground and started on back down the hill. I hurried in side, since I never know what might set your momma off mad. I figured that was her own bit of business up there and she may not want this old woman seeing of it. I just had the thought I ought to tell you what I saw and how the holler is. Send me more letters and pictures. I like them pictures you take. Be good.

Signed, your old neighbor, Mrs. Mendel

Dear Granddaughter,

Oh, Mee Maw misses her granddaughter!!! She misses all her grandchildren and can't wait to visit again. How's that son of mine, your father? He hasn't called me in two weeks!!!! I have my feelings hurt and I want you to tell him that. Tell him your Mee Maw is <u>hurting</u>! How is that saint Rebekha? That woman is too good to be true!! Tell her I got her cookies and thank you. Peanut the little devil turned into a good dog, but I miss my poor little Imperial. I visit Imper every day where he's buried out back. He always was a sickly little dear. I don't know why that Rebekha won't let you kids have a dog!!! <u>Best</u> thing for kids, I say. You hear from that mother of yours? I bet not. I bet that thing won't bother to talk to her own children!!! Always was <u>nothing but trouble</u> for my son and his kids. I don't owe her not <u>a cent more</u>. I say good riddance!! Well, Mee Maw has to go. I got so many things to tell Hank to do it can't even be funny. Old ladies shouldn't have <u>nothing</u> to do. We should be putting up our feet whilst someone

else does the work!! That's why I got married again!
You need to get married so <u>all your troubles are over</u>
and if they are not, then you find yourself another one!
That's what Mee Maw does! Loves and kisses and hugs
to my beautiful granddaughter! Love you more than
anyone in the whole world!!!!

    Your Mee Maw

Dear Neice,

    Aunt Billie and I want to let you know we bought
two more horses and would love it if you and Andy
visited to ride like you did that time when your momma
was so sickly in the hospital. That sister of mine is
~~stuborn~~ ~~stubburn~~ stubborn but I know she loves her kids.
Maybe if you visit with Andy, she will see the ~~errorr~~
error of her ways and do whats right. Aunt Billie just
read this over my ~~sholder~~ shoulder and said I was living
in a dream world and that my sister wont change. She
says I spell bad, but thats not it, I just get in a hurry is
all. Aunt Billie says hi. She says you kids are welcome
any time, but she sure understands if you cant come and
why. I ~~rekon~~ ~~recken~~ reckon it would be hard to come all
this way and not see your momma. Well, just wanted to
tell you about our new horses. Tell Andy and Micah
hello. Aunt Billie says to give yourselves hugs for her.

    Your Uncle Jonah and Aunt Billie

Dear Virginia Kate,

    I got your card, but you forgot to ask the man who
was my husband and who I had his kids to put in a
check. He knows he is supposed to send something and I
haven't seen even a shadow of it yet. Ask that man who
I birthed his children if he has forgotten.

    Momma

1978-1980

Love looks not with the eyes, but with the mind;
And therefore is winged Cupid painted blind.
—Shakespeare

Chapter 9

Shiny things

The black dress Dylan picked out for me fit close. I didn't wear black much, too sad, as if I was heading on off to a funeral. Wearing it, I didn't compare to Momma in her red dress as she swirled round and round, her long hair flying, her lips parted, her arms out as though a wayward ballerina. What I wore wasn't made for twirling in, but instead for serious restaurants that Dylan said called for me to dress *very nice.*

I brushed my hair thirty-two strokes, pulled the top and sides back, and clasped it with a wooden barrette. For make-up, I barely touched my cheeks with blush, swept dark mascara on the tips of my lashes, and on my lips, patted a stain of red. Finally, I slipped my panty-hosed feet into black heels that were higher than I was used to, teeter-tottered, steadied myself, and then practiced walking in them until I felt I wouldn't bust my head to Kingdom Come and back.

I was ready for Dylan and for Galatoire's in New Orleans.

When Dylan came for me, he looked me up and down, and said, "Very classy." He wore a three-piece suit and his hair was thick, waved, and feathered back in a look I thought a bit girlish, but he liked his hair to look like that Barry Manilow. Jade said Dylan was more like a Vinnie Barbarino in tight pants that showed all he's got and then some than he was like a skinny Manilow. I figured why couldn't Dylan just be himself? He opened the car door for me and I smoothed myself in careful as I could.

My sheer black pantyhose itched on my legs and waist, tight and squeezing. I hated pantyhose and wouldn't wear them unless threatened by the fashion goddess on high, and Jade was a fashion goddess on the highest. She'd said, "For god's sake. Wear the hosiery or I'm kicking your butt from here to eternity. You cannot go to dinner in that dress in a nice restaurant with bare legs."

I'd answered, "Why not? What's wrong with bare legs?"

She'd let out a sigh as if she were tired of explaining it all to me. "Just trust me."

Dylan closed us in and started the car, slid his hand over the pantyhose. "These make the outfit polished, so do those shoes."

I imagined Jade I told you so'ing.

As we pulled onto the interstate, Dylan tapped his fingers in time to his Mr. Manilow tape. I was near sick of it, he played it so much. Dylan studied his album covers to see what Mr. Manilow wore and how he combed his hair—he said Manilow had class and style, not like some of the other singers and bands getting tired of disco and fumbling around for the next thing they'd make money on; that's what he harped on about. While doing our house chores, Jade listened to Queen, Foreigner, and Boston turned up as high as the stereo would go, until my ears throbbed.

On Dylan's tape, the song about people looking like they made it was over and before the next could begin, he said, "It'll take a little over an hour to get there, but Galatoire's is worth the drive."

I set still so I'd keep everything nice without wrinkles or tears or smudges as we headed to I-10 east, then across the spillway, on to the thrumping heartbeat of New Orleans. Mr. Manilow wished he hadn't of sent off Mandy. Dylan always sang that one the loudest. We pulled into a parking area and Dylan paid the attendant, who looked over at me, gave me a long slow wink; I betted myself ten shiny dimes I blinked five times before his one wink was over with.

When we found our spot, Dylan told me to wait and he'd help me out. He wanted everything just so. He opened my door, held out his hand, and I took it in mine and Queen-stepped it out of his car. Remembering too late that we would have to walk to Bourbon Street, I hoped my new shoes wouldn't send me in a heap onto the cobblestones. Twirl twirlity twirl went my thoughts.

As we walked hand in hand, people passed us by, some already drunker than Otis and his brother Ralph combined, while others held onto shopping bags full of souvenirs or other goodies. Three bright young girls eating pralines while they flicked their widened-eyes here there and yonder were followed by a pack of young boys who hit each other on the shoulders to show how tough they were, and tourists with cameras around their necks held tight onto tall Pat O'Brien's drinks on their way to becoming Bam-Boozed. I knew over that levee the old Mississippi churned its murky way, over two-thousand miles from Minnesota all the way down to the hungry mouth of the Gulf of Mexico. The great water held onto its secrets and I wished I could start at the end and go all the way to its beginning.

A boy danced and danced, his eyes wild and hopeful; his grin didn't reach those eyes. People in front of us threw money into a hat. Dylan tossed in a dollar.

I placed three dollars in his hat and said, "Thank you." The boy looked surprised I thanked him.

Dylan said, "We really shouldn't encourage them."

The next one was a singer. I placed three dollars in his opened guitar case, and said, "Thank you" again.

Dylan touched my back, said, "Look." He pointed to a beautiful sparkled woman holding the hand of a strutting man wearing a disco suit and platform shoes though he still came only to her shoulders. He said, "That's not really a woman."

A carload of purple piglets could have gone by and I'd not have been more surprised. She was better dressed and made up, with hair high styled and perfect, than most women we'd passed. She, or he, sure made me seem dowdy in comparison. I had to smile at that.

Someone yelled, "Ai-yipeeeee!" The other one said, "No, that's not right. It's Aiiii-yeeee!" Then they had a hollering Cajun Cowboy yell contest, even though they sounded straight from Ohio.

Just when my feet were about to whine like spoilt kids, Dylan said, "Here we are." He put his hand at the small of my back and we entered Galatoire's.

Inside the restaurant was another world from the bam-a-lam party time of tourists, frantic-eyed street dancers, and all the wild sights, odors, and sounds that were a part of the New Orleans that most people saw, smelled, and heard. Jade's daddy grew up in New Orleans and he'd said there were places the tourists didn't know about, and that suited the New Orleans people just fine. He'd said the French Quarter was a Grand Madam but some of her polish was all worn off and her tiara tarnished because the tourists vomited and teetled and sweated on her, and even shed their blood on her.

Dylan pressed my back with his palm as we were guided to our table. I wondered if anyone noticed me in my new dress and high-heels, but I didn't want to look. Every head would have turned for Momma and she'd have pretended she didn't notice, even though she didn't miss a thing. She knew her pretty. She knew it well.

After we were seated, Dylan gave the drink orders to the waiter, who'd appeared beside our table as if out of the very air. I was going to order iced tea, but Dylan asked for white wine and vodka on the rocks. Lickity spit, next I know, I sipped white wine that slid down my throat smooth as creek water over rocks. I wasn't sure I liked the thought of booze sliding its way into my blood and marrow, where old kin molecules would suck it up like water in a desert.

Dylan tossed the vodka down his gullet faster than a speeding vodka bullet. He said, "I sure was thirsty," then he laughed.

I put down the wine and took up my water.

Dylan raised his finger, and the waiter asked, "Another, sir?"

Dylan glanced at me, then said, "Add tonic and a twist this time."

The waiter nodded and slipped away, his shoes whispering on the floor. I wondered how the waiter walked at home, if he stomped and made noise, talked as loud as he wanted, laughed with his family, and didn't have to think about saying sir, miss, or madam to everyone.

Dylan was saying, ". . . and they know the difference between a twist and a slice here."

I nodded.

Another couple was led to a table near us. The woman wore a skirt so short, all the mystery of her near wasn't a mystery. Her halter-top was shiny, tight and low, and her platinum hair fell straight and glossy to her shoulders. Her date strutted as if the king rooster of all the land. They laughed and carried on until they were settled in with their drinks, then they quieted down some.

The waiter brought us crusty French bread that was crispy on the outside, but soft on the inside, warm enough to melt the butter I spread on thick. As I bit into the bread I closed my eyes, for it was the best bread I'd ever put in my mouth. It danced happy on my tongue. I took another bite, chewed and swallowed, and then another. The closest I came to French bread this good was at Soot's. Soon, a young man came to the table and scraped the crumbs away into a little silver cylinder.

The room took up to a light buzzing noise as everyone clinked their forks, sipped their drinks, or talked to each other. The waiter glided between the tables.

"Kate?"

"Yes?" I blinked at him.

"Let's start with appetizers. What do you want to try?"

What was a Sauteéd *Poisson?* What about a *Brochette?* Or a Grand *Gouté?* Whatever it all was, every waiter's food tray that passed by left behind good smells, and a couple at the table to our right were smiling and nodding their heads as they forked food into their mouths. I wondered if they were eating some *Poisson.*

If I said the names wrong, Dylan might think me a hick. I still hadn't learned all the language, even though I'd lived in Louisiana since I was near nine years old. I once asked Daddy why I kept my West Virginia in me, and he said it was because where we're born and where we stay for the first young years of our lives shapes us and stays in our memories, scorched into our brains like a branding iron had left its mark. He said my ways were held to my past, and those who came before me. I asked him, then, why was Andy changing into a Louisiana boy and losing the West Virginia in him, and he said when a person wants to change their past bad enough they shove out the old and take in the new. Like, Daddy said, how he'd forced the Texas drawl out of his voice, and had tried to work with Momma and us kids to say things just so, even though most times we didn't listen.

I'd not wanted to lose the holler, not wanted to shove out the old and take in the new, still didn't. I hoped I stayed the same, stayed connected to my kin and my Grandma Faith. If I let it go, then who would I be? The holler would never leave me.

Like you left the holler, a ghost taunted.

Dylan cleared his throat, said, "Kate? You'll have?" He looked at me with eyebrows raised.

The waiter waited, still and polite. He'd returned without me noticing.

"What's a *Poisson?*" I said it a cross between poison and possum.

Dylan laughed, and the waiter let play a smile on that serious mouth. Dylan said, "It's pronounced pwah-sown and it's fish."

"I like fish."

"Do you want me to order for you?"

I nodded, my cheeks burning.

He ordered Grand *Gouté* for an appetizer, and it didn't rhyme with out but instead with goo-tay. For the main dishes, he ordered *Poisson Meunière Amandine* for him and *Poisson* with Crabmeat for me. He explained that the *Meunière* was not only a sauce, but also how the fish was cooked, and the *Amandine* was almonds.

When the appetizer came, it was two kinds of shrimp and some crabmeat done in differing ways. Dylan and I shared that. I then understood the phrase about slapping a grandma, and though I'd never really do that, I could get up and shout to Grandma Faith and Mee Maw Laudine how slap dab good the food tasted.

Dylan asked, "Do you want more wine?"

"No, thank you. But I'd like some sweet tea."

Dylan lifted his finger, and when the waiter slipped up, he asked for tea.

When the waiter returned with my tea, Dylan sipped my wine I'd hardly touched. It was just as well, since he'd been holding that glass close to him like a second girlfriend. He said, "You seem to be enjoying the food."

I nodded, my mouth full of crabmeat and shrimp, and wiped my mouth, just in case I had greasy lips. My lipstick came away onto the napkin. Who could keep on lipstick while eating? For certain not me. Lipstick and shrimp did not go together. I looked over at the woman in the mini skirt, and her lipstick *was* still perfect.

By magic someone appeared and whisked off our dirty dishes. The waiter soon came with another glass of wine for Dylan, and not long after came our supper. My plate of food was beautiful. I took a bite, and felt as if I was eating only the best of all the Kingdom's offerings. There was fish, and lemony-butter, along with more shrimp and crabmeat.

Dylan leaned towards me. "Don't eat too fast."

My face pulled a hot blush of shame. I took smaller bites.

Dylan ate with calculated bites, and in between sipped his wine a bit more slow since he didn't have to rush through that glass. I wondered about the rushing to gulp the first glass or two, as if he was afraid the drinks would run off from him. A long-fingered fist grabbed my insides. I breathed in, then out slow, to loosen it. It wouldn't be fair to fault Dylan for having drinks in a *very nice* restaurant just because of my parents.

Dylan talked about buildings and form and how they functioned.

I listened, and had nothing much to say. I was a boring experiment instead of a new and improved commercial, even with the new dress.

When our emptied supper dishes were taken away, Dylan ordered *Café Brûlot*. He said to me, "You'll enjoy how they do this." He explained everything in a whisper as the waiter went about the business of our coffee dessert.

At our table, the waiter brought a long handled ladle, two cups, dark coffee, a silver bowl, and under the bowl was a shallow tray with alcohol that he lit afire. Inside the silver bowl he put sugar cubes, brandy, cinnamon stick, an orange peel with cloves stuck in it, lemon peel, and orange-flavored liquor. He stirred to dissolve the sugar. Then, with a hint of a smile towards me, the waiter lit the mixture in the bowl on fire, and the fire leapt. With a long fork the waiter held the long curled cloved-orange peel over the bowl, and ladled the flamed blend over the peel. The fire shot colors of blue and gold, and the room filled with spicy scent. Last, he poured the coffee into the bowl to put out the flames.

The waiter served me first.

I sipped a taste, said, "Oh!" since it was so good there didn't need to be any other words. The coffee was thick and sweet, and tasted of spice and orange. To the waiter I said, "Thank you very much," and the waiter's eyes sparkled. I saw the man he was at home and I liked that, and his coffee brew.

Dylan sipped his, and nodded solemn to the waiter to say, *yes, this is just as I wanted it to be.*

I tried not to gulp mine down, but the waiter had said the second cup would be even better, and it for sure was.

When I finished my second cup and sighed, Dylan pushed back a strand of my hair that had fallen loose from the barrette, trailed his finger down my cheek to my chin. I was about to touch his hand, when he slid his google eyes to the mini-skirted woman, who had stood, leaned over with barely enough skirt to keep her heiny covered, and planted a kiss on her date before she wriggled to leave the room.

Her hair turned golden in the low lights; she was milk and pale-honey perfect, and I was not. When I turned back to Dylan, he had one side of his mouth quirked up as if to say, *oops.* I stared down at my cup.

Dylan reached over, touched my chin to make me look at him. He said, "I love you, Virginia Kate."

He called me by that name when it suited him, I guessed. I sipped the last drops of my spiced coffee, licked my lips, and wished I had more, even though I was already so full I could pop open and spill everything I'd eaten onto the table and see what it looked like chewed to mash. Fifty-five frogs settled in my throat with the sugary sweet and I couldn't croak out that I loved him back because there was too much clogged there.

Miss Mini-Skirt came jiggling back and Dylan slid his eyes to her again. He cleared his throat, looked back to me as innocent as could be, and said, "Isn't this nice?"

I thought how she must look to him. How the light bounced off her palest of white skin, lightest of blue eyes, her golden top with its shimmers, her super-blonde hair, how she made the room brighter. My skin, dark hair and eyes, my black dress, all absorbed the light and lost it, least ways that's how I felt about things.

The waiter soft-footed it to our table with a small glass of amber for Dylan, and then glided away.

Dylan took a sip, closed his eyes, savored out, "Fran-gel-ico."

I wondered if he was talking about a person, or if that was the name of the drink.

While he sipped his drink, and I my water, Dylan talked about Frank Lloyd Wright. He said Mr. Wright had created over a thousand designs, and he had seven kids, to boot.

When the little glass was emptied, I hoped to leave, for I was sleepy and ready to go home. But then Dylan shoved his hand into his jacket and pulled out a little brown box. His nails looked better than mine ever did. I still dug in the dirt, still peeled bark from trees to see what crawled behind, pulled aside bushes, turned over rocks and logs. Sometimes the best photos came from what seemed dirty, stained, ugly, and rough. Sometimes that's where the beauty lay, in the unexpected places.

"I was going to wait and give it to you for your graduation present next year, but why wait that long? No time like a present." Dylan laughed and then opened the box.

Setting heavy was a big shiny gold ring with diamonds encircling an opal. The opal eye glared out at me like an old catfish eye. The diamonds winked, winked, winked in the candle light.

"I hope you like it. I don't know how I'll top it next year." He cleared his throat, said, "I mean . . . I'm saying, this is a high-quality ring, Kate."

I let him slip it on. It stuck at the knuckle and he had to work it down. It stared back at me, a stranger on my finger, wink wink.

He said, "There."

I knew my manners. "Thank you, Dylan. Everything's so nice. The food and the ring . . ." and wink wink, Dylan stared at the mini-skirt woman again when she and her fella left their table, her rear-end just a going east west north south.

A spirit flew in my right ear and bopped me upside my brain, then flew out the other ear as if I knew what that bop was supposed to mean.

Dylan paid the check and we went on back to his car, walking through the crowd of people, who were rowdier than ever. I couldn't wait to take off my high-heels. When we slid into his car to go home, I asked Dylan if we could leave off the music, and he sighed but nodded. Once we were back on the interstate, I cracked open my window and let in the hot night air. All the unsaid words flew about in the car with the wind.

He drove back across that old long spillway bridge where the water was black and mysterious in the night. Past swamps with cypress and cypress knees holding their eerie mystery, where wild smells tickled my nose. And once we'd left the bridge, we passed oaks that had been living for a hundred years or more, old wood-framed houses with lights beckoning to me, dogs setting at back doors under a circle of porch light waiting to be let in or to be petted one last time for the night.

When we were close to home, Dylan asked, "Will you stay with me tonight?"

My innards felt all mixed up crazy and loose. "Not yet, Dylan."

He sighed. Drove me on home to Jade's house. I was still a kid, his sigh said. Needed to grow up, his sigh said. He was tired of waiting, his sigh said. Kissing wasn't enough anymore, his sigh said. He bet his Mr. Manilow tape that golden glow Fran-gel-ico woman in the restaurant would go home with him, his sigh said.

Jade called me the oldest living virgin in the land. I'd told her to shush her mouth and mind her own. She minded her own, all right. She minded too much.

After I kissed Dylan, and thanked him again for everything, I slipped out of his car. He didn't pull out right away, just idled there. After I went inside, I peeked out the window and he was still there a full minute before he backed away and was gone. I watched the second hand on my watch, so I knew.

I was left lonely. Jade's house was dark and silent. I turned to go to my room.

❦ • ⎈

The next morning, when Jade still wasn't home, I left my lonely self behind and went to Rebekha and Daddy's house.

As I came in the door, Rebekha looked up at me from her book.

"Well, how are things, Virginia Kate?"

"Fine." I strolled over and flopped next to her on the couch.

Her strawberry blonde hair was pulled back, and her face glowed pink from the cream she rubbed in after washing her face with Ivory. The book she held was a poetry book by Rod McKuen called *Alone*. She opened it and said, "Listen to this." Then she read aloud, "'Once or twice a face comes near, and I look up and then look down.' Isn't that sad sounding?"

I nodded, even though I wasn't sure if it was sad or something else.

Rebekha put the book on the table. "You look as if you have a secret."

I held out my hand to show her the ring.

She pushed an escaped strand of hair behind her ears, touched the opal. "That's a big ring, isn't it?" She caught herself and added, "It's pretty."

I dropped the ringed hand onto my lap, let loose a sigh.

"Is there anything you want to talk about, Hon?"

"No, Ma'am. I'm fine."

"I see. Well." She twisted her wedding ring round and round her finger.

I could close my eyes and see the paintings on the wall, the leather sofa, warm wood furniture, and soft rug. Rebekha with me. Daddy in his room reading or napping. From down the hall, Bobby hollered, "You sunk my battleship!"

The attic fan was on and through the open window, the suction of the fan pulled in wet earth, doodlebug, and oak bark smells. I searched and then found a peace deep inside my bones.

Rebekha kept quiet. She was good at that.

Then my tongue flapped before my mouth could stop it. "How did you know when you loved my daddy?"

She twirled that wedding ring, said, "Well, it was the way he looked at me." She paused, then added, "Something I can't describe. Even after all the trouble; I never wanted to lose him and that look he has in his eyes when he loves me."

I touched my ring.

"He's always quoting Shakespeare and it makes me laugh and it makes me crazy and it charms me and irritates me. And he tries so hard to do the right thing." She looked at me. "Then there were you kids."

"So, it was all of that together or one thing?"

"Are you in love with Dylan?"

"He said he loves me. He gave me this ring. He tries to teach me to be better about things."

"I think you do just fine on your own without anyone's help." She gave me a look as if trying to see parts of me even I couldn't see. "You'll know when it happens, so what's the rush?"

"Maybe I won't know it. Maybe I can't."

"You're still young. When you graduate college, another world will open. You have to give things their time and due."

"But I've been with Dylan for coming on two years. I should know about . . . about some things by now."

"I didn't marry your father until I was in my thirties. He was my first . . . first husband." Rebekha's shade of pink must have matched mine.

"Jade said I shouldn't make Dylan wait so long." My face burned. "She said I act like I belong in the dark ages of yesteryear."

"Hon, if he loves you, he'll wait until you're ready for . . . whatever."

I didn't think he'd wait any longer for the whatevers. Most times, I didn't think I could wait any longer. But I was afraid of it. Every time I came close to taking that step, I felt as if I was going to die right on the spot. Everything about me pulled into a panic. I didn't want to give away that part of me. Even so, I couldn't figure out why it was so important for me to keep it. None of the other girls I heard giggling and whispering kept themselves from experiencing it all. Jade for certain had given everything away before she even graduated high school.

Rebekha said, "You're a smart girl who recognizes the need for respect, and to wait for certain things so you don't get yourself into trouble."

Trouble. That was it. As Aunt Ruby said, how my momma would lay on her back with men until Kingdom Damn Come. I wasn't my momma. I wasn't going to be like her. I would be like Rebekha.

Rebekha's face turned a brighter pink as she said, "My friends called me Old Frosty. That hurt, but I didn't let it change the course of my direction. I had plans."

"Did you finish your plans?"

The pink deepened even more when she said, "Well, not all of them. I met your father. But remember, I was in my thirties." She rubbed the cover of her book. "You aren't wrong for being careful."

I stood. "I guess I'll say hello to the boys and Daddy."

"I know you'll do the right thing." She picked up her book.

I went down the hall, soft-knocked on Rebekha and Daddy's door.

Daddy said, "Come in."

I went in. "Hey Daddy."

"Hay is for horses." He patted the bed beside him, still holding his book.

As I set next to him, I had a wonder why Rebekha and Daddy weren't reading together.

"What's this?" He took hold of my hand, turned it this a-way and that, and the reading lamp light sparkled and bounced off the diamonds. He said, "It doesn't look like you, Bug. You like simple kinds of things."

"Maybe I'm changing."

"'This above all; to thine own self be true.'"

"I am being true."

Daddy put on his wise face. "'Children wish fathers looked but with their eyes; fathers that children with their judgment looked; and either may be wrong.'"

"Okay, Daddy."

He bent his head to his book.

"I'll see you later."

He nodded, but didn't look up, so I left him to his Shakespeare, poked my head in Bobby's room, said a hello to him and Stump arguing about something, checked Andy's room and of course he wasn't there, then went to the back porch to grab a pair of Rebekha's gardening gloves.

I was down in Rebekha's garden where her spring flowers bloomed and summer flowers held promise, pulling what I hoped were weeds, and tiny grasslings that sneaked their way in from the yard. It was warm, but not so bad, and the sun felt good on my shoulders and back of my head. Andy came barreling up the steps, asking if there was any bologna and cheese in the house. I never saw anyone eat so much fried bologna and cheese between white bread before. "Ask Rebekha, she's in there reading."

He slammed inside, then opened the door and said, "She's sleeping, be quiet," slammed the door again, and before long slammed out holding two fried bologna sandwiches in his big ole paw, one already half stuffed down his gullet. His right hand held a glass of sweet tea, which he put down on the porch floor, fell back into the rocker, and began chawing the rest of the sandwich so he could eat the other one slower than the first. That's what he did, inhale the first one, taste the second one.

I took off my gloves, stuck them in my back pocket, dusted off my knees, went up the stairs to rock with him, and held out my hand to show him the ring. Even with the gloves, dirt found its way into it, so I shined it on my britches, and then held it out again.

He frowned down at it, said, "Goddamn, that's as ugly as an alligator's digestive system."

"It is not."

"What's Dil-doe trying to prove anyway?" He chewed off a hunk of sandwich, smacked it to get on my nerves. What was it about my brothers and being nasty with their food?

"He isn't trying to prove a thing. He wanted to get me something nice." I huffed out my breath.

"Where'd he get it? At one of the Campinelle's garage sales for a dollar ninety-five? Or maybe out of a Cracker Jack box?" He hee-hawed.

I jumped up and stomp-stepped down the steps, sick of everyone.

He called out, "Aww, I'm sorry, Seestor." But he was still hooting while stuffing his face with fried bologna and cheese.

I knocked on Miss Darla's door. She opened the door wide and motioned me inside. "Let me see it."

"See what?" I knew she knew.

She knew I knew she knew, and reached down to take hold of my hand with that glob of ring weighting it down to the ground. Miss Darla turned the ring as Daddy had. She asked, "Want some tea?" She didn't say anything that would make the ring feel heavier.

We headed to her sunny yellow and white kitchen. On the way there, I admired the way she showed who she was by what she loved. Miss Darla's place was full of strange and wonderful things. She'd been all over the world and the world was all over her home. Inside the kitchen, where Miss Darla put the kettle on the fire for tea, there was china, glassware, and utensils from Europe and Asia setting on her counter and inside her cabinets and pantry.

I knew to be quiet during her tea-making. It was just her way. I leaned on her counter as she took out the tea service, tealeaves, sugar, cream, and cinnamon. The teapot and the teacups came from a little shop in Sweden. On the wall next to her breakfast table was a heavy wood spoon from Australia that was gnarled and knotty, and she sometimes let Mr. Husband use it to stir his jambalaya for the football game parties that the Campinelles were famous for.

Miss Darla had masks from Africa, Indian effigy and booger masks, statues from Egypt, framed scarves from Japan. There was a glass case full of stones and arrowheads and fossils, one of which was a wolf's head arrowhead that Miss Darla said was thousands of years old. The case also held pottery, baskets, and beadwork from everywhere I could imagine when my imaging went crazy.

In another curio cabinet, there were roadside doodads from every state. It was a combination museum and Stuckey's, and there weren't only snow globes and cedar boxes as Mee Maw hoarded, but also critters and humans made out of straw, acorns, peach pits, and soap; little dolls with silk clothing; hand-painted plates; carved wood or stone boxes with the state bird or flower painted on them. There was even a Jesus figure made of soapstone, and even though I wasn't sure what I thought about Jesus, I had to admit he was beautiful. I appreciated it wasn't the dead Jesus, but the live one. On Miss Darla's floors lay beautiful multi-colored rugs that told stories of where she'd been in Mexico and in Brazil. The house swarmed with color, fabric, wood, stone, metal, and mysterious faces peeking out from masks, books, and paintings.

I knew her bedroom was just as wondrous. Miss Darla had an iron bed with a stitched bedspread made by an Indian woman who lived alone in a tiny log house tucked in a hidden cove that couldn't be found by just anyone. Every so often Miss Darla traveled there to buy or trade for herbs, for ailments and so she could *see things*.

When the kettle whistled, and Miss Darla poured the boiled water over the tealeaves, I knew it was then okay to ask, "Why do you live in Louisiana when you've been everywhere?"

She set the lid on the teapot so it could steep and answered, "Exactly." She stacked crisp butter cookies on a thin rose and white plate. "Everyone needs a place they can be themselves; where when they step into the door, they know they're Home."

"This is Home?"

"I was born here. I'll want to be left here when I'm gone, no matter where I am when I die. I have instructions. I'll show you where to find them and you will follow them exactly."

Honor filled me, then worry that Miss Darla would ever leave me.

She sprinkled a little bit of cinnamon into each of our cups. "There's mystery here, things people don't understand. Outsiders think it's ignorance, but the people here love this place, and appreciate what they have and know exactly who they are and why."

"Like my mountain people."

"Yes, exactly. I think just like my Louisiana people, your mountain people don't give a rat's patoot what outsiders think of them. They're proud of who they are and where they are and do not require the approval of anyone else."

I never felt more proud to be who I was than as I stood in Miss Darla's spiced smell kitchen.

She placed doilies on the tray. "Louisiana isn't perfect, but it's the place that calls me back when I go too far."

Even though Rebekha had made a home for me in Louisiana, I didn't feel as if it was where I would stay forever when I died. I wanted that place Miss Darla spoke of more than anything. Some places were temporary, because they had to be. I wanted to stop the temporary and have forever the place that called to me.

You aren't listening . . . Come home . . .

I wondered who had followed me to Miss Darla's kitchen to whisper their wants.

Miss Darla and I went out to her cypress swing an old Cajun man had made her (I think he was in love with Miss Darla, but when I asked, she held her tongue and closed off her thoughts). She poured our tea.

We eased the swing back with our feet, careful not to spill our tea, and let it gentle-rock us back and forth. In between sips, we ate the little butter cookies. Sophia Loren creaked up from a clump of monkey grass, sniffed the backyard, stiff with a limp. Her eyes were clouded, no longer the prissy girl she'd always been.

I wanted to ask Miss Darla how everything would turn out, or was I afraid of things as Micah and Jade said I could be. I wanted the unknown secrets to show themselves so I'd make all the right decisions. I knew Miss Darla wouldn't tell me everything, even if she could.

When our tea was emptied, the cookies nothing but crumbs on our laps, and Sophia Loren snored on a patch of clover, Miss Darla turned to me and said, "A frog jumped through my back door this morning. A dragonfly landed on my head. I heard three crow caws. All that happened at the same time."

I waited for what she'd say next.

She looked out at her garden, where things grew that didn't even have names, but for which I'd love to be the one to name them. "Sometimes life will just have its way and you have to follow it along to see where it leads, even if it leads to heartache. Even heartache offers beauty and hope if you're patient enough, and strong enough, to get though it." She stood, called to Sophia Loren, and then said, "I need a nap."

I stood, too, and felt strangeling. As if the old world turned new and I had to figure out everything all over again. When I kissed Miss Darla's cheek, she touched my cheek with her palm and then cupped my chin. She turned to go inside, and I left her porch, went through her gate, to Rebekha and Daddy's yard, and stopped to rub the mimosa tree. Trees told stories if only a person listened with all their good heart. I wondered what story it would one day tell about me, the girl who came here after leaving her sweet sister mountain, the girl who did the rest of her growing up while the mimosa scratched at the window to let her know it was right there with her, even if it wasn't a mountain throwing its shadow it could throw its shade and it could send its scent—it did the best it could with what it had.

A fat wind blew back my hair. I closed my eyes—

On my dark horse's back, I rode the wind, a little girl again, with little girl thoughts instead of grown woman thoughts. I rode Fionadala against that funny wind. For days and days I rode up my mountain, the trees smelling green, the air fresh and cool, the West Virginia soil flying out behind her hooves. When I opened my eyes, I was standing right where I had been. Nothing had moved. No magic had taken me to where I wanted to be, which was far away from having to decide about things.

There was a sigh on the wind. I couldn't figure out it if was Miss Darla, or Grandma Faith. Or maybe it was little ole Virginia Kate.

∾ • ∾

And that night, I washed myself with Jade's lavender soap from tip to toe, rinsed, listened to the water gurgle out of the drain, wishing the ring would slip off my finger and go down the drain with the soapy water.

I kept on that ring as I put on my white nightgown and snuggled under my sheets and bedspread. I had almost forgotten what Grandma Faith's quilt felt like on the feather bed in West Virginia. Momma's ornery self wouldn't send it to me, and I'd long ago quit asking. In my sleep, the ring pressed with insistence into the flesh of my finger, reminding me that it was there all though my dreams.

Grandma Faith stood tall on the mountain. She beckoned to me with a knowing look and I turned my back on her, followed the light of the ring all the way to Dylan.

A pointed whisper pierced my ear, *Katie Ivene loves shiny things.*

I answered, "But I'm not my momma."

There was laughing.

I buried my head into my pillow so I couldn't hear anything but my own heart beating.

Chapter 10

I want to know your secrets

The evening Dylan took me for a picnic supper at the levee, the just-appeared moon shone across the muddy water and turned it more mysterious than during the bright early day. Under the sun, Mississippi water showed itself dirty, old, and cranky; and beneath, tough, wild, dangerous. Moon brought a soft gleam and tricked a calm to the wild, but when the moon slipped behind a cloud, the water turned black and unreadable. Just as people, that old water was good at changing moods to hide what it was thinking. I imagined River wanted to sweet-talk me in, hungry for a Virginia Kate snack.

It had been hotter than an ornery bear's breath all day and there was just a little relief from wind hurled in by the storm that was supposed to come in the early morning hours. Even with the wind, a clinging wet heat slicked my skin and my clothes sucked to my body. It made me itchy and cranky. I wondered why Dylan chose a picnic in the dark, and with a storm coming. He was wound tight as my old clock when I turned the crank too many times. Every so often, he Louisiana-gator-grinned and his teeth shone one Mississippi, two Mississippi, all Mississippi.

He honey-voiced, "Isn't this great?" He spread a blanket on the grass, lit a Coleman lantern.

Sweat trickled between my breasts and I was too much aware of how it slid right on down. I wore a halter dress with a full skirt and the breeze crossed the dark water and lifted the hem, teased up my legs. I dug my toes into the grass, the sandals already kicked off. All a sudden, I had a want to get down on my knees and dig, see what was buried deep into black wet Louisiana earth.

"Hello? Where are you?" Dylan put the basket onto the blanket.

I lifted my hair and let the wind play on my bare back, looked up at the stars and left my throat open to anything good or bad or in between.

Dylan strode over panther-quick and pulled me to him, kissed my throat, my lips, the top of my shoulder. He asked, "Would you care for some wine?" Before I answered, he turned back to the blanket and pulled a bottle from the picnic basket. Inside was more wine, along with cheese, French bread, little crawfish pies in a heated pack, and for dessert, fresh strawberries and melon. Dylan poured the cool pale liquid into two gold-rimmed wine glasses. He put one down, held the other with his right hand, and beckoned me with his left finger. "Come here. Come to me."

I was still standing away from the heat of him. The everything so much of him. I stood pushing roots into the ground as if an old oak, my hair its Spanish moss, my fingers its branches that wanted to reach to that moon, and listened to what Dylan couldn't hear. My mountain whispering. The sugar maple leaves waving in the breeze. The pop of skin when I bit into Mrs. Mendel's tomatoes. A sudden wind rushed me, blowing my hair across my face, covering my eyes, hiding things from me. The wind always knew when to come.

"Where are you, Kate?"

To the Great River, I sent a mind message, *Tell me your secrets. Tell me what lies beneath. Take me far away, riding your currents atop a log, a gator, or your watery back.* To Dylan, I said, "I'm right here."

River sloshed at the banks. River lifted a log and carried it away. River swirled and dared me to dive in and find out its secrets.

Dylan held out the glass. "It won't hurt you to drink this."

"Okay," I said, and in that *okay* croaked about five-thousand warted frogs. I lifted my hair again, and let it fall heavy. It was hot, but Dylan liked to part the curtain and stroke my back. I walked to him against the wind pushing me away from him. Laughter, familiar and unpleasant, whooshed by. I focused on what was real, what was before me. A man who wanted me because he saw me whole, alive, and ever-wanting.

When he hugged me, still holding that glass of wine in his hand, I lost the wind and the voices. His lips and breath tickled my ear when he whispered, "What are you thinking? Tell me, Kate. Talk to me."

I stepped back, took the glass from him. He bent and took up his own.

There we stood, holding onto glasses of wine heating from the Louisiana wind, the too-warm night air slipping all around as if sneaking up to catch us unaware.

He toasted, "To us!"

Slam bam against me was a vision of Momma and Daddy standing in the kitchen after Daddy came home from his new job at the five and dime. Momma had a drink ready for him, and one for herself, and they'd say, "To us!" Then they'd sipped, or maybe they'd tossed them down hard and fast—time had a way of filtering things through softer edges when a person wasn't in the mood to remember when "To Us!" became angry words and dishes flying.

I lifted my glass and it was heavy with the weight of my wine. I sipped and the cool liquid slid smooth down my throat and into my stomach where it swirled with all the dragonflies flying and jittering me crazy. Maybe the dragonflies and greedy lapping frogs would have some wine and be still.

Dylan drank down his first glass and poured himself another. He pointed to the blanket, said, "Shall we?"

We set ourselves down to eat our supper. I listened to splashing and the call of an evening bird. From far and away like an old fairy tale, West Virginia called: the holler, the rhododendron, the distant mountains rising, the smell of earth and rain mixing together, the leaves turning to flame in the fall, and then the sepia-toned black white brown of winter. I still thought myself a foreigner. Louisiana stayed strange and eerie to me.

Dylan opened another bottle. I stopped counting the glasses and let slide more smooth wine, even though I wasn't so sure about the woozy feeling that fell over me. There had to be a magic to booze. Why else would Momma choose it over important things—like her children? I wanted the magic potion to tell me its secret. It was cool then warm across my tongue, and all the way down, entering my bloodstream, to all my mystery. All the mystery of my parents.

When the crazy old moon sneaked behind the clouds, the night covered me, a heavy dark across my shoulders. The soggy Louisiana soil under the blanket writhed with bugs, and bumpy round mounds of dirt bubbled up crawfish with bug-eyes. Mosquitoes buzzed by, mean and hungry. Dylan then lit skeeter candles to both drive the stinging bugs away and to further light the dark. Their flickering light and strong smell added to the peculiar way of the night.

River said, *Come to me, come away from men who kiss and pour wine and want want want.*

I sipped. I wanted to know.

The changeling-water laughed, and whispers slipped into my ear. My head hula-hooped, but it began to feel good in a dangerous way— maybe that was the magic.

Dylan put down his glass, reached over and took mine to place beside his. I forgot the dark, the mysterious waters, the whispers. Forgot to keep myself in a tight ball. The wine loosed me from my own grip.

As Dylan and the dark urged me back on the blanket, the rough fibers rubbed against my skin, and it made me twitchy. In the flickering glow, Dylan watched me.

I'll show him what for. I'll show him Tina. I'll show him pale girls in tight skirts. I said, "Come here, Dylan." As he leaned in close, I grabbed his Mr. Manilow hair and pulled his mouth to mine, kissed him hard. I wanted it to hurt so it wouldn't feel so good.

He pulled away a bit, panted his breath in my face, said, "God, Kate, you're driving me crazy."

Shush it.

He stroked my cheek. "You are so exotic. I wish I could see inside those dark eyes to all you are."

Hush, Dylan. Hush.

"I want to know your secrets."

I pushed my hand against his mouth and pressed, felt my power over him, turned my head to the water, away from Dylan's mouth and the words slipping out from it. River swirled mad mad. I turned the other way, and the wine winked at me big and happy. I smiled back at the wine, turned on my side, picked up my glass and tipped it, drank it down. The world turned into a kaleidoscope toy. A light rain began to fall in slow motion, and I lifted my face to it, opened my mouth and let droplets slide into my throat. The candles sizzled; two went out, then three.

I licked the rainy wine from my lips.

Dylan caught up his breath. He'd finally hushed that flappity mouth.

I stood, and my dress whipped around and up, leaving skin bared, then covered, then bared again. The wind and droplets touched my body. I imagined the rain evaporating as it hit burning skin. Standing on my toes and arching my back, I searched for the disappeared moon.

A sliver peeked out to let me know it hadn't left me. Dylan watched me with Mississippi eyes. His face was as man's had been since ancient times, a statue unchanged for a hundred-thousand years.

When he stood close to me, his breath rushed out harsh. It scorched me as he spoke. He said, "Tonight you are a woman."

My body cooled, as if I'd been splashed by a cup of creek water.

I stepped away from him, struck a pose, pouted my mouth, arched my back, heated my eyes as I stared right at him in a challenge of the women-ages.

His eyes glittered as he said, "Oh god. You look like your mother in that picture."

A gallon of cold creek water splashed across me. I un-posed, asked, "What did you say?"

Dylan came to me, ran his hand up my thigh where the wind had played before. He touched my hair. He touched too much.

River laughed and laughed.

I was not my momma. I would not make the mistakes of my women-kin.

I pushed against Dylan's chest, backed away from him. "I want to go home now, please." A critter screeched and was quiet. Something splashed loud in the water.

"You want to go home? Why?" His voice seared his talk box.

"I feel dizzy," I said to the laughing river. River stopped laughing and at the edge it licked the ground, its watery tongue dark and lapping hungry as if to reach out and taste me and take me into its mouth where I'd drown in its heavy waters.

Dylan let out a long poor old starved dog sigh and that sigh jangled my nerves.

"I've had way too much of that booze." My face flamed hot, hotter. My body burned and turned to ashes that fell at his feet, where the wind would take them up and carry them away.

He took a step to me.

Oh god. You look like your mother in that picture. I backed up a step.

He packed away the picnic, rolled up the blanket.

There I was, a brain-lacking fool. River tsked tsked because it knew I was afraid. I lifted my face to the drizzle to help clear the spider's web wrapped round my brain. Still, I didn't understand the magic of booze. Didn't understand its willful gift.

Dylan drove me home with both hands on the steering wheel. We didn't speak. The rain pounded down hard. He pulled into Jade's driveway and didn't cut the engine.

I turned to the man beside me. "Dylan?"

He patted my hand, and in that patting, I was a child. He said, "It's okay. I'll call you later."

When I slipped on out of his car, my rubber legs floppity. I ran in the rain to the house, hurried inside, and went straight into my room. A thunder clapped and an engine roared off.

I put on my gown without bathing and climbed into cool sheets with the scent of the night still clinging to me. Jade's house creaked and moaned, settling its bones. Tree branches whipped in the wind and rain.

Outside it was wild, as I was wild. I wanted to buck and whip in the wind and rain, to scream and holler and let loose everything trapped inside me, to quench the burning fire. How long did I have to wait to stay back from my women-kin's mistakes? Why did Dylan have to invite Momma to our picnic?

A shriek of lightning lit the sky, and my wild busted out of my skin. "Enough," I said to Grandma Faith. "I am tired of waiting."

Thunder roared.

Enough.

I wanted Dylan and I would have him, would have him sooner rather than later. I was not my momma, was not my women-kin's mistakes. I was Virginia Kate Carey and I would slake the fire that raged, boiling my blood, turning my marrow to lava.

Enough with waiting.

Chapter 11

So, this is the snippet you've been dating, Dylan

I rolled head-long to Dylan's house in my olive green boat-car. Jade called it my lumbering chariot. I knew looks were deceiving and that my Fury could fly. On the passenger side in a box was Dylan's favorite German Chocolate cake with a creamy pudding-based filling between the layers—a cake I'd practiced on with Andy-and-Bobby until they said it was perfect. I wondered if they'd let me bake four cakes just because they loved cake and not because it wasn't good enough two cakes before. On top of the cake box was a book about his beloved Frank Lloyd Wright. It was hard buying Dylan gifts, for he liked quality things, expensive things, things that shined and sparkled, things I had to either save up for or pass by.

My palms were slip sliding on the steering wheel. I remembered when I was a girl in the holler and we'd soar in Momma's Rambler to the library. She'd check out romance novels, and I'd roam the library, taking in the book smells, trailing my finger along the spines until I found books I didn't yet own, *Call of the Wild, Huck Finn, White Fang,* then reading them under the sugar maple or cuddled under Grandma Faith's quilt.

In Louisiana, I pedaled my trusty bicycle to the store to buy Zeros, bubblegum, and Archie comics, then, the wind in my face, I'd fly to the library to check out as many books as they'd allow. I'd curl up in my chair by the window with the mimosa scratching and read *To Kill a Mockingbird, Moby Dick, Brother Blackfoot,* and if I couldn't get to the library, I'd re-read some of my own books, *Tom Sawyer, Black Beauty, The Black Stallion* books, *The Incredible Journey.*

I lay aside all the childish time before me, and thought of the man who would be my first lover. How strange that sounded, as if someone else had taken over my body and moved it where they wanted it to go, gave it thoughts that belonged to another. As if someone brave and strong who lived deep inside of me was tired of the child who still shiver-shook in a corner. Little Virginia Kate was ornery and a big fat pest. She stomped up a hissy fit. I stuffed little Virginia Kate in a closet and told her to ride her horse all over the mountain and leave me be. There was Grandma Faith whispering her wants. The hallowed sound of my mountain calling me back to where I couldn't go. I had a storm raging inside me.

Speaking aloud, I told hovering ghosts, "You're making me insane; go away."

Enough.

Dylan could quiet the tempest. I could be a part of something I wondered about. Things that Jade told me about—how a man made a woman feel, how there was nothing so great as a man worshipping a woman, how once a woman let herself *Go* she flew to heaven and back; that's what Jade had to say, when she wasn't telling me how men were annoying gnats circling her head, or dogs sniffing after a heat, or worse, lying liars. Jade always said, "One thing I can't stand is a damned liar." Then she'd curl her lip.

Turning into Dylan's neighborhood, I passed a woman picking up her son and twirling him around as his face opened in fear and joy, but most of all joy. I let myself think about family. Mommas who spoilt their kids rotten. Daddies who went off to work with briefcases and lunch sacks, patting their kids on the head while telling them to be good. Kids who knew that no matter what, their home and their parents would be there when they jumped off the school bus and skipped on to their safe place where their feet belonged on the floor and their breath clouded the window they watched out of as they ate their snack and the bed they lay in that made shape to their body. I could be a part of those things by becoming a part of Dylan, could make a home in that way, have kids who would have a beginning, middle, and end with the same parents. I could have a home that was mine until I died. And then there was the fire inside of me that screamed for the slaking.

I wanted it all.

I pulled into Dylan's driveway, cut the engine, leaned over, grabbed the box and book, slithered out of the car, and eased shut the car door with my hip. I hoped I didn't get smudges of dirt on my new clothes. Under my clothes my new underwear scratched my skin; pretty lace that reminded me of what Dylan would see once he took off the new clothes. I'd brushed my hair until it grew a shine and I left it down, except for a red scarf to keep the wind from tangling it.

At the door, I balanced my offerings, and turned the doorknob. The door was unlocked, but I hesitated. I'd never let myself into anyone's house before and it felt wrong, but I wanted to surprise Dylan, wanted to see his eyes as he saw what was in mine. I eased open the door and looked inside. No Dylan in his living room. No Jinxie. I let myself in quiet as a flea's whisper, closed the door, and then put down Dylan's gifts on the glass coffee table.

I'd go to him with a woman's look that said, *Here I am, ready.* I shook my hair out of its scarf, then put it back up. Maybe he'd like to shake out my hair, as I'd seen men do in the movies.

Breathing in and out to calm. Smoothed my clothes. Looked at my nails. Jade gave me a manicure a few days ago, but I'd ruined it by digging in the strange garden with Miss Darla the next day. Miss Darla and I had silent-argued over love and what it meant and the things we do for it or in spite of it, until we were tired of talking about love. Then we talked aloud about the impatiens, the lilies, rooster's combs, Louisiana Iris, and the unnamed flowers, herbs, and plants. My new light rose nails had ripped and chipped. I'd fixed them best I could.

From the box came the rich sweet smell. I opened the box, took out the cake, and licked the bit of frosting from my finger.

Dylan, I baked this for you. Dylan, let's have some cake. Dylan, I'll feed you cake with my own two hands. Dylan, you can suck the frosting from my fingertips, and I'll lick the frosting from your lips. Dylan, I bought you a book. Dylan, let's look at the book later, much much later. Dylan, you can listen to Mr. Manilow. Dylan, what else do you want to do? Dylan, what comes next? Show me. Show me everything I have been missing for far too long because I have been afraid. I am not afraid. Dylan.

I stuck my right hand into my brown britches pocket, britches that fit so close to me that when I walked I felt dangerous, and pulled out my lip-gloss, dipped out a tiny dab and smeared it on my lips as I'd seen Jade do before her dates. She said men liked moist shiny lips because it made them think how those lips would slide all around them. She told me things that made my ears sear.

After kicking off my sandals, I again smoothed the cream sleeveless shirt that fit just as close as the britches did, and it draped down to show the top swell of my breasts, just a bit, just enough.

Jade had picked out the outfit. She'd said, "I'm sick of seeing you in old castaway clothes, Vee."

I'd said, "Nothing wrong with my clothes." That day, I'd had on a pair of cut-offs and a raggedy old t-shirt that used to be Micah's. The shirt had Alfred E. Neuman leering his fool head off with that missing tooth and wonky eye. Wearing Micah's shirts made him feel close to me. I'd read his letters and wonder what he was doing right then. I had other things of his, like one of those stiff and nasty Pall Mall cigarettes he'd half smoked and put back into his special drawer, a paintbrush, a tube of almost dried up red paint, a Mad Magazine, a drawing of Momma's face he'd wadded and thrown in the trash, and a stick of Juicy Fruit.

I had to take things from people sometimes, so I'd have parts of them with me no matter where they went or where I went. It was my own secret thing that didn't bring harm to anyone and brought comfort to me. Like Momma's brush, shirt, Shalimar powder, and red lipstick; Andy's Fiddledeedee the tiger; Daddy's old watch he used to wear, and a bottle of his Old Spice; Jade's Freak Brother's t-shirt she was going to throw out because it was ratty; one of Dylan's cotton over-shirts he'd put over my shoulders when I'd been cold in the movie theater, things like that.

Jade had said, "You go to class looking a ragamuffin, you work at Soot's looking a ragamuffin. I'll be damned if you'll go out on any more dates looking a ragamuffin who is trying not to look a ragamuffin but is." She spear-eyed me good.

I just whooshed out my air and rolled my eyes.

Jade and I went shopping first at the big blue jean store. I tried on five-hundred and eighty-three pairs of blue jean britches before Jade finally picked a pair she liked on me. Jade had always done interesting things with her britches. In high school, she'd ripped the bottom side seam and added paisley material inside to make the bellbottoms flare out bigger and wider. Later on, she made blue jeans into skirts by cutting off the legs, ripping the middle, and sewing material inside. She made her own halters, maxi dresses, and granny dresses. Every time the fashion changed, she changed with it. Those things were what made Jade special, but I didn't care about looking that way one speck. Seemed a lot of trouble to me.

She'd dragged me to the mall with my lower lip sweeping the floor. She found what she called three perfect outfits that I could be proud to wear instead of what I should be embarrassed to wear. Even though I'd pulled a whiny-baby fit, I had fun, and the clothes made me feel as if I might not look so bad after all. Made me feel as if Dylan would look me up and down as he did when I wore certain clothes, like that black dress.

I was stalling. The cake was heavy. My heart thumped.

Maybe he wasn't home. I cater-cocked my head to listen. Then I heard a soft noise from his bedroom. He must be napping. In his bed. Maybe he'd called out to me in his sleep. In his bed. My cheeks burned. My entire body heated.

A cake for you, Dylan. Thought I'd bake you a cake and present it to you. Are you hungry, Dylan? I am.

I sneaked down the hall. As I moved closer, I heard the music, Carol King singing about the earth moving. No Mr. Manilow. I didn't know Dylan cared for Carol King. The door to the bedroom was open a crack. I stopped. Something was wrong. The air-conditioned air was cold and still, but I heard little rustling sounds, and sighing breaths. Two sighing sighs. I pushed open the door—*oh!*—all the air left my body and rushed through the room as insane specters.

On the bed with Dylan. A red-haired girl. His arms wrapped around her body. Her arms around his body. Her blouse undone. His shirt thrown on the floor. Their feet bare. I stood with the cake held out, in my new clothes and red scarf and stupid plans. Dylan turned my way. His eyes opened wide as Momma's old Rambler headlights. He jumped up, and bent to grab his shirt from the floor. The girl looked at me with a smarmy smirk before rising slow and easy. She stood close to Dylan, her hand on his shoulder, not bothering to button her blouse. Her whiter than white skin glowed bright in the almost-dark room. I knew who she was.

"Kate!" Dylan said. "It's not what it looks like."

I threw the cake as hard as I could and watched as it seemed to fly through the air in slow motion. *Splat* it went as it hit Dylan first, and then pieces flew out and over the room and the girl; cake and filling stuck to their hair and faces. Hunks flopped from their bodies onto the floor, around their feet, leaving trails of sweet revenge. I took this in before I turned away.

Dylan scuttled behind me as I ran down the hall. "Wait! Listen! I'm sorry—"

"Shush it! Just git away. I an't listenin' to yew." Momma's old mad-woman mountain talk was ugly bird flying from my mouth. I thought that voice long gone away, buried in the corner of the old house in the holler. The mixed up slurry of words had only lain sleeping, in waiting, ready for the right moment to explode and spew.

Dylan grabbed my arm.

"Let me loose or I'll sock you one in the nose." I jerked my arm free, shoved my feet into my sandals.

The girl laughed, a sound of glass breaking against stone. "So, this is the snippet you've been dating, Dylan."

He answered, "Shut up, Tina."

I grabbed my keys, leaving the book where it was, and turned to the girl. That snarky smirk shone on her cake-soaked face. As she licked the icing from her just-been-to-the-beauty-parlor fingers, I whirled and left, slamming the door a good one so that Dylan's house trembled. From the backyard, Jinxie barked. I shook the ground with stomps back to my car. I made an earthquake with every step, hurled myself behind the wheel and slammed that door, shaking the car beneath me. Roaring up the engine, I hurtled backward and hit Dylan's mailbox, knocking it sideways. As I screeched away, two ribbons of black painted the street.

Miss Stupid rode her Fury to Jade's house, flew up the driveway, yanked her body out of her car, storm-stomped inside, tore off the ring from her finger, taking skin with it, storm-stomped to the bathroom, and flushed that ugly-doesn't-fit-no-how-stupid-no-meaning-to-it ring down the toilet—Miss Stupid's favorite place for ugly things. It took five flushes. Maybe Aunt Ruby could wear it down there in the death sewers. I stomped to my room and flung myself on my bed as if I were still a little girl who flung herself on beds, and buried my face in my pillow. No tears came. I was drier than a big flat dessert, the biggest fool in the land.

I hadn't been able to quench my fire after all. It raged and burned inside me. The fire didn't consume, but steady burned.

I had waited too long. I had tested a man until he couldn't be tested any longer.

Grandma Faith said, *Don't blame yourself for men's failings.*

Aunt Ruby flicked her tongue, *They's stupider than worms.*

I screamed into my pillow.

My body, my innards, my heart, my brain and thoughts and being burned and burned and burned.

In that way, it didn't happen as I dreamed it would when I wondered about my future and the man I would be with and what it would feel like.

It didn't happen with the pipe-smoking, soft-spoken man I dreamed about while feeling wise at sixteen. It didn't happen with Dylan. It happened in the way Aunt Ruby would shake her half-curly haired head as she snickered at me about the infected nature of men and how my momma lost her way with them.

It happened in a blur of words and images and anger and thoughts of turning hurt upon hurt.

Patrick came round sniffing, a dog after the heat. He puppy-eyed me and stroked me as a man will stroke a horse when the whites of their eyes show. Patrick picked wildflowers for me, tied them with colored yarn or thick brown string, and laid them at Jade's door.

He didn't eye wispy pale girls.

Then one warm evening after a ride down along the river, at the place where I'd almost let go with Dylan, the burning leapt up hot and fast. I turned to Patrick, stroked his leg, and said in a voice filled with heated honey, "Patrick."

He swallowed, said, "Yes?"

I pressed my lips onto his cheek, let trail my mouth to his ear, my lips brushing his ear as I whispered, "Patrick." I squeezed his thigh.

River coughed up a log it was so surprised.

Patrick almost ran off the road.

I felt that power again. All the heat and strength of it.

I'll show you Tina.

I didn't let shame, worry, or fear stop me. Not one little bit. I lifted my hand higher on his thigh, and left it there, close enough to feel his own burn.

He drove faster. To his apartment.

Once there, some of my fear sneaked in, but I shook it away. He pulled me on the couch with him, reached over and stroked my hair, then my cheek. He didn't blabber or tell me what I should do or wear or be.

I touched the top button of my shirt.

Patrick covered my hand, pulled it away, and unbuttoned my shirt. Touched my skin light.

I wondered if Dylan was with Tina right then, if he was doing to her what Patrick was doing to me.

As Patrick slipped my shirt away from my body and ran his hands along my skin, the world topsy flopped over and heat rose up, a slower burn than I'd had with Dylan, but a burn all the same. My skin busted open and the heat spilled out and over. There came the tilt-a-whirl, spinning round and round, faster and faster.

I reached out my hand, touched him. He released a short sharp keened moan.

We were up, we were walking, we were in his bedroom, we were undressed, we were in his bed, and we were together, heated skin to heated skin.

Everything I'd saved I gave to Patrick. Every bit of my secret parts of me that I'd meant to keep safe for a good man who would know me best I spilled over and out and beyond.

There was pain, and I didn't know all of the pleasure, but Patrick panted out his cries, "Virginia Kate, oh god, Virginia Kate."

I stroked his back, trying not to feel disappointment crawl the length of my spine. A mean old critter disappointment was, a critter never satisfied with its meal but always hungering after more.

The night covered us in its dark blanket as we lay tangled like branches after a hurricane.

My hair spilled dark against light on his bleached sheets, and being the crazy girl I was, I couldn't stop the thought that wished Dylan would come in and catch us. With that thought slammed home the knowledge I'd done a wrong thing with the wrong man.

I kicked myself slap raw with stupid. Everything had changed, just because of fancy words, shiny things, and the blood of my momma. What would she think of her daughter?

Patrick stirred beside me, groaned in his sleep. I watched his face. I was a big fool. But I'd acted with a sincere heart, hadn't I? I couldn't tell myself with a sure yes or a sure no.

I slipped out of bed, dressed, and dialed up Jade to beg her to come get me. I was never so glad she was home, and of course I didn't have to beg. She heard my trembled whisper and said, "I'll be right there. Give me the address."

When she drove up, I was already out to the street, waiting. Patrick hadn't awakened. I'd left him a note telling him I'd call him later to explain.

As I climbed into her car, Jade looked at me; she saw everything. She said, "Are you hurt? Are you okay? He didn't hurt you did he? I don't trust that guy."

"No, he didn't hurt me." *I hurt me, Jade. I hurt me.*

She drove us to her house and we didn't talk. Best friends didn't need to. She reached out and laid her hand on mine. Once inside, she poured two cokes and offered me one. I drank it down, the taste of Patrick washing away.

I blinked. Dry eyes. Dry insides. What earlier was wet and wanting felt dry and sorry and sore.

Some things can never be returned to a person. Once some things are gone, they are forever gone. That's just the way of the world when it spun on its wild tilt-a-whirl.

Chapter 12

You can't make someone want you

I pushed down dark thoughts, pushed them deep into the Louisiana squirming dirt. Stepped on the dirt until it was packed, and left feelings hidden. But one day after a morning at the library that left me insane, then an afternoon at Soot's where I couldn't figure out something wrong in the books and still had to waitress for the evening, I couldn't keep things buried. They wanted to rise up and make themselves known, bloom as big ugly weeds with thorns and stink and open mouths snapping.

Patrick had been coming into Soot's, and the way he watched me made me feel as if I were one of those poor fighting fish people stuck in tiny little bowls. I was in my bowl of Soot's, hanging there all limp and sad and ready to arch and bow up when something threatened me, but there'd be that glass in the way, and I'd bump against it to no availing.

The next day after Patrick had found my note, he'd come to see me before I could call him. I'd tried to explain to him the wrong of it all. I couldn't hide my shame, couldn't keep it down deep. He saw it and wanted to manipulate it.

"You're not giving us a chance, Virginia Kate."

I shook my head, no.

Patrick's lips pulled up slow and easy as he said, "We can be sort of like friends, but more than that."

Jade told me how things went. She said once you gave that to them, they lapped it up like dogs after vomit and asked for more.

"We don't have to, you know, do *that* anymore." He'd stuck his hands in his pockets. "I mean, Dylan told me how you were about it."

I stared at him, face on fire, my throat closed tight tighter.

"But I have to tell you, you were made for it, just as I thought you'd be."

My face flamed brighter, furious. I wanted to flail him, wanted to gnash my teeth and pull a big stomping Momma fit. I said, "I don't want to see you anymore, Patrick."

Patrick's mouth turned down into a fat frown. He spit out, "Why? Is it Dylan? That asshole? Give me a break!" He'd stormed off, mad dragon-breath smoke trailing.

After that day was when he began coming in Soot's, setting at the tables I waited on, watching me as I worked, eating his food slow to where he'd be there for long enough to make me crazy. I figured as the weeks passed, he'd leave me be, but a month passed, then three, then more, and on he came. He'd mailed me two dozen red roses and a three-pound box of expensive chocolates for my graduation, and I'd given them to a nursing home to be enjoyed. Sometimes he'd stay away for a while and I'd begin to relax. Then, he'd be back and it'd start all over again. It made me jumpity and nervous.

And there he was again, on a day I just about had enough, bumping my head against that glass, bowing up my fins, ornery and tired. Just as in the other times, I brought him his burger, and always he poked me with the same kinds of words. "I miss you. What did I do wrong? Why won't you see me?"

I put down his plate and didn't say one word.

He began eating, took little bites and slow-chewed, but gulped down his beer. He raised his glass and when I reached for it, he grabbed my arm.

"Let go of me, Patrick. I mean it." I pulled my arm but he didn't let go.

"We can make this work if you just try."

I jerked my arm hard as I could and he released me.

"I don't understand *you women*," Patrick talk-spewed, while pieces of chewed burger flew onto the table.

Marco called out, "Thangs all right over there, Sweet Girl?"

"Fine," I said. I went on to the next table and tried to keep myself from screaming. The things we get ourselves into, that's what I was thinking.

Patrick didn't sit and eat the rest of his burger, but instead slammed out the door with a big *kablam*.

The only other customer in the place stared after him, shook his head, then bent to his fried catfish.

The hornets buzzed louder, diving at my head, stinging, stinging stinging; must have been sixty-six of them. I gave the customer another ice-cold beer and he said, "Thank you, Babe." I didn't take offense to the *babe*, since that's what Louisiana men called women sometimes, an endearment, and even in respect. It was just their way, not meant wrong as I used to think it. It was the men who hid who they really were who were worrisome.

While putting Patrick's plate and beer glass on my tray, Soot came to me, said, "Boo, why dontchoo go on home? We're not busy today." She hugged me and stroked my hair. "My poor girl." She pointed to the door. "Go, get out of here and go rest. If you need me or Marco, you just call, you hear?"

"I'm fine, really." I set down my tray and began wiping the table.

Soot put her hand over mine, took the dishrag. "I got this. All you been doing is working." She gave me a little push. "Now *go*."

As I grabbed my keys from the hook, then headed to the door, I heard Marco say, "That fool's got no sense god give a goose. No more'n his friend does. I got taters to fry that are smarter. That boy best stay away is all I'm saying, messing with our girl."

The customer said, "He was fixin' to get his . . ."

I closed the door to whatever else was said, feeling extra double-dip with a cherry on top tired, and ready to crawl under my bedspread without eating supper. I pointed my lumbering chariot to Jade's while my radio bawled about him wanting her to want him and shining up his shoes so she'll want him. I cut off the radio, listened instead to the whir of my tires, imagined they said, "Stupid girl, stupid girl, stupid foolish girl." I was my own island of me.

Seemed I should be able to do what I wanted to do with my own self and my own body no matter what I'd done or not done. I was no longer the oldest living virgin, and what did that mean? It didn't mean I had to let men tell me what was what from here to Kingdom Come, did it? My tires whirred whirred. I wished I could talk to Rebekha, but I wouldn't dare. Just the thought of letting her know my shame, the disappointment on her face, caused my stomach to do twenty-one flops.

When I parked at Jade's and stepped out of my car, Patrick rode by. When he knew I'd seen him, he roared off with squealed tires and rubber snaking on down the road. Made me think of the day I peeled out from Dylan's house. The idea of Patrick hurting as bad as I had twisted my heart like a used dirty washrag.

I dragged inside Jade's house, turned off the air-conditioner (I didn't think I'd ever like air-conditioned air), went into the kitchen, took five aspirin, ploddered to my bedroom, opened my window to let in fresh air through the window screen, and crawled into bed.

I said, "Grandma Faith? You were right. I'm sorry I disappointed you."

A breeze blew through the window and touched my cheek. She said, *Rest, little mite, rest. Don't fret so. It's hard being a woman. It isn't you should be sorry.* I smelled apples and fresh-baked bread, just as I had most all my life, and it calmed me. The white eyelet curtains reached out to me. On the wind flew the ghosts, the good ones, the ones I had no names for, *Rest, rest, rest . . . no more worries, no more worries . . . we'll wait for you to feel better and then we'll return . . .*

I pulled a sigh and snuggled into my pillow. The floral sheets Rebekha had bought me when I moved into Jade's were soft and cool and smelled of Cheer; so did my blue chenille bedspread I'd brought with me from Rebekha's house. The cream-colored walls in my new room were soothing. I hadn't taken my bedroom furniture, but instead was using the wicker furniture Jade's momma had bought for her to use, that is until Jade found something else she liked better and gave the wicker to me. Daddy and Rebekha had given me money for my graduation to re-do Jade's room with my own furniture, but I hadn't done a thing with it.

The hornets left off, buzzing away, and I was sleepy. Outside the window, I heard a crow call and thought of how sleek they looked as if dipped in oil, how cunning their shiny black eyes were, how loud they cawed, how they were in stories and movies to mean something evil or scary, but I thought they were beautiful.

Inside my dream was Micah. He was crying in a corner of a dark room. When I tried to reach out to him, I couldn't get to him. He just cried and cried, his skinny body shuddering and shaking. I called to him, "Micah! Micah!" He became smaller and smaller, falling into a dark empty space, falling away until I couldn't see him any more. I called out again, "Micah! Micah!" There was nothing but dark, and me standing in it, Micah too far away to hear me, too far away to hug on him good and tell him his family loved him and missed him and wished he'd come to see us. To see me.

I woke to a house that was as dark as the place in the dream. My window was closed and the room cold, so Jade must have turned on the air-conditioning, then come in to check on me. That made me feel cozy, lessen she only came in to close my window so her cold air wouldn't escape. The clock read two in the morning. I slipped out of bed and went down the hall, stopped at Jade's room, cracked open the door, and saw the lump on her bed. She was asleep. I always worried when she didn't come home and was always glad when she did. She never brought dates to her house, and I was glad of that, too.

The floor was cool as I padded into the kitchen, filled a glass with faucet water, and stood in the middle of the kitchen to drink it down as if I hadn't had water in fifty-two years. The night was quieter than I ever remembered it being in that loud Louisiana town. The dark didn't even bark. I set my thoughts on Micah and my dream, about his letters and how worrisome they were to me, worse for what they didn't say than for what they did.

Rebekha would just say Micah was a phenomenon and because of his brilliance, he acted different from everyone else. Daddy wouldn't talk about him at all. Andy said he knew Micah would be okay, so I shouldn't worry, but when he said it, Andy sure looked worried to me.

That dream had seemed so real. As if Micah were trying to get a message to me, one that I missed in his letters.

I didn't understand why people had to be so far away from those who loved them.

I rinsed my glass, set it in the dish drainer, went back to my room, and turned on my lamp. From my bedside table, I took out a box that held photographs. Inside was the picture of Micah just before he left for New York, the latest one I had, and the one I used to call out to him. I held it between my hands, felt the vibration of it as it grew warm against my palms. I pressed tighter.

"Micah, come home. Just for a little while. Come home so I can make sure you are okay. Come home, big brother. I need my big brother. Please come."

The photograph shivered in my palm and then went still. I returned the photo, put the box away, and lay back down. I knew he was alive, but alive didn't mean good. Alive just meant not dead.

I wanted to open my window, but instead I listened to the whoosh of cold air-conditioned air through the vent. There were no other sounds. No other voices. Whoosh Whoosh. I wrapped myself in my bed covers and let the morning come to me as it would.

Outside, I heard an engine pass slow and I hoped it wasn't Patrick.

„ • ‟

On a beautiful morning with a hint of cool no one expected, Andy roared up the driveway to fetch me for a ride in his Mustang convertible. Candy apple red with leather bucket seats, and his radio singing out about how a girl shouldn't do him like that, and don't tell lies or cut that man down to size.

I looked from his car to mine and shook my head. Mee Maw had said Hank wouldn't let her pick out Andy's car, that a boy who was near a man had to have a man's car, one that the girls would want to jump in and go riding off into the sunset. I guessed girls who were turning into women only needed big ugly green tanks. Life wasn't fair to the women it birthed. I admitted to myself I could have bought another car for myself and had chosen not to. I was comfortable with my Fury and didn't want to give it up, even if that Mustang was mighty fine.

Andy had fixed up the car himself with the money he made at all the jobs he hopped around to and from. He'd painted it that shiny bright red, re-covered the seats, changed the wheels, and did something with the muffler so that it rumbled. He flew around town, and I didn't know how he survived without an accident, or even a ticket. He'd called me the night before and asked what I was up to. I'd about lied and said all kinds of interesting things, but he'd know I was lying.

He said, "Let's do something tomorrow. I'll drive."

"Long as you promise not to go so fast, okay?"

"You're one to talk."

As we raced down the road, fast, Andy held a far and away look and I wasn't in the mood to tease it out of him. Bobby said Andy had been out on a date with one girl five times, a record. Andy said he always made sure they knew he wasn't going to settle down and they'd just have to accept that was his way. He told me some believed him and others didn't, so he was careful what girls he went out with. I'd never seen Andy with one steady girlfriend, ever.

We stopped by Rebekha and Daddy's to fetch Bobby. He lankied his way to the car, all arms-leg-elbows and pretend-casual eyes. Those eyes didn't fool me; I knew he was excited to ride with his brother in that spiffed car. He went to the driver's side and stuck in his head, said,

120

"Hey, y'all."

"Hey," Andy and I said.

"Let me get my stuff, be right back." Bobby loped back up the stairs and into the house.

We were going to stop by Soot's for food to go, and have a picnic at the university lakes. I'd been working extra hours at Soot's and at the library, plus, Soot and Marco had given me a raise for the extra duties I'd taken on. When the new waitress didn't show, I'd help out there, too, especially since Soot was pregnant again. I was slap happy for her and Marco. Little Mae Lynn hadn't decided yet how she felt about having a sister or brother.

I didn't mind waitressing again, the tips were good and they helped with my expenses. My paychecks went into the bank for my bills. I dropped the coin tips into a big jar and when it was full, I'd wrap them and take them to the bank for savings. The paper cash tips went inside one of those plastic pantyhose eggs, and that's what I used to play with, which wasn't very often. Sometimes Jade talked me into going out with her.

Jade went dancing in bars, but I didn't like them. The air was heavy with smoke, booze, and sweat, and the bodies would press against me until I thought I'd scream. The clammy bodies pressing made me want to go home and bathe, which I always did. Once, I saw Patrick at the bar where they had dollar beer nights on Wednesday, ladies night on Friday, and all you can eat boiled shrimp or fried catfish on Saturday. His head bent over his beer and he took a small sip, not even paying attention to the woman who was leaning into him. I grabbed Jade and said I wanted to leave. Jade said she'd be leaving with someone else and I could take her car home. I hated it when she did that, but she always just shrugged her little thinling shoulders and said, "I have a knife in my purse."

I remembered Momma's black eye and split lip that time she went out with Timothy. I'd always wondered if Timothy had a bigger blacker eye and a fatter splitter lip from wild Momma, but since we never saw him again, I never found out. Jade once came home with a big ugly bruise under her left eye, and when I stomped a hissy fit and asked who did that to her, she shook her head and said, "Don't, Vee. Don't. I'm okay. I took care of it."

The things women got themselves into. Men were nothing but big trouble, and could be mean to boot. I wasn't going to let one bruise me or split my lip, not without a stomping up fight right back, that's what—

Andy flicked my ear with his thumb and forefinger. "Get out your whirly world, Sister. Geez, some things never change."

"I was just thinking on things."

After a pause, he asked, "You okay, Seestor?"

"Yeah." Then I asked, "How about you?"

"I'm doing good. I mean, I have a nice car and I'm a good looking college-boy." He laughed, said, "Life's mighty fine." He stroked the leather steering wheel cover. "But you looked kind of sad."

"I'm fine, really." I punched him in the arm.

He made his bicep bulge. "Can't hurt that."

"What's taking Bobby so long?"

"Let's go see."

Andy and I headed into the house where it was always the same, yet not. With Andy moved out it was emptier. I wondered how Bobby felt being the only child there when he'd always had us to look after him, or tease him, and fill the house with noise. Maybe he had a private life of his own filled with girlfriends and trying out life and whatever else thirteen-year-old boys like Bobby did.

While Andy yelled for Bobby to hurry it up or we'd leave him, I dumped ice into a plastic baggie and slipped in two wet washrags. Andy went to the hall closet and found an old sheet. Bobby came out of his room holding his bat, ball, and glove, telling us to hold our horses, he'd had to use the bathroom. Andy told him that was a personal problem he should have taken care of earlier. The boys argued about it while they took the stuff out to the car.

On my way out, I stepped inside my former bedroom. The mimosa scratched at the window, and I said, "Hello, mimosa. Do you miss me?"

The mimosa scratched scratched.

It did.

I left my room and went out to the car, where my brothers waited.

Andy started his rumbling engine, and off we zoomed to Soot's to get the food.

The three of us. Missing Micah. The three of us growing beyond. Didn't seem we were as old as we were. How'd I get in my twenties, out of college and working, living with Jade? It was as if I were between worlds, between ages. And Andy, soon to graduate college himself. Bobby a teenager with lanky limbs and those eyes that pretended to be bored with everything.

Andy parked at Soot's. Bobby jumped out, ran in, and by time Andy and I were inside, Bobby had already ordered enough food for three people, even though it was only his portion.

When the food was ready, white sacks full of shrimp, oyster, and catfish po-boys, fried potatoes, onion rings, and Hubig's fried apple pies, Andy pointed his bright red mustang and we hurtled full engine-speed gallop towards the lakes. He found a place to park, we piled out. The boys grabbed the food, and I grabbed the rest.

When we situated ourselves and our food on the sheet, hands went every-which-way grabbing. We ate and watched the ducks and egrets on the water. It was peaceful there. Even when the lake was full of people come to feed the ducks, or play ball, or just let off their steam, it was still a nice place. One day I hoped to take my own children, let them feed bread to the birds, let them run screeching and being funny kids while I watched them with love and pride.

When the food was gone, Andy-and-Bobby jumped up to play pitch and catch. I lay back with my eyes closed and was almost asleep when I sensed someone near me. I had a prickling on the back of my neck. I opened my eyes.

Standing over me, blocking out the blue of the sky, was Patrick.

He didn't say hello, only stared down at me.

I pulled up quick as a Louisiana second, said, "Hey, Patrick."

He still didn't say anything, just kept up that staring.

I pushed back my hair and looked around him for my brothers. They had moved far enough away that I could see them, but I couldn't hear what they were saying, and they weren't paying attention to me.

At last, Patrick spoke. "You broke my heart, Virginia Kate." He fell on his knees beside me. "You broke my heart and didn't give a shit for my feelings. I guess you just used me to get back at Dylan."

"That's not true."

"Oh yeah?"

"We've been done with this, Patrick."

He narrowed his eyes at me. "Done with it?"

"I didn't understand things, is all. I'm sorry." I looked at him with all the sorry I had in me, tried to let him know with my eyes what I wasn't saying right with my words. How I was sorry then, I was still sorry, and I'd be sorry forever and ever, A-men.

His lips set to a line, and then he said, "You can't just walk away from someone who cares about you like I do. You can't just slip out the door and leave a guy laying alone and the pillow's still mashed in where her head was. You can't." His breathing came out fast; I felt the heat of it.

When I went to stand, Patrick reached over and grabbed me, just as he had done in Soot's, except he grabbed me with both hands much harder, and pulled me back down. I said, "Stop it, Patrick!" I jerked my arms, but he wasn't letting go. He leaned over me and pushed me down against the ground, hard enough to make my breath rush out.

He said, with that hot breath, "I'm not going to hurt you. I just want you to listen to me, that's all. You never let me tell my side. You went on with things and I never got to say what I have to say."

I wild-cat arched and bucked my body, but Patrick wasn't having any of it. He laid his body over me, pinning me down. I opened my mouth to scream at him, bite him if I had to, but he pushed his hand over my mouth and grabbed my right arm with his other. My left arm was pinned underneath him. The food in my belly backed up to my throat, and I tried to calm myself. I hated right then how it felt to be a woman, hated that I could be struggled down strong against weak.

Our bodies slicked with sweat, the sun beating down on us. What was a beautiful day turned ugly and dirty. I smelled the fish in the water and mud along the edges of the lake, rolled my eyes to the left and there was a dead bird lying on the ground, covered with ants. I hadn't noticed the bird before. All a sudden, my world was scary and that made me both mad and sad all at the same time.

"Stop fighting me." His voice was calm and easy. "Come on, Virginia Kate. Be still. I won't hurt you. I just want to talk to you. I just want you to think about coming back to me and trying things, just *try*, that's all. You've been broken up with Dylan for long enough I have a chance now, right?"

I pulled breaths best I could through my nose, but everything was a little blurry. I tried again to buck and strain against him, but he lay heavy over me, pressing down a bit more on my mouth.

"Be still. I said I'm not trying to hurt you. I'm not an animal. I'm not evil, dammit!"

I stared up at him, trying to keep myself calm so maybe he'd stay calm. Had I made a good guy go bad?

"Now. There. That's better. If you keep still, I'll let go of your mouth. I want to talk to you, want you to know how you hurt me. Doesn't matter how long passed. For me it's just as fresh as if it were yesterday. I just—"

Patrick was there then gone, flying off me with an *OOMPH*.

I shot up, took in good gulps of wet air.

Andy-and-Bobby stood over Patrick, who was on his back on the ground looking up at them. Bobby held his baseball bat high in his hands as if ready to swing it across Patrick's skull if he made one more move.

I stood with my brothers.

Andy asked me, "You okay, Sister? Did this goddammer hurt you?"

"I'm fine." I brushed off my clothes, checked my mouth—it was tender but there was no blood.

Bobby said, "Want us to beat the dog-shit outta him?" He raised his bat higher.

I looked at Patrick. "Patrick, I don't want you to bother me anymore. You hear?"

Patrick didn't look at me, but instead kept his gaze bouncing from Andy to Bobby.

Andy spit on the ground and then said to Patrick, "You come near my sister again and I'll mess you up one side and down the other. Nobody messes with my sister."

Bobby said, "That's right. We'll beat the living dog-shit outta you."

Patrick nodded.

My heart was thrumming hard against my chest. My lips stung, but my pride and feelings smarted more than anything else did. I felt foolish and sorry, but was also furious. I said to Patrick, "You can't make someone want you." The words flew into the air and grew moth wings, flitting and flying and hovering about me.

Patrick was white around his lips, and his eyes held a scared look.

"I told you I'm sorry about that time before. But you got to get on with things." Fly flit fly went the moth words, into my eyes and ears and settling on my skin.

Patrick nodded again, his eyes still bouncing.

Andy said, "Go find a girlfriend and quit sniffing my sister." He jerked his head towards the parking lot. "Get on out of here." He stood aside, as if he thought Patrick a pitiful thing lying there, as if he felt a bit sorry for him, as if he were a bug he was about to smash but at the last minute just couldn't bring himself to.

Patrick pulled himself up off the ground, knocked off the grass from his britches. He turned to Andy. "I wasn't trying to hurt your sister. I love her."

I took in my breath.

Andy said, "That's a goddamn funny way to show it."

Bobby let out a disgust sound.

Patrick turned to me, "I'm sorry, Virginia Kate. I've never done anything like this before." He turned and began to walk away, then stopped and turned back, his eyes opened with a surprised look as he said, "I'm the good guy. The *good one*." He shook his head as if he didn't understand a thing in the old world, turned, and that time he didn't stop, he didn't look back at us.

We watched him as he climbed into his truck and drove away.

I let my bones unhinge, let my muscles loosen up. The moth-words fell to the ground and died, but left their ashy imprint upon me.

We grabbed our things and headed to Andy's car.

Once in the car and driving away, Andy said, "If he ever comes near you again, you let me know. That guy's got a screw loose."

"I can take care of myself."

"I know you think you're tough. But there's some guys who only know how to listen in one way, and that way is to threaten to bash his jack-ass goddamn head in." Andy pressed the gas and roared around a too-slow car.

Bobby said, "I wonder if he's been following you everywhere all this time, just waiting for his chance?"

My arms grew goosepimples.

I hoped Patrick was smart enough not to come messing around again. Nobody wants a West Virginia hillbilly-turned-Louisiana-swamp-boy and his Louisiana born brother to go crazy on them.

Underneath my skin, under those goosepimples, came shame. I couldn't sort out all the shamed feelings, but they were there. A woman always seemed to feel shamed, but what do the men feel?

Andy dropped me at Jade's house and before he sped off, he and Bobby and I all planned to get together later to see the movies or go eat at Soot's. I felt normal with them, but not with myself.

I let myself in to nothing but empty quiet. It struck me then, I wondered if Jade felt her own woman's shame and that's why she ran from it so hard. And maybe Momma, too, ran from her own shame.

Even though it was early, I grabbed my gown from my dresser and went to run a tub of bubble bath to ready myself for bed. Feeling as tired as if it were late at night, I pulled off my clothes and put them in the dirty clothes hamper, then slipped into the warm bubbled water, leaned back my head and soaked my hair. Using a soft washrag, I scrubbed the dirt and sweat away, scrubbed Patrick away where he'd rubbed against me, where he wanted to make himself a part of me, washed my hair, cleaned my fingernails, lay in the water until it grew cold and only then unplugged the stopper. Turning on the shower, I rinsed away the soap from my body and hair, trying not to think about Patrick's words. Even though he was wrong for what he did, his words hit me hard.

I thought about the moth-wings words to him, how you can't make someone want you. I knew that to be so. I'd seen it within and I'd seen it without, seen it with my momma, and with my daddy. With Rebekha. With Jade. With my brothers. With Dylan. With me. I saw how people pushed and then pulled. Wanted and then changed up their minds. Had and then lost. Found what they thought they wanted and then tossed it away. I'd seen it, felt it, and done it. And still, I didn't understand the minds of men.

After drying myself with a big blue towel, I scrubbed at my hair to get as much water as I could from it, and then combed it out, letting it hang down my back. When I put on my gown, my hair was still wet enough to cause my gown to stick to my back. In my room, I snuggled in my bed and let myself fill with regret and sad.

Outside, cicadas buzzed. Someone started their mower and the engine roared. A little girl's high-calling cry filled the air, "Here kitty kitty, where are you Suzie? Come home, Suzie!" A woman called out, "Patresa? Come inside this instant!" and there was an answering, "Mommy! I can't find Suzie!" The momma answered, "She's here with me. Now come inside."

The air held happy, regular sounds, and those sounds made me feel better, but they also made me feel as lonely as could be.

I turned on my side and curled into a ball.

Nobody could ever take back what was already done. That's why I knew I should have more care. I should have much more care in how I went about my business.

From the opened window, fresh cut grass smells flew in and I inhaled it to my marrow. That fresh green. Grandma Faith wasn't with me, or if she was, she was quiet. Sometimes she knew I had to figure out things for myself.

Only the future me knew what would come next. I closed my eyes and let the drowsy take over, dreaming of the Mississippi darkness. Then the dark waters parted and a pair of eyes shone out. The eyes watched me with sad loneliness. I tried to look away and I could not, because the eyes were mine. I saw them from the inside out, but they weren't giving up any secrets, other than that sad lonely cast to them. The eyes closed, and everything was dark again.

Chapter 13

And here's to trouble!

Jade stepped out of her bedroom wearing black britches, a purple bodysuit, and gold chain belt. She walked with a bounce on high-heeled glittery sandals; her hair swung against her face, the choppiness gone and replaced by growing layers. She was a woman with secrets. Secrets I only thought I knew about, but instead had just pretended to.

She held up a coin. "I found a brand new 1980 penny. I wonder if it's the very first one made." She slipped it into her pocket. Jade loved finding new-minted coins that matched the year we were in. She'd tape them to her journal and write about what she wanted to do, or had done, that year. Her eyes had a star-sparkled look that matched her shoes. The air filled with Patchouli. She pirouetted and then asked me, "Hey! You ready?"

"Hey! I'm ready." I wore blue jeans, the red bodysuit Jade let me borrow—lucky it was stretchy so it would fit, and red sandals. My hair was in a fat ponytail, and I let the end curl to the front. I said, "You look so pretty."

"And you're looking super-fine yourself, Vee."

I touched my ponytail. Same hair, always the same, never changing hair.

"Quit pulling on your hair and let's go."

We Princess-stepped it out to my not quite new car. A Mercury Cougar XR7, blue with white interior, that I'd bought from one of Daddy's friends. I missed my old green tank with the woody sides and the way it flew round town not caring a speck about how ugly it was. It'd never left me by the side of the road and never failed to rumble its engine when I started it. I sold it for next to nothing to a man who wanted it for his son. One day it went flying past, the boy's hair wild in the wind as he rode the Fury to wherever boys his age rode—I guessed to freedom.

I started the car and backed out of the driveway. "When are you going to tell me about this fella always dialing you up?"

"I will. Later." She pouted her mouth to touch up her sparkled lip-gloss.

"Why later? Why not now?"

Jade shrugged, turned on the radio, and began singing about that hotel in California, and how it was such a great place—Jade sang loudest on the part about dancing to forget things, and to remember them.

From far away, I saw her the day of the Great Moccasin Incident, setting on the log blubbering sad over her dog dying. She always felt things deep under her skin, pouring out as sweat and tears over her and all who were near her when she danced too long and too hard.

Over the loud radio, Jade asked, "What did you get me for my birthday?"

I pointed to the papersack I'd left on her floorboard.

She opened it. "Is this what you got me? A Zero bar, a fashion magazine, and a bookmark?" She snort-laughed, said all prissy, "I got you lots of good stuff on yours."

"Well, I'm paying for supper tonight."

"Okay. I guess that's even." Jade always worried about what was even. She punched the radio buttons, looking for more music she liked.

I turned onto a street lined with wood-framed houses that had old oaks in every yard, their branches leaning across the street, touching, intertwining branch-fingers. In some yards, men were mowing grass or watering the yard. At one gray house with peeling paint, a little girl set on a porch step, her forlorn dark eyes and bare feet reminded me of little Virginia Kate the day she left the holler, setting on the steps with her old suitcase waiting for Daddy.

Mr. Manilow's croons filled the car, and Jade poked me in the arm and laughed. I reached over and punched the button to another station. She said, all innocent, "What? You didn't like that?"

I stopped at a stop sign and without looking at her, said, "I can turn this car around, you know."

She just laughed and attacked the buttons until a woman yelled about wanting her love to call her anytime in the day or the night, long as her love called her. Jade sang with her. I let her sing songs by herself, since she said I sounded like a frog croaking out vomit.

Under the backseat, I'd hidden a picture Micah painted of Jade. I'd been saving it for her birthday. I wondered if Jade still had a crush on Micah as she had when we were young and full of our foolishness. Micah never had been interested in Jade, but he must have thought about her, to have painted her without me asking him to. There had only been a short note that read, *Give this to Wonder Bread girl. I guess she's okay. Micah.*

Micah had drawn Jade in her striped shorts and yellow top, with a pastel smile. He had remembered her boy-short choppy hair shining in the sun, long skinny legs, and her sad-stubborn eyes, standing in first position. He drew it as a brother would, not as someone who loved another. That's how I saw his painting. I wondered if my brother loved anyone. If he had someone to help him to be happy. He never said.

Jade turned down the radio during a commercial. "Hey, are you paying attention to your driving or off in la tee dah land again?"

"I'm paying attention." I straightened my back against my seat, eyes on the road, hands at two and ten o'clock.

Jade turned up the radio.

I turned down the radio.

Jade turned up the radio, opened her Zero, took a teensy bite, chewed and swallowed, and then wrapped the rest for later. I couldn't figure out how she did that, for Miss Greedy had to gobble hers like Petal Puss in pure pig happy. Jade shouted over the radio, "We're going to the new place, right?"

"Yes, that's where you harped on and on about so that's where we're going." I turned down the radio. "How was your beach vacation with your family?"

"It was okay, I guess." She pinched her nose and talked through it to sound the way her Momma talked. "Except I barely had a minute to myself the whole time because *family* should stick together on *family* vacations doing *family* things. Family, fuh-amily, fuh-fuh-fuh-*family*." She snorted, said, "I had to sneak off to see Lloyd. It was hard enough hiding him from my parents without having to get around their constant need to be all for one and one for all."

"Why'd you have to sneak around?"

"I didn't want them mad I'd invited my boyfriend." She found another station, turned up a song where a woman sings over and over about ringing a bell and even singing out the ring ding dongs.

I stopped at a red light and watched a woman on a bench eating something out of a papersack. She was sobbing away while stuffing food into her mouth at the same time. I wanted to ask her what was wrong, why was she crying? I wanted to say nothing was worth crying so hard over.

"Lloyd said sneaking around was exciting." Jade bit her pinkie fingernail.

I didn't say anything about that, but many unsaid things swirled in my head making a big mess of talk and questions that probably were none of my business.

Jade danced in her seat to the bell ring song, then sang it full tilt. A car full of fellas rode by and they shouted out their windows, puckering their lips as if kissing the air. One of them yelled, "Hey there! Y'all looking for . . ." and that's all I heard because I punched it and flew ahead of them while Jade laughed and waved her hand out the window at them. At least I think she was waving, no telling with Jade.

After we parked at the restaurant and slid out of the car, I held my camera above us and snapped a photo of the two of us grinning as though stupid had spilled all over our faces. Nestled inside the camera were nature photos I'd try to sell later to magazines, or anyone who would take them. Freelance work was hard and didn't bring in much money. With Soot and Marco's diner booming, I could do more to help them with the business side of things. I liked being a librarian, too. All those books, the smell, the quiet.

"Vee snap out of it, for god's sake!" Jade was five steps ahead of me, prancing like a Lipizzaner pony.

"I'm coming. Hold onto your horses."

Once we settled at our table, the waitress came by, said her name was Cindy, and while we looked at the menu, she tapped her pencil against her chin as if she were already bored with us. Jade said, "Can we look at this for a minute? We just arrived. Bring me some of this chardonnay and . . ." She looked at me.

"Sweet tea, please."

Cindy shrugged and bounced off and by time she brought our drinks, we'd talked about what we wanted and were ready to order. For appetizers, Jade and I both ordered tiny cups of shrimp and corn soup. For supper, I wanted crabmeat au gratin, and Jade asked for fried catfish with hushpuppies and a side of half-dozen raw oysters.

While we waited for our food, Jade went on about the new boyfriend. What I couldn't figure was why I hadn't seen hide or claw of him. Then again, I wasn't one to talk about being better with men and dating and those kinds of things.

The restaurant was noisy and bright and I had the sudden urge to be alone, away from too much light and sound. Everything rubbed my skin tender, as if I was inside out and all my nerve endings were exposed. I felt as if I was being watched, something crackled in the air, causing the hairs on the back of my neck to stand, and goosepimples every so often zippity do dahed across my arms. I figured maybe a silly spirit had followed me in and was playing around. Most of them were good to me, but some of them liked to tease.

Jade said, "Vee Vee Vee. You are not listening are you?"

I laughed, because I hadn't been and she knew it and I knew it, and that's how it was sometimes.

"I was saying that Lloyd said he'd take me to Las Vegas, maybe next month. I'm so excited."

Cindy strutted over with our appetizers, plopped them down before us, and we were quiet for a time as I spooned into my waiting hungry mouth the creamy, spicy corn and shrimp soup. Jade ate much slower than I did, dipping her spoon from front to back of the bowl, tipping the spoon to her mouth. She was a dainty eater, but I was just slap flat hungry and didn't care if I looked un-dainty.

I finished my soup first, to the last slurp.

When Jade was done (and she left some in her bowl so I finished it), she asked, "Are you dating at all?"

I fiddled with my napkin. "Men are nothing but trouble."

"You think so?"

I nodded.

"What about that guy? What was his name? Tim? He was real sweet and cute as all get out. I liked him."

"I don't like that name."

"You won't date a perfectly nice guy because of his name?"

I remembered the man Timothy Momma dated, when she came home with the black eye and split lip. "The name just sets sour on my tongue."

She blew out her breath in a huff, then asked, "Well, there was that other one, Brian. What about him?"

I shrugged. "He drove a pick up truck."

She blinked. Blinked again. "I'm not even asking."

Cindy came by, picked up our bowls, said our food would be ready in a few minutes, and then floated off on her I'm-bored-because-yawwwll-are-boring cloud.

Jade held her wine in the air. "Happy birthday to me!"

I toasted her with my tea. "Happy birthday, Jadesta."

"And here's to trouble!" She glugged down the rest of her wine. When Cindy brought our food, Jade asked for another. She said to me, "Vee, don't get that look. I'm just celebrating my birthday, okay?"

I pretended I didn't know what she was talking about, dug into my au gratin without worry (or much) over how many calories were swimming in all that cheese and cream and whatever else I was stuffing down my gullet.

Jade was a sparrow whose little mouth couldn't take in much food.

In between bites, we talked about her vacation, my photography, and of course, Lloyd the mysterious stranger. We didn't talk about me dating anymore.

Jade drank her wine too fast, and just as in the television shows, she let out a hiccup. She put her hand over her mouth.

I laughed at her.

She ordered another, and while drinking it, missed her mouth, and wine dribbled onto her blouse. She swiped at it with her napkin, said, "Oops, oh well," then grabbed her fork and pretended it was a comb-harmonica, singing, "Boing boing boing, a-boinga boing a boing boing a-boing," then fell out laughing.

The couple at the next table looked over at us. The woman had her right eyebrow raised, and the man puckered his mouth.

Jade picked at her food, said, "Isn't this good? I told you. Didn't I? I told you and I told you. Didn't I?"

"Yes, Jade. You told me. Now shush. You're talking too loud."

She put her hand over her mouth and bugged out her eyes, then took away her hand and pushed her fork into an oyster. She held the oyster at the end of the fork and studied it as if it was an alien. "Can you believe we eat these snotty things? Ever had one raw? It's just like chewing snot!"

I ate my supper as if everything was normal and Jade wasn't taking the oyster and putting it close to her eye and then away, close and then away.

Jade popped the oyster into her mouth and swallowed it. She leaned in to me. "When they're raw and I swallow them whole, makes me think of swallowing a man's stuff. Just too gross for words."

I stared at her, my fork held between my plate and my opened mouth.

She pointed a drunkened finger at me. "You should see your face, Vee! You should see it!"

Cindy sashayed over and leaned into our table. "Can y'all hold it down? Some of our diners have complained."

Jade looked up at her. "Who complained? Show me so I can explain how we're celebrating my glorious birth."

"Just lower it down, why don't you?" She slit her eyes and then pranced off.

Jade widened her eyes like a Hollywood starlet and with dainty bites began eating her food again, but her eyes sparkled monkey-mischief.

I told her, "Don't drink any more of that booze, you hear?"

"Aw, Vee. I'm just having fun."

I let it go; how could I not? She was my friend and, after all, it *was* her birthday.

I'd just finished my supper when Jade stopped in mid-sentence telling me about a date with Lloyd. She looked up at someone behind me, and then back at me all owl-eyed.

Those hairs on my neck were straight out.

Jade said, "Well, here we go."

A familiar voice flew over my head and landed smack across the table. "Hello, Jade. How have you been?"

"Oh, uh, wunnerful to see you again. Long time no see. I thought you were dead."

The voice crooned, "No, I'm alive. I saw you two from across the room, but I didn't want to disturb your dinner."

I smashed my fork into a glob of cheese that'd been hanging on to the side of my dish. Jade wouldn't look at me, but I was staring a big fat hole in her. Every part of me was still and tight. I wanted to fold inside out and hide inside myself.

She said, "It's my bird-day and we're celebrating. Now me and her are both twenty-three going on eighteen and eighty, respectively." She laughed.

I didn't laugh one little bit.

He said, "Happy birthday, Jade."

"Well, gee willikers." Jade glanced at me again, then raised her eyes to the one behind me and asked, "You remember Virginia Kate, don't you?"

I gulped down five gallons of tea that was so cold my body froze to my chair.

A rumbled voice blew my name close to my ear, "Kate?"

A shrimp swam to my frozen throat.

"Virginia Kate?" he tried.

I turned to him, slow, because my body clamped up, and frog-croaked, "Oh, hey there, Dylan. Jade thought you were dead."

He stared down at me until my heart thumped so hard, it came out and landed on my empty dish. I almost asked Cindy to take away my heart and dump it into the garbage, before Dylan tried to put it there himself, again. I hated feeling as if I could jump up and slap him, or run away, or hold on to him until Cindy came and pried me away with a spatula. I turned back to face Jade, my neck stiff and creaking, my spine had a pole stuck in it. My bones went stiff and I lay bet seventy-seven shiny dimes everyone in the restaurant could hear them creakity-crick groan.

"Why Dylan, old chap, if you'd care to join us, we were just about to order dee-ssert." Jade wasn't looking at me when she spewed out that.

I could have killed her with my killer x-ray beam eyes. She ignored me by busying herself with the dessert menu. I waited for Dylan to say no.

"I'd love to join you for a sweet. I just finished my meal—alone."

He touched my shoulder and I jerked away. He said, "Do you mind?" Then without waiting for an answer from me, made himself right on at home, picking up the dessert menu Jade put down.

The familiar heat from his body slammed into me. His leg brushed mine and I jerked my leg away, scooting my chair to the right, farther away from him. "Go ahead, what do I care." I spit out nails to impale him. "Seeing as you're already setting down." I sucked up a piece of ice from my tea and crunched it loud and rude.

Jade snickered and I shot her another laser beam. I tried to keep my mad good and alive, so I pictured him and Tina, wrapped like snakes in a blanket. But the image of Tina kept turning into an image of me close and hot with Dylan.

Cindy came to take our dessert orders, giving Dylan a wink and touching him on the shoulder. "What'll it be?" She sure wasn't tapping her pencil that time.

"I'll have the silk pie," Jade said first. "I wanna see if they make that pie as good as Lloyd does." Her eyes dreamed, "Oh, he makes great pie." She looked at me, and then at Dylan, "Okay, what are y'all getting? There is *so* much to choose from. This is a great restaurant, don't you think, Vee? *Reallly* dee-licious." She batted her lashes at Cindy. "Oh, thank you Cindy Lou Who, for taking my order first. You're a *doll*. Isn't she a doll?"

Dylan nodded his head at Jade until she stopped talking. Cindy looked as if she'd sucked on a lemon until she stared at Dylan's lips when he said, "I'll have the cheesecake with pecan praline topping." He said it like pee-can pray-leen.

Cindy Lou Who put a hand on his shoulder, and squeezed it. "Say it this way, handsome. Puh-cahn prah-leen." She had her just-glossed lips close to his face.

I told myself it didn't bother me at all. I didn't wish it were my right hand on his shoulder, and my left around Cindy Lou Who's throat. Rolling my eyes, I said, "Well, you picked the exact thing I planned on ordering. I'll have that, too."

"We only have one piece of cheesecake left. Sorry." Cindy shark-toothed me, then added, "You'll have to pick something else fattening to eat."

I stared at her, said with a stiff-mouth, "I'll have the bread pudding with rum sauce, hold the raisins please." I hated bread pudding, but my head was all muddled. With a shaking hand, I reached for my water glass to wet the fire in my stomach.

Cindy Lou Who bounced off on her toes, her curls thousands of auburn rubber bands, her hips to the right, the left, roll roll, right and left. I stole a look at Dylan to see if he noticed, but he was talking to Jade. His breath smelled sweet from that amber liquor he sipped as if it would disappear from the earth if he didn't hurry and finish it.

He said, "Jade, you look fetching."

"Of course, I do." She laughed, and then in a few throat-bobbing gulps, downed my untouched glass of wine she'd ordered for me. She then said, "If you all will *excuse em moi*, I must retire to the ladies room for *Le Tee Tee*." Jade stood, caught her balance, said, "Oh, no more wine for this girl," and then tottered off on her heels.

Dylan burned his eyes into me. "How are you?"

I decided I wasn't going to talk to him. He could set there and have his coffee and *my* cheesecake, but I didn't care.

He leaned back in his chair and didn't speak again.

The air in the room crackled and sparked.

Jade came back walking a bit wavery and said, "Well now, isn't this *niiiice?* What a nice celebration time."

Dylan held out her chair.

She gave him a big fat grin.

I pretended my spoon was more interesting than the two of them. It had a nice rounded part and a straight part and curly cues on the end and it was silver and it held food and I could sort of see myself in it. Interesting spoon.

Our desserts came riding on the Cindy Lou Who hip roller coaster. My rum sauce was full of raisins.

After she walked away, Dylan said, "I remember how much you love cheesecake, and I love bread pudding." Before I could say anything, he pushed his fork into my soggy bread dessert, lifted a big glob to those lips, pushed the dessert in, closed those lips, chewed, and said, "Mmmmmm."

Jade snickled.

I snatched my eyes from Dylan's lips and gave her a *Look.*

Dylan reached over and traded our desserts.

I looked down at the cheesecake with extra praline topping and fought the urge to throw it at him just as I'd done the cake that day, but I didn't want him to think I cared that much. Because I didn't care one speck. When I saw Cindy Lou Flooz staring at me, I took a big bite of the dessert just to be ornery. It was so good, I decided spite was tasty.

Jade picked at her dessert. "This pie's not quite as fine as Lloyd makes, but it's still good. How's your dessert, Vee?" She hadn't a bit of sense.

I shoveled in a mountain of cheesecake and didn't answer her.

"What do you two think of the restaurant?" Dylan asked.

"The waitress has whipped cream for brains," Jade said, laughed big and loud, caught herself and then said, "Lloyd brought me here last week. We *love it.*" When she said *love it,* she threw up her hands and let out another laugh.

I was getting right tired of hearing *Lloyd* this and *Lloyd* that.

Dylan took a sip of the coffee Cindy Boo Hoo brought over.

"Yeah, I like it here. The food's yummers." Jade took another teeninesey bite of her dessert, swallowed it with a sip of wine, and then said, "Oops, I forgot. No more wine for this girl." She pushed away the wine glass.

Dylan cleared his throat, then asked us, "What I meant was, what about the building itself?"

"Elegant, but with a *rough* touch to it." Jade then sighed out, "just like Lloyd."

I rolled my eyes. I'd never seen Jade act so goofy about a guy before. Maybe she was taken over by a pod alien.

"Kate? What do you think?" Dylan asked.

The mood was cozy, warm wood and old-timey lights. It was a nice place, but I didn't say it. Ornery ornery.

"The firm I'm working with designed it. Meaning, I mostly designed it. I'll open my own business before you know it. Things are looking good for me . . . professionally speaking, that is." He looked over at me.

I attacked my dessert, taking big ugly bites, not caring how I looked. Scalding my tongue on hot Community Coffee that I was sure Cindy Lou Pooh boiled before serving it to me.

"You have cheesecake on your chin." Dylan reached over and wiped my chin, then stuck his finger in his mouth and licked off the sweetness.

"I think I can wipe my own face." And that's what I did, wiped right where it burned fire at his touch. My body burned; I was a raging furnace. Blazing from the tips of my toes to the top of my scalp. I couldn't stop my breath from scorching my lips as it escaped from my lungs.

Jade stared at us with her mouth hung part-a-ways open as if we were behind glass at a scientific experiment fair.

I finished my coffee and asked for the check. When Cindy Lou Boob brought it over, she handed it to Dylan's outstretched hand, but I snatched the ticket away. I said, all prissy, "I'm paying."

"Yeah, 'cause it's my e-special day and she didn't get me a good present so this is my present." Jade then hiccupped again. She threw back her head and hen-cackled.

After Cindy Lou Snoot gave me back my change, and I left her a good tip even if she did try to ruin my dessert, we all stood to leave. Jade had a grin plastered on her plastered face.

As we moved out into the breezy evening, Dylan turned to me. "Kate?"

Jade made some excuse about going back to the bathroom and drunk-rat-scurried inside. An instigator had to pee a lot, I guessed.

He said, "For the longest time, Jinxie looked for you out of the front window."

I frowned thinking on Jinxie and how much I'd missed him.

"You could visit him. He'd love it. I know he'll remember you."

I crossed my arms over my chest and then looked behind me at a couple arguing about which one was the worst driver. The woman had the keys and she was dangling them in front of the man, as if she really wanted to smack him one with them. When I turned back around, Jade was peeking out of the door.

Dylan was saying, ". . . and Jade could come if she wants to."

"Jade can come where?" Jade asked, as she stepped out all full of too much wine innocent.

"Kate wants to visit Jinxie."

"You do?" Jade's eyebrows flew up to her hairline.

"I didn't say that." My feet were heavy on the pavement. I was sinking down, down.

"Well, I gotta date with Lloyd."

"You have a date?" I sighed a big fat sighing sigh.

"I'm s'posed to meet him at his house at ten. He couldn't join us 'cause he had business to take care of." She checked her watch. A frown touched her lips, then flew off. She leaned on the wall of the restaurant, looking all casual and smashed. "Maybe you can come by after you visit Jinxie."

"I'm not going to visit anyone."

"Oh, stop it, Vee. Look at him, standing there like he's lost his bestest friend. Poor thang." Hiccup.

Dylan leaned over, kissed her on the cheek, then said, "It's okay, Jade. Thanks for letting me have dessert with you." He turned to me. "I guess I'll be going. It's good to see you again."

I studied a spot on the sidewalk as I listened to his shoes sludgering away from me.

"What're you doing?" Jade asked as I walked and she teeter-tottered to my car. I unlocked her door first, and she flopped in, yapping about *Jinxie and Dylan and forgiving and . . .* I unlocked and opened my own door . . . *and that's what I learned about that,* as if I'd heard everything she said while I walked behind my car to my door. I climbed in. Jade slumped against the seat. She said, "He looked like a little boy walking off with his shoulders drooping."

"He can droopalate his shoulders till the cows come home." I started the engine, and out of the corner of my eye, I saw Dylan drive off.

"I'm just saying to think it over, so you won't have any regrets."

I drove the long way out of the parking lot, just to make sure I wouldn't pull up behind Dylan and be tempted to follow him to see Jinxie. "Where does this Lloyd live?"

"Drive. I'll tell you where to go." When she said, "Drive," she pointed her finger straight and kept it there as if forgetting to put it down.

I reached over and pulled down her hand, and she laughed.

After a few turns in a quiet neighborhood I've never been to, Jade told me to stop in front of an Acadian style house. It didn't seem the kind of house where a Jade stud-date would live. It looked the kind of place families live. She said, "I'll be home la-la-la-la-late." She snatched her purse from the floor.

"Hold up. I got a surprise." I reached in the backseat for her package, then handed it to her.

She put her purse in her lap then tore into the package. When she saw herself staring out at herself, she became still. The car was still, like before a big storm comes, when the trees don't move and the critters and bugs don't make a sound. Then a wet droplet appeared on the painting. And another. Then three more.

My own eyes itched and stung.

"Oh, Vee," she said. She reached over and hugged me, and the smell of her Patchouli and wine mixed with my soap smells. "Look at what he did. He remembers that part of me." She wiped her eyes. "Would you take it back to the house and put it in my room?"

"I will."

She opened the door, stepped out, steadied herself, then stuck her head back in the car. "Well, guess I'll see you later." She hesitated, then said, "Thanks. I hadda great time."

"Me, too." Except for that one part. I didn't like that part, did I? The Dylan part? Of course I didn't like it.

She was still standing there. "You're the best everest friend I everest had."

"You too, Jade."

"I mean it, Vee. The bestest of the best of ever ever ever."

"You, too."

She started to turn, then said, "Oh! Wait here a minute and see if Lloyd will come out to meet you."

I wondered why he wouldn't.

She shut the car door, trudged-tripped to the house, and knocked.

The door opened, but I couldn't see who answered it. She pointed to me and grabbed at a hand that appeared out of the door, but the hand pulled at her. Then, with a little wave, she was inside and gone.

The air stirred, the wind picked up.

I watched the door for a while before I drove away. I wanted to go back to her, though. Go inside and pull her away from that Lloyd. If she wanted him to meet me, why didn't he come on out?

Once back to Jade's, I scrubbed my face, brushed my teeth, and changed into my yellow cotton pajamas. Jade laughed at my cotton gowns and pajamas, since she wore sexy satiny things. I asked her who ever saw me in them but her? That made her shake her head and ask me whose fault that was.

It was only ten o'clock and I was ready for bed like an old country granny in my old country granny jammies.

I went through the dining room to go to the kitchen for a glass of water. There on the dining room table lay Momma's letter that she'd sent to Rebekha's house and Rebekha had given to me. I'd earlier read it while eating a potpie for lunch.

All it read was Momma asking if I'd taken a picture of her and Aunt Ruby in their matching blue dresses (I had not and didn't know what picture she was talking about).

I poured a glass of water from the faucet, went back to the dining room table to read her letter again, as if it would tell me something I needed to know, and then lay my head down, it was so heavy with thoughts, the imprint of Momma on my cheek.

The ringing of the telephone woke me and I stumbled out of my chair to answer it. Miss Frog croaked, "Hullo?"

"Did I wake you?"

"Yes, you did. I fell asleep on the dining room table."

"Wouldn't the bed be more comfortable?"

"Is there something you want, Dylan?"

"I just wanted to hear your voice." A hesitation then, "You could say hi to Jinxie." There was a muffled sound and I heard Dylan saying, "Say hi to Kate. Say hello to your friend Miss Kate."

I heard snuffling. I felt sillier than silly, but I said, "Jinxie! Hey boy! Hey there boy! Remember me?"

Dylan's voice slithered into my ear. "You should see him. He's wagging his tail like crazy. He would love to see you."

I didn't answer because ornery Miss Frog still set on my tongue, and no telling what she'd have to say. Sometimes that frog surprised me with what it croaked.

"Are you still there?"

"I have to go, Dylan." But I didn't put down the phone.

"Nothing happened with Tina that day."

"You think I care a speck about that mess that happened a million years ago?"

Breathing on the phone, clearing of throat, then, "Okay, maybe you stopped me from my own foolishness, but nothing happened that day, and that's what's important, right?"

I squeezed the phone, tight-tighter. What did he mean by *that day*?

Clearing of throat, then, "I had no impulse control, but I'm different now." Breathing, breathing. "Kate? Virginia Kate?"

"Who cares? I do not and never will."

"Yes you do. You do care." His voice was pulling me right into the phone.

Miss Frog opened her big fat mouth and said, "And what if I do?" The food must have been poisoned with stupid sauce.

"Let me come over. We'll talk. Let's fix this." Breathing. "Look how much time we've wasted apart."

I held onto the phone and pushed it to my ear so hard I had an earache come on sudden and hurtful.

"I'm coming over. I'll bring Jinxie."

I put down the phone without saying no, stood in the middle of the room while a storm built. Voices flew all round my brain, until I couldn't hear any one voice, especially not my own. I pressed my palms to my eyes, pressed harder. Lightning flashed. Thunder roared. Trees whipped their branches to the ground and up to the sky. The wind howled. Old Moon poured its light down and then was shadowed by dark clouds. The house lifted and then slammed down. The walls blew outward and then sucked inward. The windows rattled. I was a tree with shallow roots that a twister would tear away and blow about. I stood, digging into the earth, holding on against the tempest.

Lights glowed into the driveway. A car door opened, closed.

The lightning disappeared. The thunder faded.

Footsteps clomped up the steps.

The house quit its shuddering.

A soft knock.

The wind calmed.

The sounds of my slippers sluffing to the door. The creak of the door opening. Dylan's voice saying, "We're here."

Jinxie whining and wagging his body, slipping his cold nose into my palm just as if nothing had changed, as if no time had passed at all.

All my voice caught up where I didn't have any words.

But others had words. Plenty words that had blown in with the storm and hadn't left.

Give in, murmured a voice all the way from the holler. Momma's voice. *Give him another chance. He's a big strong man. He'll give you things. He loves you. Be happy with what you got. You might not get better. Look how lonely you've been.*

Grandma Faith's voice was lost behind the louder one.

I fell into him, fell hard and fast into him and he into me, fell against and in and out and through each other.

I was minding my momma, and I was minding my women-kin.

Chapter 14

Today

Old letters read in the holler while leaning against the sugar maple's trunk

Dear Vee,

Here in big New Yawk City, damned kablamed if I'm not feeling alone. How long now since we've seen each other, one year, two, three? I forget. All my life ahead to fuck up, right? You know, I could never admit my fears to you cause you always thought me a hero. Maybe it's easy to be a hero in someone else's head but not your own. But I wasn't ever a hero. I'm sure not one now. What was that little kiddie book you read to Bobby? About the rabbit being real? I want to be real. Micah.

Dear Seestor,

Hey, I was just thinking how you were 16 when I left, now you're a young woman. I haven't kept count how long I've been gone, but I bet you have. You keep track of everything. I've punched out those numbers to Lousyanner so many times. Once when Rebekha answered, I heard her soft breathing, and Bobby laughing in the background. It hurt so bad I couldn't stand it, couldn't stand to lie about how good things are in this big city I thought would be my saving and seems, not. So I hung up. Your big brother, Micah

Dear Veestor Seestor,

You'll be wondering why I haven't come home. Guess I'm afraid everyone will look at me like I'm a failure. What a long journey to my real life this is turning out to be. Maybe you'll read my letters and start crying over your dumb luck brother. Well, don't you dare do that, brat. I'll be fine and when I visit you I'll have cash in my pocket to spare. Well, later gator, see you in the movies. Love, your incredibly fucked up, but genius and going to be famous brother, Micah

Dear Vee,

I miss everybody pretty bad today. I can even muster homesickness for Looseeaner. Spanish moss hanging down. I try to paint that from memory. I crave gumbo, crawfish pie, oyster po-boy, and pralines. (Has Mee Maw croaked yet?) How's Bobby? Andy-bo-Bandy? How's Rebekha? Dad? You always thought Dad only had some character flaw, like in them books you read. Did he give us the same introspection? He expected something out of me I don't understand (is he still guzzling the brew?). Time is a funny thing, when it's happening seems it goes by slow, but when I look back on it all, it's a speeding train whizzing by so fast I can hardly make out the faces as they look at me from the windows. Most of it goes that way, except the crappy-go-sick shit slicks along with a smirk. I wonder if you'd recognize me. (Is Momma still being a selfish bitch?) Here's lookin' at you kid! (I always wanted to say that.) Love, your brother, I know I've been gone a long time, but don't forget me, Micah

Dear Veester,

Send Momma's address to the post office box where Rebekha sent the cookies. I got things I got to say. Don't worry about me, I'm fine. I sold another painting. The money means nothing. Not much means something. But it will, won't it? I will. Love, Micah

Dear Virginia Kate,

Your brother sent me a letter that I reckon weren't too nice. I expect you kids are mad at me for doing what I had to do. If you kids can't say nothing nice, then just don't write me a letter. Tell Micah what I said. That I don't need all that trouble on top of my own troubles. Your Momma

1981-1982

The revelers are entering, brother: make good room
—Shakespeare

Chapter 15

Virginia Kate Carey, will you marry me?

I was thinking on that photo of Micah the day before he left for New York. He stood tall and dark against the big granddaddy oak in Rebekha and Daddy's front yard. He struck a pose, knowing he looked handsome with his black hair grown long and pieces of it flying across his face. His eyes burned into the camera with untold mysteries. He wore his favorite brown corduroy britches, a white shirt, and black boots. All the shadows and light of him played in and out of him, swirling spirits I'd captured. In that picture, he reminded me of Momma more than he did of Daddy. The two of them looking far out and away from where they were, eyes burning with a hunger for what they thought they were missing instead of what they already had.

Dylan grabbed my hand. "Are you still with me?"

Fastened my eyes onto Dylan.

"Just a little over three years before I'm thirty, can you believe that?"

Shook my head as if I couldn't believe it.

"The age men think about things, you know?"

Didn't know, but nodded my head.

He cleared his throat, took another sip of his wine. I knew Dylan had something Very Important he wanted to tell me, knew by the way he set ready in his seat, playing with his wine glass in his right hand when he wasn't drinking from it, the way he kept sneaking his left hand into his pocket. In his pocket, where things lurked to take me off guard and put me on the spot. I hoped it wasn't another big gold ring with a winking catfish eye. He said, "A beautiful night, isn't it?"

"Yes, it's a nice night."

"Did you finish your coffee table book yet?"

"Almost."

He nodded, cleared his throat.

I'd never heard Dylan so quiet.

Since that night he'd come over with Jinxie, we'd gone back to where we were before. Except different. I was different in ways I didn't want to explain to Dylan. He was different because he knew I'd changed in ways he didn't want to find out the details. The time we'd spent apart was a mystery to the other. I'd promised myself I'd never ask about his time apart, and I knew he wouldn't ask about mine. Men didn't like to know things and women liked to know too much. I wished to break the spell of women, but I figured most of us thought we'd do things different just as we stepped into the same messes we always had.

The restaurant ceiling lights were low and the candle glow bounced off the white tablecloths, leaving our shadows closer than we really leaned in to each other. Everyone spoke in low voices, couples held hands at their tables. Soft violin music played where it was barely heard at all, as if the restaurant wanted to suggest the music, not really have us listen to it full out.

We'd finished our grillades and grits and I could have licked my plate clean but I wouldn't. Dylan asked for another glass of wine. I think that was four glasses. But I wasn't counting. Much.

"Kate? Virginia Kate?"

I blinked.

"The places you go off to. I wish I knew where they were so I could go, too."

The waiter brought our desserts and coffee on a tray as big as a politician's ego. I don't see how he carried it since he was as small as Rhode Island. I liked his dark blue eyes and the way his mouth quirked, especially when Dylan spoke to him. I think he was sweet on Dylan. The waiter called me Sweetie, and I didn't mind a bit.

"This Bananas Foster sure looks good." Dylan liked to order food he said was "authentically Louisiana," so he could copy it in his own kitchen.

I took a spoonful of the dessert into my mouth, let the sweet slide across my tongue and then down my throat and into my stomach. The greedy frogs slurped it up and that kept them from hopping around and making me feel jittery. I said, "This is better than any I've ever had," and smiled to show I was paying attention and how everything was wonderful and how I appreciated all he did and was.

Dylan reached his hand into his pocket and pulled out a black velvet box, similar to those in jewelry commercials where the man holds it out with a grin while the woman says, "Oh!" and looks all glowed with happy thoughts of the future. He prepared to open it, cleared his throat another time; it was as if my frogs had jumped inside his throat. He sighed out, "I love you. You know that."

I took a bite of the melting ice cream, a sip of coffee, and the cold and hot mixed, the sweet and bitter, the darker and the lighter. Then I figured I ought not to be eating and drinking when something important was happening. I shouldn't be doing a thing except keeping an eye on that box and what was inside, and what would come out of Dylan's mouth.

He opened the box.

Nestled inside was a ring I had tried on in an antique store when I thought Dylan wasn't looking. It was a slim platinum ring with worn etchings, but the imperfections of it only made it more beautiful. I'd liked it because it reminded me of Grandma Faith's ring. Sometimes she'd take it off and let me hold it. I knew the ring Dylan held wasn't hers, but it was so close I couldn't help but be drawn to it. Grandma Faith's ring had perished with her in the fire. The fire that I wondered if Grandpa Luke had started in all his fiery meanness. Her ring was the only thing horrid old Grandpa Luke ever did for her that had beauty to it, besides the children he lent his manhood to by way of his own pleasures and nothing else.

Dylan hadn't moved. His breath was drawing in and pushing out. His hands began to shake.

I said, "It's beautiful."

He took the ring from the box.

I sipped water and some dribbled down my chin. I didn't wipe it off; a droplet slipped and fell onto the table, and it was as if I heard it loud as the crash of a wave. Every little thing became as if through a magic magnifier. I could see molecules rushing. Smells shot into my nose. My right hand held onto my left hand. My pores opened and wept.

Dylan leaned across the white tablecloth. He said in a low, graveled-voice, "Virginia Kate Carey, will you marry me?" He touched my clasped hands and they had a life of their own as they sprung apart; I saw them do it, felt it, but my brain didn't seem to be in charge.

Dylan then took hold of my left hand and slipped the ring onto my finger. It fit without force. My finger tingled and grew warm. I held up my hand to admire it, wondered, wasn't I supposed to say yes first? Before the ring was slipped on? I didn't know about those kinds of things.

He went to blabbering, "I saw you at the jewelry counter, so I went back the next day to find out what you gave back to the owner." He drained his wine, then said, "I know how you don't wear a lot of jewelry. And you like, ah, understated things. I hope I did all right."

"Dylan," was all I frogged, still hypnotized.

"Please say yes." He took my hand and covered the ring with his palm so I'd wake up and look at him. He stood, came around the table and bent on one knee.

"Don't, Dylan." I hated the way the others in the restaurant watched us.

"Please say you'll be my wife."

It was all too foolish.

Rivulets of moist trickled into his collar, his mouth turned down, and the corners of his eyes followed. When he took my hand again, his fingers were cold, the palms moist.

I stared like a dumbed-up mule, looked at the ring again, looked around the room at everyone looking at me, looked again at Dylan's worry-face. Look look, look at the looking fool Virginia Kate.

His eyes stayed fastened on me. And the ring, it was just what I had picked out for myself. He learned to pay attention to things I loved. He was doing it for me. He would make me love him back and I would be a part of someone, a half to a whole. I would make my own home with my own children, would ask Dylan to smoke a pipe and the air would fill with bay scent. The children would run through the house laughing and breaking things and I'd fuss at them and then I'd tell them it didn't matter since things were just things, and we'd all be happy.

I'd never again be see-through or worry about being lonely again.

The world held its breath; we all together held our breaths. Grandma Faith sighed on the wind. But Grandma Faith was not an alive woman. *I* was an alive woman.

And then my mouth opened, my tongue moved, words hopped out and fell at Dylan's feet. "Yes, Dylan, I'll marry you." There was clapping at the other tables as the ring squeezed hot and tight around my finger. I wanted to put the words back into my mouth and swallow them, but I didn't because I wanted that house with the pipe smell and the sounds of children. Home.

Dylan stood, leaned over, and kissed me full on my lips, then flopped back in his chair as if he were a tired old man. Then he let loose words, "You've made me the happiest man in the world. Our children will be beautiful. I hope they have your eyes and my coloring. I've always wanted a houseful of kids, like Frank Lloyd Wright. I know most men don't want kids weighing them down, but I do. I—"

"Hush," I said, gulped some tea, then said again, "Just hush now, Dylan."

And that time he did. He pulled wine into his mouth to stop the words and watched me over the rim of his glass.

That night, I wanted to tell Jade all about it, but she wasn't home. I waited until one in the morning. No Jade. I climbed into bed, touched the ring. My head rushed round and round. I refused to listen to any ghosts, refused to listen to any voices at all, and wrapped the pillow tight around my head.

I only wanted quiet.

⋙ • ⋘

The next morning, after I made coffee, I checked Jade's room, but she still was not home. I never relaxed my worry until she was home and I could make sure she was okay. That's what should happen when a person lived with someone or with their family. They were watched over and worried over.

I poured a cup of Community, drank it down, and poured another. I popped a slice of bread into the toaster, and from the ice-box I took the strawberry jam and butter. When the toast popped up, I buttered and jammed it, and ate it nice and slow, enjoying every bite. I was still hungry, though.

After I washed my dishes, cleaned my face and brushed my teeth, I dialed up Rebekha to tell her the news. After three rings, someone picked up and at first all I heard were bumps, as if the receiver was being banged against the furniture.

Then, "*Hell*-o, Carey's In-sane Asylumarian, may I he'p yew?"

"For lord's sake, Andy. I could be someone important calling."

"But you aren't."

"Why are you there so early?"

"Goddamn! Can't visit my own house?"

"I was just wondering is all." When he didn't say anything else, I asked, "Where's Rebekha?"

"In her garden."

"Can you tell her to come to the phone?"

"I don't know, can I?"

"Will you please go fetch Rebekha for me?"

"Can't even talk to your brother for a second?"

"Well, then. What are you doing?"

"None of your beez-wize."

"I don't have time for your orneriness."

"All right, if you're gonna be cranky about it. Bobby and me are headed to New Orleans to mess around. There, now you know what I'm up to."

"Have fun and don't get into trouble."

"Uh huh."

"May I talk to Rebekha now?"

"What about, Virginia Grouch?"

"Just some stuff I want to talk about. You wouldn't be interested." I poured another cup of coffee, put a leftover piece of peach pie into the oven to warm. Sometimes a girl just had to have pie.

"Well, I'll just hang out right here until you tell me." He hummed and then whistled, knowing I hated whistling more than glass underfoot.

I spilled out, "I'm getting married." The whistling stopped and Andy didn't say anything for so long I thought he'd put down the phone. "Andy?"

"Yeah, I'm still here."

"Well, what are you thinking?"

"I'll get Rebekha for you." Breathing in the phone.

"Hello?"

"Yeah?"

"I thought you were getting Rebekha."

"Don't do it, Sister!"

Before I could answer, he plunked down the phone and I heard the sound of his shoes clomp across the floor.

I'd turned into a statue of a woman with all kinds of worries chiseled into her face.

When Rebekha came to the phone and I told her the news, she said, "Congratulations! I'm happy for you, Virginia Kate."

We yappered on about wedding dresses and receptions and parties, but I was on the ceiling looking down at myself. *Virginia Kate is on the phone. Virginia Kate is taking a sip of coffee and then swallowing it. Virginia Kate is pulling the pie from the oven. Virginia Kate takes a bite of warm pie while Rebekha talks. Virginia Kate is a crazy woman.*

Rebekha was saying, ". . . and let's plan an engagement party."

A couple of hornets flew by giving me the don't-you-think-we've-forgotten-you buzz.

"Just a small party, as you like it."

"Sounds great, Rebekha."

"Have you set a date?"

"No Ma'am, not yet. But it won't be anytime soon, I don't think. Maybe next year."

"Well, let's see. What if we plan the party when it's not so hot? In October or November? That's just a few months away. We'll just have to make sure the party is on an away game day. You know how bad football traffic can be."

"Sounds fine."

While Rebekha went on about planning the party, what kind of food, how she hoped the weather would turn cooler, since sometimes it stayed hot even through Christmas, Jade trudged into the house. Her hair was a mess, her clothes wrinkled, her eyes droopy with Mississippi mystery turning them muddy where it was hard to read her. She raised her hand in a hello-I'm-here-and-don't-ask-me-any-questions wave. I waved back. She poured herself a cup of coffee and dropped down into a chair.

While I *uh hummed* and *that sounds good* and *that'll be fine*, Jade watched me with a quizzable look.

After I hung up the phone, I told Jade the news. She scalded-bald-cat screeched, hugged me, and said we'd have to have some champagne even though it was still morning. We toasted with three sips and then put down our glasses, preferring instead to drink the rest of that pot of coffee. While I poured hers and then mine, stirred in cream and sugar, and divided the last of the slice of peach pie so Jade could have some, we were quiet, but that comfortable quiet of friends. Even though I could tell Jade was for true feeling happy for me, I could also tell someone or something had sucked all the innards out of her and left her without bones to hold her upright.

We set ourselves down at the table and peered at each other over the rims of our cups. I thought of Momma and me drinking our coffee while the breeze drifted in from her kitchen window, the checkered curtains square-dancing skirt twirling. I'd earlier opened the blinds to let in the Louisiana light to Jade's kitchen, where no curtains danced from a cool breeze.

Jade yawned, then said, "I'm pretty tired. Mind if I take a nap and we'll talk all about your wedding when I'm feeling better?"

"You go on and rest yourself. We'll talk all about it later on."

She stood, put her cup in the sink, went to her room, and closed the door with a soft click. I finished my coffee, washed and rinsed our cups, the pie dish and forks, put them in the drain to dry, and then went to my room, took out two pieces of white paper, two envelopes, and two stamps. I wrote to Momma first.

> Dear Momma,
>
> I am getting married. I hope you will come. We haven't set the date yet, but you have plenty of time to plan. We're having an engagement party in a couple of months. Maybe you can come to that, too. I'm sure Daddy will pay your way. Mrs. Mendel is invited, too. So are Uncle Jonah and Aunt Billie. I will call or write them to let them know. I'll tell you all the plans when I know them. I also thought you should know Andy's graduating college, too, in the case you want to send him a nice note or when you come to the wedding you can tell him you are proud of him, or maybe you'll come to his graduation instead of the wedding. I don't mind if you want to do that. Well, that's it for now. Hope you are feeling all right.
>
> Love, Virginia Kate

And then to Micah.

> Dear Micah,
>
> Well, I'm getting married! What do you think of that big brother? I can't believe it myself. It's as if I'm in a movie where everything is happening to someone else. I hope you will come. I invited Momma, too. I hope that won't keep you away. Please say it won't. Say you'll come. Come home and see your sister get married. And the engagement party. And our Andy's graduation. You can't miss all these events, can you?

Guess what? I had some photography published in a little magazine and they paid me! What about that? And I'm finally finished with my photography book, but haven't looked where to publish it yet. Rebekha says Bobby has been buckling down in his studies and talks about getting into medical school instead of baseball, can you believe that? He's only fifteen and already setting big goals. Rebekha is the same as she always is. Daddy, well, what do I say about Daddy? He's the same, yet he is not. I know that doesn't make sense but that's how it is. He still has his Shakespeare but he isn't guzzling down the booze as much and Bobby says he stays home more often than he used to. I wish you'd come see for yourself. We can go get a shrimp po-boy at Soot's. Write me soon.

Love, your Seestor

I put a picture in each of the envelopes. For Momma, the picture was of Dylan and me at a party for my twenty-fourth birthday where I wore an off-white dress and my hair was down. I hoped she'd appreciate seeing me in a dress. For Micah, I had a picture of the both of us at Dylan's house with Jinxie's nose pushed in my hand. I was wearing blue jeans and a gypsy top and I'd kicked off my shoes. In both I was grinning to split my face in two, so they could see how hap hap happy I was.

I didn't know if Micah would come. I knew Momma would never come. Not in a zillion years would she leave the holler where she hid out, since she thought she'd lost her pretty. She cared more about her pretty than she cared about her daughter getting married. Maybe I should tell her I forgave her for taking money from Mee Maw in that deal that mommas shouldn't make. But I didn't forgive that. I was as ornery as she was. I missed her all the same.

The last time I called her, a few months ago, she'd surprised me by answering the phone.

I'd said, "Momma. It's Virginia Kate."

She'd said, "I know who this is."

"I want to talk to you. About things."

"What sorter things?" Her voice was slurry and thick.

"Did you love Daddy, and if not, why did you marry him?"

Momma's loud laughing turned into a sour-frog cough. She said,

"You call here asking me a question like that?" She said something to someone in the room, "Pour me another one of those. I reckon I'm dry as the Savannah dessert." There was a man's voice rumbling something, and then Momma said, "Savannah, Sahara, what the hell you care? And light me one of those Marlboro's while you're at it." There was more rumbling man voice. Momma laughed a low laugh, a woman's flirty-voice laugh, her Queen of West Virginia laugh. She let out a whoosh of air. I could see her, her hair still long and tangled, her body strong and tall, her lips red and pouting as she blew out clouds of cigarette smoke, arching towards the man. I could see him staring at her, just as men had always stared at my momma, with a hunger deep in his belly. She'd not lost her flirt, or I bet not her pretty. She'd not lost a thing—but us kids.

I held onto the phone, even though I knew I should slam it down, said, "Momma? I'm still here."

"I know you're still there. I was taking care of something." Then the sound came of ice rattling in a glass, and I knew she'd up-ended whatever the man had just brought her. She said, "What do you want, Virginia Kate?" That time I heard something in her voice, something that made me stay on the line. I heard something that maybe was missing me, just a bit, maybe?

"I just wanted to know things, about you and about Daddy. I want to understand things."

"Understand what? I reckon I don't get what you're saying."

"I . . . I just wanted to hear your voice." I held the phone pressed to my ear. "How are you?"

"I expect I'm doing just fine." She said *just fine* as if it was the greatest thing in the world, as if she was doing so great she didn't have need for anyone or anything, except maybe that glass in her hand, and whatever man was there to hand it to her.

The man's voice was close. It said, "Who you talking to, woman?"

Momma said, "Just a girl I used to know." She laughed that low laugh again.

I put down the receiver and disconnected the line that held us. She didn't call me back and couldn't even if she wanted to, since she didn't have Jade's number. Maybe I shouldn't have asked her to come, since I was just some girl, but she was my momma and mommas were supposed to be at their daughter's weddings. Still.

In a fit of mad, I took out the letter from the envelope and tore it in half, then soon as I did that, I re-wrote the same letter to her. That's what Momma did to me. That's how she kept me going between mad, sad, and crazy, loving her and hating her. Why couldn't daughters outgrow their mothers, was what I wondered.

I knew Micah would come only if he could come without bringing along his darkling spirits that followed him and made him so sad. From the sound of some of his letters, I wasn't keeping up my hopes.

I lay upon my bedspread and tried to imagine myself a wife. I didn't know what kind of marriage I'd have. One like Soot and Marco, with their little Mae Lynn and sister Peggy Elaine. Maybe like the Campinelles, who couldn't live without each other.

The ones I studied from the closest most every day view were my birth parents, and then Rebekha and Daddy—I didn't think either one of those would be my choice at all.

I sure didn't.

Chapter 16

I'm giving up on men, Vee

I climbed out of my bed with my head full of rocks. Slapping my feet on the floor to the kitchen, I put on the coffee and watched a dark cloud drift across the sun. A storm could be coming, but sometimes the Louisiana sky fooled me. And other times the storm was in my head, blowing my thoughts and feelings in a mad confused rush and whistle of wind.

While the coffee perked, I went to Jade's door. Pressing my ear against the wood, I heard the sound of a drawer open, close, and then her slippers shlopp shlopping on the floor. Hurrying back into the kitchen, I took out two cups from the cabinet and hoped Jade would at last come out of her room.

Since the night she'd come home so boozed up she'd slipped to the floor and I had to carry her skinny body (the weight she'd gained going, going, gone) to bed, she'd stayed fastened up in her room. The tea along with saltine crackers with butter slapped on would be gone the next morning, but not the soup.

I had finally banged on her door and wouldn't let up, said, "I'm not leaving until you talk to me."

She'd called out, "I'm just tired, Vee."

I rattled the doorknob. "Best let me in or I'll bust this door wide open."

When she opened her door and stood in front of me, I hardly recognized my old friend with her dark-stained hollowed eyes and greasy hair.

I pushed a limp strand back from her face, as if I was her

momma, said, "Oh Jade," and handed her Miss Darla's special tea I'd brewed hot and steaming. Miss Darla told me to make sure she drank it all, not to leave a drop, so I told Jade, "Drink it all, every bit."

Jade took a sip of the dark tea, made a this-tastes-weird face.

"I said drink it all. Miss Darla's orders."

She sucked it up fast, handed me the cup. "Any coffee by chance?"

"I'll bring it to you."

She turned and perched herself on her bed.

I went back to the kitchen, poured us two cups of coffee, added cream and sugar, and put the cups on a tray. Also on the tray, I shook three aspirin, Jade's favorite Hubig's lemon pie, and a glass of water, then headed back to Jade's room.

When she sipped her coffee, Jade made the same oh-it's-hot-but-good face Momma used to make. She looked like Momma had after her accident, even though Jade was lamb-white and Momma was not. It was how her light had dimmed so that she turned dull opaque, just as Momma's light had. She took the aspirin with the water, and then mouse-nibbled the fried pie along with sips of coffee.

I was quiet, making circles on Jade's furry deep purple bedspread. Micah's painting of her was on the wall, along with another painting of his I'd given her. There were shades of red, purple, gold, orange, and those bright colors were calmed with cream, tans, black, and brown— she'd taken the colors from Micah's paintings and matched her room. Those two were meant for each other, but I'd learned that just like the planets and sun, some things would forever circle each other round and round, never allowed to come together.

Jade pushed the barely nibbled pie aside. "Thanks for the pie. I guess I was hungry."

I sipped my coffee.

"I did things I'm not proud of, Vee. Put up with things I never thought I would."

I waited. I knew I wouldn't want someone trying to dig thoughts out of me, but I also knew some secrets shouldn't stay trapped where they'd fester and pus and make a person sick inside.

She took hold of her cup with both hands. "For one thing, Lloyd's married. I mean, I didn't know at first, and when I knew . . ." she sighed, continued, "I don't know. I just kept seeing him. He said his wife traveled all the time, staying gone for months, and he was lonely, like that was good enough reason. He always had these reasons and excuses and I always fell for them."

"You deserve better."

She looked up at me, then down. "You think too well of me."

"And I always will. You're my friend."

"Maybe I don't deserve to be thought well of."

"Yes you do, too." I sipped coffee, waited to hear what else she had to say.

She wiped her nose with her lavender-colored and -scented sheet. "It wasn't just that he was married. It's how I let him control everything. It was a relief to let someone older take charge. He seemed to worship the ground I walked on; that's pretty heady stuff. But, I think that's the game, the way they trap you." She shivered, put her feet under the covers, the hot tea and coffee not enough to warm her. "I quit dance because of him, not just because of my back and knees like I told you."

I swallowed words and coffee.

"And to make things worse, I wasn't the only one he was fooling with. When I confronted him, he'd either act hurt, or he'd get mad, as if I was the crazy one." Her mouth thinned out, then she said, "I'm smarter than that. I don't understand what happened."

I smoothed back her hair again. "He's no good and that's that."

"Now I see how he's like my dad in a lot of ways. Boy is that Freudian, sick."

It was as if a bird flew out of her nose. I thought she had a *Leave it to Beaver* or *Father Knows Best* television family, that their house was calm and perfect, that it was the very kind of house I wanted to have when I had a family of my own with Dylan, except louder.

She nodded at my surprised look. "Yes, my dad isn't perfect like you thought. He was controlling and Mom did whatever he said. He never hurt her. I mean, he loved her and she loved him, but he had to control everything, it had to be his way all the time. And I know for a fact he cheated on my mom with that Mrs. McGrander; remember her? I saw them go into a hotel. I never told Mom. Maybe I should have, but I couldn't. She would have pretended it never happened anyway." She thought a bit. "Besides, it would have hurt her worse for her to know I knew."

I remembered Mrs. McGrander, and the time I saw my own daddy driving his silly little car with that woman riding beside him, the top down, her bleached-out hair barely moving in the wind.

We both watched out her window as two blue jays flew off

making a racket. That's what made blue jays happy, making racket and being big and handsome blue. Maybe some couples were like that, only happy when they were squawking at each other.

I said, "He's not worth getting sick over."

"The sad thing is, I thought he would save me."

I leaned to her. I needed to know. "Save you from what?"

"I don't know exactly. But he made me think I was better off with him than without him."

How did women get themselves all in a fix over men? They let men take away their insides that made them who they were until they weren't the same person any more. And they'd make a woman somehow feel happy to have it that way. It was like the parasites I learned about in the sciences at school, how the little critters took over the host bit by bit and made the host behave in ways that fashioned a better world for the parasite, but not for the poor old host. I asked, "Did you love him?"

She didn't answer at first, then said, "No. I guess I didn't. I think it was how he seemed so sophisticated, like he had all the answers. At least at first." A corner of her mouth lifted as she said, "You know what, though? He dyed his hair and beard and wore lifts in his shoes. How vain is that?" She quirked her mouth higher, said, "What kind of name is Lloyd anyway? I hate that name. Two l's together with an oyd trailing behind; *whoopee*; I'm Big El, tiny El, with an Oyd! A Him-R-oyd more like it." She busted out laughing.

I laughed, too.

"And, he was a horrible lover, now that I think about it. He let his big old poodle watch. Gross!" She laughed harder.

I laughed harder with her.

She stopped, wiped her eyes. "I'm the joke. I'm the one let him play with me like I was his own personal Barbie doll."

"You aren't going back to him are you?"

"No way. I told him I didn't want to see him anymore." She poked her finger into the pie, sucked the lemon from her fingers, and then said, "It was a really bad scene, one I won't replay. But, it's over."

"Promise, Jadesta?"

"More than promise. I pinkie swear."

We hooked our pinkies, like little girls again.

"I never want to feel that way again. So . . . so *used*. I'm just hoping I can get myself in shape again." She looked at me. "There was a lot of drinking and . . . sometimes other things besides drinking." She shrugged. "I'm a mess."

She'd reached over and hugged me; smelling like Miss Darla's tea, and fried lemon pie, and sweat and hurt. After that day, she began to come out of her room and eat better, and she wasn't as shaky. Each day she became stronger.

It looked as if the Jade who shlopped in with her big fuzzed slippers, lavender shower soap smell, and pink scrubbed face, was back to my old familiar Jade. She heaved herself on the stool at the bar.

I placed two pieces of peanut butter and jelly toast in front of her. "Eat this, please?" Then I reached her a cup of coffee.

She took the cup I held out. "Are you excited about the party tomorrow?"

"I guess."

She picked up a piece of toast and bit into it, chewed slow. Strawberry jelly stuck to the corner of her mouth, she licked it away. "Have y'all talked about a date yet?"

"He keeps harping on about it." I turned to the framed print over the dining table of the Starry Night. It always made me sad, but peaceful at the same time. It made the mysteries in the painted night sky flicker their secrets. I thought how Van Gogh didn't realize that waking the next day to paint again could have been enough. That's how easy it was to think on things after they were already done.

Jade and I made a grocery list for our offerings to Rebekha's table. We didn't talk about that Lloyd one speck, but I still wished I could go over to his place and smack him silly. I betted fifty shined dimes that Andy would beat him senseless. I wondered what Micah would do? If he'd see how hurt Jade was and go to Him-R-Royd and give him a swift kick to his rear end from one side of the planet to the other.

Jade looked up at me from her list. "I'm giving up on men, Vee. They're too much trouble, just like you always said. Maybe I'll become a lesbian."

"Finish your list, Jadesta."

ॐ • ॐ

That night after Jade had gone to bed, I stared at Starry Night, making wishes on Van Gogh's stars lighting his forever night. Wishes for Jade, for Micah, for Daddy and Rebekha, Andy, Bobby, and even for Mee Maw and for Momma. It wasn't until deep into the night when I awoke that I realized I hadn't remembered to say a good wish for Dylan and me.

Chapter 17

Goddamn! Her name's Virginia Kate

I wore a top as blue-green as the ocean, with white shorts, and pushed back my hair with one of Rebekha's white headbands. I flipped flopped to the living room and looked out the window. The sun peeked out from behind a cloud.

Behind me I heard, "So, do you like it?"

I turned to Jade. Her hair was chopped to within an inch of its short. The ends were jagged, pieces stuck out, and the bangs that had been cut straight across to hide her eyes she'd scissored short and uneven. She struck a pose, wearing that hair, a slinky lilac top, a blue jean skirt with flowers she'd embroidered, sandals, and shimmers of her old self.

I said, "It looks just right."

Jade took my hand and led me over to the wall mirror. She leaned her head on mine. "Look at us. We couldn't be any more different, could we? But we're the best friends in the universe."

I smelled her Flex shampoo as we stood together.

She said, "We're cookies. I'm the vanilla filling while you're the rich crunchy part." She laughed.

"There's nothing vanilla about you."

She hugged me and her bones pressed against me, sharp and sad. She said, "We won't have much time left just to be friends, not once you're married."

"What do you mean we won't have time?"

She looked as if she knew things.

We grabbed our stuff and hopped into Jade's new Bug that looked a lot like the old one. She started it, turned on the radio, and said, "Thank god the shaking booties of disco seem to have faded away, Vee. Disco really does suck." She found a station playing a beautiful song about time going from the river to the sea and she sang it so sweet I wanted to cry.

Jade drove with the top down so that our hair blew about. No problem for Jade since she didn't have much hair left. I didn't care if my hair tangled into a mess, I was more thinking on the worry bone that poked me. A worry bone that wouldn't tell me what it was worried over. When we pulled into the driveway, Dylan's car wasn't yet there, but then right as we parked, he pulled up to the curb out front, honking the horn and waving out the window as if he left all his sense at home. It made me scrunch into a knot just hearing that horn and seeing that arm stick up and wave.

Jade slithered out of the car holding the box with her banana pudding and my macaroni salad. I figured Andy would have a fit when he saw her looking soft and pretty. Except rumor flying round was his five dates with the mystery girl had grown to more, so maybe he was over his childhood crush with Jade. He'd also been working at a bookstore for more than six months, also an all-time record for any place he'd ever worked. Andy was just Andy, no figuring him out.

"You coming, Vee?" Jade asked.

"I best wait for Dylan." She nodded, slinked towards the backyard. She had the best molecules in the land, all of them fitting together to make her look just right, even when she was too skinny. I couldn't feel envious of her, since she was my friend and I loved her. Soot was the same way; like Jade, she had a way about her when she walked or talked or even just stood there that made her gorgeous and alive. When I practiced their walk it was as if I walked on loose pebbles, all wobbled. I figured I best just accept my molecules for what they were and my walk for how it walked.

Dylan had parked at the curb, grabbed his stuff, and made his way to me. He wore pressed tan britches, brown belt, and a tucked-in denim shirt with sleeves rolled to his elbows. His hair was combed just so and his eyes glittered. In the papersack he carried, he showed me the two bottles of wine and a package of steaks he brought as his offering.

When Dylan leaned down to kiss me, I smelled something old and familiar. I smelled life in the holler. But then, when I put my face into Dylan's shirt, there was bay-rum aftershave and fresh-smelling clothes detergent, and the holler flew away.

When I stepped back, he said, "You look sweet, Kate."

"You look handsome. Your hair looks like Mr. Manilow's."

He preened, as I knew he would.

"Dylan?"

"Yes?"

"Let's don't set the date today. Let's just eat and have fun."

"Why are you putting it off? I was thinking in the spring. I'm not getting any younger you know." He smiled, but it didn't reach his eyes. His sort-of-grin said he'd been patient enough for quite long enough. That he'd been patient with too many things, and he was tired of patience.

"I just don't want to do it in front of everyone."

"Okay, I guess that's fine." He followed me to the backyard, rustling that sack of his.

We circled around to say hello to those who'd come to the party. Mee Maw wasn't there because she was in Mexico. I knew I'd be getting a box of strange things from her that she'd buy off the streets. She'd be at the wedding, and that was more than enough for all of us. Our down-the-street neighbor and Amy Campinelle's best friend Mrs. Portier-turned-Engleson wasn't able to fly to Louisiana with her twins, their son, and husband, of course, but they'd sent flowers and a nice card and promises to be at the wedding. Dylan's parents said they had all-a-sudden houseguests and couldn't get out of it, even though we'd planned the party months ago.

I'd met Dylan's parents when they came to visit him, and to meet me. Dylan prepared Louisiana food for them: corn and crab bisque, fried oysters, stuffed mirlitons, and salad. For dessert, I'd baked Rebekha's old family recipe *Crème au Beurre* Cake.

All Dylan and his parents seemed to talk about was business. I figured maybe it was boring because I was used to my kaleidoscope family with words and sounds fractured everywhere. Figured I was being ornery because they had eyed me up and down and sniffed, just a little, enough for me to wonder if I had heard that sniff at all. Rebekha's momma had sniffed at Micah and me in that same way.

"Oh where oh where has my little Kate gone?" Dylan looked down at me as if I were the silliest thing ever.

"Just thinking about the night your parents came to supper."

"That was a wonderful night. Everything went perfectly. They just loved that cake you made."

I nodded, for why wouldn't he think that way? They were his parents, he loved them, and that was how it should be.

I waved to Rebekha looking peach-cream pretty in linen britches, a cotton top, and sandals. Daddy, wearing his tan britches that almost matched Dylan's, and a white shirt, was reading a Shakespeare passage to her, "'Close pent-up guilts, rive your concealing continents, and cry. These dreadful summoners grace. I am a man. More sinn'd against than sinning.'"

Rebekha always listened to him as if he was the smartest man she knew, unlike Momma's smart mouth shooting out things like, "Who's this Shakesfool think he is anyway?"

Daddy held Shakespeare before his face whenever it suited him to hide from everyone and everything.

Dylan put his papersack on the long picnic table, and stood straight-backed in front of Daddy. He put his right hand on his chest and the left he held in the air and said, "'If music be the food of love, play on!'" Then he grabbed and shook Daddy's hand. "What a day for dreamers, eh, old chap?"

"Old? Who's old? I'm not fifty, yet." Daddy broke off the hand-shaking, then came to hug me tight. "You look pretty, Bug. My little Ariel grown up before I had time to get used to it."

My eyes burned. I fought the urge to press my palms to them. A woman's daddy always made her feel like a little girl. I said, "Hey, Daddy."

"Hay is for horses." Daddy's shirt was crisp from the cleaners, blinding me with its white. It scratched against my face when I turned into his hug. When I looked up at him, his hair had slivers of gray that I'd never noticed before. I couldn't picture us all as old, graying, and turning into the years.

Daddy left me and went over to a smaller table where a pitcher with drunken ice sweated. The cool November weather we'd hoped for the party hadn't come about. It was near eighty degrees.

"I'll just get these steaks salted and peppered." Dylan grabbed his sack and headed into the house.

Rebekha had decorated the yard and garden with tiny lights. On the tables were black tablecloths and white napkins, and there were clear containers of differing sizes with white candles inside ready to be lit once the sun went down. The skeeter candles' strong smell danced by every so often, reminding me of that night at the river with Dylan. A shiver pulled me up tight, thinking of what I'd denied that night, but what I denied no longer. I heated from tip to toe, turned thoughts away from Dylan's burning touch, and turned instead to the table. I rolled napkins into their holders; the breeze was picking up.

Near me, Andy was busy sneaky-eye watching the path that led to the backyard. How different from that boy Momma dropped off in the front yard without a bye I'm leaving. His hair had grown out over his ears and in the breeze it blew about, he jiggled his leg, cracked his knuckles. Everything about Andy moved. His skin shimmered, his bones clicked and clacked, his eyes searched, his blood rushed through his veins.

Bobby hadn't grown comfortable into his gangling height yet, and his auburn hair was shorter and neater than Andy kept his, but he was changing a lot, too. He had a calmer way about him, and since he'd had to start wearing glasses (when he remembered), it made him look older and more serious.

My brothers. I studied them and wondered after them and worried over them. I never thought how they might do the same for me, but I supposed they did in their way. Especially after Patrick at the lake and how they came to my rescue. If Micah had been there, he'd have done the same. Maybe Micah was the one needing the rescue more than I did, he—

Rebekha said, "This is your day, you don't do that."

"I want to help." I picked up another napkin.

The phone rang and she hurried inside to it.

Amy Campinelle and Mister Husband made it across the street without spilling the tons of food they carried over in a red Radio Flyer that had a rope attached to the handle so they didn't have to bend over to pull it. Amy Campinelle wore a Muumuu that looked as if every shade ever invented had been splashed on it and then swirled round into a big colorful mess. Her cotton-top hair frizzed out in a permanent wave gone wrong. Mr. Husband stroked her upper back, proud as lemons in a sweet lemonade punch.

Miss Darla floated over, looking timeless in a long flowing purple Infinite dress, which she wore as a halter. At her throat was a necklace made of silver and small amethyst stones. Her low black sandals had a square silver buckle. Her long gray hair was in a twisted up braid. Tucked into the braid was a peacock-tail comb. Dangling from her ears were silver hoop earrings. On her index finger was her ring with the large black stone that looked as if things swirled, an eye, or a figure of a person, or fire leaping—it was the strangest ring I'd ever seen. She'd once said the old Indian woman gave the ring to her, and it was in her will to give it to me, but I told her to stop talking about such things as wills. I didn't think Miss Darla would ever die, and she for certain didn't seem to age and never was sick or tired. Micah had said she was an enigma, and it was true.

I caught her eye and pointed to the green-eyed horse locket. Miss Darla nodded when she saw I was wearing the gift she'd given me when I was a girl. I didn't have a wish folded inside even though she'd said I was never too old to place wishes there. I wanted to believe her, but sometimes I forgot to open the clasp and place a wish. There were many things to being a woman that meant forgetting the magical parts. I stroked the locket and promised myself I'd always remember the magic. Miss Darla did, remembered the magic.

Rebekha came to me with a worried look, said, "That was Soot called. Soot's mother fell ill so they went to see about her. They send their love and will talk to you later."

"Is her momma going to be okay?"

"I don't know. Soot wasn't sure what was wrong."

"I'll call after her momma later on then."

"Me, too." Rebekha picked up a bowl, set it down five inches from where it was, then slid it over an inch, cocked her head, and then slid it half an inch. She nodded at it, as if to say, *Yes, right there.*

I poured potato chips into the bowl, careful not to move it from the spot Rebekha wanted it.

Jade was tucked in a lawn chair, her head rested against the back, looking at the sky. She was as her old self when she didn't let her face take on too many thoughts. The others drifted around the backyard, or slipped into the house to find more food or play another record. Rebekha would put on her Elvis; Daddy liked his piano or violin music; Andy would find anything that was loud and had electrical guitars; Bobby listened to Andy's records; Amy Campinelle and Mr. Husband were gaga over Hank Williams and Porter Wagoner and Dolly Parton; Miss Darla had strange music with languages I didn't understand; Jade, anything she could dance to. Momma used to dance to the greatest hits that blasted staticy from the old orange radio. I never thought before about what I liked. I most always listened to whatever someone else played.

Everyone was blabba-dabba-dooing.

I set upon the grass and pulled blades into a tiny pile.

Dylan had volunteered to cook the hamburgers Rebekha had

already shaped into patties, along with his steaks. As he slapped meat onto the grill, his hair didn't move much in the breeze and I wondered if he'd sprayed it, or put some kind of hair-jelly in it. When I was his wife, I'd know all the secrets of him. If he snored (bet not), if he stayed up late to watch television or went to bed right after the news, if he put his left leg in his britches first or his right. Jade said men let their habits out of the sack one piece at a time so women wouldn't run out screaming if they just dumped them all out on the counter at the once.

Something smacked me upside the head. I looked up and Andy was mouthing, "Whirly Brain!" while Bobby snorted in his hand. Stump raised his half-pinkie fingered left hand and silly-finger-waved at me.

I picked up the roll Andy had filched off the table and threw it back at Andy, but it missed. They laughed.

Daddy tapped a knife against his glass until everyone was still and quiet to hear what he had to say. "A toast to the to-be-weds; 'Love is not love, which alters when it alteration finds, or bends with the remover to remove. O, no! It is an ever-fixed mark, that looks on tempests and is never shaken. It is the star to every wandering bark, whose worth's unknown, although his height be taken.'" He paused, looked at me as if he wanted to tell me something important. His eyes changed, flickered with a decision, and he finally added, "To my Ariel and her beau, good fortune," then took a long drink.

Those who held drinks raised glasses, those who didn't pretended to.

Rebekha said to me, "Tell everyone how you met."

Dylan cleared his throat and then laughed one of those *oh this is a great story* laughs before he said, "I saw her around campus from time to time. Then I went to the theater, and there she was." He looked over at me. "I tried to catch her eye but she stayed in her own little world."

Amy Campinelle said, "Oh, that's our sweet girl, yeah. That's her for sure, on a stick and dipped in honey!"

"*Any*way," he gave a glance to Amy Campinelle, "I was on my way to class and saw her taking photos of tree bark. I stood not two-feet from her and she didn't notice anything but whatever it was she saw through the viewfinder. Right Kate?"

"Goddamn! Her name's Virginia Kate." Andy rolled his eyes. "Is that so hard? *Virrr-ginnn-niaaa* Kate."

"Andy!" Rebekha said.

I looked down at an ant crawling to the top of a blade of grass.

Dylan pretended he hadn't heard Andy. "After three performances, it was obvious she wasn't seeing anyone, so she wasn't ignoring me because of that. I was intrigued. Why was she most always alone? Why would she ignore me?"

Andy made a snorting sound, and Bobby snickled.

Dylan went on ignoring them. "There she was, this exotic girl standing under an oak tree with a bunch of sunflowers, her toes digging into the dirt. I made my move."

Amy Campinelle sniffled. "Oh, young people. I am about to pop with happy thoughts hearing this love story."

Mr. Husband said, "That sounds so sim-u-lar to our love story, doesn't it?"

"Yeah, except for the camera part, and the theater part, and the sunflowers part, and I was the one who came to you all handsome in your band uniform." Amy Campinelle little-girl giggled.

I stood, went to kiss Dylan on the cheek.

He turned his head so our lips touched instead.

A sudden hot wind smacked me stupid.

Daddy said, "'Journeys end in lovers meeting'" and then stepped to the sweating pitcher and poured liquid into his glass. He called out to Dylan, "Young man, want some of this?"

Dylan asked, "What is it?"

"Why, it's my special concoction. Come on; try some."

"Sure." Dylan downed the last of his wine, closed the top to the barbeque pit, and walked over to Daddy with a light-hearted step.

Daddy tasted it, and then said, "Wait, hold on. It may be watered-down. Let me freshen it up." He took the pitcher and went into the house with it.

Dylan called after him, "Can't wait to try it, Sir."

From inside, Daddy called out, "Be just a second."

I guessed that was how Daddy and Dylan got along. Over concoctions.

Dylan went back to the barbeque, opened the lid. "Almost there . . ."

Bobby said, "My stomach's caving in from *huuunnnger*."

"The meat should be ready soon." Dylan pressed a steak with his index finger.

Bobby and Stump staggered, holding onto their bellies as if dying of starvation.

Everyone laughed.

Daddy came out with the filled pitcher and laughed, too, even though he didn't know what we were laughing about. That was my daddy, always trying to belong in places he was coming late to. Daddy filled two glasses from the pitcher and said to Dylan, "Okay, got it tight now."

Dylan rushed over to Daddy, took the glass held out to him, tasted it, then said, "Oh yeah. This is fantastic."

Daddy nodded, then swilled. Dylan swilled. Swill swill.

Miss Darla leaned against the magnolia tree, her dress swirling about her ankles. Her black ring caught a glint of light from a skeeter candle. She asked Andy, "Where's that girlfriend of yours? I want to meet the girl who captured my best guy."

Andy pretended he hadn't heard her.

Miss Darla sipped her wine, her eyes knowing and true.

"Well, he sure hasn't been by here much lately." Bobby looked hurt.

"Aw Bobby. I'm sorry, just been busy working and stuff."

"What *stuff*, Andy?" Daddy gulped back a load, the ice clinked.

"Yeah, give us the scoop. What, or who, have you been getting busy with?" Dylan winked at Andy.

"None your beez-wise, Dilly-land." Andy's face was ten shades of red.

I was curious myself over Andy's girlfriend he'd kept quiet about. The girls he usually went out with were always blonde and skinny— same as Jade.

And as if we'd conjured her out of our curious, a girl came round the corner and straight to Andy. She didn't look a thing like Jade.

Andy jumped up. "Beth Anne!"

The girl smiled and she was someone I wanted to know all about. Her hair was to her chin, golden brown, and her eyes were a pretty hazel. Her cheeks spread out and puffed and it was so cute I wanted to pinch them. She wore dark blue shorts, a blue and orange top, and blue tenny-shoes. Her jangling bracelets sang as she hugged on my brother. They stood together looking at us.

We all came out of our trance and said, "Hey!" and she answered, "Hey y'all," then became shy as a newborn kitten.

Andy didn't even glance at Jade, who all a sudden decided she was interested in the goings-on of Andy's love life and walked over to introduce herself to Beth Anne.

Miss Darla went over to Beth Anne, too, and they all began yapping away. I knew then that Miss Darla liked Andy's girl.

I heard behind me, "Make sure the meat's not overdone. You have to be careful with steak. I think that's cooked long enough."

"Yes sir. Most of them are medium. The others are with the burgers in the warmer." Dylan began placing the meat on a platter. He had another glass of concoction in the hand that wasn't taking off the meat.

"I want mine medium, or just under that." Daddy sipped his own concoction and stared at the meat Dylan had on the plate.

"Yes sir. I got it all under control." Dylan looked over at me and shrugged a tiny shrug.

I felt sorry for him so I went over to give him a hug. He hugged me back and kissed me on the cheek. His lips were cold and wet.

There it was again. Daddy's glance at me, his looking away before I could read his eyes.

Rebekha came out with two pitchers, a lemonade and a sweet tea that she put on the small table. She came to Daddy, kissed his lips and rubbed his back. She loved him when he drank. She loved him when he quoted Shakespeare instead of talking to her. She loved him when he came home with guilty eyes. She loved him even when she suspected he still loved Momma. I never knew such love existed. I didn't think I could ever love like that, with blind eyes and too much hope.

Andy said, "Goddamn, I'm with Bobby. I'm about starved." He grabbed his stomach, growled like a hungry bear, and Beth Anne laughed, her face opening like a big flower soaking up the sun and rain.

"I know, that's what I'm saying," Bobby said. He stood near Andy, giving Beth Anne sideways glances, but I think he liked her, even if she did take his big brother away from him more than he was already gone away.

"The meat is ready for thy table, Sirs," Dylan said as he bowed toward Andy, and then to Bobby.

Everyone goggled at the food on the long picnic table we'd borrowed from the Campinelles, including the wagonload of the Campinelle's famous football party chicken jambalaya, crawfish bisque, rice, fried catfish strips, fried shrimp, hushpuppies, a pan of dewberry cobbler, two bottles of muscadine wine, a six pack of beer, and the fried potatoes that were almost gone from all us picking at them while waiting.

Rebekha placed desserts on the smaller table with the drinks, except for Jade's pudding that needed to stay cold. I also knew Rebekha had baked a lemon pie and whipped together a Hershey bar pie.

Miss Darla had prepared potato salad as she always did, with extra onions. She said to me, "Your guy's trying hard to fit in."

"I know."

I wasn't sure if we'd spoken aloud or in our old way.

She nodded her head, as if by nodding it settled everything.

Daddy settled next to me, smelling of Bouquet De Concoction. Dylan to my left side, smelling the same as Daddy. Rebekha was on the other end of the table passing food and plates and looking happy, even with Daddy's booze-breath.

Andy nestled in close to Beth Anne and they spoke low to each other. Jade looked almost disappointed that Andy no longer sweet-eyed her. People sure were funny.

Everyone settled in, and we ate as if it was the last meal we'd ever again have. That was what a person had to do in Louisiana, or else people thought something was wrong, or a person was sick, or crazy, or a yankee.

Dylan and Daddy argued over the Peloponnesian War, then about Alexander the Great. Dylan said Alexander the Great was in a coma and not really dead when they all thought he was dead. Daddy said, *Prove it.* And on and on they sparred.

Rebekha asked to see my ring again, and I stuck out my hand to show it to everyone. Dylan grabbed my hand and kissed where the ring was and it was wet where he kissed so I wiped it on my shorts.

Just as I'd worried, whenever I was with my family, I looked at Dylan with different eyes than when I was with him alone. Seemed he drank more, talked more (if that could be true), argued more, everything more than when we were alone. And then there was Daddy's eyes, like he wanted to say something but didn't want to. I couldn't figure it out, so I pushed doubts down into Rebekha's garden to see if they'd grow. Maybe if I buried things they could take up to blooming answers I'd need, peculiar fruit.

After dessert was over and everyone had about enough of food and of each other, we all began cleaning up and making plates to take home. Rebekha rubbed her flat stomach and told Amy Campinelle to take home any leftover food they wanted in the red wagon because her pants were getting tight.

Amy Campinelle laughed at that one, rubbing her own not at all flat stomach.

Dylan, Daddy, and Mr. Husband took the Campinelle's picnic table back across the street. I could hear Daddy and Dylan arguing over something else, probably the best way to hold a picnic table, while Mr. Husband belly-laughed at them.

Miss Darla spoke to Beth Anne for a long time under the magnolia tree. Beth Anne looked back at Andy with softened eyes. I wondered what Miss Darla was telling her, since those private thoughts with others were always closed off, but whatever it was, it made Beth Anne *very happy*.

I wanted that *very happy* look. I was going to get that *very happy* look. I was. If I had to stomp my way over ornery thoughts and crawl over my worries, then that was what I'd do.

Miss Darla came to kiss me goodbye, took the plate of food from Rebekha, and levitated back to her house. Beth Anne and Jade slipped inside Rebekha and Daddy's house, yappering away.

The rain that had stayed away during the party threatened; I lifted my face to the coming wind and let it smooth the worry lines away.

Andy slipped up next to me. "Well?"

I turned to look at him. "Well what?"

"You know good and well *what*."

"I like her a lot, Andy."

His eyes lit bright. "I figured you would." Then he patted my arm. "Dylan's okay, I guess. He acts like he wants to make you happy and that's all that matters, right?"

"Thank you for saying that."

He shrugged and then smoothed away to find his girl.

When Dylan came back with Daddy, they were still arguing. Daddy said something about the sonnets and Dylan said something about he hadn't read them critically and Daddy said then you can't call yourself an expert and Dylan said he never said he was, and there it all went between those two.

I stood amongst my family and friends—those near and almost near, amongst the spirits, amongst the family and friends who weren't there but their memory and thoughts were, amongst the trees and grass and the quickening wind, amongst the flickering candles that were melting away, amongst voices and smells and touches. I'd planted my feet in the Louisiana ground, but no roots had grown. Yet, there I was. And there they all were.

Dylan slammed back the last of the concoction from the emptied pitcher. Daddy slammed back his. I was the one turned my eyes away that time.

Everyone and everything swirled about me.

I was to be married. The party was the glue that sealed the envelope.

I was to be married. It was on everyone's face as they took food from Rebekha and remembered why we all were there.

I was to be married. There was a roaring in my head. The wind blew a napkin across the yard in a dance. All about me swirled leaves and twigs. The storm that had held off decided it was tired of waiting.

Rain fell in fat drops on those who'd come back outside, and as everyone hurried back inside, I stayed to face the sky. I opened my eyes wide and let drops fall, then I closed my eyes and let the drops run down my cheeks. It felt like tears but it was rain.

⇛ • ⇚

Into the fresh dishsoap- and water-filled sink, Jade and I added our snack dishes to the dirty ones that had been soaking since before the party.

"I wash, you dry?" I asked.

"Shoot, let them soak some more and we'll get them in the morning."

"I can't stand to leave them. Please?"

She lifted an eyebrow. "Well, if you want to wash them, do it. Leave them in the drainer and I'll put them away tomorrow."

"Pretty please with sugar and spice and all that's nice?"

She grabbed a dishrag from the drawer. "I swear, you and washing dishes."

"It helps me think."

"Uh huh. Well, it helps me be bore bored booorrringly bored."

"Hush."

As Jade and I stood side-by-side washing and drying, I looked out the kitchen window and admired the rainy night. I wished I could see the stars and moon I knew were still there, just beyond the storm's end. Those stars and moon shone down on everyone I loved and everyone I missed and that made the world seem a lot smaller than it really was.

"You sure are quiet." Jade began putting away dishes.

"I told you it helps me think." I scrubbed at the last pot.

"Well, at least talk to me so I won't be so bored."

"What do you think of Beth Anne?"

"She's sweet and I'm really glad for Andy." She grunted as she reached to put up the macaroni bowl.

I rinsed the pot, unplugged the drain and let the dirty soapy water glug down.

Jade took the pot to dry and put away, said, "Y'all didn't talk about a wedding date."

"I told him I didn't feel like it."

Jade gave me a look, shrugged, and then told me about how in dance the entire body has to be together as a team, breathing, steps, body aligned, focused. How if one thing is off, then it's not going to be a perfect dance performance. She said that's how she thought about a good marriage.

Later that night, I lay awake and since the storm had passed, was able to stare out at the moon and stars. It shone on my face, across the room, over the house, the entire city, the universe. It was trying to show me something, but I turned to my pillow instead, weary from the day and all of my wayward thoughts.

From far away, Grandma Faith called to me, from up top her mountain high.

I was too tired, too tired, too tired to listen.

Chapter 18

Deny was a woman's word

Rebekha kidnapped me in her brand new but still serious Dodge for a day of wedding shopping. It was a pretty not-quite-spring day in Louisiana Land. The azaleas were blooming, and though most of Louisiana stayed green in the winter months, spring would lush out with a big happy shout and cry.

Dylan had set the wedding date for spring and that was that.

We first went to Soot's for breakfast. Soot fussed over Rebekha as if she were a movie star come to visit. I knew Soot was trying to keep her mind off her momma and the cancer lump the doctor found. Her momma had been so sick, and I'd been helping out as much as I could in the diner. Soot had said talking about cancer was off-limits in the diner, since that was her one cancer-free safe place, so no one said a word about it.

"You two look like spring breezes." Soot led us to a table with a flower in a vase.

I knew what I wanted and ordered sweet potato pancakes, fresh-made strawberry syrup, and scrambled eggs.

Rebekha's eyes grew wide. "Well. Let's see." She shrugged. "I think I'll have the same."

While waiting for our food, Rebekha took from her purse a list and a yellow pencil. She checked off the word *Breakfast*, and said, "After we eat, let's go by the drug store. They're having a sale on lipsticks."

Sure enough, *Drug Store* was the next listing.

The air filled with good smells. Marco sang a song in his strange-sounding French. Soot called out orders to him from the other customers. Little Mae Lynn helped by filling salt shakers, getting more salt on the counter than in the shaker. She looked just like her momma. I hugged her little neck, then went back to my table. I couldn't believe how big and smart she'd grown. Peggy Elaine wasn't there. She was louder and had more energy than Mae Lynn, and first crawled and then toddled about the diner making a racket and pulling on things with her pudgy arms so that Soot and Marco had to have the babysitter come fetch her away. She'd been mad, her face red and unhappy, but Soot said she always settled down and was excited and happy once she had something else to do.

Each time those little girls had slipped from Soot's body I'd seen the light of Soot's face as she'd held them, eyes shining out with love and wonder. And big man Marco with tears running down as he stroked his daughters' faces. I wondered then if children could make a marriage bind tighter instead of breaking it apart. It sure seemed so with Soot, Marco, little sweet Mae Lynn, and tiny feisty Peggy Elaine.

When our breakfast was ready and Soot brought it to us, she leaned over and said that Marco was nervous over what Rebekha would think about the food. Soot grinned at us, and then left to take care of someone else.

Marco had taken extra care with our plates and I thought to go hug his neck, but didn't, since that would embarrass him. There were sliced strawberries fanned out on the plate, and he'd dusted powdered sugar over them. The pancakes were fluffy and light and were served with his own fresh homemade Louisiana strawberry syrup that came in a little creamer pitcher. The eggs were golden, light, and fluffy.

We both dug in.

I drank two cups of Soot's dark coffee that was so strong it could have jumped out of the cup and said *hello wake up wake up wake up!*

While we ate, I caught Marco looking over at us several times.

I cleaned every bit of my plate.

Rebekha left a few bites of pancake and a bite of egg, and said if she ate any more she'd explode.

Marco called out, "How was it? Did you like it? I'm the one fixin' to blow a gasket over here."

We all laughed.

Rebekha said, "Those were the best pancakes and the best syrup I have ever eaten in my entire life. Marco, you are a genius! Please tell me I can have the recipes."

Marco's face turned as red as the syrup. I'd never seen him look that way before and I had to try hard not to laugh at him. He said, "Okay, for you. Nobody else, so's don't tell nobody else."

Rebekha promised she'd keep his recipes safe.

After Rebekha slapped away my hand and paid our bill, I hugged Mae Lynn and Soot, while Rebekha took from Marco the hand-written recipes. We groaned our full selves into the car and took off for Eckerd's, where we bought a mud mask, tubes of creams and buffers to rub on our feet to make them smooth and pretty, lotion with extra emollients to make the skin extra emollied, new lipstick that was on sale, and a red fingernail polish for me and rose for Rebekha.

In the car, Rebekha took out her list and pencil, and this time checked off *Drug Store*. The next item read *State Capitol grounds.*

She drove me downtown to the capitol ground gardens where many brides had their pictures taken. We walked along the big oaks with their heavy old limbs, the magnolias, the big old statue of one of Louisiana's peculiar governors, and towering over it all, the art deco capitol building that Jade had said was nothing but that statue governor's phallic symbol.

Rebekha watched a girl pose in her wedding finery, said, "Maybe you'd like to have your photo done here, too."

"Maybe."

"It's a beautiful spot."

We watched the girl fake-smiling in a dress that was a lace explosion. Her piled hair was so big and high, I bet I could hide in there where no one would find me.

It *was* a pretty place, and the oak trees bent over the girl as if they wanted to touch her and tell her all her dreams would come true so she should have on a real smile instead of a bratty scowl that was supposed to be a happy-day face. Those oaks were old and wise, like grandpas. I'd always wanted a wise old grandpa, one with candy in his pocket. He'd pat his knee and I'd set there while he told me stories about when he was a young dog strutting in a world war or when he met his true love or when he had his first car and drove it to a dime dance or sock hop or whatever grandpas did back then.

Instead, I had Mee Maw Laudine's parade of men, and Grandpa Luke who was cruel to Grandma Faith and then in jail and then dead. Until the end, he wasn't sorry. The only letter I'd ever written to him just to ask him to see me, to know me, to give me some small gift of a grandpa, and he was still the same. Not even death banging on his door made him good enough to write me back a nice letter that wasn't full of hate and sorry spite. Death and cancer didn't make all men noble. Only those who were noble to begin with.

Rebekha touched my arm. "Hon, you okay? You look sad."

"I'm fine."

"Is it the wedding? I know how stressful it can be." She reached to stroke a bit of Spanish moss hanging from the oak tree we passed. The giant arms of the tree rested on the ground; it was an old old man of a tree.

I told her, "I'm just thinking on some things."

We walked along for a spell, headed back to her car, and then on to the mall, *check*, to look for anything that called to our eye. Rebekha found an outfit for the wedding, and shoes. Then we went to the University Club for lunch, *check*. She said we could think about having the reception there. We ordered shrimp salads since we were still a little full from breakfast.

When we were near done with our lunch, a honey-haired girl stopped by the table and asked, "Aren't you Professor Carey's wife?" She licked her lips.

Rebekha gap-toothed-smiled up at her, answered, "Yes, I am."

The girl licked her lips again, tossed back her hair and smarmed out a, "I thought so. Well, tell him Alexia said hey." She turned and wiggled off.

I took a sip of water.

Rebekha opened her purse, took out pencil and list. "So. Well. Let's see." She pressed her finger into the paper and followed along as she spoke, "We've had breakfast, Eckerd's, the Capitol grounds, the mall, and now lunch."

"I'm having a great time," I said, then sipped water again.

"Next is your wedding dress and shoes at the boutique."

"That sounds like fun." I took to finishing off my salad.

Rebekha pushed away her plate.

The room filled with how things had been before with Daddy's tomfoolery, and how I hoped things had not remained. It could be nothing, nothing at all.

She smoothed the list. "If there's anything I left out, just tell me." She grabbed her pencil and held it over the list, waited.

"You've thought of everything."

"Yes. Well." She put the list and pencil away.

I glubbed down the rest of my water.

Rebekha paid the bill, and put on a happy face as we headed towards the table where the honey-haired girl was tittering with her friends. All of them with hair perfect, their make-up just so, even their food looked fashionable.

Rebekha outshined them all, made them look like little fools.

Rebekha chitter-chattered all the way to the boutique. I hated how the mood had changed and hoped her light-filled eyes would return.

I had my wish. When we stepped into the boutique, Rebekha shucked off her worrisome mood as if it were an old rotten cornhusk. She checked off another word in her list and tucked the list and pencil in her purse, and turned to me with her face cleared of bad things. I breathed out a breath of glad.

The boutique was full of dresses. I tried on one that had lace that came up to my neck and scratched like crazy. Another one had a skirt that billowed in a *Gone with the Wind* way. Another plunged down until my breasts were two loaves of bread to be admired behind the glass at a bakery. Still another was slithery and tight and better for a singer in a nightclub.

Each time, the saleswoman poked in her head and asked, "How's that one? No? Then try this."

When I was about to give up and wear blue jeans and a t-shirt to my own wedding, she handed me a simple gown that had pearled buttons down the back. When I slipped it over my head, it flowed over my body like water.

The saleswoman said, "That's the one."

She helped me button up, then left the changing room so I could ready myself to step out.

I regal-walked into the room where Rebekha waited.

Rebekha's said, "It's perfect for you."

I felt as pretty as a bride in a magazine, unlike any girl I'd ever been or any woman I'd lived with. I was a mystery in all that white.

The saleswoman clucked her tongue. She rushed over and lifted my heavy hair. "Imagine exposing your lovely neck." She cater-cocked her head right, then left, said, "Your coloring is perfect for this dazzling white. And with those dark eyes and hair, are you . . . what?"

Rebekha said, "She's a beautiful girl who came to us from West Virginia," and eyed the woman as if to say, *and don't ask questions that aren't your concern.*

I was used to people asking me where my kin came from and I for sure did not know all the stories of their lives. Maybe one day I'd find out, when it was important enough for me to have all the answers to everything, if that day ever did come. Maybe I didn't need to know, because I'd be making all the kin to come and they'd be part me and part Dylan.

The woman pulled, tugged, and pinned the dress to make sure it fit right in all the places it should fit. She said, "This won't take much altering. Make sure you don't gain or lose any weight." She unbuttoned me.

I figured I better lay off the extra Zeros, and eating Soot's, Dylan's, and Rebekha's cooking, at least for a while. When I went back to the changing room and slipped off the dress, I became regular old Virginia Kate again, but it was all right.

As the whole day had been, Rebekha wouldn't let me pay for a thing, not the dress, the satiny shoes, or the pretty underwear the saleswoman recommended a bride should wear. Rebekha said she'd been looking forward to having our day since I'd told her Dylan asked me to marry him. When we left the store and slipped into her car, she turned to me and said, "I couldn't be happier for you, Virginia Kate."

"Thank you."

"It doesn't seem all that long ago you came to live with me."

"I know."

"You were so quiet, so hurt."

I remembered that girl.

"You and your brothers lit up the house with all your personalities. I feel incredibly lucky."

"I don't know what would've happened to us kids."

"Your daddy made it happen, too. He wanted you to come."

"I know."

"He tries so hard to do the right things. He really does."

"I know."

She pulled out her list, looked at it, put it back into her purse, started the car, and said, "Well. Onward we go! Next stop, we'll go look at the church Dylan likes."

We rode on with the wind blowing our hair—hers red-blonde and light; mine the opposite. Our strands mixed. I had always wished our bloods were mixed. As soon as the thought nibbled at my brain, I felt bad. I couldn't deny my kin, couldn't deny sweet sister mountain and the holler and the little white house where Momma was. The mountains where Grandma Faith was born and then died. I could never deny it all. It could never deny me.

Rebekha's knuckles were relaxed on the wheel. Her face wasn't tensed or strained and she hummed a happy tune.

Deny. I thought how funny a word that was. Deny was a woman's word. Deny kept us huge-grinning with relaxed knuckles and cars flying down the road to churches where men and women joined as one even when one of the joined wasn't certain.

Chapter 19

Crock of sages, ain't for me, let me side of beef to eat

My wedding day began with the old hornets buzzing my head. I creak-boned out of bed, swallowed four aspirin, and drank three cups of sugary-creamed coffee. Last night, Jade had given me a hot oil treatment with olive oil, and it took two washings of dishsoap to get it all out. The detergent made it dry, so she put mayonnaise in it. The smell made me want a sandwich, so I rinsed that out and told her to leave my hair alone. I woke smelling like a salad. In the shower, under a spray of hot Louisiana water, I soaped my hair with shampoo and used extra conditioner to get the nasty smells out.

I turned the bar of Dove soap over and over in the washrag and took in Momma's smell. She loved Dove and kept the bars hidden away in the cabinet, just for her. Except the night she let us all use her Dove and we danced to the music from the orange radio. I'd bought bars for myself and both loved and hated what it brought forth as it released its scent. I'd wanted to take a bath and soak in the tub, but was afraid time would get away from me. Jade took showers all the time and couldn't understand why I favored baths. We'd have arguments about whether baths made us cleaner than showers, and whether baths used more water, and whether our skin was better off soaking in a tub of water or hit by stinging showers.

I lifted the bar of soap to my nose and took in Momma farther down into my innards. The steam from the shower was as the mists on my mountain. A tiny wind swept round from the water and steam built up. The West Virginia wind blew us kids as if we were dried leaves fallen from the branch, until we settled in the house in Louisiana, settled at least until we blew about again. Funny how things worked out in life.

Out of the shower and dried off, I slathered on the new lotion from the drug store, put on my robe, and went on back down the hall to my room. The floors creaked out a good morning until I stepped on the scatter rug to quiet them. I didn't pay attention to the white dress hanging from the hook on the door, yet it hollered loud at me all the same. Turning to my dresser to find my new satiny lacy wedding day underwear, I saw Jade had left me a white box with a note on top.

The note read, *Here is something blue. Actually, silver and blue, but who cares? Enjoy! Love, Jadesta.*

Inside the box was a Zero candy bar. I hadn't had candy since Rebekha bought my wedding dress. I tore open the wrapper and gobbled it while looking at what else she'd put in the box. Underneath pink tissue paper, she had placed a picture of a hee-hawing Mee Maw wearing a snarled wig, placed in a pink polka dot frame to match the pink polka dot pantsuit Mee Maw wore. Jade knew I hated pink, so I knew she was being funny.

The note taped to the photo read, *And, here's your something old!*

She must have pilfered Mee Maw Laudine out of the box of memories I'd pulled from under my bed the other night. We'd gone through those photos, laughing at some and not so laughing at others.

I slipped on the lacy underwear, and pulled from my dresser a glob of clothes, threw on a pair of Rebekha's gardening britches and an old t-shirt that showed the New York skyline dark against the red of the shirt. Micah had sent it to me when he'd first moved there. He was as mysterious as he ever was, and his being that way worried me more than gnats flying in my eyes. Sometimes wishes came true and sometimes they did not. Recognizing that was what grown women did, but really, I'd known those things since I was a little girl.

Jade called to me from the living room. "Would you hurry? I still have to get ready."

"I'm coming. Can't you hold onto your horses?" I grabbed things, here, there, yonder.

"You should have been ready twenty minutes ago."

"We have plenty of time."

She was right outside my door when she mad-dog-barked, "Get out of that room and get your *butt* out here and let's get your *butt* to the church and I don't want to hear any whining or I'll *Kick. Your. Butt.*"

I opened the door, laughed at her standing there with her brows all pushed together.

"I swear, Vee. You'd drive a Baptist preacher to drink."

Baptist preachers did worse things than drink, but I wouldn't think about Momma and Preacher Foster Durant and lost babies who may or may not have been from that union or whatever had happened too long ago to set my mind to whirling on it.

Jade rushed me to her car, practically tossed me into it by the seat of my britches, jumped in the driver's seat, shoved her keys into the ignition, started the car with a *vroom*, roared backward down her driveway, and headed with haste to the Methodist church. I wondered if Dylan was rushing around.

He couldn't see me until I walked towards him down the aisle, since it was a tradition. Dylan wanted most things to be about someone's tradition. He wanted me to quit my jobs and take care of a house and fifty-galleven kids. Dylan laughed when I said I wasn't so sure about fifty-galleven kids. I almost felt as if I was a brood mare and he'd picked me for my sturdy hips.

When Dylan's parents came to town, his momma had harped on about traditions, too. I told her I didn't think too much about traditions, and she'd said, "Maybe because you don't have any of your own, but we do."

"Me and mine have our ways that suit us just fine."

She sniffed. "I'm sure *you and yours* are just fine, but *my family* has done things in a certain way for generations."

Dylan had cleared his throat and asked his daddy, whom he called Father when he was mad or Dad when he wasn't, if he wanted another drink. Dylan's momma and I stared each other down. I was feeling ornery about the whole thing, until I watched Dylan's momma watch Dylan's daddy tip that booze drink and let it slide down his gullet. Her eyes were so familiar to a little girl's dark eyes who watched her parents give love to their booze that I wanted to reach over and take her hand and squeeze it, to tell her I understood those shattered hope eyes.

Dylan's daddy began yapperventerlating about properties and houses, and Dylan joined in to talk about where we could live after he sold his house, and about property in California. I'd hoped he wouldn't sell his old wood-framed house with the glassed in sunroom, the warm wood floors, and the kitchen with the pots hanging, but I also knew Dylan was itching to build with his own plans, just as he was itching to move back to California one day.

All the years I'd wanted to leave Louisiana for the place that called me Home. But California?

A wizened ghost had slipped up and said, *Not for you. Not for our Virginia Kate* . . .

It had slapped me then how I was marrying a man who had different thoughts than I did. Who wanted different things than I did. I wondered if that's how all marriages started out. Two people who tried to become one and instead butted heads until one gave in, and then they'd take turns on who gave in to what until it was all settled and compromises were made and one day they were old and just didn't remember whose thoughts were whose any more.

Jade pushed my shoulder. "Are you listening to me or off in your own world again?" I noticed then that Jade hadn't turned on her radio.

"What?"

"Oh good god, Vee. I just told you the meaning of life and now I'm not going to repeat it, so you'll have to figure it out on your own."

Pooched-lipped, I answered, "Maybe I already did."

"Huhn. You wish." Jade rolled up to the side of the church, turned off the engine, and leaned back against her seat. "The Methodist church looks nice."

"I guess so." It looked as if it'd been standing there for hundreds of years, even if it hadn't. At least the church had a personality that said, *Hi there, come on inside and get married. Come inside any old time; I'll be here waiting. I might get old Jesus to show up, unless he's busy, which he most times is.*

Jade fiddled with her keys. "I can't believe you have to move out now."

"Yeah. I know." A hornet dive-bombed my head.

"Well, we can't sit here forever." She reached into her purse, pulled out a stick of gum, opened it, and popped the gum into her mouth, chewed like a cow with cud. When she'd worked that gum enough to speak, Jade asked, "Are you sure this is what you want?"

"What?" A crow landed on a crepe myrtle and shrieked at me.

"Never mind. I'm just being the cautionary friend. That's my job. Yes-in-deedy-do." She chewed chewed, then said, "Well, I guess I'll see you after I get showered and all."

The crow scuttled back and forth on the limb, its beady little eyes staring right at me. It let out a husky caw that sounded like some kind of warning to me.

Jade said, "Wrigley's spear-a-mint is good, but those commercials are annoying."

The crow moved its head back and forth, back and forth, then jumped to the right, the left, cocked its head, and let out another fat caw.

Jade leaned over and plopped a kiss on my cheek. Her lips were cool against my hot face. Her spearmint breath was soft.

I thought maybe I was getting a fever, and then I would be too sick to get married. The crow opened its mouth, but that time no sound came out. It shook its head no no no.

Jade said, "Go on. Get inside."

The crow flew off and disappeared.

"It's getting late," she said.

All a sudden, the church didn't seem an old friendly place anymore, but a place that would swallow me and keep me in a dungeon where I'd howl out my pitiful existence for thousands upon thousands of years, wailing and gnashing my teeth to nubs.

"Vee?"

I looked for the crow.

"For god's sake. *Get. Out. Of. This. Car. Now.*" Jade pushed at me. "If you don't, then I'm taking off and we'll just drive and drive and the whole thing will be called off. You'll be one of those jilting brides who leaves the groom standing at the altar pulling at his collar and he'll forever hate women and weddings for the rest of his sorry life. He'll climb to the top of the Capitol and pick off people with his rifle, and it'll be all your fault." She quirked a brow. "Of course, that may be something we could live with if it secures your freedom today." She laughed.

"Well, Dylan doesn't believe in guns."

"That's not the point I was—"

"And he says he loves weddings so's he'd have another one if it wasn't me I bet."

"Figures." Jade let out an I'm-the-only-one-who-could-ever-be-your-friend-because-you'd-drive-them-insane-sigh, then said, "Either get out or I'm taking off and driving into next week."

"One more minute?"

Jade nodded, then looked away from me and out towards the road.

Finally, I slung myself and my things out of her car and stepped to the church, turning once to wave at her. She waved at me, and then sped away. My feet moved back toward the curb, my heart hammered ready to jump out of my chest, my lungs tried to suck up thick wet Louisiana air. She was gone. I turned back to go inside.

I couldn't step into church without remembering that long ago Easter with Preacher Foster Durant's handkerchief just a going as he mopped his brow once he had a gander at the power of Momma. I wondered if he thought of her sometimes and blushed during his sermons at the Baptist church with the cross Momma had stared at so long and so hard. Daddy had sure climbed to the lonely house on the hill to think on things much more often after all that happened.

Momma had made lots of bread that day I'd overheard her telling Daddy about another child coming along to ruin everything. She used Grandma Faith's recipes as she always had. Momma told me baking bread helped her to think. She kneaded the dough until it gave up answers. She thought things over while creating the sponge for her salt-rising bread. The house smelled so wonderful, it didn't seem as if anything bad could come out of it, or into it. The bread baking must have offered a solution, for Momma drank the potion Aunt Ruby gave her, and then cried and held on to her womb. She had gone to the hospital and came back later, emptied.

As I walked between the pews, the stained glass allowed golden light beams to filter through. One touched the top of my head, as if Jesus tried to pull me to him because I was so far away from him. I took in big lung-exploding gobs of air, wanted to believe in something that powerful, wanted a saving as people who went to church said happened. I wanted the answers to secrets. I wanted many things. There I was, soon to be married, no longer my momma's little girl (*or aren't you?* came a whisper). There I was in a church with light falling on my head like a daddy's touch. There I was. If I'd ever learned how to cry, I'd have cried then.

I put down my wedding day things, draped the dress over the back of the pew, eased myself down on the hard wood, put my head in my hands, pressed my palms to my eyes, and let the world go dark. *Oh Fionadala, if only I were a girl again, riding you up sweet sister mountain, the wind in our faces. I miss you, though I know I shouldn't because I'm a woman not a girl, but still I do. I miss riding upon your strong back, the wind mixing up your mane with my hair, your tail flying out behind you. Up we'd fly, farther than anyone could see us, away from my thoughts, away from the sad and fights.*

Everything was still until I felt a hand on my shoulder. I thought maybe Jesus had finally come to give me all the answers I needed. It was Andy gazing down at me with a worry crease between his brows.

"Hey," I said. "Well, we're in a church."

"Hey," then, "Yeah, church." Andy kicked at the carpet, looked over at the stained glass, and tapped his fingers on the wood. "Remember when I was a little kid and kept yelling for Uncle Jesus?"

"You sure were cute then. What happened?"

He flicked me on the ear with his thumb and forefinger. "Ha ha, very funny."

"That was the best Easter ever. And later, it was the worst."

He dropped down beside me, then fiddled with the Hymnals. Opening it to a page, he began singing in a screechy off-keyed voice, "Crock of sages, ain't for me, let me side of beef to eat . . ."

"Good god, we're in church, you fool." I laughed, though, slapping my thighs.

"You're just afraid Gawd will smote you to Kingdom Come if you aren't perfect."

"I am not."

Andy fell on his knees with his hands held in prayer. "No, *puh-leeze* Uncle Jesus, I didn't mean to fornicate and pontificate and sordidificate."

"Andy!" My face burned.

He hee hawed, then jumped up and crowded close to me on the pew, pushing me over with the weight of his body.

We set there for a bit, then I asked, "Do you ever think about Momma?"

"Why would I?"

I wondered if the church knew all our secret wants and our secret hurts. If I believed that wishes or things whispered in the dark were listened to, I may have said some prayers, but I didn't. I checked my watch. It was past time to meet Rebekha in the bride's room so she could help me dress.

Andy thumped his fingers on the pew in front of him.

"Where's Beth Anne?"

"She's getting all prettied. As if she can get any prettier." That time it was Andy's turn to redden.

"You two seem serious."

Andy shrugged, but the corners of his mouth lifted.

"I hate weddings," I said.

Andy stood and grabbed my arm. "There's still time to change your mind. We can zoom off into the wild blue yonder, go fly a kite like when we were kids, and forget this wedding crap. Dilly can find another wife. Does Barry Manilow have a sister?" He brayed, let go my arm.

Maybe I could run away. Out the door. All the way home. Tell Jade I changed up my mind. We'd laugh about it. The dress could go back, or could wait for another time. There was still time to change everything.

Andy ran to the preacher's podium. He turned to me and held his hands in the air. "I sayeth to you, bruthahs and sistahs, this-a woman is making a big mis-take-ah." He did a jerky jig, and then flopped on the floor, flinging about his hands and feet and yelling, "I'm healed! Good gawd a' mighty, I'm healed of my ah-flic-tu-ons!"

"Andy! Stop it!" But I was laughing, holding on to my stomach as if I'd laugh it right out of my throat and it would land on the church carpet.

He moseyed back over to me, an innocent lamb look scrubbing his face clean. He said, "Well, I guess I'll let you go on and do what makes you happy."

I stood and hugged my younger brother. He didn't break the hug. I flicked his ear with my thumb and forefinger as he had me, then grabbed my things. "Well, time for me to go get doodied up."

Andy sunk into the pew. I turned to leave, and he said, "Sister?"

I turned back, baby-cradling my dress to keep it smooth. "Yeah?"

"I do think of Momma sometimes." He looked right into my eyes. "But, I don't know that she ever thinks of what *could* have become of us, and that's what bothers me most of all." He then folded his hands in his lap and lowered his head. I wondered if he was praying, or remembering, or hiding the rest of his thoughts from me. He was my brother. I was his sister. We'd lost each other for a time before, and then found each other again. I had the urge to grab him tight, as I'd done to Micah that day in the holler when I didn't want him to leave. As I'd have done to Andy the day I left the holler if Momma hadn't of taken him off to town with Mrs. Mendel, tricking him and me.

I left Andy alone and headed myself on down the hallway. Through the open door of one room were the flowers. I stepped in to have a look and the air filled with sweet smell, as if I'd opened my window in the holler on a nice spring day when it seemed as if everything was blooming scent, even the dirt. There were white dogwood blossoms, lilacs, roses, and lisianthus, along with a box of corsages and boutonnières. I touched the petals, took deep inhales of flower. I'd make sure everyone took home all the flowers so they'd be loved, at least until all their pretty left them and they'd then be tossed away. It was time to start the wheels to rolling. Rebekha was waiting.

Chapter 20

I'm a wife

When I at last made my way to Rebekha, she had her back to me, looking out of the window. The fitted tea-length dress we'd found on our shopping day shimmered over her slim body. She turned and when she saw it was me, she said, "There you are." Rebekha was stunning. The emerald green dress made her green eyes pop. Her hair was in a French twist and around her neck was the single-pearl necklace she wore the day I first met her, and all the days after that. The pearl lay against her chest where I imagined it thrummed with her heartbeat.

"Yup, here I am." Then, "You look beautiful."

"I thought maybe you weren't coming." She turned a telling shade of pink. "I mean. Well. Anyway, let's get started." She took my dress from me and caught the hanger on the hook. I put down my other things. Rebekha pointed to the chair. "Sit."

I did as told.

She took the hairbrush from my bag and ran it from my scalp to end. "Your hair is so long."

"Maybe I should cut it." Momma kept hers long, as least the last time I saw her it was. I imagined all her pretty had come back with the force of a big wind slamming against a mountain rising high. The mountain could take anything thrown at it and still hold onto its beauty. That's what I believed about Momma. No accident or on purpose could take away her shine.

"If I had hair like you instead of my fine hair, I'd grow it out to my collar bone." Rebekha pulled out hair doodads from her big make-up case and placed them on the table. "Did you hear from Micah? Is he coming?"

I shook my head.

"Maybe he'll come."

I didn't think so. I just didn't *feel* it.

She smoothed my hair with her left palm, pulled the brush with her right, smoothed, pulled, smoothed, pulled; I was sleepy. After a time, when she'd finished brushing my hair way past when it was already smoothed, she put down the brush, picked up four bobby pins, and handed them to me.

I told her, "He isn't coming. I know it."

"Maybe he wants to surprise you."

"No, I *know* he isn't."

"Well, people say siblings have connections that can't be explained. I imagine that's what you're feeling about Micah." She took two bobby pins from me and pushed them into my hair as she twisted it and molded it and made it feel as if it might be pulled out of my ever-loving scalp. She took and pushed in the other two, and then handed me more bobby pins to hold. She said, "This will be really pretty, but are you sure you want a twist, too?"

"Yes Ma'am." I held up the bobby pins.

She worked away. "Your brother must have felt so haunted after what happened that day. He was just a little boy to have witnessed such a horrible death."

I pictured phantoms poking at Micah, making him remember what happened to Uncle Ar-vile over and over. The hole in our Uncle's belly. The blood. Aunt Ruby screaming. Micah's hands tingling from the push. Daddy coming to get us.

"Oh, listen to us. Let's talk about happy things on your wedding day."

I nodded careful, so I wouldn't muss what she was doing.

Rebekha talked about Amy Campinelle and her new garage sale shopping addiction. After pushing about forty-eight bobby pins into my hair, Rebekha picked up a pearled comb and hammered it into the fold. She then took up to talking about her wedding to Daddy, while she stuck baby's breath into the comb, then sprayed a good bit of Adorn over my hair, diddly-doed with the bikini brush, and then sprayed more Adorn.

I hated hair spray, hated my hair pulled tight (even though I'd told her to do it), hated bobby pins pushing into my scalp. I was full of ornery crankiness.

After I went insane three times and came back again twice, she said, "There. All done. I've never seen so much hair fit into this severe a style. I hope it stays put." She held the mirror in front of me.

I stared at the woman looking back at me. I thought the hairdo would make me look like Rebekha, but I was still me, Momma, and Grandma Faith. I said, "It looks perfect. Thank you."

"One thing is still missing." Rebekha took off her pearl necklace and clasped it around my neck, where it lay above the horse pendant with a note inside with two names written: Micah. Momma. Rebekha said, "Here's your something borrowed. My father gave this to me when I graduated high school and it means the world to me. I'd be honored for you to wear it." She stepped back to admire my hair and the necklace.

I touched the pearl. "Thank you." My throat thickened with fifty sobbing frogs.

"You'll be the most beautiful bride." She fiddled with leftover bobby pins. "I was worried at first, but I know we all have to make our way."

"Yes Ma'am."

"I trust you to know what's right for you."

"Yes Ma'am."

"And to go towards a good happy life, right?"

"Yes Ma'am."

"Now, let's see what's next." She rifled through the bags she'd brought.

I didn't check the mirror again, because I was Rebekha's daughter right then, and I didn't want to lose that magic. In the holler, my own momma was living her life. Was she thinking about her daughter's wedding day? I was angry for even thinking that, since I wanted the time to be about Rebekha and me without Momma butting herself in with her jittery loud and itchy nature, all her wants and whining and carrying on. She was tucked in my locket with Micah but she never stayed where I put her.

Though I knew she'd never left far from the holler, I'd written Mrs. Mendel to let her know about the wedding. She'd answered how she sure wished she could come, but she was afraid to leave Momma alone, and please send plenty of photos and a letter with all the details. I'd asked about Momma, but she didn't write much about her. I supposed there wasn't much to say that hadn't already been said. There'd be no Momma at my wedding. Momma would stay far away as she always had. Even when I tried to touch her as a child, she scooted away from me. She was still scooting away. She'd scooted so far away, I might never see her again.

I'd hoped Uncle Jonah and Aunt Billie would come, but Uncle Jonah wouldn't leave Momma, either. Uncle Jonah worked hard, loved his horses, and took care of his sister when she should be taking care of her own baby-whining self. I laid bet of a million shiny dimes he'd never get back to the farm he'd loved so much, because of Momma.

Rebekha put her hand on my shoulder. "Are you okay? You look a million miles from here."

I was. But I said, "I'm glad you're here."

"I am, too."

I stood and we hugged and it was all mooshy-good.

Jade walked into the room and said, "Awww, I'm going to cry!" Then we all laughed so we wouldn't cry. She wore a silky blue dress, with a small blue and white flower pinned to that short hair, and was my one and only bridesmaid.

Rebekha went over to my dress, admired it again, turned back to us, and said, "I just adore this dress."

"Yeah. It's not fussy at all. Good job, Vee." Jade studied herself in the mirror. "If I ever get married, I'm going to make my own dress. Something different."

I could see Jadesta doing that. That dress would be unlike any other and she'd wear it as if she was the Queen of all Brides.

While Jade and Rebekha fussed over me, I stood as if a JC Penney's mannequin. I hadn't even taken off my old clothes. How would I remove my shirt and not ruin my hairdo? It all was really happening. I was getting married. My stomach did the ferris wheel that breaks off and rolls over and away with all the people on it screaming to their deaths.

"Hey, you okay?" Jade asked.

"We keep asking her that, poor thing. It's just wedding day nervousness, right Virginia Kate?" Rebekha patted my shoulder.

I opened my mouth and a squeak came out.

Jade eyed me. "Maybe she's got frigidly cold feet."

"Most brides do," Rebekha said.

"Oh. Do they?" Jade asked.

Rebekha looked at me. "But, really, if you aren't sure, it's not too late to stop everything."

"Yeah, Vee," Jade looked at me, too.

I opened my mouth and nothing fell out.

"Listen to us, Jade! My word. Well. Both of you girls, just know that you have choices even up until it seems as if you don't."

Jade slapped her hands together. "Okay, let's get busy. If this things happening, she needs the full treatment."

Rebekha opened my bag. "Let's see what we have here."

Jade pulled out a make-up pouch from her purse. "I brought extra, just in case. You know how she is."

They fluttered around looking for cosmetics as if they were crazy birds on silly-seed.

Rebekha held up lipstick and eyeshadow as if to say *ta daaaa!*, said, "Let's get some of this on the bride."

Jade nodded her approval.

They patted, fiddled, swiped. When they'd finished painting me, Rebekha said, "Oh dear."

"What?" Jade asked. "What's wrong?"

Rebekha laughed with her hand over her mouth, lowered her hand and asked, "Could we be any denser?"

Jade pulled her eyebrows together in a *what do you mean?*

"She'll wreck her hair and make-up when she takes off her t-shirt."

I wanted to roll my eyes, since I'd figured that out long ago (even if I'd not said a word).

They both stared at me, studying a puzzle.

I stayed a statue, afraid to move anything for fear something would slide off, pull out, mess up, or smudge.

Jade said, "*Wait, hold on,*" and I heard her rummaging. She lifted the shirt away from me, and then I felt something cold and heard the snip of scissors.

I jerked away, no longer caring what went wrong, and turned to look at the back of the shirt. Too late, already cut. "What have you done, Jade?"

"That shirt is revolting and has a hole in it." She blew out her breath.

Rebekha said, "We'll get you another one."

"But I want this one." I pooched out my lip until it hit the floor.

"That thing needs to go. You shouldn't be wearing it in public," Jade said.

Rebekha began putting away make-up, comb, brush, mirror, so she wouldn't have to be in the middle of it.

Jade clicked the scissors open and shut.

I let out a sigh and dropped my arms by my sides. No use fussing about what was too late.

Jade cut the rest of the shirt so it would slip off my shoulders, threw it on the table, and then pointed at me. "Look Rebekha, at least she has on a pretty bra. I'm sure Dylan will appreciate it." She snorted.

"She picked it out herself."

"I think I'm going to be sick," I said.

"Well, yes, weddings make everyone crazy. Just complete nervous wrecks! What bride would react differently?" Rebekha patted a piece of my escaping hair.

"No, it's not that. That was one of my favorite t-shirts." I grabbed the shirt from the table and held it to my face.

Jade snatched it away, blabbing something about my make-up and to just grow up and stop being a baby because today was my wedding day, for god's sake.

"But Micah gave me that shirt. From New York."

"I see. Well." Rebekha took it from Jade as if it was a tiny bunny for a little girl, folded it, and stuck it into her purse. "Maybe I can make a pillow out of it."

I smiled at her, at least I think it was a smile, my lips were twitching and trembling all over creation.

"Off with those awful pants before I cut them to shreds." Jade wrinkled her nose. "And those nasty flip flops. For god's sake, Vee."

I didn't even make a fuss, just stepped out of everything else. I didn't like being left half-naked, so I grabbed the long slip to step into.

Jade said, "And she's got on prissy pretty panties to match. Well, I'll be ding-donged. Little Vee is actually a sex kitten . . . *Meowarrrr.*"

She and Rebekha laughed, but I didn't make a lick at a laugh.

Rebekha took the dress from the hook, slipped it off the padded hanger, and then they both held out the dress for me to step into. They buttoned me up, smoothed me out, twitter, flutter, squawk. I heard the crow caw for me outside the window.

When they'd fastened the tiny pearls and the dress fell just how they thought it should fall, they stepped back and nodded as if they were mirror-twins.

There was a knock at the door, and Amy Campinelle's voice blasted through the wood, "Hey! Y'all all right in there? Y'all need some help?"

Rebekha opened the door a crack and when she was satisfied no one else was there, she let in Amy Campinelle, who took up to bawling before she crossed the threshold. Her mascara ran down her cheeks, her face turned red as a newborn rose. She hitched and cried, garbling out something about beautiful brides and wedding days and Mr. Husband.

Jade brought over my shoes and laid them at my feet. "Thy shoes, Cinder . . . wait, was it Cinderella that had the glass slippers?"

"Yes, it was. She married her prince and they lived happily ever after." Rebekha sighed, said, "Those old fairy tales set women up for disappointment, don't they?" She busied herself smoothing down her dress, straightening a stray hair that hadn't strayed.

"I for sure married my prince, yeah." A dreamy look slipped across Amy Campinelle's face. "He was a frog and I kissed him and he turned into my handsome fairy prince."

I pictured a four-hundred pound frog turning into a four-hundred pound prince who married an almost-four-hundred pound Cinder-Amy Campinelle. I loved every inch of every part of them and was glad someone in the old world believed in fairy tales, and lived them. I wanted to hug on Amy Campinelle, hug her tight and tell her to love and live forever, her and Mr. Husband.

Jade began singing the song about how one day some guy who'll be her prince would come round. She twirled with her arms over her head and I remembered all her days of dancing. She remembered, too, because she stopped and took in a breath, her eyes as dreamy as Amy Campinelle's had been. Except her love was dance, not a man.

Rebekha said, "Slip on the shoes so your feet will get used to them some more."

I'd worn the shoes for hours the other night, back and forth walking until my feet sobbed a surrender song. Rebekha and Jade said it was better than wearing brand new shoes on my wedding day. I had to do the same thing again the next night, and the next.

I slipped into the shoes, and thought instead I should have Dorothy's ruby slippers to click together and go no place like Home. As if by magic, I'd disappear in a swirl and wake with an Auntie Em at my bed saying, "Child, we were worried about you." I'd tell her fantastical stories about where I'd been, when all along I'd never left Home at all.

Jade said, "I'm going to wear ballet slippers to my wedding."

I wished I'd thought of slippers for myself. I wished brides could wear flip flops to weddings.

Amy Campinelle handed me a soft pouch with a drawstring at the top. "Here's your something new, cher." She sniffled into her hankie.

Inside were two little pearl earrings. They had an antique look and would go perfect with Rebekha's necklace. I thanked Amy Campinelle, screwed on the earrings, and then turned to the mirror to see what I had become.

Amy Campinelle let out an, "Ohhhh, *yawwwlll!* I'm fixin' to cry all over again, yeah."

I stared into the full-length mirror. The dress's satin-whiteness shrouded my skin. My hair and make-up, shoes, the earrings, Rebekha's necklace—all of it hid the girl I was and made me into the woman who would marry Dylan. That's what I needed. That's how the world turned round and round, spinning my head all whirly twirling. I even felt beautiful, but a different pretty from Momma's pretty.

It was time.

Amy Campinelle wiped her eyes, and then leaned to kiss me, her lips stopping just shy of my cheek, so she wouldn't leave her pink lip-gloss imprint. She said, "I hope y'all are as happy as Mr. Husband and me are. Y'all deserve the best." She went out the door, sniffling away.

It was time.

Jade hugged me, whispered in my ear, "You're the best friend I've ever had. I will miss you being at my house. I love you forever, Virginia Kate. If you ever need me, you call and I'm there."

I whispered back, "I love you, too."

She left the room; from behind, her neck was tender and sweet.

It was time.

When Rebekha said, "It's time, Hon," I turned to her.

Her mouth trembled. She came to me and hugged me and all the days I'd fought to stay out of her arms came back, and then the days since then when I'd accepted her rushed to me, and I didn't want to leave that circle of her arms where I was safe.

There just were no more words to say right then. Nothing to do but release, and then enter another set of arms.

∾ • ∿

Churches made people whisper, unless you were Bobby, Andy, or Mee Maw. When I peeked into the sanctuary, the three of them were talking too loud and laughing twice as loud as that. I about laughed my lipstick off when I saw the back of Mee Maw. From what I could see, she wore a bright orange dress with lots of organza poufed everywhere as if she wanted to attract everyone's attention who weren't already noticing her loud mouth. A feathered hat perched on her head and I expected it to fly off and flutter to the ceiling to escape Mee Maw. I could hear her screeching, but couldn't understand her.

I searched. Micah wasn't there. I knew he wouldn't be, but I'd hoped all the same. The locket felt cold at my chest, not warm when a wish came true.

Jade pulled me back and we all stood in our places. The music changed. The doors were opened wide by someone. The aisle looked as long as the road that led to the holler. Little Mae Lynn held tiny Peggy Elaine's hand as they made their way to the front. Little Mae Lynn tossed flower petals, but Peggy Elaine took handfuls and threw them at people. I laughed at that.

Jade and the best man began their walk down, their arms linked.

Daddy stood beside me as we waited for our turn. He'd worn my favorite Old Spice, to help hide the unfavored Old Booze.

He turned to me and said low, "'I wish you all the joy that you can wish.' Happy wedding day, Bug, my dainty Ariel." He squeezed my hand.

"Daddy?"

"Don't worry, I'll always be here."

I squeezed his hand back.

We began the walk to Dylan, who watched me with a look that soaked me into him as if he were a sponge and I the entire ocean. His best man cut his eyes to Jade. I bet Barry the best man and Jade the best bridesmaid would dance up a storm at the reception, and no telling what all else. I saw the look that passed between them. Barry was more than a good guy, so Jade could do worse, and she for sure had. Yet, she said she'd sworn off men, so who knew what she'd do, maybe she'd go for Barry's sister. I had another laugh to myself over that.

Jade eyes said, *just put one foot in front of the other until you are beside Dylan.* I worked my way to him, slow, almost sure. And before I was quite ready, I was there and Daddy had to let me go. I looked up at my daddy; he looked down at me. All the time before us fell away. I was no longer his tiny Ariel, his Bitty Bug; I was to be a wife. I wondered if he'd look at me in a different way from how he had before or if I'd always be the same little girl to him no matter how old I was or where I went. He leaned down and kissed my cheek. His eyes glittered, but he didn't cry. I'd never seen my Daddy cry but Micah had.

The ceremony was short as a butterfly's breath, just how I wanted it. Dylan and I kissed, and the fire raced from my toes to my scalp, frightening me as it always did with its intensity. As I turned to the smiling faces, they all blurred together like one of Micah's paintings.

While Dylan and I headed back down the aisle to leave, individual faces sped by me. I snapped the shutter in my mind, taking inner photos. Snap. Rebekha crying. Snap. Daddy with a strange far and away expression. Snap. Snap. Andy smiling sad with his suit beginning to rumple, Beth Anne beaming beside him. Bobby giving me a thumbs up. Snap-snap-snap-snap. Stump looking bored. Soot, Marco, and their two flower girls huddled together. Amy Campinelle still sobbing her heart away while Mr. Husband rubbed her back. Dear Mrs. Portier-turned-Engleson, with her family. There was Miss Darla, who called out, *Oh Girl you are on such a journey* and I called back, *A journey to where?* But she didn't answer, or if she did, I couldn't hear because the roar of claps and sighs and ghosts and Grandma Faith calling to me to love wise and well or not at all and the sound of my feet on the carpet and the wind blowing wild into a window someone had opened and a hymnal's pages flapping like a wild frenzied bird and the satin in my dress wisping and my blood thundering in my ears and cameras popping and so many more smiling faces flashing by flashing by flashing by carried her thoughts away from me.

Dylan and I busted out of the church door that like magic opened before us.

I thought I would fall onto the ground in a heap of satin. That'd I disappear under it all and when they looked for me, there'd only be a shell of a wedding dress. I'd have clicked together my heels, called for Home, and disappeared.

Dylan brushed my ear with his lips, said, "My wife. The new Mrs. Watersdown."

I said, "I'm a wife."

He kissed me hard, kissed my cherry-colored lipstick off onto his lips. His momma came to stand beside him, swiped at his mouth with her hanky, said something to him, and then began crying. His daddy shook his hand, and led Dylan's momma away.

Rebekha hugged me; Daddy hugged me. Another hug, and another, and all the hugs and voices and sounds howled up a tempest.

People surrounded us as we made our way to the car. Cameras clicked and flashed. I heard Andy shout, "Hey! Wait! Sister!" as rice rained down upon us.

I tried to turn to find my brother, to give him a big hug. To tell him I wasn't leaving him behind forever, but would always be his big Seestor.

I was pulled along by the crowd and by Dylan and then into the car.

As we drove away, I looked out of the back window. Andy stood in the road. As we headed away from him, he became smaller and smaller, younger and younger, until he was the little boy I had to leave in the holler so long ago.

I turned back forward, and through a haze, I watched the road ahead.

Chapter 21

I'll have a white infidel!

I remembered a story Rebekha told me about when she was a girl. She would stand under a sweet gum tree in her front yard and pick at the sticky gum that leaked out. She'd put some into her mouth and bite down with her young strong teeth. As she chewed, she said she picked at her mind for any worries. Had she done all her homework? Would she make an A on her test? Had she done anything to embarrass herself at school?

On down the list she went, standing still as dark night under that tree with her jaws working. She said sometimes picking at her brain led to nothing to worry over, and then she'd feel a snappy freedom to go play. Other times, she counted the worries that had been hidden and forgotten, reliving them until she became trapped like a little critter in a cage.

I knew I must not pick for worries. It was my wedding day and I must go out and play. The chauffeur parked in front of the Faculty Club building. It was time for the reception party where everyone would drink, laugh, eat, and congratulate.

Dylan jumped out of the car first, and I knew I was supposed to wait for the chauffeur to open my door, as we'd talked about. When Mr. Chauffeur opened the door for me, I stepped on out and stood next to Dylan in his nice suit and shiny shoes, blue tie, combed down hair, and smooth-shaved cheeks. A photographer took more pictures. I'd never had so many pictures taken of me; I was always the one taking the photographs.

Dylan stroked my cheek, said, "I love you."

I kissed him on the lips.

He pulled back. "You've got to tell me you love me back, today of all days. Tell me you love me as if you really feel it." He gripped my shoulders, squeezed, urged me with hot breath, "Tell me. Say you love me. *Say it.*"

That I had never said I loved him as he wanted me to took me by surprise. I had, somewhere along the way, hadn't I? I parted my lips to let breath and words release—a car door slammed and a loud voice filled the air with screeching and the moment passed, sucked into a Mee Maw Laudine vortex. She and Hank had bounced out of a white Cadillac as if on rubber.

"Oh, you are so beautiful! And such a handsome man. I'm so happy I could run around the world in my underdrawers shouting A-*Men!*"

I managed to keep my eyes from frog-bugging at the sight of Mee Maw. She'd changed clothes. For all I figured, she may have done it right in the Cadillac on the way over.

She grabbed hold of Hank's hand as they hurried to us.

I kissed them on the cheeks they offered like wrinkled gift paper, drowned in Brut versus White Shoulders.

"My baby granddaughter is married! I can't believe it." She shook a spiky platinum-blonde horror that I hadn't earlier seen under the bird-hat. She wore blue eye shadow, dark thick false eyelashes, frosted orange lipstick, and two stop sign smudges of rouge. Her pantsuit was blue to match the eye shadow and she had a pink boa thrown around her neck. Gold earrings the size of a buzzard's head completed Mee Maw.

Hank was lion's head proud and handsome in a gray suit and black cowboy boots, his black cowboy hat tilted back.

"My baby granddaughter is safe at last. She won't have to do a thing for herself anymore." Mee Maw sparkle-eyed Dylan, then screeched, "She can take her pretty pictures without having to work at that diner or that li-berry. I'm going to cry me a river and float it all the way to heaven!"

"Mee Maw," I said, "I *want* to work and—"

"Well, you aren't giving it a chance." Mee Maw grabbed my hand. "Once you have a man taking care of you, you can play with your camera all you want."

"It's not playing, Mee Maw. The photography is my work, too."

"Well that doesn't make any sense." She shook her horrored-head. "Not any sense a'tall."

"Let's go inside now, shall we?" Dylan said, pulling on my other hand.

Maybe they'd wishbone rip me in two pieces. I released my hand from Mee Maw, but Dylan held tight.

Mee Maw cocked up an eyebrow at Dylan. "This handsome hunk of man is too good to be true. I can't wait to meet his family. Can you, Hank? I've been curiouser and curiouser about them. I tried to get their attention before the ceremony, but I guess they didn't hear me because they kept on going like they were running from a stink."

"They'll be waiting for us. Come on, Kate." Dylan tried to back away from Mee Maw's tentacles, but she stepped up as he backed away.

"Kate? Who is this Kate? No Kate here. You can't be changing names. I tried that." Mee Maw winked. "I tried my dandiest to get them to name her Virginia Laudine or Laudine Kate and they wouldn't hear of it. Would they?" She eyed me as a chicken does a chicken yard.

I tried to act as if I felt bad I wasn't named Laudine.

Dylan said, "It's just a nickname." He was turning red from his neck up.

"Well, I guess that's what y'all do in California. Make names shorter so you can hurry off to do something else. Don't have time to say a whole name out, do you?"

Hank nodded his big head, said, "That's for sure how it is in California. I seen it with my own two eyeballs."

Dylan opened his mouth, but Mee Maw kept on flapping her lips wild and furious about names and California versus The Great State of Texas and the weather.

It was the first time Dylan couldn't wedge a word in side ways or up down over.

Mee Maw grabbed his left arm with her right and my right with her left. She asked, "Hank, doesn't my granddaughter look pretty?"

"She shore does. Perty as a picture."

Dylan and I inched toward the building, pulling Mee Maw with us.

"Oh, the traffic was horrid once we left Texas. Wasn't the traffic horrid, Hank?"

"It shore was. It was cattle mooing through a feed-gate."

Dylan mopped his face with his handkerchief.

"Oh dear me! Here I go making everyone miserable out here in this terrible humidity. Mee Maw just doesn't think straight sometimes, does she Hank?"

"She gets her head all in a wind sometimes, she does," Hank answered.

Mee Maw at last let us go, and Dylan practically slung me to the door, Mee Maw and Hank galloping along beside us, while Mee Maw went on and on about the ceremony and the people and how her girdle was cutting off her blood flow.

Dylan jerked open the door to enter a party that was already going full steam blast ahead.

Everyone turned our way. Dylan's parents looked at Mee Maw as if their eyeballs would fall out of their sockets and roll out of the room to get away from the sight of her. His sisters snickered at Mee Maw behind their hands, their light brown hair falling straight and shiny to their shoulders, their just-been-to-the-beach skin glowing under the lights. They wore matching yellow dresses. Momma had once told me that yellow dresses made women look like either sunny lemons or too-sweet bananas. Momma squeezed her sunny lemons in vodka or bourbon and sliced her too sweet bananas in pudding.

Dylan's family made their way over to him.

I searched the room for my family. Daddy stood in a corner, holding onto his glass of wine. Rebekha headed my way. Bobby's long lanky arms were just a going as he stuffed his mouth. Andy and Beth Anne were at the table, talking to each other with their heads close. Andy looked serious and Beth Anne sleeping kitten calm.

Rebekha asked, "You doing okay, Hon?"

I whispered, "Just a Mee Maw attack."

Rebekha nodded with the understanding of the ages of Mee Maw.

"When can I get out of this dress?"

"Your change of clothes is through that door, second door on your right. Just make a quick circuit and then you can escape to change."

I pulled my lips up up up.

Rebekha turned to the Queen of Texas, who was yodeling to a flabbergasted Mr. Watersdown. Rebekha touched Mee Maw's arm and as soon as Mee Maw turned to Rebekha, Dylan's daddy hightailed it away.

Mee Maw caterwauled, "Why, he's as handsome as my granddaughter's new husband! What a catch!"

Rebekha said to her, "Mee Maw, why don't you put your purse at your table right over there and I'll get you and Hank something to drink."

Mee Maw's purse was the size of a suitcase with her home state sewed in multi-colored rhinestones, and *God Bless Texas* spelled out in diamonds. She kept opening and closing the clasp as she stood sunbeaming at the back of Dylan's daddy, who, along with the rest of his family, was speaking with Dylan.

"Mee Maw? Are you thirsty?" I asked.

"Oh, let's see now. I want a glass of that wine I heard some girl at the wedding talking about. Let's see." Mee Maw's brows pulled in, then she brightened and said, "I'll have a white infidel!"

Rebekha's lips twitched. She said, "I don't believe we have that. What about a chardonnay? Or a Pinot Noir?"

Mee Maw cocked her spiked-haired head. "I'll take a peanot newert, whatever. What'll you have, hon-bunch?"

"You know me, bourbon and water. I brought my own, right here with me in a flask." Hank patted his pocket. "Just need me some water."

Rebekha turned to me. "You go on. I have this under control." She guided Mee Maw and Hank to their table.

Dylan grabbed me to spin around the room so people could gawk and take more pictures.

Jade snapped a photo of Dylan and me. I said to her, "I am deadfrog tired already."

"It's time to party, Vee! You can't be tired at the fun part."

Barry reached over and pulled Jade onto the dance floor. The band played some song about celebrating and having good times.

Dylan and I separated as the crowd pulled us every which-a-way. I had a first dance with Dylan and with Daddy. And then Hank. Mr. Husband swirled me about the room in a waltz that surprised me with how graceful he was. When I danced with Barry, he said that Jade was sure something else. Mr. Watersdown held me a little too close and put his hand a little too low on my back for someone who didn't seem to like me all that much.

I threw the bouquet. Beth Anne caught it and ran to hug Andy, who looked happier than I thought he would be. After cake and more dancing, at last, before I lost every last bit of my mind, I was able to sneak away to change into my going–away blue linen suit.

I next stumble-stepped my way to the bathroom, closed the door, pushed up my skirt, pushed down my underwear, and set there on the toilet where it was quiet. I wanted to hide forever, but of course, I could not.

The bathroom door opened, closed, and I heard Dylan's momma and sisters talking about Mee Maw. How she had no class and was a loud mouth. Made me so mad I wanted to bust out the door and start swinging. I stood, trying to fix my clothes, while shouting out, "Mee Maw doesn't mean a thing wrong. She's a sweet old woman who just has her ways!"

It turned quiet, the bathroom door opened, and then closed. I stepped out to a room without a soul in it.

That's how it was with family. I could say my Mee Maw was an insane old woman with a big flappity mouth, but no one outside of family best be saying it. There was a crazy-mad woman looking at me from the mirror, most of her French twist untwisted and pieces of hair slung all over creation, lipstick near-gone.

When I stepped out of the bathroom, I stopped short and quick, almost turned and ran back inside.

Patrick and a pretty woman with a big head and a skinny body stood in front of me. I didn't think I could take much more of my wedding day and the people in it. And who had invited Patrick? I hadn't and I felt pretty sure Dylan hadn't.

Patrick said, "Hello, Virginia Kate."

"Hey."

Patrick put his arm around the woman. "This is my girlfriend, Janet."

"Nice to meet you, Janet."

"So, how are you?" He touched my shoulder and then pulled back.

Janet's lips coyote-curled.

"I'm fine."

"It's good to see you again," Patrick said. "You look great."

"*My* Patrick talks about you all the time," Janet said. "Blah blah Virginia Kate this. Blab blab, Virginia Kate that." She put her hands on her hips and gave me the evil eye.

"Can I get by, please?"

They moved just enough to let me walk back into the room, but they didn't leave my side.

On the dance floor, Miss Darla waltzed with Dylan's daddy to a sweet sad song without words. His lips were just a-moving and Miss Darla only nodded, nodded, nodded, her eyes once catching mine and twinkling an inner wink. Soot and Marco danced close, her head on his shoulder, and an envy tried to grab me in its claws. Something broke apart inside me at how their love was strong and sure. The pieces flowed jagged in my veins and I hurt all over because I didn't recognize all I needed to when I looked at them, then looked inside me and my soon to be life.

It was good to see Soot have fun, though. It broke my heart to see her worry all the time about her momma so sick with the cancer. I had two mommas and she had but the one, and I worried her momma may not be long for the world. Life did peculiar things to the people who lived it.

I thought about how Grandpa Luke had cancer, and how Soot's momma did, and how it didn't matter if you were mean as a ornery snake as Grandpa was, or as sweet as a spring rain like Soot's momma—that cancer didn't care about sweet and it didn't care about mean, it found a way inside a body and did it's dirty work all the same. Took the good ones with the bad ones, always had and always would.

Janet was saying something about having a history, and Patrick was saying something about how everyone had a history so could she just shut up about it. I'd almost forgotten they were there.

"I'm sure you both have lots of *history* to talk about," Janet said. "Maybe I should let you two *alone* to talk about your *history*, huh?"

Patrick said, "I'm truthfully happy for you, Virginia Kate."

I searched the room for Dylan. He was dancing with a fresh-scrubbed-look girl with sandy hair and breasts that spilled out of her fire-pink dress and slapped onto his chest. Dylan looked as if he was having way more fun than I was.

Patrick patted Janet's back. "Janet is a dental assistant."

"Can we go now, Patrick? I'm bored and I need another drink and something to eat." Janet yawned wide, showing off her dental assistant teeth.

"I just wanted to say congratulations." Patrick gave up a splintered grin.

"Thank you, Patrick."

Janet grabbed Patrick's sleeve and pulled him away.

I let out sucked in air. Men were the strangest of critters.

Dylan stayed with the fresh-faced girl for another dance, to a song about don't be standing too close and being wet at a bus stop. I searched for my brothers, except the missing one who decided to stay himself in the big city. Andy was busy shoving down ten pounds of boiled shrimp while Beth Anne danced with Stump. Andy said Stump had told Beth Anne the story about the firecracker that caused his missing finger part and since she had listened and asked question after question, Stump had a crush on her. Bobby gobbled a tiny pecan pie, and had four more on his plate that he would gobble just as fast. He'd said he didn't have time for girls, so had come without a date.

Andy asked, "What's Patrick doing here?"

I shrugged.

"Who invited him?" Bobby asked.

I shrugged again.

Then my brothers shrugged. That's just how things went sometimes, not a thing to do but shrug.

Rebekha and Daddy danced to a song about getting kicks from a woman and not champagne. Dylan danced with one of his sisters, and they laughed at something. My brothers looked at me and I said, "Don't worry; we don't have to dance together." They didn't hide their relief.

Jade had stopped dancing with Barry and had three dances in a row with the bartender's helper while Barry kept on an I'm-pretending-I-don't-care look. During the band's break, someone played tapes. When a woman throated out her song about a man going to her head, Dylan fetched me to dance. When he held me close to him, his breath was hot with liquor breath, his eyes glittered, his lips wet, his jacket thrown across a chair, his steps a slow one two three four one two three four that didn't quite match the music.

Mee Maw had a little too much peanot newart and slung the twist, then kicked off her shoes and stomped up a jig to the thousand dances land song. She flopped into a chair and fell asleep with her mouth hung open. Hank woke her and led her out the door, first stopping by to tell us how much fun they had.

Dylan went to the microphone, toasted his parents, and said we'd be leaving for our surprise honeymoon trip in the morning. I don't know why I couldn't know where we were going so I could prepare myself. Dylan had said he'd taken care of everything, including my clothes. How he'd done that was a mystery since I still had all my clothes as far as I knew. Dylan registered us as Mr. and Mrs. Watersdown at the hotel. Watersdown sounded like watered down. I decided I would keep my own name.

Dylan grabbed my hand and we headed outside. The limousine had shoes, cans, and a Just Married sign hanging in the back. The driver stood at attention and I wanted to tell him to slump if he wanted to, I sure did feel like slumping myself. We stepped inside the car, and the driver closed us in. I opened the window so I could breathe and waved at everyone waving and shouting at us. Daddy stood wearing that same far off look. Rebekha had tear-tracks running down. Bobby stared into the bushes, pointing at something there—when I looked closer, I saw it was Janet heaving sick while Patrick patted her back. Andy was behind Daddy and I waved to him, but he was smiling down at Beth Anne. Jade blubbered away as she waved to me, Barry close by her side.

Miss Darla gave me a wave. I didn't hear a thing she said, if she even said a thing. She was beautiful in her sea-foam green dress and sandals, her hair pulled back into a low ponytail. I knew she'd go home, pull on her britches and her loose men's top, and sit on the back porch sipping tea, happy for the quiet. I tried not to wish I were going to be there with her.

The chauffeur drove us to a hotel by the airport. Two suitcases were already in our room, with a big bouquet of flowers on the table. A bottle of champagne chilled in a silver bucket. Everything taken care of, except for the bird mad-fluttering inside me. I felt sorry for it, banging against my chest.

↔ • ↕

That night when the moon hid behind a cloud as we lay in bed, I climbed on Dylan and rode him all the way to my mountain. He was the bull from mythological stories, and hot steam blew from his nostrils. Higher and higher I took him, the moisture from my face gathering like the mountain's mist around the trees. I urged him to the top, but he reared beneath me, anxious and impatient. I was wild, and needed to go all the way and to the other side and back again. I threw back my head and my hair fell heavy against my back. Up up up I went, higher and higher. Forest critters' sounds flew from my tongue. I leaned down, put my tongue to his, gave him my sounds. I took in his taste and swallowed it down to mix with my marrow.

I left him sweaty and wide-eyed and full up with himself. He pawed the ground, snorted, marked his land, and curled beside me. His cooling breath rustled the hairs on my neck as I panted, rolling the whites of my eyes.

He turned me to him and said, "I love you." He waited while the air stilled as if the entire world came to a stop in the second before everything could go one way or the other.

I said with all I could bring forth, "I love you." I didn't die, the world didn't explode. I was still me. Of course I was. The words had dripped off my tongue and fallen liquid gold onto the tangled sheets.

Dylan swallowed my golden words, lapping them up like cream from a never-ending bowl.

Chapter 22

Going again

I turned a circle in the room Jade and I had fixed up for me and where I'd not stayed long enough to leave something of myself to imprint the room forever. How many times did I have to be the one packing my things and moving on? Why couldn't I be the one to stay for a change? That's where my ornery thoughts flew like black bird's raving. Into my suitcase, I placed a bottle of Jade's spiced-patchouli scent that was almost gone, a small round rock from her yard, one of her favorite pens she used to write grocery lists, and a hair bob she wore when her hair was longer. I closed the suitcase.

I'd saved packing my things from Jade's house until after I'd returned from our honeymoon, which turned out to be a trip to California. Dylan had bought me all new clothes, toothbrush, cosmetics, everything. Not a thing of my own was in the new suitcase. He said it was to keep the surprise a surprise. We'd stayed in his parent's vacation beach house. It was beautiful and wild at the ocean, and I loved how the surf pulled at the sand, the salty smell, the little crabs, the water that seemed to go on forever without ending, the way the earth curved where ocean and sky met. I dug my toes into the sand and wondered what it would be like to live on my mountain with the sea surrounding it.

Even with its ocean, I knew I'd never want to live in California. Some places just didn't feel like home, but only for the visiting. It was too far away and too different from all I knew. With pride, Dylan had shown me around his town, his high school, all the places he loved. I was afraid when I heard the longing sound in his words. I knew that longing sound, I for sure did.

We'd come back to Louisiana and I took my new things with me to Dylan's house, our house, he with a suntan and highlights in his Mr. Manilow hair, his still wistful eyes. And me with smoothed sea-glass, shark's tooth, pieces of sand- and water-polished wood, shells, and other interesting doodads I'd found while walking the beach and strolling through little shops.

Jade came into the room and looked around. Her swollen eyes showed me she'd been crying. She'd said living alone hadn't mattered until I'd come there to live and filled up the spaces with light. I thought maybe Barry would be a man she'd find light with, but she'd said he wasn't right for her. No one was ever right. Poor Barry had packed up his broken heart and moved back to California. He'd told her he was thinking of going to Canada.

Jade's marble-colored eyes were too big for her thin face, and her long legs were sticks, matching her stick arms. I didn't want to leave my friend. I was afraid of what might happen to her. She'd gone back to dancing, but instead of it making her strong and beautiful, it was parasiting her. I knew her legs and back hurt her and some nights she paced the floor, back and forth back and forth.

We didn't speak as we walked outside with the last of my things. We'd said everything we had to say when I'd come over the night before. I'd told Dylan I wanted to spend the night at Jade's, and he'd sighed, but he said to have fun. Jade and I had talked about when we were kids, the day we met, the times she'd come to our house and laughed at how loud we were, the times I'd gone to her house and tiptoed around in the quiet.

I stood in front of the respectable car Dylan bought me for a wedding gift. The boring white Chevrolet stood steady ready on its steady ready tires to take me to Dylan's house. I hadn't picked it out, and if I had, it wouldn't be a white Chevrolet, but instead a blue or a green car with interesting details flashing by as I roared down the road.

Jade touched my shoulder, said, "Call me and we'll go do something after you get settled in, 'kay?"

I nodded; I had a clog of frogs jumbled up in my throat.

We hugged, tight, tighter. Then she stepped by to let me go.

Going again. That's what I did. Go go go. Always go. I wanted one day when I could stay. Forever. One place until my end.

A ghost called sweet, *You know where that is . . . Why do you deny?*

I climbed into my car, started the engine, and backed down Jade's driveway. She didn't move, but if a wind came, it might just blow her away, swirl her about, and who knew where she'd land? It took all I had to back out the rest of the way and then drive off. I couldn't look at her in the rearview, couldn't see how alone she looked. Who would take care of her and bring her coffee, Miss Darla's healing tea? Who would make her eat? Who would she talk to when she came home from a date gone bad? Who would bring her aspirin when her back and knees throbbed?

Leaving people behind was the worst thing in the world.

When I pulled into Dylan's driveway, a brown-paper-wrapped package leaned against the door. I pulled myself out of Ready Steady, leaving my stuff in the car until later, and made my way to the front porch. An envelope taped to the package had Rebekha's handwriting that read, *Virginia Kate*. I tore open the envelope. *Virginia Kate, this came in the mail for you from Micah. I'm sorry I missed you. Call me whenever you feel like it. Love, Rebekha.*

I hurried inside. Jinxie grunted from his bed and came over to sniff the package to make sure it wasn't anything that could hurt me. He was my guardian. I tore off the brown paper. Under that was more wrapping, newspaper from New York. My hands shiver-shook as I ripped away the newspaper. The blast of brushstrokes flew out as if alive. I sucked in my breath. The swirls on the canvas danced and musical notes flew up, out, and to the sky. A group of children huddling inside a circle. A dark-haired girl riding a dark horse up her mountain. A woman standing as the wind pulled her hair out to the beyond.

There was more hidden than imagination could allow. A woman in red swayed to her own music. Eyes that told secrets. A galaxy, and in it the moon all pale-full and mysterious. I saw those things in the painting. The chaos led me to more of Micah's mystery, and to his universe, and beyond to my own mysteries. My brother was the prodigy Daddy had said he was so long ago.

I turned it over to see if there was a wire so I could hang it and found another package taped to the back. I opened it to find a small oil painting of the three of us kids when we were little children in the holler. I wore a yellow sun suit with teddy bears on it, the elastic bands leaving bitty bird tracks on my legs. My eyes were wide and dark. Andy was an infant, wrapped in a blue blanket, lying between us. Micah wore his rolled up blue jeans and checkered shirt, his skinny arm thrown across my shoulders so that he protected both Andy and me. In his other hand, he held something. Looking closer, it was a picture of Bobby. Micah had included the little brother we didn't know we'd have at that time, the time in the holler. Child Micah stared right at the grown woman me as I looked down at him from my grown woman height. Micah's look seemed to dare the world to try to hurt us.

I took the small painting into Dylan's, our, bedroom and rocked in the rocker with us held in my lap. I hugged to me the little children. Back and forth, back and forth. I rocked the ages; I rocked the children; I rocked my brothers and I rocked me; I rocked until time didn't mean a thing. I held tight so we would feel warm and safe.

I didn't cry, never.

The world opened wide with possibility. Micah gave that gift to me with his paintings.

I smiled to myself as I rocked and rocked. One day I would have my own children to hold. One day I would keep my little one's safe so they would never be hurt or lonely. I would keep them with me until it was time for them to find their own place.

Dylan and I would have a family. I would have and love our children and always stay where they could find me.

That's where my fractured thoughts splintered, pieces flying outward and outward and beyond to places they'd never before been.

Chapter 23

Today

In the holler while setting cross-legged on Grandma Faith's quilt

If I were to look into the mirror, I know what I'd see. I'd see a middle-aged woman who is near the same age as her momma was when she wrote to her young woman daughter and said how she was in the holler alone because she was losing her pretty, getting old, as if that was the worse thing ever to endure, and that one day her own daughter would, too, be old. I do not feel old. I do not worry about all the things my momma did.

In that mirror, I'd see a still-dark-haired woman with just a few threads of gray. I'd see a tall strong high-cheekboned woman who wonders if she looks anything at all like her momma did at this age, or any age. I'd see a woman who pretends she released her momma to the winds come down from the mountain ridge.

I'd see a woman who wasn't here to celebrate birthdays when Momma turned thirty-five, or forty, or fifty, or sixty. She'd given me up as a young girl, let me come back as a teenager, and after that, banished me for the rest of her life. She missed my birthdays, my graduations, my wedding, my divorce, my own lost babe, and all the things both good and bad that came without her by my side. Now she's left the world and that is what brought me back to this holler, where I began my storytelling journey, prompted by Grandma Faith. I'm here in my childhood home, without Momma.

What manner of women are we, momma and daughter? How could I hug an urn of ashes? I couldn't; I can only release her to her soft dance.

Oh, I knew if I looked into the mirror, I'd see a woman who did make many of her women-kin's mistakes. Who lived, loved, and lost, and had regrets come calling. A woman who, although she has seen fifty even if not for long, still misses her momma, still smells her Shalimar, and sees glimpses of her if only she would look into the mirror. But I will not look into the mirror.

I think about the tales told of the circle of our lives. How everything goes round just as the earth does. What is up becomes down, what is east becomes west, past is now present. Things meet themselves coming and going and in the middle. And then there are the things that make not a lick of sense. Those circles make things come round to meet a person again and again, round and round even when we'd rather them not.

On my childhood bed is an envelope full of photos. I stare down at one of Momma and Daddy when they were first married and had moved into this little white house in the holler. Their teeth shine white and strong as they stand under the sugar maple. Momma has her head tilted to the right towards Daddy's shoulder. They are for sure unaware of the years before them that will wipe the Happy from their faces. I wonder who snapped the photo, but then I always wonder who takes the pictures.

There is next a photo of my wedding day. Dylan has on a Hollywood smile, and I had no real expression at all. I never noticed that before, how I looked as if something distracted my attention and I forgot where I was. I put down that photo, beside the one of my parents.

I shuffle through memories. There are photos of my parents' lives unfolding in black and white and sepia. Momma and Daddy with their mouths open wide with laughter. There's one of Momma's strong body posing on a towel with her sexy pout on. Daddy's shadow eases behind him, his arms lifted to take the picture. Momma eyes Daddy from over the top of her sunglasses with a look that says, *put that camera down, and get yourself on this blanket, mister.* I can smell her Shalimar simmering in the heat.

Then we begin to show up, my brothers and I, and the wide-open laughter fades on away from Momma's and Daddy's faces. The recognition of that makes my stomach do a somersault flip. I don't want to see the evidence of their trouble, but I keep searching—us kids in our pj's loving Christmas, Momma yawning wide in the background;

Momma and Daddy dancing in the backyard and I remember it was my birthday that day. They look stiff together in that dancing photo, as if the photographer had to beg them to dance for the camera. It is little Virginia Kate behind the camera, and I *had* begged them.

Andy swing-swing-swinging on the old swing, with me pushing him. He is laughing and I look worried as an old woman who knows what comes next because she's lived it before. I trace with my finger the years of Momma and Daddy before and after us kids. It is as if I am looking at different people. As if it is all our fault.

And an image of me, when hope was Queen. I'm empty and ready to be filled, my hands down at my sides, my belly slim, my eyes hope filled. Every month Dylan had sighed at me as I trudged out of the bathroom with my eyes down to the ground and my lips pulled into a frown, the bright red evidence of my failure washed out of my underwear. The photos show the evidence of his need and my want and the lack of it.

I put all the pictures back into the envelope except for the one of my parents under the sugar maple in the yard where I played with my brothers. I'll frame that one to remind me there was a time that held love. I slip off my little girl bed, and ease out the back door, say hello to the sugar maple, and gaze at my mountain rising as it always does. Then I stroll to Mrs. Anna Mendel's house. She's there in her garden with her funny hat and spiffy cane decorated with a yellow bow. She's old and gray and she doesn't care.

I hail her, "Hey there, Mrs. Anna Mendel."

She turns to me, holds out a pretty purple flower. "Come here and let me give you some flowers." With her pruning scissors, she cuts away. I take the flowers, one by one. She says, "So, have you talked much to my nephew lately?" She tries to sound casual, but I know better. I do.

I answer, "Not much."

She straightens, looks me full on, says, "Gary's a good man. You could do worse, you know." She doesn't act embarrassed one speck by how bold she's being. "And by the way, please call me Anna instead of Mrs. Anna Mendel."

I push my face into the flowers and inhale. There's sweet, there's bitter, there's the West Virginia soil. When I look at her, she's shaking her head.

"You are as ornery as ornery can be, but I know you'll come round." She wipes her hands on her gardening apron and says, "Come to supper with us."

"I'm a little busy with things."

"I'm having pintos, cornbread, and apple pie. No person is too busy for that." Anna Mendel leans on her cane, waits.

I nod, because I can't hurt her feelings, even if I'm in no mood for supper with that Gary being there.

"My nephew had a wife years back. She took off and he never heard hide nor hair nor spit from her ever again. Never did get another one, always said he was too busy for it, just like you. All I know is he's been hurt too much for such a good boy, just like you." She touches a flower's petal. "I think that boy's been waiting for you since he saw your picture when you were nothing but teenagers."

"You are too much a romantic. That's the silliest thing I've ever heard."

She cackles, says, "I'm going in to cook. See you at six." She totters away.

I watch her, feeling mad at myself for saying I'd go to supper. I have other things to do. I have photos to look through, journals and letters to read, memories to write, ghosts to listen to. I go back inside Momma's house to find a vase for the flowers, fill it with water from the stuttering faucet, plunge in the flowers, and take them back to my room.

The mess is everywhere, memories spilled. I hold my hand over a pile; my palm tingles, grows warm, warmer. Where my hand feels the most tingle, I pull out an old journal, place my palms to the front and to the back, feel the warming of my palms, the vibration of the words and memories inside. When I open it, a hospital bracelet with my name on it falls out. I don't need to read the words to know who it is. The pain comes sharp, even after all this time. I can feel everything all over again. The pain. The empty.

I smell bread and apples. *Be strong, little mite.*

I have to finish this part. Get though it before I lose my nerve.

I again hail Anna Mendel and tell her I can't make it to supper after all. Too much to do, I say to her. Too many voices to listen to.

This part must be done first. Then, I will rest for a while.

For you and I are past our dancing days
—Shakespeare

1983-85

Chapter 24

If you can't give me children, then will you give me this?

Dylan rolled out of bed, and grinning as if he were a kid on Christmas morning, went out the bedroom door. He soon came back with a long cardboard tube, and plopped on the bed with it. Taking out the paper as if it were national documents of greatest importance, he unrolled the thin house plans flat, and began pointing at what looked like squiggles, squares, triangles, and half-circles to me, but were rooms and doors and windows to him.

The sun was full out. I rubbed the sleep from my eyes. I hadn't been able to rise early as I always used to. Even my bones were tired. I'd never felt so sleepy in my entire life. I pulled myself up.

"And here is the master bedroom. Isn't it huge? I made you a huge walk-in closet." He pointed to the bluish paper.

I nodded, yawned.

"Over here we can put in double-doors leading to a personal patio where we can have coffee in the mornings. We'll have a bigger patio out from the living room for parties." He smoothed the paper. "My friends and family give fantastic parties. You'll learn how to do it the California way, too."

"California. So far away." I stretched out my legs, pointed my toes.

"We'll be closer to my family."

"But far from mine."

"It's just a thought." Dylan rolled the paper back into its tube. His little boy grin turned into a little boy pout.

I slid from bed, put on my robe, and went to the kitchen.

Dylan followed me and I imagined he dragged a blankee behind him instead of that tube. "You always said you didn't want to stay in Louisiana. Now here's your chance."

While I made coffee, Dylan went outside for the newspaper.

As soon as he was back, he flappervated his lips all over again about it. "What if we kept this house? We could, you know. Have a place to come back and stay when you visit your family."

When *you* visit your family. Where was the *we*, I wondered. From the ice-box, I took the cream, poured a bit into the creamer. Opened the sugar jar. Smelled the coffee brewing, glad it didn't make me sick.

". . . and the weather is . . ."

Opened the breadbox and took out the store-bought bread. I'd yet to bake Grandma Faith's recipes, or Momma's. Maybe it was time to get over all that, since I sure missed that bread. I'd bake some later today. That's what I'd do. Maybe like Momma, I could knead answers out of the dough.

". . . love the beaches there . . ."

I placed two pieces of bread in the toaster. Opened the ice-box again and took out the eggs. The date showed they were still good eggs. Mee Maw said white eggs are from white chickens, brown eggs are from brown chickens, and they all come from the same place: a chicken's nasty butt. She'd said chickens were the nastiest of critters that ate their own waste and would as soon peck out a person's eyes as look at them cross-a-ways.

". . . and my sister said . . ."

I cracked three eggs and dumped the innards into a bowl, scooped out the squiggly white slimy thing I hated so much, tried not to think about what Jade said it reminded her of.

". . . anyway, where else would you want to live? We could go anywhere. Think of your photography! And I can find a firm anywhere, or better yet, open my own." He rolled the tube back and forth across the kitchen table, and the sound was like fingernails on my brain.

I added salt and pepper to the eggs, a bit of milk, a squirt of water.

"But California. I miss it, Kate. I do. I want to go home."

Home. I whipped the eggs, fast faster fastest. Slapped butter in the skillet and waited for it to melt. Poured us both a cup of coffee, added cream and sugar to mine.

Then he said it, "If you can't give me children, then will you give me this?"

The room went still. It was a still so sudden and so complete, that it felt as if even my blood stopped flowing and my heart stopped beating. When everything began to move again, I swallowed fifteen hideous snapping sharp-saber-toothed frogs, each that wanted to tear at Dylan and shush him up. It made my news feel as if it was rusty, as if it'd been out in the rain and lost all its shine.

I poured egg mix into skillet. Eggs were dead babies, or maybe it was eggs that weren't fertilized. But they were most certain baby chickens who weren't allowed to make it. My stomach squeezed. But some chickens hatched and grew into more chickens and on the world turned turned turned doing what it was supposed to do and maybe at last my body was doing what it was supposed to do.

Everywhere I went, I saw pregnant women with beaming faces, their bellies poked out as they waddled. Still, my own emptied life had passed. I worked at the library, my freelance photography, helped Soot and Marco, especially when Soot was with her momma, who had rallied and said she wasn't ready to die and would will herself well. I hoped that would be the case.

I tried not to take picture after picture of babies and mommas and swollen pregnant bellies.

Dylan's disappointment in my empty womb sent him to his best friends in a bottle more often. One night, I poured a bottle down the sink while Dylan worked late. Another bottle showed up. I should have known, since I'd long ago learned those bottles always came back, a never-ending parade of them crossed my life-path at every turn. The more the world turned, the more it stayed the same.

Then one morning I awoke smelling fresh-baked bread and apples. Grandma Faith said, *Stop fighting so hard, Granddaughter. Stop fighting life so hard. Let it be as it will be.*

I listened to her, wise wise Grandma. I left my troubles by the side of the road, and when I did that, something took. I'd wanted to tell Dylan the good news from the beginning, but I'd stayed quiet until I felt stronger.

I'd planned to tell him right before he brought in his Tube of Dreams.

"Hello? Kate? I *said*, I guess I shouldn't have said that." He sipped his coffee in a way that made me think he wasn't so sorry.

I pushed over-scrambled eggs back and forth. I wanted to make him a family. I wanted to offer up gifts from my body, one after another. He wanted five, six, a Frank Lloyd Wright seven. I wanted whatever would come when it would come. Maybe at last there was something happening that would be the beginning. Maybe at last my body knew what to do.

He was then behind me, kissed the back of my neck. My piled up hair had pieces falling all over themselves. I looked a mess. He said, "I suppose there isn't some formula for life everyone is supposed to follow, much as I want it that way."

His apology.

The toast was ready. The eggs more than scrambled. The second cup of coffee ready to add to cooling cups. I wanted to tell him, but I was afraid. Afraid of how molecules did strange things in our bodies. Afraid that I was wrong and there was something else going on. Afraid that I was wishing so hard that I'd somehow made a fake baby to believe in. I'd heard of those things, women who yearned for something so bad they conjured them from their want.

". . . ole E W E may just pull this off . . ."

Grandma Faith brushed my cheek, but it didn't calm me.

I thought of Momma giving up her children, even the unborned one, and how I wanted one so bad and it had seemed I couldn't even make one. A woman had to have that purpose, even if she decided not to use it, it had to be there. At last, maybe I was finding the possibility of that purpose.

I made up our plates with food.

". . . and that's why traffic is so bad . . ."

I put breakfast on the table, set myself down to eat. My stomach squeezed bile. Chickens and their eggs. Chickens that didn't make it. That were on my plate. That were broken open and scrambled.

"What's wrong? You seem tense."

"I'm fine." I took a bite of toast, swallowed it past the sick frog, took another and swallowed, and another. Took a bite of egg but it wouldn't go down. The baby chick that was never to be gelled on my tongue and grew sour-nasty. My stomach boiled up and over. Pressing my hands against my mouth, I ran out of the kitchen to the bathroom, leaned over the toilet, and let the toast surge up and out, the piece of egg fly, let coffee spew up, let the bile heave from me. I thought I would roll inside out.

Behind me, Dylan called my name. I heard water running as he cut on the faucet.

I flushed, turned from the toilet to the sink, wiped my trembly mouth, washed my face, sipped water from my palm, cut off the faucet, leaned over and rested my head on the cool sink.

"Do you need a glass of water?"

I shook my head, straightened, turned to him and parted my lips to say it. Saying it would make it real. Saying it would make the whispery feeling inside of me strong and brave, and it would grow and grow, and then a full baby would form inside of me, and I'd hold it in my arms and rock and rock and tell it all the stories of our lives, things to come and things behind—but only the good things. My eyes held the story, they must have because Dylan's smile began at the corners and then spread.

"Are you pregnant?" He reached out and put his hand on my stomach, searched my face as if reading it for signs. "That's what's been wrong, isn't it? The sluggishness, the preoccupation. Kate? Are you?" He put both hands on my shoulders.

I wanted to cry. No, I never cried. Though, it was all too much. The secret I'd held. The want to tell him.

"Answer me. Are we having a baby?"

"I don't know," I said. I knew. I knew the baby was a tiny bug inside of me. A little being who looked like a shrimp or some other critter that didn't look human, but one day would.

"You don't know?" He lifted his arms, waved them around. "Then go to the doctor. Find out. Why haven't you said? What are you doing? I don't understand you at all." Dylan pushed back his hair and it stuck out wild. "I'm making an appointment with Dr. Hammermill. This is ridiculous."

I let him dial up the doctor, while I went back to bed feeling as if I hadn't a brain to call my own. I lay there while he talked to the doctor's office, his voice falling in waves into the room, up and down up and down. I felt a little sick again.

Dylan came back into our room with a wet washrag. "I have an appointment for us tomorrow morning."

I barely nodded, but wouldn't turn to look at him since moving my head made things worse.

"I don't understand why you didn't tell me. You know how much I've wanted this."

"I wanted to be sure."

"How can you be sure until you go to the doctor?"

I sighed into my pillow.

"This is happening, isn't it? You're having our child." Dylan eased himself on the side of the bed, his weight pulling me to him. He put the cold washrag on my forehead.

"I don't feel right."

"Well, what pregnant woman does?"

I couldn't explain to him how I was afraid the baby wouldn't be mine to hold, after all. How afraid I was that the whispering would stop. How the emptiness would then return.

"You rest. I'll clean the kitchen."

I pulled the washrag over my eyes so I wouldn't see so much hope in Dylan's eyes. I knew that same hope was in my own.

The next day, when the doctor said, "Congratulations!" Dylan let out a happy shout. Dr. Hammermill said to me, "Well, isn't this wonderful news at last?"

I opened my mouth to answer, but Dylan said, "Yes! I can't believe it. We've tried so hard."

"That was probably the problem," Dr. Hammermill said, and laughed.

Dylan slapped the doctor on the shoulder and laughed with him.

I grinned. I whoop-dee-dooed. I pushed down the bad feelings and let the good ones rise up and spill out into the room.

Dylan said to me, "You'll quit work now."

Dr. Hammermill said, "I'm sure she'll be fine. Many women—"

"I don't want her on her feet and pulling and tugging on books and driving back and forth from that greasy diner and the library."

"Well, that's between Mom and Dad and you two can discuss it at home." Dr. Hammermill made notes in his folder and snapped it shut. "Make a follow up appointment at the desk." He looked at me. "And congratulations, Mommy."

Dylan grabbed me in a hug, then loosed his grip. "Oops, don't want to hurt the Mother."

Mom. The Mother. Mommy. I was going to be a Momma, the best Momma of all of the Mommas who ever lived. I would be the most loving wonderful Momma in all of Momma Land. I held onto my womb.

We did it, little one.

۞ • ۙ

Dylan had the baby's room painted a pretty yellow. He'd already bought baby toys and baby furniture. Rebekha and Jade jabbered away about baby showers, baby clothes, baby this, and baby that, and I laughed at how excited everyone was for me. The whispery feeling became a flutter and the flutter became a rolling motion. The little one was there, I felt it.

I quit my job at the library and at Soot's, since Dylan wouldn't let it go, and I was afraid if I didn't do everything he said just as he said it, something would go wrong and it'd be all my fault. With my new camera Dylan bought me to celebrate, I took photos of my belly so I could record it for all time and one day show my child what I looked like as it grew inside of me.

Dylan wanted a boy because that's what men most times said they wanted, so that boy could carry on their name, and not their mistakes. A little boy would be grand, with sturdy legs and mischief in his eyes; but I wouldn't care if a little girl came crying into the room with chubby cheeks and pretty eyes. The boy names I thought of had my daddy in them, or my brothers, or Uncle Jonah. I wanted the girl to be named after Grandma Faith and Rebekha (or Momma? a thought sneaked in), and Dylan had said, Well, we'll talk about that. He wanted a baby girl named after his momma and grandma, who had the names Barbara and Audrey. I knew Mee Maw Laudine would have a fit if there was a girl child and we didn't name it after her; oh, but how could we?

Rebekha took me to the mall once a week and we walked all around the stores gawking at baby things. She wanted to buy a portable crib to keep at her house so she could babysit. Everything had happy stars shining with all the sparkling light.

But at night, when everyone was still and the world was sleeping and Dylan soft-breathed at my side, I laid my hand on my womb and felt the fear rise up as it had before. When I tried to talk to my little one, its sighs and whispers seemed to me weaker than I thought they would be.

One restless worrying morning, I eased myself into my car, and drove to Miss Darla's house. When I knocked on her door, she threw it open and asked, "Tea?"

I nodded, stepped into her sanctuary.

In her kitchen, she poured tea she'd already had steeping as if she knew I was coming. She put the hot tea and her cookies on a tray and I followed her outside. We lazed on her back porch and sipped.

At last, I said, "I'm a bit scared."

"I have never had a child, so I don't know how that feels."

"It feels as if there is something inside of you that either wants to stay, or wants to leave. Some babies stay. I feel as if mine wants to leave."

"You're being protective. I do know that many pregnant women feel that way. They want to protect what's growing inside of them."

"I have bad dreams." I took a bite of a cookie, thinking I should be eating a piece of fruit instead, for the little one's good health.

"Oh, pregnant women have bad dreams all the time. It's the hormones."

I took a sip of tea.

Miss Darla held the palm of her hand over my belly. "Do you mind?"

Part of me wanted her to do it, and part of me didn't. "No, I don't mind."

She laid her hand on my belly.

I didn't care for the shadow that passed in her eyes.

"This baby is sure a quiet one."

I nodded.

"The child is far beyond the years of our knowledge and understanding. It has lived many years in many places." She took away her hand and began talking about the trip abroad she'd soon take.

I didn't ask her anything more about my little one. We sipped our tea and talked about the fresh mint she'd grown and added to the tea and didn't it give it a fresh taste? Yes, I agreed it did. And weren't those cookies good? Oh yes, those cookies were the best in all of cookie land. Miss Darla stroked my hair, as if I were her child. I closed my eyes and wished Momma was there with me. I didn't care what she'd done or said, I wanted her. I made no sense to me.

That night I dreamed my baby was born without eyes, and it turned its head this a-way and that a-way as it tried to find my voice while I called to it. The empty places where its eyes were supposed to be were pitiful and dark and its searching head was horrible. When I woke, I felt a little cramp, as if the baby was scared of the dream, too. I stroked my stomach, told it, "There there, there there, don't be afraid, Momma's here."

I wished the bad feelings away, but they crept in the dark, scrabbling their feet across my brain.

Chapter 25

Little one, stay with me

I settled into my routines. Taking my photos and sending them off to magazines and papers. The baby room was done, because Dylan had worked on it every night after work, his talk about California postponed.

Uncle Jonah and Aunt Billie sent gifts, and one of them was a beautiful carved bassinette made of oak stained dark that must have cost a fortune to ship. Mee Maw sent baby clothes and shoes, and bottles she said were just like a woman's niplets (that's what she called them). Daddy wanted me to call her Ariel if it was a girl and William if it was a boy. Bobby moved into Andy and Micah's old room and Rebekha used Bobby's room as a baby-come-to-visit room. Mrs. Mendel sent crocheted booties in white, yellow, green. Soot and Marco gave me some of their babies' old clothes, and bought new soft toys, little books, and rattles. Amy Campinelle knitted a bitty sweater. My little one was already spoilt rotten.

I'd written Momma and she'd sent a wrinkled five-dollar bill with a note telling me to buy something for the baby. She also written, *Now your life's going to change and you'll understand better.* I would never understand in the way she did.

I was laughing with Jade on the phone, talking about something else that wasn't babies, at least at first because really the baby was all I thought of. She told me a story about a man she'd been dating who asked her to marry him after two dates.

"I couldn't believe it, Vee. He got down on one knee and had a ring and everything."

"Did you say yes?"

"What? No!" She said, "It was uncomfortable to say the least." There was the sound of clinking, and I knew she had on her bangle bracelets, seven of them, silver and gold. "I don't think I'm going to be seeing him again." More clinking.

"Whatever happened to Barry? He's a great guy. Maybe you can move to California. I mean, if we go there after the baby is born."

"I'm selfish. I hope you don't go there. Please don't move."

"I was asking about Barry and you."

"It just didn't work out."

"Well, he sure liked you a lot."

"Oh, he got over me fast enough. Last time we talked, he made that move to Canada and is dating a very nice woman who is better for him than I could ever be."

"Stop it. He'll never get over *you*, Jade."

"You love to dream up stuff, don't you?"

"I do not."

"So, how's Dylan? Is he about to drive you crazy with all his plans for the baby before it's even born? Has he figured out what college it'll attend? When is he going to stop haranguing you to move to Cal-ee-for-ni-a." Her bracelets jingled. "And the other day he was already talking about the next kid. For god's sake, you haven't even squatted out this one yet."

"Jade, that's nasty." But I laughed.

"Well, I've never met a man who wants children as bad as that man does. Let's hope he wants to take care of them as much as he wants to have them, huh?"

"Well, I suppose he will." I leaned over to grab my glass of sweet tea. A cramp sneaked across my belly. I'd had little cramps before. As I straightened with my tea, the next one made me breathe in sharp and hard.

"Vee? I asked if you wanted to go get something for lunch?"

I couldn't answer her, my whirled brain latched on to what was happening in my womb. What the little one was trying to tell me. What was happening where I couldn't see so that it may as well have been a million miles away from me. Another cramp hit and I dropped the phone and the tea. The glass rolled across the wood floor, tea and ice spilling out. I heard Jade calling to me from the phone receiver, but I couldn't answer. I held onto my stomach, tight tighter. *No, little one, no.* There was wet between my legs.

The phone squawked with Jade's voice, then went silent.

I slid careful slow down onto the floor, asking of my baby, "Don't go little one; don't leave me. Hold on tight."

Grandma Faith brushed my forehead with a finger, sad sad sad. Sighs on the wind. Heavy sad sighs. The spirits surrounded me, unable to help. Helpless helpless ghosts. Helpless me. Helpless babe.

The next cramp hurt bad, and a sound ripped the room. It was my own voice crying out. The sticky wet feeling spread. I curled tight tighter, as tight as I could, held onto my womb with all I had. The world was topsy turning, and I was going to be sick, but held myself even tighter, afraid that if I heaved, it would force out my sweet one.

"No, little one, no."

Another bad cramp came to tear me asunder.

We'll take it. We'll take the babe and care for it for you. Don't worry.

"No," I told the ghost. "I want my little one to stay with me."

The babe sighed, slipping away, sighing. Beyond my knowledge or understanding. Sighing, slippery slipping, wet, warm, then cold, then hot, then aching aching aching. Shivering. Sticky. Lonely.

The ghosts sighed, held out their arms. *This wee one's not ready to come back to the old world again. We'll take care of the babe for you.*

Grandma Faith cried, long low laments.

The room filled with moans. Lamenting weeping moaning.

The door pounded open and Jade's voice came from far away. "Virginia Kate? . . . *Oh no!* Oh my god, oh Vee. Oh, sweetie. Are you . . ."

And I fell, down down, faster and faster I fell. I fell away. Fell down deep and hard, fell into the black hole, sucked up and away. I searched blind, like my little eyeless one I'd dreamed about, turning my head this a-way and that a-way. I searched the ever eternal for my baby, but all I found in the old wild world was dark.

Chapter 26

The ghosts were quiet

The phone rang but I ignored it since I didn't want to hear anyone tell me they were sorry for my loss. Sorry I was emptied. Sorry I wasn't a woman who could hold onto her little one. I'd not picked up my camera, and I'd not gone to see Jade dance while she tried to pretend it didn't hurt her to do it. Soot and Marco sent food, as did Amy Campinelle and Mr. Husband, as did Rebekha. The food smelled rancid, looked rotten and old. I pushed some into my mouth, chewed, and wondered how rancid rotten food could be tasteless.

Miss Darla came. She said, "Drink this . . ."

I drank. I didn't know what it was supposed to do, since I still had an echoing empty in the center of my body where most women grew fertile gardens. She said, "Oh Girl, my heart's heavy with you." She lifted my pendant where it lay cold against my chest, poured something into it, closed the clasp, held it between her palms, and laid it back against my chest. I felt a warming then cold then nothing.

The ghosts were quiet. They had my baby.

Grandma Faith was silent, as she sometimes was, for her own reasons—maybe she was thinking on her own little one born wrong and twisted. Maybe she was thinking it better to lose them before they were born pitiful and then taken away wrapped in nasty workshirts by horrible husbands. Maybe she thought it better to die as neverborns than as her boy Ben, who left the world on purpose with his head blown to bits. Maybe that was what Grandma Faith thought on. I hoped she'd find my little one with the spirits and take it into her arms, the arms that held her own.

A day came to mind during my pregnancy when I was full of my possibility. I had photographed a woman who painted tiny angels onto pebbles and then put them into soft leather bags. The angels represented different things: love, warmth, kiss, and hug. I'd bought a few of them for gifts, cradling them in my hands while she figured out how much I owed her. I remembered how she had photos of children in her studio and when I asked her about them, she said they were all her children and grandchildren. She had ten kids and so far fifteen grandchildren. So many. And some had few. Then, after all, some had none.

I thought of who belongs, who doesn't, where we belong, and where we don't. Who gets a chance in this old world and who doesn't.

The phone rang again. I let it howl.

Dylan wasn't there to answer it. Maybe he had to work late, maybe he had to go to supper with clients, maybe he had a flat, or maybe he wouldn't even bother to come home. The first time Dylan stumbled into the house with glittered eyes and casual mouth, I hadn't said a word; he tried to pretend he wasn't boozed up more than ever, but I hadn't cared a speck of nothing about that.

The second time, I threw the supper Rebekha brought all down the garbage disposal, gurgled it on down the pipes, one spoon at a time. Dylan came in and watched me. Later, when he stood in the bedroom with his sandwich, watching me as I lay there, he'd said, "You don't have to cook dinner you know, not if you don't want to." I'd turned away from him. He said, "I cook better anyway and I enjoy doing it." I didn't even tell him Rebekha had brought it.

The third time he came home late with the booze breath and the halted steps, I was in bed with a book, pretended to read, pretended I hadn't known what could happen with men and their trouble. Pretended I hadn't known that men couldn't handle the bad, that they only wanted the good. That when we aren't perfect visions of what they desire, they become petulant and ornery and search for answers in bottles, or other beds, or through work, or all of it. I wondered where Dylan's searches took him, but I didn't wonder enough to ask or let it pull me from my bed of sorrows.

He'd said, "Do you ever get out of this bed?"

I turned the page of the book. It was page eighty-one, and I couldn't repeat what the book was about because I wasn't really reading it.

He said, "Kate?"

I turned to page eighty-two.

"And you wonder why I don't want to come home."

I looked up from my book, opened my mouth, but no words would come. I wanted to tell him how I hurt, wanted to tell him that he was making things worse, wanted to tell him I was a failure and couldn't he understand how sorry I was I let him down, let my women-kin down, let woman-kind down. I wanted to tell him I needed him to tell me everything was all right, and to mean it, wanted to ask him to forgive me for something that wasn't my fault, that my body was against me, and how could I change that? Nothing but soured breath came from my open mouth, so I closed it. Even the old mouthy frog was quiet.

He tore into a chicken leg with his teeth, chewed, swallowed, took a slug of beer, and then said, "This house depresses me."

I lowered my eyes, turned to page eighty-three.

He walked away. There came the sounds of ice clinking against the glass. Those sounds that I'd heard most my life. The comfort and the disappointment bound together as one.

There had been days when Dylan and I laughed together, cuddled together and watched favorite television shows, times he showed me the plans for the house in his Tube of Dreams; the one he wanted to build that had many rooms for the many children he wanted, the children I couldn't hold in my ornery womb.

There were days when we took Jinxie for long walks and then went to Calandro's and bought groceries so Dylan could cook a feast, or we went to a nice restaurant and ate hallelujah crab, where the crab had its claws all up in the air as if it were praising Jesus instead of dead, fried, and put on a plate. We had Jade and her latest over, or if she was off men for not-really-good, she'd come alone. We'd set at the long mahogany table and talk about everything under the moon. Dylan and his buildings. Jade dancing and her teaching dance.

I'd even yappered on about my photography, how I loved the library smells, and even the greasy fry smells from Soot and Marco's diner. We laughed at how lucky we were to be doing what we wanted. We lifted glasses into the air and clinked them—they with their drinks and me with my sweet tea. Clink clink clink. Those times, I could ignore how sometimes there were too many clinks.

The seventh time Dylan came home with boozy breath and a sly way about him, I pretended I was asleep. I wondered things. Wondered why men did the things they did. Why they wanted and wanted and asked and asked and then when they had what they wanted and wanted and asked and asked for, they no longer wanted it and they no longer asked. Or, if they didn't get what they wanted and wanted and asked and asked for, they punished by pretending it was the woman who punished.

That seventh time, he'd slipped into bed and I kept my back turned. He didn't touch my shoulder. There were no words. There was no riding to the top of my mountain until my breath was ragged and torn.

The tenth time Dylan came home late with soured breath and the hooded eyes of those old birds of prey, I'd lain quiet. Waited for the things that would soon come to a horrid head.

A voice from down in the death sewers flicked its pointed tongue. *This ain't all that man's fault. You scarce didn't love him proper. You just loved the idear of it all. You made this happen. You did, Fattie Mae. You did. You did.*

I had pushed the pillow around my ears so I wouldn't have to listen to the voices I ran away from, but still heard the sad soured breathing of my husband.

k • k

The phone caterwauled again, until it stopped. The darkened room had pinpricks of light, but I didn't want to let in all the light. In the dark I saw my baby's face in shadow, the little one who hadn't been safe inside me. It had left me because I wasn't strong enough. It hadn't wanted to be a part of who I was. It was just too tired to hang onto a womb that couldn't carry it to its term. Maybe the spirits were right, that the babe had been in the old world before and decided it didn't want to be there again, and instead, would try again later, with someone else.

Never again with me, was what the doctor said. Never. "I'm sorry," he said. "So sorry." No more. Ever again.

I let myself slip on away. Let the hours pass me on by. The phone finally stopped yowling.

Jinxie put his head on my bedside and I petted him. He climbed into the bed with me, something he'd never done before, and I let him stay there beside me, his warm body and soft doggie snores helped me in the way those things will do when nothing else or no one else will.

The twelfth time of his arriving home late, Dylan slurred, "Enough's enough." He moved into the guest room.

My bones creaked and moaned. I said, or maybe only thought,

"Wait! Please, Dylan. My husband. Understand. Help me. Help your wife. I'm so tired." My hair spilled across my pillow.

Daddy came, said to me, "'How far that little candle throws his beams.'" He stroked my hair, as he'd done to me when I was his little Bitty Bug, his sweet Ariel.

Oh Daddy.

Rebekha helped me up, brushed out my lanked hair, long and slow, her lullaby.

Thank you, Rebekha.

Jade lay beside me, hugged me to her, rocked rocked rocked me. "Vee, please. Please don't be so sad. I love you."

I love you, too. The love of a friend was more pure than ever the love of a man and a woman. It would always be so.

Someone opened a window, the curtains reached out to me, and I turned my head away. My marrow emptied. All that was left was empty skin and emptied bones lying flat on the sheets.

Bobby read to me from my old book, the one I used to read to him when he was little. "'There was once a velveteen rabbit, and in the beginning he was really splendid. He was fat and bunchy, as a rabbit should be; his coat was spotted brown and white, he had real thread whiskers, and his ears were lined with pink sateen. On Christmas morning, when he sat wedged in the top of the Boy's stocking, with a sprig of holly between his paws, the effect was charming . . .'"

Did he become real, little brother?

Andy said, "Oh Seestor, please get up," and I did for him that day. But I was dead frog tired and as soon as he left, I slipped back between my rumpled sheets.

Once I thought I'd died as I floated in a black space, high above the earth, where even the stars couldn't shine. I looked for my little one there, but I was alone. I woke, realizing it was but a dream, and found I missed the black space and wanted to return.

Dylan stood in the doorway, holding his magical tube that he wanted to carry him all the way back to California. He said, "You never could give me what I wanted. You always held it back from me."

Dylan, how could you never understand the power of my women-kin? Dylan, did you ever really know me?

ॐ • ॐ

There came the sound of pots and pans banging loud, the sound of off-tuned humming. I'd not heard Dylan make a happy sound in that way in a long lonely time. We didn't use the kitchen much lately, unless it was Dylan pounding ice in a glass, and when I wandered about the house at night, there were booze bottles standing at attention with their amber liquid both beautiful and terrible. Sometimes Old Moon shone through the bottles, and it made the magic sparkle. How wicked and tricky it was.

The banging was so loud and the humming wore on my nerves so fierce, I slipped out of bed to tell Dylan to leave it all be.

When I sludged into the kitchen, he was there.

I cried out, my voice exploding out of me as old blood vomit. I rushed forward, the floor cold beneath my bare feet.

"Hey Vee!" That's all he got out before I grabbed him and hugged him hard enough that I heard his breath go *Omph!*, felt his ribs though his shirt. Micah grunted out, "You're going to . . . break me in half . . . Seestor."

I stepped back to look at my big brother. Micah was skinnier than ever, so skinny I could almost see through him. He and Jade could have a skinny contest and I don't know who would win. He cocked an eyebrow at me still in my cotton gown even though it was afternoon, at my hair hanging messy and greasy. He gave a half-grin and I laughed because I just couldn't help but laugh. The sound plopped out of my throat and into the room. It croaked and jumped and blinked in the sunshine.

He said, "Don't you ever answer your phone?"

I wondered which time had been him. I wondered why I hadn't known.

"Look at you, in your nightie. Lazy go crazy!"

I croaked out, "Look at you, brother."

"As you can see, I'm still alive, mostly. Are you?"

"Oh Micah."

He put up his right hand, palm to me. "Let's talk about something good. Like what're we going to eat? I'm starved for Louisiana food. I was trying to make you a grilled cheese and tomato soup." He pointed behind him with that hand.

I looked at the sandwich and soup. Then back at him. He had dark smudges under eyes that searched for something, and I wanted to erase those dark things. Maybe he saw the same with my face and wanted to erase my own.

Jinxie eased into the kitchen and went to Micah for a pat. The old dog had arthritis and didn't wiggle to his guests as fast as he used to, but he was still my strong warrior dog. Micah hunkered down and put his face into Jinxie's coat. Jinxie didn't move, he let my brother stay there as long as he needed to because he was just that kind of dog. I'd put my face in Jinxie's coat too many times to count.

I ate the grilled cheese and slurped the soup while Micah took a shower. It was the best tasting thing I'd had in forever. While I ate, Rebekha's red beans and rice heated on the stove for Micah. There was some of Rebekha's cornbread, too, and I'd sliced two big pieces for him, sprinkled a bit of water on them, and slid them in the oven to warm.

Micah came back in with a fresh shirt and blue jeans hanging on his skinny be-hind that was the skinniest ever. "Vee, you don't look so hot."

"'Vanity, thy name is woman' isn't me, huh?"

"Shakesshit, as Momma used to say."

I went over to stir the beans.

He looked comfortable at my kitchen counter. "I came soon as I could."

I stirred the beans more. "I'm glad you're here."

"I'm sorry. Really sorry."

I didn't say anything. Too many words would vomit out and make a mess all over creation.

Micah ran his hands through his hair, still long.

I stirred the beans and stirred the beans and then I spooned them into a bowl. The steam rising looked so normal I about cried, except I hadn't cried during it all. That thought slipped up and hit me upside the head. How I'd learned not to cry. Crying was for weaklings; crying was for pig-tailed girls who were lost. Rebekha said that crying emptied out the poison. I wondered how often she'd cried.

I opened the oven, took out the cornbread, put two heated buttered slices on a plate.

Micah ate the beans and cornbread. Every bite. Afterwards, we went out to the porch, and Jinxie curled at Micah's feet. Micah had a drawing pad on his knee and drew with unrestrained strokes of his pencil. An image of Jinxie began to appear. Sometimes when there was too much to say, it was easier to say nothing at all. I kept my eyes on the drawing. I was safe from the words Micah didn't say. The things he didn't say aloud had been in the letters he sent and in his tired eyes. The things I didn't say were all around as ghost whisperings with their arms full of my child.

My brother was there beside me. I couldn't stop looking at him and at his drawing. I couldn't stop listening to the pencil scratch on the pad, all the memory in that sound. I tried not to notice the marks on his arms. They made my insides feel as if I had worms crawling.

I went inside to fix us some tea, took the frosted glasses back out.

We sipped. I waited for Micah to tell me what all happened with him, but I didn't think he ever would tell it all. The only thing I asked was, "How long can you stay?"

He stopped drawing for a moment. "A week. Is that okay?"

"You can stay forever."

He gave me a look that said of course he couldn't do that, and we both knew it.

When Dylan came home, I introduced them. When my husband said hello, the booze breath shot out and slapped Micah in the face. I saw it in Micah's eyes, what I already knew. Even in all that, it was hard to let go of the marriage, since that would be a failure heavy upon my head. It would mean another abandonment, no matter who left whom. What manner of woman was I?

Dylan said to me, "I'm going to bed."

And he did.

Micah and I stayed up long into the night, rocking; all those unsaid words that didn't need to be said were as the stars over our heads.

When we both yawned so hard our jaws popped, we said our goodnights. I made my way to the bedroom to lie against my pillow until the sun broke and spilled its light. Maybe I slept some and maybe I dreamed. Then I went to the kitchen, made the coffee, and then went back to the bedroom. I stripped the sheets and put them in the washer, then took a bubble bath, scrubbing the sad from my skin and hair, and letting the sad go down the drain, then toweled off, scrubbing until my skin pinked. I then put on soft cotton underwear, soft cotton britches, and a soft cotton shirt, since my skin was raw, and combed out my wet hair.

Back in the kitchen, I decided I'd try to make Rebekha's biscuits, and serve them with her homemade blackberry jelly. After drinking a cup of coffee, I found the old bowl to start my biscuits in, cut on the oven, measured flour in the bowl, and made a well in the middle. From the cabinet I took the shortening, from the ice-box the butter. I went to work making the biscuit dough, adding a pinch of salt and a pinch of sugar, mixed the dough with my hands, but not too much so it wouldn't be tough. I rolled it out with an old glass rolling pin filled with ice water to keep the dough from becoming too soft. Using one of Rebekha's old biscuit cutters, I cut the dough and put the rounds on the baking sheet, and then put the sheet into the oven.

I sipped more coffee, thought about the two men in the house. I waited to see who would rise first and what would happen next with those two men.

But what I knew was that both of them would soon be leaving. Knew that as well as I knew the Louisiana air was wet and the oaks had moss. That Jinxie would soon be in to beg for a treat. That the mountains were older than what I knew old to be. That Rebekha's biscuits would rise up high in the oven and would taste perfect with lots of butter and strawberry jam.

ॐ • ॐ

We'd eaten crab cakes with a hollandaise sauce, stuffed potatoes, and baby greens salad with vinaigrette dressing, and for dessert, Micah's favorite big fat chocolate chip cookies made into ice cream sandwiches. Micah had beamed at us as we devoured our food. Everyone was there, except for Dylan. He'd said he had too much work to do. I didn't beg him to come; I didn't even ask him twice. I couldn't decide if my heart was cut out, or if my heart had never been with him just as he said. I shook thoughts of Dylan away. My big brother was home, even if for such a short time.

When I brought the prodigal son to Rebekha and Daddy's for our reunion party, Rebekha hugged Micah so hard, he said his guts were squished out. He laughed, told her she was a sight too beautiful to behold. Rebekha turned bright pink, cried, touched Micah's cheek as if he were a mirage and she had to check again that he was real, then she wept again.

I wanted to imagine our own Momma weeping for joy for us as Rebekha was.

Daddy had first shaken Micah's hand, then half-hugged him quick, mumbling Shakespeare, or maybe it was I love you or I've missed you, but I do believe it was Shakespeare.

Jade was shy around Micah, but he grabbed her up and swung her silly. She laughed until she cried.

It had been far too long since our Micah had been with us.

The Campinelles and Miss Darla had come for dessert. Micah almost was lost between the two Campinelles as they hugged on him.

Miss Darla had kissed Micah right on the mouth. There was too much noise and confusion and I loved all of it.

Andy had to take Micah for a spin in his Mustang. Bobby jumped in the back and off they went, whooping like warriors off to the hunt.

Daddy had looked at me, said, "'Doubt that the sun doth move, doubt truth to be a liar, but never doubt I love.'"

"I know, Daddy." I hugged his neck but good.

Andy screeched to a stop at the curb and hollered out, "Daddy! Hey, why don't you hop in and take a spin with us?"

I hadn't seen Daddy move that fast in some time, as off he flew, calling out, "'We few, we happy few, we band of brothers!'"

Beth Anne stayed behind, talking with Rebekha as the Mustang's tires peeled off, my brothers, and Daddy, hollering their fool heads off.

If only time could stop right at that moment. I stilled myself, to capture everything in a mind's stilled photograph. Micah laughing. Andy whoop whooping. Bobby throwing his head back in joy. Daddy hollering out in wild abandon. We women pointing and laughing at the men. All us together again. My mimosa waving to me as it'd done from the beginning. The oaks along the street. Rebekha's garden. The green grass, the blue sky. I ran to grab my camera, so I could take real photos when the men returned.

The night before my brother went back to New York, we set on the porch a last time and watched the world turn and turn and turn. The moon was always there, even when I couldn't see it. We sipped a Coke-Cola with lots of ice. We talked about his art, but not about his journey to get where he was. We talked about my photography, but not about Dylan. Sometimes there was no talking, just safe quiet of two people who happened to be brother and sister.

I saw myself mirrored in Micah's remembrances. Maybe he saw himself in mine.

"Nothing in this old world is always easy, is it?"

"Seems that way, I guess," I answered.

"But it sure feels like it is now."

I nodded, touched my brother on the hand quick and then away.

He leaned back his head and a small smile touched the corners of his mouth.

The morning of my brother's leaving for New York, he handed me a canvas wrapped in brown paper. "Vee, I hope you understand this painting. I hope it brings you some comfort. Open it later."

I hugged him tight, then took him to the airport.

He said, "I'll be calling soon. Things are getting ready to happen for me."

"I hope so."

"I know so." He strutted off, looking back only once to give me a wave.

Back at my house, I unwrapped Micah's painting, blinked back the burning in my eyes.

He'd painted me setting in my rocking chair, a tiny smile touching the tips of my lips. The moon shone through the window, a great round orb of mystery. There, floating beside me was a tiny naked baby, kissing my cheek, its tiny angel wings spread as it hovered at my side. The painting was in soft colors, not his usual bold and wild way, and it had a dream-like quality. I held the painting to me, and rocked, rocked, rocked my little one. Then all the veiled secret tears came rushing out. My heart thundered and stormed, my eyes rained and poured. With the painting I was able to say goodbye to my baby, but I also was able to say hello.

Chapter 27

Today

Old letters read while sipping coffee at Momma's kitchen table in the holler

Dear Virginia Kate,

I told your sad momma what all happened with your poor marriage and your sweet little baby. She is sorry, she really is. She would write you, but she does not feel like doing much atall. She got her own poor heart broke by memories and men. I bet she will soon write and let you know how much she hurts because she is your momma. And our mommas are always our mommas, right? I am hurting for you. I know the pain of not having babies. I surely do know the burden of it. I wish I could tell you some thing that would make you feel better. I wish you could see the tomatoes in my garden. I think of you when ever they turn ripe, how we eat them up like apples. If I had a way, I would send some to you for your supper. Well, that is all I got to write. Write me any time.

Your old neighbor, Mrs. Mendel.

Dear Vee,

I'm getting ready to be rich and famous cause some guy bought one of my paintings and then come back a week later and bought another one. Then he was back with another man and that man bought a painting. Then they were back again and talked to me about my own show! I'm going to have my own art show and I want yawwwl here for that. I'll send word as soon as I know. I told you, didn't I? I told you and everybody else I'd be famous one day. I got to get busy painting but let Rebekha and everybody know

    Love, your soon to be famous brother who says I told everyone so! Now I can see everyone again without feeling a failure. Love, your big brother

    Dear Virginia Kate,
    I'm in Kyoto, Japan. It's a beautiful morning. I've been thinking heavily of you since last night. Though I am enjoying my visit, I must get home. Home is a little sad without my Sophia Loren, oh how I miss her! People say I should get another dog and yes perhaps one day I will, but one cannot replace one thing with another, for each person, each animal, everything on this earth is its own unique being and cannot be replaced, only can things be embraced as something new, even if familiar. I have bought you the loveliest kimono. When I return, please come so that we can sit on my back porch and have tea. I have had such good tea here and wish to share with you.
    All my friendship and love, Miss Darla

    Dear Seestor,
    Guess what? Chicken BUTT! Aww, quit making that face. Guess where I am? I'll sit here a minute to give you time to guess. (Cue in Jeopardy theme.) No, that's not it. Nope, that's not it. No. No. Okay, since you can't guess, I'll have to tell you. I bet I'm the only one taking spring break in . . . Alaska! Mom had a fit, said I was too young to be traipsing around the wilderness. I told her I'd be going to medical school in a few years and that qualified me to do every fun thing I could do now. She can't stand it we're all leaving her. Well. Life,

huh? Anyway, everyone else wants beaches in Florida. Bor-ING. I know this will shock you, but I put up my bat and glove for a while. It's for a good cause, since I will have to knuckle down in my studies without much time for practice. Stump is upset, since he says he'll go pro and thought I'd be there with him. That's just how life is, huh? We leave people and things to their considerations. Well, as Micah always said, got to flee, see?

Later gator, Love Bobby

PS: MAGGOT MEAT!!!!!

Dear Sis,

I'm thinking about buying this old bookstore. What do you think? I'm heading on the backslide to thirty in a few years and feel like I need something. Beth Anne says hey. She wants me to do it, but isn't pressuring me. I want to do it, too, but I'm scared. I mean, I know I don't always act mature (I can see you laughing at this, rolling your momma eyes and you can just stop it, Seestor), but you also know when it comes down to it, I do what I have to do and what I want to do and I'm as ornery as you are. Still, I'd like your opinion so give me a call.

Love, Andy

PS: You still getting whirly-brained?…haw haw!

PPS: Bobby says to tell you: MAGGOT MEAT!

Dear Vee,

I can't believe I'm in NEW YORK! I just had to write you a quick note and say how AMAZING it is here. Your brother is being so sweet, showing me around when he can, which isn't often enough. I can't wait until you get here. I mean it, I swear by all that is holy and good and right that I'm MOVING HERE. This is where I belong. Anyway, hurry up and get your butt up here. The art show's right around the corner. He told us, didn't he? He told us he'd do it. I gotta go. I'm going to a BROADWAY SHOW tonight. Your brother set me up on a date. Um, okay, Vee, is your brother STUPID or what? He is. He's the most insufferable stupidest man ever when it comes to some things!

Love you, Jade

Dear Kate,

I know you said you don't want my money, but I'm enclosing a check anyway. Take it. It will pay off the mortgage on my house, our house, well, yours now. We'll settle up on all the papers. My business is doing well, and that's another reason you should take the check because I'm doing extremely well out here. By the way, remember that old tube with my house plans, have you seen it? I know I have asked a million times, but if you ever do come across it, will you mail it to me?

I hope you'll find it in your heart to be happy for me, but Suzanna and I are expecting twins. Laila will have twin brothers to boss around. We're on our way to a houseful!

I'm happy, and I hope you're happy as well. I saw where you published the coffee table book on trees and flowers and what not, and I couldn't be more proud for you. Believe that, even though it never quite worked out for us, did it? Well, that's all I had to say. Quite enough, right?

Take care, Dylan.

Dear Virginia Kate,

I expect you aren't even reading my letters no more, since I haven't heard from you in a long while. Mrs. Mendel says to tell you hello and she ate a tomato yesterday (and that's the silliest thing I ever did hear). Does that man who was my husband still say all that Shakescrap? I reckon you aren't going to tell me since you don't seem to be talking to me. I was up in the attic and found the things your grandma sent me the longest time ago. That apple don't fall far from the crate with you two. Tell that man who I had his kids and cooked for him and made him a home to stop sending me notes with the checks, I don't need to hear him tell me how to live. Tell Laudine to kiss my West by goddammed Virginia ass since she don't have a call to ever write to me ever again and I'll never open another of her letters. I lost my pretty in the accident and now I'm losing my pretty to getting old. I was once 20, then 30, and even 40. I guess you'll get there, too one day, old. I don't need anyone see me get old and ugly so they can gloat. Well, don't know that you'll get this, but here it is.

    Momma

1987 . . .

Why, then the world's mine oyster
—Shakespeare

Chapter 28

Well. Here I am

My high heels click clicked on the sidewalk. There were other high heels clicking: Jade's, Rebekha's, Beth Anne's, Miss Darla's; and there was the clomping of men's shoes: Daddy, Andy, and Bobby. We were dressed in all our finest, our hair shining with our brushing, the women with lipstick and the men with aftershave. I had on a new red dress that swirled about my knees, and my hair was up.

Just another block and we'd be there. Everything he'd said was true, just as he'd been saying since he was a little kid. Our Micah had been noticed. His art was in a show. I was about to bust wide open with pride. All about me people stormed and swirled and I wanted to shout out to them that my brother would be famous.

Jade said, "I've had such a good time here." Her eyes shined. "There's always something going on. I just may not leave."

I shot a look at her and she was so excited, I didn't say, *First Micah, then you? But I'll miss you.* I didn't say it because where would I end up one day my own self?

She glanced at me, said, "This is *my* city. I feel it."

I laughed, in a way that showed I believed her.

Rebekha's eyes sparkled, and she reached over to touch my arm, light, then away.

Daddy, Bobby, and Andy were loping along like giraffes. They were smiling. Everyone was smiling.

When we reached the door of the gallery, we all stuck out our hands at once to open it, then we laughed, then reached out again, then stepped back. Someone inside opened the door and we piled in—right into the world of my brother. He was everywhere, everything about him in his chaotic, wild, and beautiful color on those canvasses. We were everywhere, too. Us, family, before and after and in between. Everywhere was our story played out across the room. As we walked about, our proud and star-struck eyes glittered with wonder at what Micah had done.

I searched for my big brother, wondering where he was, imagined he was doing what he'd always said he would, getting ready to be famous. I caught sight of him in the middle of a crowd of people, all of them pressing near to him. He looked wild from the attention. He looked better than I'd seen him in forever and a day. I remembered the time long before in Rebekha and Daddy's yard, when he'd told me about Uncle Ar-vile, and the nightmares that came. I'd told him to paint out his demons. Maybe he finally had. But he'd painted out the joy, love, and family, too.

I lifted my hand in a little wave, and that was when he saw me. He didn't even tell those people goodbye, just ripped out of the middle of them and galloped over. He stood in front of me, in his favorite color brown. I was glad he didn't wear all black, was glad he didn't wear a beret, was glad his hair was long and dark against his shoulders, and his eyes were glittered from excitement and not from something he put inside his body. His face left cleared of his mistakes, that's what I saw. I hoped it would stay that way.

He said, "Well. Here I am."

"You're everywhere."

"We all are."

The rest of our gang hurried over, so I hugged my brother, and then stepped back to let them gaggle over him. Micah grabbed Jade and squeezed her, then swung her, just as he'd done as the prodigal son returned, while her face glowed. I saw in her eyes how she loved my brother. The only thing I saw in his eyes was sparkling out like fireworks booming. I wanted to bomp him a good one for not seeing what was right before him. Love.

While everyone was just a going on and on, and while Micah laughed at Miss Darla's kiss on both cheeks, I slipped away so I could study Micah's paintings. I started at the beginning, because I knew they told a story, just as a book does, just as photographs do.

There was Micah, Andy, and me, little kids in the holler. There was Momma, her painted back was to me, her face barely turned and in shadow—it said everything about her. Micah had painted Daddy during his salesman days, holding onto kitchen utensils, his hat low over his eye. There was one that reminded me of the drawing I'd found in Micah's closet at the holler, a man full of holes, blood rushing from his wounds, his eyes losing life. Aunt Ruby was there, but no one would know it was she unless they knew that story. The woman in that painting was banshee wild, her hair curling into Medusa snakes. There was the house in the holler, the mountains rising. The lonely house on the hill.

Farther along, the paintings changed to the eerie wet of Louisiana Land, and as the paintings changed, so did the faces of us kids, and of Daddy. And there, Rebekha came along, and her painted face with her gap-toothed smile shone out.

I saw these things even in the paintings that seemed at first to be nothing but swirls of mad color. That was Micah's gift. Within what seemed madness and chaos was beauty, family, friends, love. Truth.

My Family. My Friends. I turned to them. The real them with the painted ones behind me. My heart near to full and bursting.

Before I walked to the other paintings, I wondered, what was next? What came after? Where would Micah's paintings take me? Where would the wind blow everyone?

Where would I take myself?

I entered the circle of family and friends and we took our journey backward and forward.

Momma stayed missing, hiding away in the little white house in the holler.

Chapter 29

Today

The lonely house on the hill over the West by God Virginia holler

I pick one of Anna Mendel's tomatoes, lift it to my mouth and take a bite, let the juice run down my arm. I watch as Gary pulls weeds from his aunt's garden. He looks up, waves at me, and I pretend I don't see him. I should not have done that, for now he's up and comes my way. I have tomato juice on my shirt, on my arm, on my face and chin.

He hollers, "Good Morning, Virginia Kate!"

I watch him walk to me, and I wipe at my mouth. I don't care a speck of nothing that I have tomato juice all over me. He's only an almost handsome man, and what is any man in this big old world?

When he stands in front of me, I say, "Good morning, Gary. How's your aunt?"

"She's feeling poorly this morning, but she'll be all right. Stayed awake too late."

I try to imagine what Anna Mendel would be staying awake late to do.

Gary pushes back his hair, and I almost laugh at the streaks of dirt he leaves on his forehead and the dirt dusted in his hair. He asks, "Are you doing okay?"

"Yes, thank you." I look over his shoulder at the lonely house on the hill. Gary looks back to see what I'm looking to. I say, "My brother bought that house."

"What will he do with it?"

"Fix it up, I guess. So it won't be lonely. He seems to think I'll be helping to do that." I slap shut my trap. Then I square my shoulders. Who should care what I say or do? I didn't have to answer to a soul but myself.

Gary steps closer to me. I step back. He reaches down and plucks a tomato, takes a bite of it, and juice dribbles everywhere. Chewing, he says, "Mmmmmm," his eyes crinkling up. He understands the importance of a fresh-picked tomato.

I stare at him, then look away because my belly does a little wiggle and a flop at how that lopsided grin and that tomato juice spilling and those crinkly eyes pull at me. I do not what to be pulled. I do not want to fall ever again.

Gary says, "I sure liked your brothers. I guess you hated to see them go."

"Yes."

"And your momma, too."

"Yes. My momma."

He shuffles his feet. I knew he was trying to think of things to say to keep me there. He says, "Aunt Anna said you adopted Adin. She's a beautiful young woman. You've done a good job."

I look at Gary to see if he wants to know what's what and decide he does and he doesn't. He does because he is standing too close and has interested eyes. He doesn't because he wouldn't put his nose in another's business. That's what I decide anyway. Soon I'll write down Adin's story, but it's not time for that storytelling, not yet.

Gary wipes his hands on his britches, leaves a trail of tomato seed. He looks down and brushes them off. When he looks at me, his face is pinked.

"Well, I'm about to go on up to the old house."

"Want company?"

I'm about to say, "I do not." But the big fat busy body frog blurts out, "Sure."

Gary's smile shows a tomato seed on his tooth.

I wonder if anything is on my tooth. I do not care. Why should I care if anything is on my tooth?

I walk fast, ahead of Gary. He doesn't try to catch up and I'm glad. He doesn't talk and I'm glad. He doesn't smell of booze and I'm glad.

At the top of the hill, I stop and twist my head to look down at Momma's house. I think for a moment I see her looking out of the kitchen window, her face split in a mischievous smirk, but then I blink and she's gone. A burst of wind brushes back my hair and I hear a sigh of a laugh on the wind. Ghosts are a pain in the rear end. Always sticking their vapor-noses in my business.

When we come to the door, I put my hand on the knob and it feels warm, as if just held by a hand. It feels as if it wants me to come in, the house does. As if it's been waiting for me. Behind me, Gary is soft breathing.

I turn the knob, open the door, and step inside. The house accepts me, has wanted me to come inside for so very long. This I know. I catch up my breath. Its empty needs filling.

Gary stares down at a hole in the floor. "It's going to take a fortune to get this place fixed properly." I see him working out in his mind how he'd fix that floor, and then the windows, and the doors, and the roof.

"I can't believe Micah bought this old house." But I can. I can imagine when he was a boy, how he must have come up here to think and worry on things and have some peace. The way I rode Fionadala, Micah climbed the hill to stow away here. On the walls are his drawings, one after another. I never even knew. I always thought he was up to Buster's house, or down to the creek, or hiding out in the woods. He must have seen Daddy crying that day while hiding inside the empty house. I can imagine him creeping to the window and watching as Daddy buried what remained from the hospital. That spot calls to Daddy and to Momma, but not to me. I have my own little one who calls soft from the arms of the spirits.

All a sudden, I want to help repair the old house and make it like new again, except still like old. Micah must have known this. Must have bought this house knowing his sister would feel the pull of the lonely house needing the fixing. The house knew. The ghosts knew— they'd been calling me back.

I step across the old wood floor and it creaks, but in a pleasant kind of way.

Gary walks towards the other rooms, and I hear his creaks.

I say to the house, "First thing I'll do is get some of this dust and dirt out of here."

The house sighs, *yes please, thank you.*

At a place on the wall that doesn't have Micah's drawings of Momma, me, Daddy, Andy, I peel a long piece of wallpaper. It was once full of bouquets that are almost faded away to nothing. I decide I want to spend the night here. I don't worry about what I'll do with Momma's house.

Gary steps back into the room, and again I almost laugh at the dust and dirt on his face, his hands, his arms, on his clothes. I am irritated at how he makes me want to laugh, but then I can't help it, I point to him and laugh. I say, "You look like a dirty boy who's been playing out all day and his momma's going to get his goat when he comes home."

He looks down at himself, shrugs, looks at me. "And you look like a girl who hides how beautiful she is, inside and out, because she's afraid."

I stare at him; he stares back. I look away first.

He puts his hands in his pockets and turns to study Micah's work on the walls.

To his back, I say, "I'm going to clean this up a bit. I'm going to spend the night here and . . ." I don't tell him I feel a sense of belonging here. I look out one of the windows. They're dirty, but still sturdy. I look down at Momma's house, wonder if that house will remain a sad house in the holler, and the lonely house on the hill will come alive and happy. Maybe I should tear Momma's house down and build a corral for a horse, a horse named Fionadala. We'll ride up the mountain, fast as the wind. The grass will grow back, the wild flowers will come. I'll have a dog, too. A big soft-furred dog. Maybe two horses, two dogs.

Gary has turned to me, smiling. He doesn't look impatient. He doesn't ask me what I'm thinking about. He doesn't look at me as if I should be paying attention to him. He is only there, patient, quiet.

My heart gives a flutter and I try to ignore it, but I'm glad he doesn't ask me where I go off to and to hurry and come back to pay attention to him.

He says, "I'll help you clean it up."

I decide to let him.

We go down to the houses below to grab cleaning supplies, then climb back up and busy ourselves with sweeping and scrubbing. Anna Mendel comes to help for a little bit, but we tell her to go home to rest. She says, "I'll make some sandwiches then."

Gary answers, "And don't climb back up here with them. I'll come down shortly."

When my stomach sets to rumbling, Gary's must have, too, for he goes down to Anna Mendel's and soon returns with tomato and mayonnaise sandwiches, with salt and extra pepper, oatmeal cookies, and a container of fresh-made lemonade. Nothing will ever taste this good.

With care, Gary says, "I don't have any wine, but if you want some to go with your supper tonight, I'll drive into town for you."

I remember Anna Mendel writing to me about the drunkard who killed his daddy. I tell him, "I don't drink."

His eyes spark as he says, "Neither do I."

I get the feeling I was tested in some way, and I don't mind it.

Something unclenches deep inside of me. A release. I finish my sandwich, trying to keep a sappy smile from lifting my lips. Trying not to think about lips. Trying not to think about his lips with a speck of mayonnaise at the corner that he licks away.

He says, "Are you still hungry?"

Yes, I want to say. Yes, I am. I am hungry, Gary. I need filling. I have been empty for far too long. Instead, I say, "I'm fine. Thanks."

We pick up our wrappers, comfortable in the quiet.

Gary turns to me and touches my cheek. I hold my breath, afraid of what smart aleck words might come out of that old frog's mouth because I'm afraid. I hold myself still. He leans in and places his lips against mine, then pulls away.

My lips tingle. We are face-to-face.

I turn away. Behind me, I hear his breath leaving his body. His inhale, exhale, without force, without asking anything else of me I am not ready to give.

My own breath leaves my body.

We breathe in each other's breaths. Taking in of each other.

The air crackles and pops. Maybe a storm is on its way.

Behind me, I hear him walk to the other room.

I want to follow him to find out more, but do not.

Not yet.

❧ • ☙

It takes hours to get the living room clean enough to where we aren't sneezing and to where I can put down a pallet to sleep.

I say, "This is good enough for now. Thank you."

"My pleasure." He has the crinkly-eyed look again.

"I'll take you and your aunt some supper tomorrow. That okay?"

"Sounds more than okay." He goes to the door, then turns back to me. "If you need me, Virginia Kate, you just holler." He stands there, as if waiting for me to need him right then so he can come running right then.

A thought, like a small wren, reminds me of how Jade told me the same thing, because that's what friends say, and then do. I tell him, "I'll be fine." Then before I can stop the happy frog that keeps hopping over the ornery one, I add, "But I will holler good and loud if I need you, you can sure bet."

His face lights up moon-bright. He turns to go back down.

I go down to Momma's house to bathe with her Dove soap in the old claw-foot tub, and then gather what I need. It takes two trips to get what I want back to the old lonely house. I make a nice soft pallet on the floor. I have a jelly jar of iced tea, a dishrag with another tomato sandwich wrapped inside. I'm a girl camping out without a speck of care in the world, and feel as if I'm filling the lonely old house with a live voice, and with my secret desires, and my life.

After I eat my sandwich and drink the tea, I snuggle in Grandma Faith's quilt and think on things. Like how my car is full up with the memories I placed back in boxes and bags, but now I'm not so sure I will be leaving any time soon. Or ever. I'm thinking I want to stay in the holler. The ghosts have always wanted me here. The lonely house on the hill wants me here. Maybe I want me here. I have surprised myself, but then again, I should have known I'd always wanted to return to where my sweet sister mountain called to me.

This can be my belonging place until my end.

I have filled many blank pages in my memory books. There are more blanks to fill, but not as many as when I began. Grandma Faith will be proud of me. Soon, my past scribblings will find my present scribblings, and then I will be done. Grandma Faith says, *The storytelling goes on until your end.*

I snuggle in, cozy with a soft wind blowing in through the windows, and the hole in the floor. A fog has settled in, and drifts by the windows. Not a speck of tired is in my bones. I'm glad for the journey I made here, even though it was hard. I thought I'd be all alone with Momma's ashes, with her memory, and all the spirits of the house in the holler. I was never alone.

The last days in the holler are as close to Momma as I've been since I was a little girl setting beside her at her vanity table with clouds of Shalimar floating. No, even closer than then, since Momma never let me fully come to her until she was already gone.

My family; how it changed and morphed, how it was and wasn't and then how it is. I know my family in Louisiana will miss me, but I know they will understand my need to stay here. I shine the lantern Gary gave me on Micah's drawings. They waver in the shadows. So far he's come from these crude drawings to the art he sells now.

I lie back on the pallet, prop my head against the pillows I brought up from my bed. Under me are blankets and bedspreads, including Andy and Micah bedspreads with the rootin' tootin' cowboys running about with guns and lassos and wild bucking horses. Cover up with my white sheets with the little yellow flowers and Grandma Faith's quilt. These pieces of my childhood home surround me. There's more in Momma's house I'll have to worry over, but for now, this is all I need.

An impish ghost says, *Almost all you need, Miss Virginia Kate the Ornery.*

"Hush now," I say, "hush." Yet, I slip out of the pallet and go to the window, look down at Anna Mendel's house. There are lights on. I wonder if Gary can see the light from my lantern. I go outside, stand with the lantern and listen to the night frogs and insects, the wind through the trees, the mountain darker against a dark sky. An owl flies across the orb of the constant old moon, a dark silhouette between its glow and me.

There's a movement at the window below, and then someone walks out of Anna Mendel's house. I can tell it's Gary since it's for sure a man and not his dear old crooked aunt. He waves. I lift the lantern and wave back, my face burning because I realize I'm full fool face grinning. Like a scared little girl, I hurry to go back inside, but stop before the open door.

I think about how my fears have held me a prisoner, and how I have been releasing them. Or have I? Have I released everything? I released Momma, or at least the parts of her I couldn't hold onto. I released my mad at Daddy for things he couldn't help. What else am I holding on to, I wonder.

My face flaming hot, I wave the lantern, holler out, "Hey! Gary!"

He waves, and doesn't hesitate.

I close the door quick, go back to my pallet, put down the lantern, and set upon the soft of my makeshift bed.

Night insects sing happy.

I watch the mists mosey on by the window. I close my eyes, Dylan's face floats behind my lids. I think on him for a moment. How I have to admit my own part in our unhappiness. My anger and disappointment flies out the window with a sigh that scatters to all the corners, hidden and shown, of the universe. My fear lingers, but I feel it loosening inside of me, loosening so it can fly away, too. There are sighs all around me.

I open my eyes, and say to the ghosts, "It's good to be Home."

They murmur, a humming.

I hear Gary's footsteps.

I could change up my mind.

His footsteps are at the door.

I don't have to let him in.

The door opens.

I could tell him never mind.

He stands in the doorway, waits for the word from me, in no hurry, not demanding of me.

I had never wanted to remember things that insisted on remembrance. The things that could make me cry I had always kept pushed deep into the earth, buried there with ancient ancestors. Now, here, everything erupts, pushes up from the ground and exposes the sharp angles of white bone. The mountain, the spirits, Momma, Grandma Faith, all, must feel it, too.

The spirits of my kin, my women-kin, and the spirits of those who lived in this holler, those who lived in this lonely old house, look to me as if I have all the answers. As if I have answers to all the questions of all the past swirling in my brain. And maybe I do.

I have borne the past, but I also could have the future—even the one waiting at the door.

I reach out to the man standing in the doorway, "Gary, come here."

He comes to me.

So much is here for the taking. So much for the leaving behind.

After me, before me, all around me are the whispers, the stories, the imprint of my family, of what came before, and what comes next.

There is more to remember, and there is more to find.

I am still the storyteller of our lives.

The ghosts sigh. The mountain shadows let in light. The spirits sing me to sleep, to sleep, to sleep. Songs of my mountain, of the holler, of Home. Sleep, sleep, the ghosts sing, sleep until we wake you once again. They hover near, whispering, their long low laments now high songs of home, family, love, life, endings of things, beginnings of things. I rest my head upon my pillow, and no longer have to dream of Home.

Virginia Kate's Recipes

Marco's Sweet Tater Pancakes

Ingredients

Near bouts 3 quarters pound of sweet tater
2 eggs that you beat with a fork, but don't be beating it to death
1 and one half a cup of milk and not that skim kind but real fat milk
Half stick of butter you melted and don't be using no margarine
1 and a half cup of flour
3 and a half teaspoons of baking powder
Thereabouts a teaspoon of salt and thereabouts a touch of fresh
ground nutmeg, don't be using that stuff been on your shelf for fifty
years, and add a tiny bit of cinnamon and cloves—but I won't tell you
exactly because that's my own secret. Maybe I got another secret
ingredient, too, but it's a family secret and I won't tell it.

You got to cook them sweet tater until they're fork tender. Drain
them, let them cool, and then take off the skin. Then you mash them
up. In a bowl, mix them mashed sweet taters with the eggs and milk
and butter. In another bowl, sift the flour, baking powder, salt, and the
spice. Blend them two bowls together, but be sweet about it, don't
want them pancakes to be tough, do you?

On your greased griddle, spoon out the batter to the size you looking
for and cook them until they are a pretty golden color. Look for that
bubble, that's how you know to turn them. I like to serve mine with
grandmere's strawberry syrup, but I won't be telling you that recipe, no
sir and no ma'am.

Miss Darla's Crisp Butter Cookies

Before you even go any further, gather all your ingredients! You don't want to be started on the cookies and then realize you are out of something. Then the cookies-making joy is ruined. Gather then begin.

1 cup butter, softened
1 cup of sugar
1 egg
2 tablespoons lemon juice (you can use orange if you want)
Teaspoon of good vanilla and I mean the good kind—some things are worth it.
2 1/2 cups all-purpose flour
1 teaspoon baking powder

In a bowl, stir together the butter, sugar, and the egg, and then beat at a medium speed. Now, you'll need to scrape the bowl every now and again, for you don't want lumps or bits of flour finding their way into your cookies, do you? Of course not! When the mixture is creamy, add the citrus and your good vanilla I urged you to splurge on, and mix well. Then, turn your mixer down on low or else you'll have flour flying everywhere—add the flour and baking powder and mix until blended.

Divide dough in three pieces, wrap those pieces in wax paper, and place in the refrigerator a couple of hours until firm. While you are waiting, sit on the porch and have some tea, meditate, or have you read a good book lately? Or sat quietly and thought about things? Or taken your dog for a walk? Then do so while you are waiting for your cookies to chill.

Heat oven to 400 degrees. Roll the dough on a light-floured surface— just one dough ball at a time! The others must remain cold! Don't make the cookies too thick, you want them thin and crispy. Cut with the cookie cutters that make you happy. Put about an inch apart on an ungreased cookie sheet. Bake anywhere from 6 to 10 minutes—just until the edges of the cookies are lightly browned—don't over cook! Paying attention when baking cookies is important. But so is having fun eating them—enjoy them with a good tea!

Amy Campinelle & Mr. Husband's Fried Catfish:

Go to Tony's and get some cleaned catfish. Cut it up in strips and soak them strips in buttermilk. Put some cornmeal and spices in a paper bag. Toss the catfish in the paper bag and shake shake shake shake. Fry the strips in hot lard—now our sweet Virginia Kate will get upset at the lard, yeah, so if we make the catfish for her, we don't fry them in no lard, but in the Crisco. Fry them catfish until crispy and serve with some hushpuppy and some French fry. That simple is that good, yeah.

Reader's Guide

1. Virginia Kate says, "Reminding some girls about their mommas made their eyes pinch up with sad and mad and hurt and hope." Why is her reaction to hearing about other girls' mothers such a jumbled mixture of emotions?

2. "Why couldn't daughters outgrow their mothers, is what I wondered." Virginia Kate raises an excellent question. Why do you think it is so difficult for daughters to outgrow their mothers?

3. "I was part of her, no matter how late I came around." Virginia Kate thinks of Rebekha as "sanctuary." How is Rebekha salvation to Frederick and the children?

4. Micah closes his letter to Virginia Kate with the words "don't forget me, Micah." Explore the desire to belong so apparent in both Micah and Virginia Kate. Does Andy have those same feelings about belonging? What about Bobby?

5. Virginia Kate compares herself to "a tree with shallow roots that the storm would tear up and blow about." What does she mean?

6. "Come home," Virginia Kate hears her beloved West Virginia Mountain spirits call. Discuss the universal longing for home.

7. "I would be a part of something, the half to a whole," Virginia Kate thinks after Dylan proposes marriage. She imagines a home with her own children. "We'd all be happy. I wouldn't be lonely anymore." Discuss the faulty reasoning that leads us to think another person can make us happy. What does our culture teach women about marriage?

8. What is the importance to Virginia Kate to be the storyteller of her family? Explore the idea of storytelling as a preserver of culture and tradition. Why do you think storytelling is such a valued activity in the South?

9. Virginia Kate shares a powerful bond with her deceased Grandma Faith. Explore the possibility of supernatural communication. In addition, what of Miss Darla, for whom Virginia Kate has a spiritual or extra sensory bond; how does their relationship help guide Virginia Kate?

10. How does Virginia Kate delude herself into thinking Dylan's alcoholism is somehow different from her father's? Explore this paradox repeated by so many of us today.

11. After Jade tells her a secret, Virginia Kate thinks, "Men didn't like to know things and women liked to know too much. I wished to break the spell of women, but then most of us thought we'd do things different just as we stepped into the same messes we always had." Explore the "spell of women." Do you think Virginia Kate repeats her women-kin's mistakes? Have you ever deluded yourself into "messes," as Virginia Kate terms them?

12. Jade says, "Men let their habits out of the sack one piece at a time so women wouldn't run out screaming if they just dumped them all out on the counter at once." Is this true? Are men secretive by holding back their true natures? What about women's secrets?

13. Explain the symbolism of the old green Plymouth Fury station wagon Mee Maw Laudine gives to Virginia Kate. What does the vehicle represent for Virginia Kate?

14. Virginia Kate feels a kinship to the one sunflower that looks in a different direction from the others. In what ways does Virginia Kate look in a direction different from other people? Is she secure in her difference? Explain.

15. "I hope I stayed the same, stayed connected to my kin and my Grandma Faith," Virginia Kate says. Discuss the importance of family.

16. Virginia Kate is afraid of Gary's affection for her. Is she being smart? Or just afraid?

Reader's Guide written by Mary Ann Ledbetter, Baton Rouge, Louisiana

Where Virginia Kate's Story Began

Book One
Tender Graces

Excerpt

Between Pocahontas and Summers County, where Momma was born, where Grandma Faith lived and then died on her own mountain, I look up and beyond at my heritage. All the mystery, all the secrets, all the loss and gain of our lives.

When Momma was a girl, she ran on the mountain wild and dirty until my daddy came to fetch her away. I see my momma just as clear as if I were there myself. The old house perched on the mountain, and Daddy walking up to knock on their door.

I shake away the memories so I can concentrate on what's ahead. The address Uncle Jonah gave me is easy to find, right off the highway. I park, go inside to fetch Momma, walk with my head up and my feet clomping hard. There's no one else here. I'm alone.

Grandma Faith says, "No, you are not alone. I'm here."

When I see how it is with Momma, I'm relieved she made Uncle Jonah take care of things before I got here. But it makes her even more unreal as I put her in the car with me and set my wheels turning towards the little white house where we all lived for a time, where Momma stayed behind alone when she let us go, one by one. I take her around the curves, down the long weaving road, between mountain and memory. Then I'm there. The two hills stand guard over the holler; my headlights glow before me as I pull into the dirt driveway.

Nothing has changed.

Ɇ•ɇ

Grandma Faith wavers in the mists, the wolf calls, the owl flies, the mountain is. Up up I go on Fionadala's back, her hooves thundering. I see my child's eyes only, through the closet keyhole, dark eyes are open, then closed. Thundering hooves, up the mountain we ride. At the ridge I stop, take Momma from my pack. And there, with mountain song rising, with fog wetting, with Fionadala nodding her head, with the fiddles of the old ghosts of old mountain men crying, with the voices of all I've lost and all I've gained, with the mountains cradling, with the West Virginia soil darkening my feet, with Momma's cry of "Do It!" I open her vessel, and as I twirl, turning turning turning, I let her out—she flies out with a sigh, with forty thousand sighs. As I come to rest, she settles upon me, settles upon the trees and mountain and rock, settles, then is finally stilled. The owl cries, the wolf calls, the mountain is, Grandma Faith nods. Momma is a part of it all now.

Chapter 1

Today

All my tired flies out the window when I see Grandma Faith standing in the mountain mists that drift in and out of the trees. She's as she was before, like one lick of fire hasn't touched her, whole and alive and wanting as she beckons to me. Grandma whispers her wants as she's done all my life.

I put my hand out the car window as Momma used to do, and say "Wheeee . . ." then holler to the owl flying in the night, "I'm Virginia Kate, and I'm a crazy woman." He keeps his wings spread to find his supper. I don't feel silly one bit. I rush headlong into the night in my gray Subaru, a tangible addition to the darkness. The tires seem to hover above the road as if like the owl I am also flying. I could let loose my hand from the steering wheel and my car would find its way to a little holler that lies in the shadow of the mountain. Inside the unused ashtray my cell phone lies silent, for I've turned it off, pushed it into the little drawer, closed it as much as I could. I am in no mood for voices telling me any more bad things.

The last time I allowed it to ring, Uncle Jonah had called and said, "Come home and fetch your momma." I haven't called West Virginia *home* for longer than what's good, but I left before light to do as he said without giving myself time to think too hard on it.

Grandma Faith used to say, "Ghosts and spirits weave around the living in these mountains. They try to tell us things, warn us of what's ahead, or try to move us on towards something we need to do. But most of all, they want us to remember."

Momma never told stories much, since it hurt to do it. She said looking behind a person only makes them trip and fall. I understand why now in a way I didn't as a girl.

I touch the journal Momma sent two weeks ago. I should have

gone to her right after I read her letter, but I was too ornery for my own good, always have been. I didn't want her to think she could crook her finger and have me scurry back to West Virginia after she gave me up as she did when I was a girl who needed her momma. I had set my teeth to her words and carried on with my own business.

Momma wrote, *I know you'd want to have this diary from your Grandma seeing how you are two peas in a pod. I made a few notes alongside hers. She didn't have everything written down, so I had to fix parts of it. Come soon. I got lots to talk about. Things I reckon will explain what the notes in the diary won't.*

I wrote back, *Dear Momma, I'm busy. You can mail my stuff to me (I'm enclosing a check that should be more than plenty for postage). You have your nerve writing me after all this time and expecting me to drop everything. That's all I have to say right now. Signed, Virginia Kate.*

I didn't open the diary until a week later. And only then because Grandma took up to poking at me until I had enough.

Now I'm full of regret. Momma didn't tell me she was so sick; how was I to know? And the diary notes would have changed things, changed the way I thought about my momma. I'm almost to the West Virginia state line, but I already know it's too late for Momma and me.

֍ • ֎

In Grandma Faith's journal is the story of how Momma and Daddy met. How I began. In the pages are tucked pictures—one of Grandma with me on her lap, another one of Momma when she was a young girl of seventeen, and one of my parents after they were married in 1954. The journal burns my right palm warm as I rub the tooled leather and pass the sign that welcomes me to the state of West Virginia. But I don't need the sign to tell me. The pull of my mountain calls me home. Oh, how I've missed these mountains, even when I didn't know I did. They'd been tucked away inside, hiding behind my heart, pulsing with my blood. Waiting for me.

Between Pocahontas and Summers County, where Momma was born, where Grandma Faith lived and then died on her own mountain, I look up and beyond at my heritage. All the mystery, all the secrets, all the loss and gain of our lives.

When Momma was a girl, she ran on the mountain wild and dirty until my daddy came to fetch her away. I can well imagine Momma the day she met Daddy, from Momma's scrawled notes off to the side of Grandma's slanted ones. I see my momma just as clear as if I were there myself. The old house perched on the mountain, and Daddy walking up to knock on their door.

I shake away the memories so I can concentrate on what's ahead. The address Uncle Jonah gave me is easy to find, right off the highway. I park, go inside to fetch Momma, walk with my head up and my feet clomping hard. There's no one else here. I'm alone.

Grandma Faith says, "No, you are not alone. I'm here."

When I see how it is with Momma, I'm relieved she made Uncle Jonah take care of things before I got here. But it makes her even more unreal as I put her in the car with me and set my wheels turning towards the little white house where we all lived for a time, where Momma stayed behind alone when she let us go, one by one. I take her around the curves, down the long weaving road, between mountain and memory. Then I'm there. The two hills stand guard over the holler; my headlights glow before me as I pull into the dirt driveway.

Nothing has changed.

My sweet sister mountain waits, mysterious in the moonlight, rising up as it always did. I get out of the car and take deep breaths of clean summer air, listen to the night insects and frogs call to each other, and remember a lonely girl, who grew up to be a hopeful woman. Holding tight to Momma, I walk into the door of my childhood home and the ghosts of a thousand hurts, loves, wants, and lives rush against me. I hug on to her so I won't drop her, and say, "Momma, I'm home again."

She doesn't say, "Stay awhile."

"You can't send me away this time, Momma." But I know she can. She sent me away twice before.

I hurry through the shadowed house, straight to my room. I'm stunned. It's still the same. I place Momma on my dresser, say, "There Momma. There." I turn my back to her, head out to my car again. Outside, the cool air clears my head. Once my bags are from car to room, I don't bother unpacking. Now that I'm here, I want to leave soon as I can.

I open the window and breathe in earth and childhood smells. A breeze lifts my hair and plays with the strands. The mountains are shadows in the distance and I shout, just to spite Momma, "Hello! Remember me? I'm home!"

I hear an echoing, "Stay awhile, Virginia Kate." Maybe it's only the rustle of leaves, the blowing of wind, but I smile to possibility. Pretending I'm brave, I open the journal to the page with my parents' picture and read Grandma's slanting words, along with Momma's scrawled additions, by moonlight.

Our mothers and their mothers and the mothers before them do the same things over and again, even if in differing ways. Not me. I close the journal. A blast of wind rushes in, pushes against me, and causes something from the nightstand to fall over. It's the Popsicle-stick photo frame Micah made me. My hands grow warm and tingly. The photo inside is of Micah, Andy, and me, grinning without a bit of sense. The Easter picture. We're all dressed up—with bare dirty feet—and my bonnet is tilted on my head ready to fall off. We look so happy it makes my stomach clench.

Grandma urges, "Go to the attic, little mite. More waits."

I put the frame back, and go out to the hall. The stairs make the same loud scrangy sound as I pull them down, the same rattle as I climb. Daddy's old flashlight still hangs on the nail at the entrance, and I use it to look around. There are Christmas ornament boxes, book boxes, unmarked boxes, and a box with *Easter* written in big black ink.

Inside *Easter*, folded in tissue paper, is Momma's green dress, her hatbox with the wide-brimmed hat, and her white gloves. I recall Momma sashaying down the church aisle while everyone stared at her, dim bulbs in the bright shine of her light. I press Momma's dress to my face and inhale deep. Shalimar. I still smell it. I put everything back before too many things are remembered too soon.

Shining the light in a corner, I find the dirty-finger-printed white box. My Special Things Box. I pick my way over to it, and cradling it in my arms like a baby, take it down with me. Up and down the rickety stairs I go with pictures and mementos, until I have the things I want scattered about my room. I know now I'll stay until I finish the remembering.

When I open my dresser drawer to put away things from my suitcase, some of my childhood clothing is still there. Underneath the white cotton panties there is more—letters, notes, and smoothed creek stones, tucked away as if I just put them there. Inside the cedar robe are two dresses I never wore unless Momma made me. I pick up the Mary Janes and see my sad in the shine.

The room is filled to overflowing with the past—like a broken family reunion. It's hard to suck in air; the bits of ghost-dust choke me. My eyes water, but I know it's not time to cry. Grandma Faith wants me to remember, not to weep. She knows about truth and the pain it can heap on you if you keep hiding from it. Momma knows now, too, I bet.

I say in my croaked voice, "Crying is for weaklings. Crying is for little girls in pigtails." I know I speak strong to the spirits who are watching me. I want to show them what I'm made of. I do.

I empty my Special Things Box onto the quilt. Inside are items I thought important when I was innocent. I up-end paper sacks, a cigar box, envelopes, *Easter*. I'm a crazy searching woman as I go through years in a gulp. The wind blows in and scatters papers. I hear laughter. Everything is willy-nilly as if there's no beginning and no end.

All around me are child's drawings, Daddy's old Instamatic camera, photographs, a silver-handled mirror and comb set without the brush, school notebooks, river and creek rocks, letters, diaries, a bit of Spanish moss, whispers, lies, truths, crushed maple leaves, regrets, red lipstick, losses, loves, a piece of coal—all emptied from dark places.

Everything will be emptied from dark places, even the urn of ashes full of Momma's spirit that can't be contained. Momma always said she never wanted anyone to see her look ugly, and Momma would think *dead* was ugliest of all. She made Uncle Jonah burn her down before anyone could say goodbye. That's what she wanted, that's how she is.

I stop my mad tossing aside, pick up a photo of Grandma standing next to her vegetable garden. She's holding Momma when she was a baby. The same West Virginia breeze that rustles the secrets on my bed pushes Grandma's dress against her long legs. The sun behind her shows the outline of her body. I can sense the smiles that would be there if she had been given a chance to breathe. She reaches out to me. We are connected by our blood and love of words and truth. She's chosen me to be the storyteller. I can feel her. I can.

I will start with a beginning, before I slid down the moon and landed in my momma's arms, those same arms that let me go without telling me why, or at least a why I wanted to hear.

"The stories are made real by the telling," Grandma whispers.

I smell apples and fresh baked bread. I inhale them into to my marrow.

Gazing out the open window, I wish on falling stars of hope. Far off a flash of lightning breaks through the night—a coming storm? I want to remember my life as falls, springs, and summers. I don't like seeing things in the winter's dead and cold. I'm like Momma that way.

I situate myself cross-legged on the bed and the ghosts guide my hands where they need to go. I dig deep into the secrets. I will begin with Momma and Daddy the day they met. The beginning of them is the beginning of me. I hear a hum of voices, like dragonflies and cicadas buzzing.

I'll record our lives, my life, as Grandma Faith wants me to. I look out my childhood window at the moon and the stars, at my mountain, at the rest of my life stretched before me, and the one behind me. Spirits urge me; a clear path opens, up to the top.

My life begins again.

Coming in Fall 2010 From Kathryn Magendie

SWEETIE

*Let me tell you I am better acquainted with you for a long absence, as men are
with themselves for a long affliction: absence does but hold off a friend,
to make one see him the truer.*
—Ovid

ONE

This is not the beginning. . .

I smoothed my thumb over the tiny wood-carved bird lying in my
palm, closed my hand around it, and recalled the day Sweetie became
my friend. She stood, feet rooted in the grass as she gazed down at her
cupped hands held against her chest. Her blonde hair blew in the wind,
pieces of it whipping across a tough face. Those intense hard lines
were only reflexes of preparation, a bracing against her secrets. She
wore a cotton dress of faded yellow, scattered with once bright roses
that had turned old blood colored.

I'd held my tablet at eye level, as if studying my lessons, and
secretly watched her by peeking over the top. She brought her hands
to her right eye and peered inside, and I wondered what was there, a
butterfly, or a wish? I pretended to be distracted by my reading, and
shuffled in inches to stand closer to her.

When she looked at me full on, I was captured by eyes that
reminded me of my brother's favorite cat's eye marble. She held out
her hands to me. I hesitated, for I had been tricked before. Not only in
western North Carolina, but all of the places my father moved us to
from north to south, east to west—no one could resist tormenting me
over my chubby body, thin brown hair, and the ugly thick-framed
glasses I wore. I was a walking cliché from daytime movies—always
the awkward new girl in town. One would hope I took that cliché to
the limit, grew to be beautiful and showed them all, but I was at best
unremarkable, average. Unlike my brother, tall and handsome, his dark

hair thick and shiny, his eyes clear and intense, his fingers strong as he held up x-rays of bones crooked, broken, or bent.

In the schoolyard that day, I stood watching a girl who wore her strange beauty like an afterthought, one that defied the imperfections that mottled her body. I'd never seen or known anyone like Sweetie before, and would never since.

Sweetie kept her hands held out, enticing me to her. My feet continued to her as if they were independent of me, as if I were pulled to her by the force of those compelling eyes. When I at last stood by her side, I smelled mint and moist earth smells.

"See here what I got?" She thrust her hands to my face.

I put my right eye to the tiny hole she made between her thumbs, closed my left eye, and squinted through my glasses. She opened the backside of her hands a bit to let light filter through. A baby bird nestled in her palms.

"This here bird fell out its nest, and I got to put it back so its mama can take care of it." She eyed me up and down, as if trying to make up her mind about me.

I stared at the scabs marching across her knees, the puckered skin racing up her right arm, the reddened zigzagged scar that ran from her ankle, up her thigh, to disappear under her dress. She didn't try to hide her imperfections, as I would have.

"You want to watch me climb up and give this here bird back to its mama or you want to stand there gawking?"

I tore my eyes away from her hurts. "Nnno. I mean, yyyes. I . . . *oh* . . ."

She narrowed her eyes. Then a grin lit her mouth, as if she then did make up her mind about me, after all. She tossed her head to a herd of girls on the playground. "Them girls would keep it, like a pet." She snorted, then asked, "It belongs where it belongs, right? If things don't stay where they belong, they die, right?" Without waiting for an answer, she pulled up the hem of her dress, gently placed the bird in a fold, tucked the ends into the cut-off dungarees she wore underneath, and climbed up the tree. When she at last arrived at the nest and put the baby bird inside, she waved to me from the limb, and then scuttled down as swift as an animal.

Standing beside me again, she said, "Up to Mama Bird now. Little Bird might be sickly, or busted up inside, and Mama Bird pushed it out the nest to spare it from dying slow."

I croaked out, "Bbbut you tttried." I stood still, waiting for what usually came next when I couldn't control my words. Teasing, shoving, or worse, pity.

"You got to breathe, Miss-Lissa." She inhaled through her nose, filling her thin chest, and then blew out through slightly parted lips.

"It's *Me*lissa, nnnot *Miss*-Lissa."

"Just try what I said, Miss Stubborn-brain."

I breathed, in and out as she'd done.

"That's right. Don't get in no hurry with your words." Sweetie looked up to the nest. "All a person can do is give it all they's got. Right, Lissa?"

There was no turning back from Sweetie then, and I followed her to the ends of her earth that summer. Sweetie was a mountain creature who could not be contained, and when they tried to take her from her mountain, she fell away so they would never find her.

She said she would wait forever. She said she would wait for me. How could it be so?

I squeezed the wooden bird and let its beak cut into my palm. When I opened my hand, a spot of blood beaded in my palm. Another memory came sharp with sound and image—the crowd of shouting people, my sobbing face, and Sweetie asking for her mother's healing even though it meant she sacrificed her own.

I would find Whale Back Rock, where Sweetie made me pinkie swear I wouldn't tell a soul any of her secrets. It was a massive boulder, rising up out of the mountain with its back full of moss and lichens. It looked like a great humpback whale curving back into the ocean after its breath released from its blowhole. There were natural signs to lead me to the great rock of our friendship: Bear Claw Rock, Turtlehead, Jabbering Creek, Triplett Tree, all the places we'd roamed on the mountain.

I pushed the bird deep into a pocket of my backpack, and walked up the blacktop road, which used to be a dirt and graveled road. The road that led to the old log trails was only two miles or so from my old neighborhood, where I'd lived that summer before Father and Mother raced me away from the mountains to another temporary home. I'd cried all the way to Ohio and by time we'd moved again to Boston, I pretended to forget about Sweetie. It wasn't until I came across the old box of memories that she spoke loud to me, from the distance of time and space.

About Kathryn Magendie

Kathryn Magendie, a West Virginia native & adoptive daughter of
South Louisiana, lives tucked in a cove in Maggie Valley, western
North Carolina. She spends her days writing prose and poetry,
photographing nature, and as co-publishing editor of the Rose &
Thorn.

Photo by: Christy L. Bishop

LaVergne, TN USA
28 November 2010
206539LV00005B/12/P